I0822284

# The Dead Leaves

*Stories*

Rich Varner

Disclaimer: This is a work of fiction. Names, characters, places, and events portrayed in this story are products of the author's imagination. Any resemblance to actual persons, living or dead, or events is purely coincidental.

The author and publisher are not liable for any loss, damage, or injury caused by the information contained in this work. The views expressed are solely those of the author and do not represent the publisher or any affiliated entity.



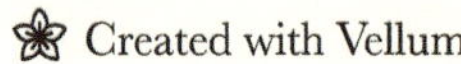

Created with Vellum

*For Khim, who allowed me to suffer this art.*

# Contents

# Preface

This book began its life in the summer of 2007, when "Tuesday Law" inflated into a 100,000-word, incomplete first draft. I set it aside for a time, and when I returned to it, I hated it, and so it lay dormant. But it wasn't forgotten. Over the years, first through a process of sporadic editing, then through a daily ritual, the story condensed to a 30,000-word final version, 15 years in the making, which now forms a part of *The Dead Leaves.*

Writing "Tuesday Law," and the three stories that followed, taught me that the creative process is not a deliberate, linear progression. Instead, these stories unfolded as a series of revelations, struggles, and moments of transcendence - some conscious, others not.

I have no doubt that many of us feel this magnetic pull, the awakening of our creative spirit, only to be confronted and eventually defeated by the harsh reality of our own perceived limitations. This struggle between the desire to create and the fear of inadequacy can be all-consuming, as it was for me over those 15 years. Despite this, the compulsion to finish these stories remained so potent within my mind's eye, that ideas, sentences, characters, appeared before me like vivid dreams. And yet, when I wrote them onto the page, they remained flat, hollow, and lifeless. For a time, this destructive cycle was relentless: Inspiration. Write. Edit. Hate. Repeat.

This dissonance, I believe, stems from the inherent resistance we experience when engaging with the creative process. It manifests as self-doubt, anxiety, and sometimes, suffering – powerful emotions that can deter otherwise brave people. However, it is essential to recognize that this resistance does not signify a judgment against our ability to create. Rather, it serves as a reminder that the full potential of the work is not yet complete. There is more to be done. This, I learned, was the next crucial component in the process of creation: dedication to the craft.

Embracing this, I immersed myself with these stories, often at a personal cost. Through my devotion, I gained a heightened awareness to the creative consciousness that we all share. The awareness did not improve the technical craft of my writing, necessarily, but it did motivate me to persist, to suffer through the failures of writing until I had received all I needed to complete the work.

When I finished each of these stories, I experienced a wide range of emotion: fleeting euphoria, brief melancholy, and then a realization of my changed relationship with the story. It felt less like creation, and more like discovery, like I was handed a jumble of words, and my only job was arranging them until they were in order. A codebreaker, not a creator, and with no comprehension for the quality of the code I had broken. I did not know if my writing had intrinsic value, or if I wrote merely to add a contribution into the communal source of creativity, where it might inspire someone else to create a superior piece of art. You, perhaps.

Regardless of the true purpose, this revelation led to the eventual destruction of my ego and the erasure of self-doubt. It was only then that I felt truly free to share my work, because it must be in the act of sharing, in the connection between creator and audience, that the purpose of art is realized. Where the audience craves to be enlightened or entertained, the artist craves evaluation, for it is through the eyes of others, in their conscious critique and their unconscious creativity, that I hope to learn and hopefully improve as a human being, a writer, or both.

But, if *The Dead Leaves* should be all I am capable of, then I am at least proud to have faced the resistance and overcome it. In doing so, I found the essence of art: unselfish awareness of creativity and devotion to craft. This simple equation transcends the subjective evaluation of merit, and instead focuses on the commitment of the artist to their work. As such, I present *The Dead Leaves* not as a testament of talent, but as a promise that I have poured my heart into these pages, a human heart fueled by unwavering dedication, a heart that now beats with a developed and profound ability to perceive the humanness and creativity in you - a distinction that will grow increasingly important in the age of AI.

# Tuesday Law

Professor Becker always carried a mechanical shuffler in the briefcase he brought to his lecture. As the class drew to a close, he placed it on the lectern and produced a deck of playing cards from his jacket pocket. He deftly mixed the cards in three quick snaps to demonstrate his skill, then loaded them into the shuffler, and pressed the red power button. The machine hummed and the cards fluttered together in a rapid burst. Becker snatched the top card when they settled, displaying it at eye-level, its red back-side facing the captive audience of law students. For those of us cursed with an assigned seat on the front row, our compromised vantage point, necks strained upward at him, added an exaggerated air of authority to a man who, despite his academic flair, had never practiced law a day in his life.

Becker spun the card around and revealed the three of spades. In the white margin, a name was scribbled with permanent marker. He announced, "Mary Khong."

Normally this ridiculous ceremony created a great deal of anxiety among the first-year students in Becker's Torts class, because the person drawn would be the Socratic participant for the next session. But today, when Mary Khong heard Becker announce her name, she didn't flinch. The entire class had snapped into a silently attentive, fearful harmony, with all eyes focused on the exam booklets Becker had arranged on the table, as if their concentrated stares might telepathically transform a C into an A.

Becker wrapped a rubber band around the cards and replaced them in his jacket pocket, then he packed the shuffler into his briefcase. He snapped the case shut and held it in his hand, then finally addressed what everyone was so keenly interested in.

"There were only four A's, mostly B's and C's, and five…others," he said. "Overall, slightly disappointing but I say that every year." He moved a few more paces toward the stairs. "I did my best to offer substantive input in each exam. I will keep regular office hours through Wednesday, next week." He was halfway up the stairs at this point. "Arrange to bring me your questions or comments regarding your work, but once we reach that deadline, I will not speak of these again. Onward, ever upward," he added – his usual valediction – and exited the room briskly to avoid being bombarded with questions from the usual cast of tryhards.

In Becker's absence, a nervous murmur trickled through the room. Solemn silence followed, until Phillip Fantuzzo, seated at the far end of the second row, gathered his things and confidently found his exam. He looked at the cover, nodded respectfully, tucked it under his arm, and left. The rest of my classmates followed and filed in front of the table like funeral mourners observing an open casket. After finding their Blue Book, they hustled up the steps and into the hallway where they huddled in the safe confines of their study groups. I watched the theatrical procession to the last man. Worried faces nodded to somber passersby. Impatient rage built up when someone struggled to find their exam. Mary Khong sobbed before she had even looked at her grade.

When the aisles behind us cleared, the first row emptied but for me. I loafed to the table where a solitary booklet remained. I grabbed the Blue Book, rolled it up, and stuffed it into my back pocket. I left the classroom and walked through the hallway, avoiding eye contact from the fretful groups who gathered and surely lied to each other.

The cold wind slapped against my face as I stepped out of the law school. Grit blew in my teeth. I wiped the dirt away with the sleeve of my fleece jacket then dodged a few Section Two students in the courtyard. They laughed as they inched their way along the wall, avoiding the overhanging tree branches where birds nested and filled the entry space with their excrement. The law school legend went that, if pooped on by the infamous birds, a first-year student would be doomed to a failing grade in at least one class. I ignored the feathered judgement, zipped my jacket up to my neck, and quickly walked away. As I cut through a courtyard, I overheard several more frightened Section Two classmates complaining about their performance:

"I never made anything less than a B at Vandy."

"Did you hear who got the A's?"

"Phillip Fantuzzo for sure."

"That guy creeps me out."

"He stares at me in class."

"Thank God it was just a practice exam."

Two weeks ago, Becker announced that he had pulled an essay question from a previous year's examination and was offering it to us as a voluntary trial run. All the pale faced handwringing and worry was over a practice exam, but because he was the only professor to do so, this was the first time Section Two of the 2007 graduating class would learn how they stacked up against each other. This motivating taste of competition, however inconsequential, had riled everyone up. Finally, we had a way to rank ourselves. Finally, there was blood in the water.

I walked until I was far enough away that, when I stopped and looked back, the Briscoe College of Law resembled a small garrison on the main campus' outer reaches. The building was boxy, brown, boring, with prison style slits for windows that seemingly mocked everyone trapped inside.

Since most law students earned their undergraduate degrees elsewhere, they brought with them the snobbish idea that the main campus' dubious academic reputation was beneath their noble status as budding doctors of the law. I knew this was a disguise for their own mediocrity, however, because like many of them, I had also been rejected by law schools with better reputations, so I rather enjoyed walking campus, where unremarkable scores were not considered immutable measures of worth.

The sidewalks near the BA building were clogged with people pouring out of class. I weaved through the masses along a maze of bland, tan bricked buildings and gray pavement, until I reached Memorial Circle, where ornate Spanish Colonial-styled buildings capped with bell towers surrounded an expansive, tree-lined lawn. I repeatedly reached in my pocket where the weight of the exam booklet had grown heavier, but each time I touched it, I'd find some excuse not to peek at the grade – a snooping person over my shoulder that could have been a Section Two eavesdropper, or a gust of wind that might blow the embarrassment into the wrong hands, like the group of attractive sorority girls walking close behind me.

Where its academic reputation lagged, the university's repute for its coeds rivaled any school in the state. In this instance, I found myself among a group of Kappa Kappa Gammas who, like me, just missed the light at the corner of University and Broadway. We waited together, bracing against the biting wind, and it was at this very spot where I achieved a moment of clarity regarding my critical decision. If I was being honest with myself, I knew what needed to be done.

I was only a couple months into my first semester, but I saw the curtain lifted higher than ever, and got an unpleasant glimpse of the show that would be the next three, 15, even 50 years of my American life. I saw the wearisome details that would consume my time, and the tedious individuals who would undertake this devotion with me. The only uncertainty that remained was a predetermined ceiling symbolized by the red letter burning a hole in my pocket.

I should have been nervous about this test question, as it might reflect my ability to understand and apply what I've learned to a standard worthy of future clients' trust and money. However, practical concerns had no sway on my current state of apathy. I wasn't interested in outshining anyone or making a name for myself in this arbitrarily cutthroat environment. The whole enterprise seemed meaningless, and from the moment I sat down to complete the exam, I couldn't shake this feeling of disillusionment.

Professor Becker gave us a week's notice and provided the general subject matter covered in the practice question. I reviewed summaries on an outline that was several years old. The prompt called for a self-imposed 90-minute time limit. I spent about an hour writing my answer, distracted by the surfer movie *Big Wednesday* playing on the TV in my apartment for reasons I don't recall. If intent and respect for the exam had anything to do with my grade, surely, I deserved to fail, and with so much on the line now that it was my money and my reputation on the line, I felt like a failure whether I was one or not.

"I'm gonna quit," I whispered just loud enough for the idea to be thrust into the world and validated.

"What did you say?" one of the Kappa girls asked, leaning in. She had been spying on me.

I glanced at the crosswalk sign, wishing it would suddenly turn green.

"Nothing. Just talking to myself."

The other sorority sisters gathered around their leader. I recognized her, probably from the bars.

"I thought I heard you say you were going to quit something?"

"I'm going to quit staying out so late," I said, then checked the light again. Still red.

"I've seen you before," she added, a flirtatious, confident tone in her voice.

There was an easy segue here, but I wasn't interested. I didn't want their sympathy, or their attention. The pedestrian light finally turned green, and I darted across the street, heading straight for a trash can. The Kappa girls followed, their laughter echoing in my ears, like little daggers while I fumbled for the Blue Book in my back pocket. I got hold of it, rolled it tightly, and tossed it in the trash can. As it slipped through my fingers, a wonderful, orgiastic rush of relief swept over me. The decision felt consequential and final and real. I had no intention of conforming to others' expectations anymore, and I certainly wasn't going to reach into that awful trash can to resuscitate that other life now.

But the euphoria was short-lived. The sounds of traffic and chatter returned, and I felt a tap on my shoulder that jarred me back into reality.

"Right on time, Shep," a familiar voice said. "It's cold out here. Let's go."

It was James McClure, and I followed him down the block to Rocky Larue's. Rocky's was our usual collegiate dive that had a Tuesday lunch special we never missed. Five bucks for a burger and a beer. Mike, the bartender inside, shielded his eyes from the daylight that burst into the dark bar when we walked in. After the door slammed shut and a comfortable dimness returned, he recognized us. "Law Dogs," he said and nodded as we bellied up in front of him. "Usual?" he asked. The place was empty but for us.

"Medium-rare. Jalapenos. Budweiser," McClure reminded him.

"Same," I said.

McClure had been assigned to me as part of the law school's mandatory mentor program. He was a third-year student who had shed any delusions about the function of law school and his place within it. His cool candor was refreshing compared to the tense attitudes of my fellow first year classmates, but had the school known how he conducted the mentorship, they would have ended the program at once.

Mike punched our order into his computer. He popped the top off two Budweisers and slid them down the bar in front of us, then he grabbed a bottle of Jägermeister and poured shots into three shot glasses. Our frequent patronage at Rocky's earned us various privileges. Among them, shots of collegiate booze.

"Cheers boys," he said, tapped his glass on the bar top, then downed the shot.

"Why do people do that?" I asked after watching McClure mimic the same. "Does anyone know?"

"Do what?" McClure asked.

"Tap the bar before drinking a shot."

"Beats me."

"To pay respects," Mike said. "I think."

"Respect to what?"

Mike shrugged.

"Just drink the damn thing," McClure said.

"Fine. But this is it for me. I told Diablo I'd drive for him this evening," I said and downed the shot.

McClure's shoulders shook like a cold chill had run down his spine. "I can't believe you're still working for that psychopath," he whispered.

"How else can I afford a $5 burger and beer special without taking out another loan?"

"Well, if you were any good at darts or foosball you could make a few bucks off me every Tuesday, instead of the other way around."

"Which would you prefer today?"

McClure nodded his head to the beat of a Ween song playing in the bar, then he smirked and grabbed his beer as he slid out of the barstool. He claimed to have earned a national ranking at a foosball tournament in College Station, so naturally he went straight for the Tornado table in the back of the bar. He had an unstoppable pass-pass-shot combo, and I had only beaten him once, when he was so drunk he could only hold one eye open.

McClure scored first using his patented move. The ball zipped through my defense and clanked against the back of the goal.

"Remember I mentioned that Becker gave us a practice exam?" I asked.

"What about it"

"Got the grades back today."

"Is that why you were staring into a parallel universe hovering over that trash can outside? Your fake grade was that bad?" he asked. "You threw it away in shame?"

"Not exactly."

"Then why so glum?"

"I always look glum, don't I?"

"Glummer than usual today."

"Is that a word? Glummer? I've never heard it spoken."

"Well, that's how goddamned glum you look," he said as he snapped his wrist and sent another rocket through my goal.

I took the moment between points to observe myself in a mirror hung on the wall near the foosball table. The mirror had an image of a smiling Ozzie Smith, former shortstop for the St. Louis Cardinals, imposed on the foreground. We had attempted to steal it several times and now the frame was screwed into the wall. I did not recognize any more or any less gloominess in the reflection. I looked less happy than Ozzie Smith, but otherwise it was a face afflicted with the general tedium of a 23-year-old graduate student with no place to be and no real drive to get there either. It was all so cliché and pathetic and there was no hiding from it now.

"I didn't look at the grade," I said after finally making a shot. I slid one bead on the scoring Abacus in my favor. "I don't care anymore, so I just threw it away."

McClure sighed. A deep, annoyed sigh. "We've all seen that movie, man. Are you being coy with me?"

"What movie?"

"The Paper Chase."

"I thought he got an A?"

"In the movie or the book?"

"There's a book?"

"I think everyone assumes he got an A because he was an asshole. Did you really not look at your grade?"

"I really didn't."

"What are you so worried about? Did you prepare and like…try?"

"How do you prepare for an open book question?"

"You don't really have to, so, it's perfect. You applied minimum effort and now you know what kind of effort it takes to make a… well, never mind. It would've been perfect if you looked at your grade, which really, if you think about it, not looking is the opposite of not caring."

"I don't follow."

"If you really didn't care about your grade, you would have

looked at it, because it wouldn't have mattered. All you're admitting by not looking is that you care so much it made you scared."

"It's worse than that."

"How?"

"Because I didn't want my grade, whether bad or good or middle of the road, to influence my decision. I'm going to quit."

McClure gently placed the ball through the hole in the side of the table and wedged it against his nearest yellow player. He inhaled sharply, ran his fingers through a salt-and-pepper Kennedy coif, and quietly said, "Quit? Did you say quit? Quit what? Drinking? School?"

"Yes, I want to quit school." The words sounded hollow now that they were spoken above a whisper. This was my wet finger in the wind to see how someone I trusted would react to the decision, or better yet, how someone I trusted might guide me in the right direction. He was my mentor after all.

"Mike!" McClure shouted. "Shep is having an existential crisis. We need another round!"

Mike punched an order into the system but needed clarification. "Just the one? Or both of you?" he asked.

"One for me," McClure answered, "and one for Albert Camus over here."

"No, no," I protested. "I've got to work this afternoon. And it's not an existential crisis." I checked my reflection in the Ozzie Smith mirror again. I didn't look convinced. "You know what, Mike, forget it, bring me another beer," I said after the moment of reflection had passed.

McClure nodded with approval and finally let the ball slip into play. He scored another goal five seconds later, then Mike brought us two more beers. McClure downed half of his in one dramatic gulp.

"It's a little weird, isn't it? Being bummed out by a practice exam?" McClure continued. "The law of averages says you clearly got a B or a C."

"I'd rather not base my personal growth on the law of averages, which is somewhat beside the point. It feels like my grade could be anything from an A all the way to a Dragon Tail, and since I can't tell the difference, what's the use of a grade? Average or otherwise."

"What's a Dragon Tail?" McClure asked.

"D+."

"Is that really what people call it?"

"That's what I call it."

"How many D+'s have you made in your life?"

"My roommate in college carried a 1.3 GPA through his freshman year, and he had a lot of them."

McClure won the first match of foosball handily and we reset the Abacus on both sides of the table.

"What would you even do if you quit?" he asked.

"Get a job, I guess."

Bewilderment slowly spread across McClure's face. "A job doing what?" he asked.

"I've got a degree," I reminded him. "That's got to be good for something."

"Mike!" McClure shouted again, "It's worse than I thought! We need more Jaeger this time! Stat!"

"10-4!" Mike said.

"Shep, you have a political science degree from a land grant school," McClure continued. "What are you going to do with that besides deliver steaks for a maniac? Work nights stocking grocery shelves? Substitute teach? Open a political science laboratory down on Main Street?"

"Actually, I think the pinnacle of success for poli-sci dorks is to be a state senator, though most of them would probably accept just sleeping with a state senator."

Mike walked over to us and placed two shot glasses on the ledge of the foosball table.

"Better yet," McClure went on, "Mike, you guys hiring? This frail thing won't make much of a bouncer, but I bet he can bar back until he learns to pour a decent drink. What do your guys typically make working here?"

Mike blinked several times and reset his glasses on the bridge of his nose. "A barback? Fifty bucks on some Thursdays, Fridays,

Saturdays. Seventy maybe. During the school year anyway. Not so much in the summer. And it's hard work."

"You guys need any help?" McClure asked.

"Who's asking again?"

McClure pointed at me. "Shep here is staring down a second career path now that he's decided to quit law school. All because he felt a little pressure from a fake test with a fake grade that he was too scared to look at."

"Sounds complicated," Mike said, "but you're probably overqualified. Plus, like I said, it's hard work."

McClure nearly spit beer from his mouth. "Overqualified? Did you not hear me say he has a political science degree?"

Mike blinked several more times, readjusted his glasses, then slowly walked away.

"I object to this entire line of questioning," I said to McClure, which drew a quick reprimand.

"Don't try to talk like a lawyer," he said. "It's obnoxious, and have you considered that you might be some kind of a Torts Law savant? For all you know that trash can on the street is hiding the highest grade in the class, and I mean, of all things to be an accidental genius in, Torts isn't the worst thing. My first year I sat next to a guy that was a Property Law savant. His name is Peter something or another. First semester, Peter was average at best, but then out of nowhere he AmJur'd Property Law without lifting a finger. This dude was a mess, too. He missed several classes, slept through several more. We had a midterm and after he aced it, the professor thought Peter had cheated, so he started calling on him in class, and Peter always answered flawlessly. And you know what he was doing in class the entire time? Playing online poker. Live hands. Anyway," McClure nodded, "Natural talent in Torts would be high on the list of lucky breaks. Imagine being unnaturally gifted at something stupid. Like Constitutional Law." McClure shuddered at the thought of it.

A cook delivered our food from the kitchen and set the dishes on the bar, so we left the foosball table and returned to our seats, where we ate in silence, briefly. The only thing McClure did more voraciously than speak was eat, and the only reason he ate so quickly was so that he could hold court while everyone else chewed. McClure had devoured his entire meal before I had reached the middle of my burger.

When Mike returned with another cold beer, McClure asked him, "Hey Mike, here's a question for you - do you support the death penalty?"

"I guess so," Mike answered without much thought.

"Shep?" McClure asked.

"Which answer will more quickly end whatever harangue you're working up to?"

"For the majority of my life," McClure continued undeterred, "I would have agreed with you, Mike. I believed in capital punishment. Know what changed?"

Mike shook his head and guessed. "You learned how to think like a lawyer?"

"Oh, Jesus," McClure said apologetically. "You've been listening to our bullshit too long, Mike." Then McClure turned to me again. "Do you study their faces, Shep?" he asked. "Your classmates, do they look intelligent or noteworthy to you in any profound way? Any of them? These are the people who will one day be responsible for putting someone to death. *To Death!*" McClure cleared his throat. "I had a professor who polled our Tax class with one simple question: what kind of law do you want to practice? He went student-by-student and listened to their answers, and now think about this – we're only two hours away from a major oil and gas hub yet I was the only person in the room of 75 that said they wanted to practice oil and gas law. The other morons said criminal defense, criminal defense, criminal defense. We get it, you've read every John Grisham novel, you've seen every Boston Legal episode, but then one girl," McClure stopped and took a long drink of beer. He was getting revved up. "Then one girl," he repeated, "the one who never wears makeup because makeup would obscure the permanent scowl on her face and trust me, this girl wants us all to see the contempt she has for us. She's the same girl who wheels her books around on a rolling backpack. A gunner, of course, and she is the one person who wants to be a prosecutor. Imagine it! All these weirdos saying criminal defense or something else they'll never be, one practical oil and gas lawyer, and the only person that absolutely nobody, and I mean *nobody* likes – truly a rare law school occurrence as I'm sure you're now aware – and she's the one who will reinstate the firing squad one day." McClure paused and went to take another drink of his beer but stopped short, too repulsed to even sip. "In the end, they'll do divorces, wills, title, or if they're lucky they'll work in-house for a company that hires the hard parts out..." McClure trailed off. "What was I trying to say?" he asked.

"Something about capital punishment and a girl with a rolling backpack."

"She is the exception, Shep. She means business, which is why we need to end the death penalty in this state."

"That was your point? The death penalty?"

"No, but here's another point, Shep, we're not exactly at Harvard here. You're not competing against future Supreme Court aides or taking classes from professors with highbrow reputations to defend. The bare minimum is all you need apply until the law school has collected its full tuition from the banks you borrowed from. They're the ones who really own your ass. Worry about them and the interest rate you cannot even begin to fathom yet. It's all bullshit, man," McClure said, rubbing his thumb and fingers together, "but it's entirely possible to treat it as bullshit and still get through it. I am a prime example. Here I am knee deep in my third year of it, enrolled in Maritime Law, Museum & Art Law, Sports Agency Law..."

"Did you say Maritime Law?" I asked.

"Yes, I am studying Pirate Law, Shep. I mean I could be billing hours at one of the firms that offered me a job. You know, learning to be an actual attorney? Instead, here I sit, drinking beer on a Tuesday afternoon dishing out free advice."

"You sure this is advice?"

"Yes, Shep, it is. You do it. That's the advice. You stay in school. This is the long game, so you play along and do it, because you're good enough to be here in the first place. Make your money a priority, and when you've got enough of it, then you'll have earned the right to look back and bitch about the bullshit route it took to get there. That's the American Way, and your JD is your presumption of intelligence, so forget about grades. Sleepwalk through a C+ average. You can do it easy." McClure looked at me and raised his beer. I had a hunch what was coming next, and so I did not reciprocate the offer for cheers. He finished anyway. "In the meantime, how about a toast? Here's to two damned handsome men on scholarship who don't have to suffer the misfortunes of the peasant class."

"You're picking up the tab today, asshole."

This was McClure's most overused joke at my expense. Where McClure was on a full ride based on his accomplishments in undergrad, he knew I paid my own way. The full rate.

"Oh," McClure added, mocking embarrassment, "I forgot you aren't on scholarship, are you? Well, I'm sure there's some other handsome man at this school who meets the criteria. Cheers to him, anyway," he said and drank.

"I know you're proud of yourself for being the best of the mediocre, but you can also already see your future in the profession. You have job offers. You're beyond grades. Even if I make it to that point, I'm not convinced I'd be fulfilled, so your appeal to the American Way isn't convincing."

"You don't have to trust me. You got any old people in your class? Like older than 28?" he asked.

"Sure, there are a few."

"Go ask those people if you should quit on this opportunity. If you should prematurely give the working world a shot. Because I guarantee you the jobs available in that world are exactly what pushed the old people to apply to law school. They learned that you're going to have to grind anyway, and some of us would rather grind in a profession where you occasionally get to fuck somebody else over and get paid lots of money to do it. Now, you want another drink?" he asked and pointed at my empty beer.

"One more. Then I need to catch a ride to Duck's to sleep it off."

"What's going on at Duck's?"

"We're supposed to review for the Order of Barristers competition that's coming up."

"Order of Barristers!" McClure wretched. "No wonder you want to quit."

"Duck asked me to do it. I gave him my word. Besides, I'm just along for the ride at this point."

"Yes! That's the perfect attitude, Shep. I'll drink to that."

"Which reminds me – what are you doing on Thursday around five o'clock in the evening?" I asked.

"Why?"

"We need someone to play the role of our client in the Order of Barristers thing."

"Shep, there's not a goddamn chance in hell," McClure said.

RUSSELL "DUCK" Williams was an All-America law school candidate. Well-traveled. Scratch golfer. He graduated cum laude from TCU where he lettered in football, just like his father, who Duck had quite a bit in common with. The size and athleticism, the handsome face, and the great expectations to be a litigator at the prestigious firm of Tisinger, Williams, and Scott, LLC. Seeking employment at a prestigious firm, even one bearing his own last name, meant he had to try for Law Review, and that meant he had to care supremely about his grades. To deal with the mounting pressure, he was stoned roughly 95% of the time. It was a habit he could easily afford because the stress of being a Williams came with several benefits, most especially Duck's standing as one of three beneficiaries to the M.A. Williams Estate Trust. Duck lived in University Terrace in a two-bedroom, three-bathroom, two story house that felt like a mansion to a 23-year-old college kid. Any day now I was due to move in, except there remained an outstanding impediment. Duck's uncle from his mother's side – an eccentric named Abernethy Green or "Uncle Ab" – currently occupied the upstairs bedroom. He showed up during the summer after he became embroiled in family drama over what Uncle Ab described as the theft of his inheritance. He was hiding out at his favorite nephew's house, unbeknownst to the rest of the family, until he could arrange a more permanent place to stay. Due to a perpetual lack of motivation, made worse by a terrible drinking problem, he wasn't going anywhere any time soon. Until the problems facing Uncle Ab were resolved, I lived in a one-bedroom dump of an apartment with a shared coin-op laundry room that doubled as a safe space for light drug deals.

I knocked on Duck's front door and let myself in. I had a key.

"Anybody home?" I announced. "Uncle, you up there?" The staircase leading up to Uncle Ab's bedroom was just off the foyer. I heard his voice boom.

"Hello, Shep, gangs all here!" he called, then he appeared at the top of the stairs. He wore a white guayabera shirt and held a purple TCU mug that in the middle of the afternoon likely contained more Irish whiskey than coffee. He was a large man, who walked pigeon-toed, and he had his *Wall Street Journal* folded under his armpit. He read the paper from cover-to-cover every day, among others if he had the time, and he usually had the time, so when he was good and drunk in the evenings, he became enraged with political conspiracies.

"How was class?" he asked.

"Class was fine."

"You look tired, Shep, are you okay?"

"I am tired. Nothing more."

"Duck looks tired, too. Tired and maybe a little disappointed." Uncle Ab's eyes narrowed. He looked at me and with a softer, paternal inflection in his voice, he asked, "Did you come out okay?"

I avoided the crux of the question and used banality instead.

"I'll be fine," I assured him. "I'm working on my ability to skate by."

"Listen, Shep, I don't think I'm going to be out of here by the end of the semester," Uncle Ab admitted. "I do feel terrible about it, so I decided to get you boys a little something. A stress reliever. And...well, I'll let Duck fill you in," he said and smiled. "I need to hit the head. Adios." He stepped across the hallway and shut the door.

The scent of weed wafted through the house. I walked down the hall and through a beaded doorway curtain into the Entertainment Room, where *American Beauty* spun on the record player with the volume set low. There was a weed grinder on the coffee table and an ash tray with two spent joints in it, but no Duck.

I heard a groan in the backyard and pulled back one of the green velvet curtains covering a window. Duck was outside on his hands and knees looking for something underneath the porch deck. I knocked on the window and he waved me out there.

As I stepped outside, I was hit by a noxious odor so overpowering that it masked the thick scent of marijuana in the doorway. It smelled like fertilizer and death. I put my jacket over my mouth and said, "My God, Duck, what the hell is that?"

"I think a raccoon died under here. I saw one yesterday in the tree, but I can't find the damn thing." He stood up and knocked the dirt off his jeans. "Help me look?" he asked.

I checked under the deck but didn't notice anything out of the ordinary. We looked behind the shed, in the trees, along the porch, behind a stack of firewood. We walked the fence line. Found nothing unusual.

As we were headed back inside to escape the stink, Duck looked at me and said, "You bailed on me today."

"I couldn't handle how everyone was acting so intense," I explained. "I kept my head down and got the hell out of there."

Based on his sunken demeanor, I don't think Duck performed well on Becker's exam question. He had been a nervous wreck about it, too. We went out for drinks the night after turning the exam in, and Duck debated with himself about his answer the entire time, making multiple trips to the bathroom to vomit.

"So, what'd you make on the exam?" he asked.

But before I could answer, the sudden roar of an engine caught our attention a few blocks away. We could hear the car accelerating through the neighborhood, the noise getting louder as it approached

Duck's block. And then, as suddenly as it had started, the engine went silent, leaving us both wondering what had happened.

My cell phone buzzed ominously in my pocket. I answered. His voice was calm. Direct.

"Shep, you got a minute?"

"What's up?"

"What's the name of your friend in University Terrace? The one with the good weed?"

"Duck?"

"Yeah, Duck. He in your circle of trust?"

"He is. I'm with him right now."

"At his house?"

"Yep."

"Listen…shit…hold on," he said and for a moment there was silence. Then he came back on and said, "There's a cop out in front of his house. I need you to let me know when he leaves."

"Hold on," I said, and I immediately rushed inside with a panicked Duck trailing on my heels, asking what was going on. I ignored him, and peeked through the small windowpane on the front door where I saw a cop car parked near the stop sign. "Still here."

"Is he out of the car?"

"Nope. He's in it…wait!" I said, as the cop car started moving. "He turned down Essex Ave. Sped away."

"Your friend's house has a garage on the west side, right?"

"Correct."

"Listen, I'm having some car trouble. You think he'll let me park my car in his garage until I can get a mechanic over here to look at it?"

"Car trouble, huh?"

"I need an answer in a hurry."

"Yeah, we can make it work," I said, though I knew I had no choice.

"Hurry up," he said and hung up.

I put my hand on Duck's shoulder and said, "We have a problem."

"Who was that?"

"Diablo."

"Oh, no."

"He needs to park his car in your garage."

"Why?"

"I don't think I can say no to him at this point."

"Dude."

"Trust me?"

Duck nodded, then followed me into the garage where we moved boxes full of records and old law books that his father had loaned him. I mashed the garage door button on the wall and the door jolted open. Just as it did, the engine in Diablo's black Z06 Corvette rumbled from the alley catty-corner to Duck's house. Diablo coasted quietly toward the driveway and expertly backed in next to Duck's Land Rover. We saw no other cars. No police. Only a gray afternoon mixed with the rancid smell of a dead raccoon dipped in pig shit.

Diablo casually stepped out of the car wearing his usual getup. Blue jeans. Luccheses. An untucked, white, Oxford button down with the sleeves rolled neatly below the elbow, gold Rolex, but this time, he also had a busted lip and red welt over his right eye. He had a real name, Ryan Leppich, but around the restaurant we preferred to use his old Army nickname.

"Go ahead and put that door down, if you don't mind," Diablo said.

"You look like you need a drink," Duck said.

"Man, you said it."

"What would you like?"

"Whatever you place in front of me, barkeep, I'll drink."

"How about an easy bourbon and soda?"

Diablo agreed and Duck kindly ushered him inside. While Duck poured a cocktail, I showed Diablo to the bathroom, where he cleaned himself up. I led him through the beaded curtain into the Entertainment Room, and with Duck's blessing, Diablo sat on the couch and adeptly rolled a joint. He lit it. Toked from it. Passed it to Duck.

I was worried how Duck was going to react, until he took one long hit. He sat down on a walnut Eames chair, and propped his feet up, then took another hit and contemplated the smoke suspended in white streaks hovering in front of an LCD Soundsystem concert poster. He adjusted the collar on his grey corded cardigan and a red glaze covered his foggy blue eyes. I think he was happy to have the distraction from law school.

"All right, Diablo," I said, "why were you running from the cops?"

"Who said I was running from the cops?"

"Easily implied."

Diablo took a deep breath and sunk into the couch. "I put my chin in front of her and dared her to do it," he explained. "And she did. First with a right cross that connected, followed by a backhand with a Louis Vuitton bag I bought her. The bitch had the nerve." Diablo smiled at the thought of it. He touched his lip and winced.

"So, she beat you up? But then she's the one who called the police?" I asked.

"There was some yelling before the punch was thrown. In front of her mother, no less, the real bitch in this situation," Diablo said. He put his fist to his mouth and coughed. "She called 9-1-1 before I could slap the phone out of her hand."

"I know I'm just a student, not a real lawyer," I said and raised my hands, "but I think you made things a lot worse for yourself by running. I mean, if you were the victim here."

"What the hell are they teaching you in law school?" Diablo growled.

"Nothing this exciting."

"What do you think happens when the cops show up to two crying women, one of whom prematurely called the cops and said her daughter feared for her life? I'd rather take my chances leaving. And so, I left."

"Did she have reason to fear for her life?"

"Of course not."

"What are you going to do when the police show up at your place looking for you?"

"That's the reason I'm not at my place. There's an extenuating circumstance that I'm more concerned with."

Duck slowly raised his finger and interrupted Diablo. "Sir, I feel obligated to reiterate that, like Shep said, we are just law students. There is no confidentiality between us. No lawyer-client privilege. Do you…do you understand what I'm trying to say?"

Diablo grinned a wide, intimidating grin, and he stared at Duck long enough to make the extended silence uncomfortable. Then he winked and lightened his attitude. "Here's some real-world advice, boys, that they won't teach you in school: don't ever talk to the police. Ever. Even if you're innocent. Especially if you're innocent. I didn't talk to the police today, and tomorrow morning, when everyone comes to their senses, there won't be any charges pressed. There won't be any domestic dispute. There won't be anybody to open the trunk of the Corvette."

"The problem is, if I may," Duck said, "there's a difference between not talking to the police and running from the police. In the eyes of the law."

"Wait a second," I said quickly, "What do you mean the trunk of the Corvette? Do Corvette's even have trunks?"

"It's little but it holds a sufficient amount of compromising evidence," Diablo answered. "And if the cops listened to my old lady and her bitch of a mother, had I stayed around, they would've searched the car, and…" Diablo held his hands up like they were in cuffs.

Duck looked queasy. He asked to be excused for a drink of water, but he changed his mind and returned to the Eames chair when he nearly fainted after standing up.

"I'm going to get it all taken care of and out of your hair real soon. Don't you worry," Diablo assured him. "It's all white-collar bullshit, other than…" he added, and first he ran his finger along his nostril and then he touched the cut over his eye and checked for blood. "Do you mind if I get some ice for this, boys? It's starting to swell up on me."

"No problem," Duck said. "Freezer in the kitchen. Just use one of the towels on the counter."

"Mind if I also…?" Diablo shook the ice in his empty glass.

"Make yourself a strong one."

Diablo thanked us, and when he left the room, Duck leaned toward me and whispered, "Does the underlying crime have to stick for the charge of leaving the scene to apply? That's a felony, isn't it? Leaving a crime scene?" Duck wondered and looked to me for reassurance for reasons I knew not.

"How would I know? We haven't had Criminal Law yet."

"Might we be accomplices after the fact?"

"Can we please not law school this one?"

"Speaking of law school," Duck said. He relit the joint and took another hit, then he reached into the green backpack at his feet and found his Blue Book. He flapped the booklet around before he threw it aside and said, "C+, man. Not going to cut it with Mr. Tisinger, Mr. Williams, or that prick Mr. Scott." He placed the joint on an ash tray and added, "I'm going to smoke enough dope to ricochet off one of Jupiter's moons, then I'm cutting back. I wanted to hold off on the Adderall regimen until closer to real exams, but I'll start now and put in some extra work." He suddenly shot up violently in his chair, "Shit, what about the Order of Barristers? That's in two days. Why did you let me drag us into this mess?" he said and fell backward against the chair and closed his eyes.

I had reluctantly agreed to be Duck's teammate in the competition after initially declining. Duck asked several other of our classmates, the few he trusted, who either declined or had already partnered with somebody else. So, he came back to me, and offered self-pity, booze, and drugs. The competition involved an interview with a potential client in our make-believe law firm, and we would have to perform the interview in front of a panel of judges who would declare winners using metrics like poise, clarity, and the knowledge of a minimal amount of law.

"Are we sure we want to do this?" I asked. I couldn't bail on Duck even if I intended to quit school, but maybe I could convince him to back out by using his own volition against him.

"I could be talked out of it. I'll convince my dad that I need to refocus some time and energy on Torts. Besides, we don't even have a client."

Diablo poked his head through the curtain. He had ice wrapped in a dishtowel that he held against his eye. "You guys mind if I make a few phone calls?" he asked and showed us the cell phone in his other hand.

When Diablo left the room again, Duck looked at me and said, "What about him? He owes us now."

"I don't think we want this going off the rails."

"They would probably assign us an upperclassman to be our witness."

"Oh no, I'm not dealing with some sanctimonious upperclassman," I said.

"Just promise me this much - ask a few more people if they'll help us out. I'll do the same. If it works out, it works out, because if I'm going to make shitty grades, I better beef my resume up with extracurriculars," Duck said, then quickly transitioned the spotlight back on me. "Are you going to tell me what you got on the damn exam or not? That's what you owe me for this Diablo mess," he whispered.

"I'm going to have to owe you something else, because I can't tell you what I got on my exam."

"Don't play games, you prick."

"I'm not playing any games. I don't expect you to understand this, but I threw my exam away before I looked at the grade. I'm going to quit the law school."

Duck got very serious and peered at me. "What do you mean you don't expect me to understand? Is this a joke? Are you talking about reenacting that movie? What was it called?"

"Duck, I'm not any good at law school. Let's be honest."

"How do you know!? You didn't look at your grade!?"

"Even if I got a good grade, I'd owe it to dumb luck. I'm not interested in Torts or Contracts or any of it," I continued. "The fact is I'd make a terrible lawyer. It's all about details and deadlines and procedure. Little nuances and patterns for nosy people to apply to a population full of the emotionally compromised. I'm not good at dealing with any of that. Why put myself through debt and stress over grades in the meantime? I'd rather be honest with myself and quit."

"You'd be throwing your life away, man. It's crazy."

Diablo poked his head through the beads again. "What's the address here?" he asked.

Duck hesitated. I reassured him with a gentle nod, and I patted my hand upon my chest to let him know it was on me. "2915 21st Street," he said and gulped.

"Thanks," Diablo said, and returned to his phone conversation.

"Don't you ever dream about what life would be like if you escaped the pressure of being a litigator in your father's firm?" I asked.

"That's a daydream that fades pretty easily when I consider the possibilities flying around the country in the firm's Citation." Duck leaned forward and studied me again. "Did you really not look at your grade?" he asked.

I just shook my head, no.

"It's going to be a real shame when a rumor flies through Section Two because one of the A's isn't accounted for, and then I'll have no choice but to explain that one of the A's is delivering steaks for a living."

"I won't be around to care."

"Maybe not," Duck began, quietly, "But you'll be close by. At the intersection right outside of Hannagan Hall, waiting on a red light so you can drive the cheap steak steaming in your backseat to some guy that tips in coins. You'll pine for that ugly Hannagan building, and then you'll notice your odometer has reached 200,000 miles and you'll get nervous about the check engine light that's been on for six months, and you'll wish you were around. You'll wish you cared."

Diablo returned to the room and sat back down. He placed his drink on the table and asked if Duck wanted him to roll another joint. Duck agreed, so Diablo took a rolling paper from the stash box and laid it flat, then he said, "I've got a ride coming. Should be another few minutes."

"Tell him," Duck said.

"Everything okay?" Diablo asked.

"It's nothing. I've decided that I'm going to quit law school," I answered.

"Why would you quit law school?" Diablo asked.

When I didn't immediately volunteer an answer, Duck informed him. "We took a practice exam. Got our grades back earlier today. This idiot apparently didn't even look at his fake grade and still he decided to quit."

Diablo looked at me curiously and said, "Don't be an idiot, Shep."

"Let's get back to the matter at hand, please? Diablo, did you leave before the cops arrived? Did they see you at all?" I asked.

"Nope. I was long gone. I was home free until I blew through a red light. I was probably speeding, too. Traffic cop was nearby."

"Speeding? How fast?"

Diablo shrugged.

"Hundred?"

Diablo pointed his thumb higher, then explained, "The cop was a couple blocks over. He might know the make and model, but that's it. Like I said, by tomorrow morning, it'll be over with. No crime. No crime scene. No scene to flee. Right?"

A loud noise thudded in the ceiling like Uncle Ab had dropped a bowling ball upstairs. A startled Diablo flew out of his chair, and said, "Who the hell else is here?"

I reassured him. "It's Duck's roommate. His uncle. He's probably drunk and he's definitely old and not a problem."

Duck nodded approval of my description.

"Shep, I'm really out on a limb here," Diablo said. He took a deep breath and sat back down. "Is there anybody else hanging around I need to know about?"

"No, but that reminds me, Duck. When I walked in, Uncle Ab mentioned he got us something. What was he talking about?"

I could see Duck's brain working by the way his eyes suddenly jittered. A small smirk formed on the side of his mouth. "Uncle Ab is leaving for Vegas today, but he has very generously decided to throw us a little party during his absence, and as the host, I have decided to be very strict about the invitees."

"What do you mean strict?" I asked.

"Only currently enrolled students are allowed to attend." Duck said. "Law students. No plus-one. No dates. No undergraduates. No nothing. Except law students."

"You're telling me if I brought a waitress from Chimy's as my date, you wouldn't let her in?" I asked.

"No, I wouldn't, because your hypothetical is flawed. First, nobody gets a number from a waitress at Chimy's except for athletes."

Diablo pointed at Duck and said, "That's true."

"Second," Duck continued, "you won't be invited to the party in the first place. Assuming, again, that you aren't full of shit and that you really are going to quit."

"When's the party?"

"Originally, it was supposed to be Friday."

"Fine, I'll quit on Monday."

"I said originally, but something has just come up Friday, so I'm moving it, to the week before Finals. In December."

"I do love watching those nerds get drunk," I sighed, "but if that's the price I must pay…" I knew full well Duck couldn't wait until December to throw this party.

"You might want to see this, too," Duck added. He reached into his back pocket and withdrew a folded piece of paper. "Based on Uncle Ab's budget, I've assembled a list of basic necessities for the party." He dangled the paper between his fingertips until I grabbed it from him and read it. It included two kegs, several handles of booze, two ounces of weed, three kinds of wine, and 15 cases of Andres Champagne.

"How many bottles are in a case of champagne?" I asked after looking over Duck's list.

"Six," he answered.

"That's a lot of champagne," Diablo said.

"I think I'll name the party – Bring the Pagne," Duck added and waved his hand over his head like it belonged on a brightly lit marquee, but then his shoulders dropped, and he pleaded with me. "Please don't quit, Shep. I really want this party on Friday. I already told Mary Khong about it. Mary Khong! She got a B+ on Becker's question, and…"

Before Duck could finish, a bone-jarring knock shook the front door with authoritarian force.

Diablo jumped out of his seat again, and this time he put his finger under his nose to keep us quiet.

"Is that your ride?" I whispered.

"That's a cop knock," he whispered back.

"What the hell?"

Diablo looked at his watch. "There's no fucking way."

The bedroom door on the second story opened, and the stairs squeaked from the weight of Uncle Ab, who walked down the steps, whistling some tune, headed to answer the door. Duck and I scrambled toward the foyer while Diablo ran for the back of the house, but it was too late. Uncle Ab opened the front door.

"I'm running a few minutes behind!" Uncle Ab said to the Chinese man at the door. There was a yellow cab parked on the curb. "A few more minutes, okay? You can keep the meter running."

The driver agreed, and when Uncle Ab turned around, he looked shocked to see me, Duck, and a stranger twice our age blinking at him down the hallway. He gathered himself, nodded, and walked back up the stairs without another word.

We took Diablo back to the garage. He opened the trunk of the Corvette and removed a small briefcase. He reached into his pocket and removed a billfold, pulling out five crisp $100s. "For you," he said to Duck, "if you let me keep the car here overnight. My mechanic won't be able to make it until morning, but I want you to know I'm taking the heat with me," he said and patted the briefcase.

I nudged Duck with my elbow. He hesitated at first but came to his senses and took the money. "What time will you be back for it?" he asked.

"Open the garage precisely at 9:00am, and I'll be out of your way. Do you have class then?"

"No, I'll be here."

Diablo's phone rang. He answered it and stepped to the side. After a short conversation, he returned to us and said, "Rides here. You mind opening the garage door?"

I hit the button and we all three stood there as the door jolted open and the garage filled with the rancid smell lingering outside.

Duck wretched his face. "Aww, that smell again," he said, "It's nauseating. What is that?"

Diablo grinned and said, "There's a feed lot outside town. The wind blows out of the northwest just right, and voila, Shit Smell." His chin was up as he strutted out of the garage, briefcase in hand, and got into the passenger side of a black Suburban that immediately sped away.

"Damn," I said, standing in the driveway, still perplexed.

"What?"

"Just remembered I left my car at the law school."

"Weren't you at Rocky's before this? How did you get here?"

"One of the bartenders drove me."

"Of course he did."

"What do you think was in the briefcase?"

"That's your boss. What do you think?"

"My guess? Some faulty paperwork. Maybe some blow. Like he said, mostly white collar shit. Can you give me a ride?" I asked.

"You know my rule."

Duck's rule was that he never drove, under any circumstances, while under the influence of a substance stronger than a single cup of coffee.

"Maybe you can catch a ride with Uncle Ab," he mentioned.

We went back inside the house and found Uncle Ab lugging a large suitcase down the steps. He agreed to drop me off at the law school as it was on the way to the airport anyway. I left Duck, weary, quiet, and stoned as he was, and accompanied Uncle Ab to the back of the taxi. He gave instructions to the driver, then put a stubby cigar in his mouth but promised he would only chew on it.

"What was that all about?" he asked.

"Apologies, but I can't talk about it."

"You'll make a fine lawyer one day, Shep."

"I don't know about that," I said. "You're very generous, Uncle Ab. For the ride and especially for the party. Duck is assembling quite the list of party favors."

"Don't mention it. I owe it to you."

"You go to Las Vegas often?"

"Used to."

"Where do you stay?"

"The MGM."

"What's your game?"

"I play poker. Do you like to gamble?"

"Not normally and especially not poker. Takes more patience than I'm willing to commit," I told him. "Uncle Ab, you ever do anything crazy? Like, purposefully crazy?"

"Well, if all these people filling up the world are considered the sane ones, then yeah, I've done a lot that qualifies. The difference for me is that I'm allowed to be nuts, because I'm wealthy. Is your family wealthy, Shep?" he asked and leaned closer toward me so that he loomed over me in the backseat.

"No sir," I answered, intimidated and uncomfortable. I hated talking about money.

"Then you better be a little more careful about your crazy decisions. How about rich? Is your family at least rich?"

"Is there a specific valuation cutoff?"

"If you're honest with yourself, I think you just know."

"I think my parents have money, but they aren't rich. Does that make sense?"

"It does," Uncle Ab answered. He straightened back up in his seat. "In my more recent experiences, I have discovered wealth doesn't necessarily involve a number at all, but that's a lifelong lesson I do not have the words for. It can only be experienced, by a person of any class. Though, I wasn't able to achieve it myself until I had already accumulated so much money that I had the leisure to contemplate the mystery in the first place."

"Mystery is right," I said.

"Rich people, and some people who just have money, you will interact with regularly, because they spend their money and like to be seen spending it. Often, they are assholes, and some of them, unfortunately, turn their kids into assholes, too."

"Do you think I'm an asshole, Uncle Ab?"

"Of course not, Shep. But your parents might be."

"That was my boss in the house by the way."

"Your boss?"

"I work at a little steak restaurant to help pay my bar bills and what have you. He owns the place."

"My guess is he's into something else other than just steaks. What do you think?"

"Maybe. Maybe not."

"I suppose that's honorable of you. Working and whatnot," Uncle Ab added. "But I must admit I wouldn't really know much about responsibility. The silver spoon is so firmly implanted up my rear end that I am unable to empathize with common folk, if you catch my drift, so I like to stay out of most people's way, especially the sober ones. If only they'd reciprocate," he added and chewed on his cigar.

We arrived at Hannagan Hall and pulled into the front drive where the taxi squealed to a stop. Busybodies with backpacks full of books walked by, studying the cab with curiosity. I couldn't wait to step out and reveal the kind of wildcard who took a cab ride to the school on a random Tuesday afternoon, but first, Uncle Ab gave me one more piece of advice.

"Keep your aspirations small, Shep. Concentrate on the task at hand. The day. The class. The case. This is not mere diligence I am describing, because if your dreams get too far ahead of you, the space between your dreams and your reality will be filled with anxiety, regret, and fear. Focus on what's in front of you, and I promise it will be your first step toward a fulfilling life of wealth."

I thanked him, though I didn't understand him, then I walked to my car, where I found a pink slip folded under the windshield wiper. I removed the parking ticket and stacked it with the others in the glove compartment, then I turned the engine on and let the car run until it heated up, and I drove toward the restaurant. The sun peeked from behind the gray afternoon and when I faced the unencumbered western sky, I flipped the overhead shade down to shield my eyes, and I cussed the unabated horizon. I missed trees. There weren't any trees here. We had trees back home that blocked the sun in the evening and filtered the light into soft colors along highways that cut through the forests like tunnels.

One of those tunnels led to my childhood home, my parents, and their straitlaced regime of GPA benchmarks, extracurricular activities, resume builders, and a social status with a perpetually vertical trajectory. I was never allowed to be curious, argumentative, or uncertain, because once there was an iota of proficiency in an area that might lead to an acceptable career, I was forced to dedicate myself to it, whether I remained interested in it or not, whether I believed in it or not. There was no time to explore self-serving beliefs. Those were wasteful endeavors.

In college, I tricked them into believing my liberal arts classes were to achieve a minor degree in political science, but that was my major area of study. I was merely chasing grades. Once they found out, I had little choice but to apply to law school in order to salvage what they considered a meaningless diploma. I tried sabotaging the decision by limiting the scope of my law school applications, but once I was accepted into the Briscoe College of Law, my parents were so relieved that they bought me a brand-new suit, a few ties, and threw me a party, inviting all their friends. Even though I was the one footing the bill for three more years of school, I played along.

They would be surprised to know that since junior high, I would begin each school year the same - eager to learn, enflamed by great expectations, and excited that it might be the year they finally revealed something I'm truly interested in. But year after year, by the time temperatures cooled and autumn rolled around, what little motivation I had was drowned in procrastination, tardiness, and vice. Over the years I developed noticeable physical effects, too, as a manifestation of this attitude. The mere thought of having to dedicate time to study for something I never cared about to begin with created a nauseating pit in my stomach. If I opened an uninteresting book, my ears filled with a distracting, high-pitched ring.

When I walked to class, my muscles ached with lethargy. Some of this was surely owed to laziness, or juvenile cynicism, but there was something more serious present that, as I matured, I interpreted as a warning, especially when my pessimism about school and the physical malaise reached the point of self-hatred. I was a coward who refused to hear the calling, whatever that calling might have turned out to be, and I dutifully lived the life that had been laid out for me instead. The life where all I had to do was keep my head down and grind. But I felt like a fraud and the better I performed, the more I achieved, the more the fraudulent feeling intensified.

Now that the cold weather had taken over campus, and the few trees around Hannagan Hall grew bare, these cold colors of autumn, the browns and yellows, were unavoidable reminders that I was under duress, stuck in a place incapable of recognizing the holistic beauty of a simple life driving a simple car around a simple town with the simple task of delivering people their dinner.

Steaks-2-Go was located in a little strip mall next to a reclaimed furniture store and a cash advance business. Where the law school still felt distant from the actual practice of law, the law was often on display at the restaurant, especially Criminal Law. There was a manager with a felony, a sugar daddy going through parole hearings, and Diablo and I once bailed a waitress out of jail after a public intoxication arrest.

A cook checked the temperature on three steaks, flipped two cheeseburgers, then lifted a basket of fries from hot oil. When the food was ready, he added it to Styrofoam containers holding salads and baked potatoes, and I loaded them into paper bags and stapled them shut when they were full. I sealed them in an insulated bag and checked the receipt for an address only to see, to my horror, my very first order of the shift was for the bitches on the sixth floor at the University Hospital.

Making a delivery to the hospital already creeped me out. A near constant pall exists out of respect to those who might be suffering and to honor the hard work of the professionals doing their best to make people well, but walk in wearing a hat featuring a restaurant's logo, carrying an armful of delivery food, and not only do the solemn formalities vanish, the food acts like a skeleton key that opens every door in the entire building. Nurses would frequently speak to me. *Steaks? To go? Can I get a menu?* They'd invite me on the patient elevators where I'd be crammed next to some medicated stranger on a gurney and a nurse grilling me about the best things to order. I made deliveries into the Burn Unit, where employees wear a mask, a scrub cap, and medical coveralls. Every door is covered with a laundry list of warnings, images of stop signs, and secured access, but once someone in the Unit notices the food, the doors unlock, and I, and my insulated bag that hasn't been sanitized in months, are allowed unfettered access to deliver well-done steaks.

But they wouldn't dare trust the bitches on the sixth floor with burn victims. I found them in their break room seated quietly around a table watching *Days of Our Lives*, waiting for their lunch or dinner or whatever the hell their shift was. The lead nurse, the old one, the fat one, gave me the usual business. Not enough A1 packets, soggy lettuce in the side salad, an upcharge for extra sour cream even though she's a regular customer. I nodded, smiled, took my $2 tip, and left. Once I made it through the hospital maze and got back in my car, Diablo called.

"We good?" he asked.

"Anything you want to talk to me about?"

"Nothing you need to know other than it'll all be over with tomorrow morning. Your friend won't squeal, right?"

"He's cool."

"Listen, I've got an order I need you to take care of. This doesn't have anything to do with the car, but I still need you to be discreet about it." He gave me an address not too far off University Ave and added, "The order will be ready by the time you get back to the store, and Shep, don't you dare take any money from her. I'll cover you later."

"You going to be at O Bar tonight?"

"Not tonight," he answered. "Shep, tell her I'm sorry I couldn't make it, and tell her I'll be at the club later," Diablo said, then he hung up the phone.

I drove back to the store and picked up the order. The bag was sealed but the receipt wasn't unusual. Lexi F. She lived in the Alphabet Neighborhood – a hodgepodge of geriatric locals, suspects, and college students willing to risk burglaries in exchange for lower rent. The address was fronted by a small house with faded green paint and several panels missing on one side. Plastic grocery bags were tangled in the dead shrubbery and the mailbox mounted next to the broken screen door was overstuffed with colorful newspaper advertisements. The delivery was to the "B" lot, so I carried the brown paper sack of food and the jug of sweet tea down a cracked driveway overrun with weeds to a shaded backhouse covered in ivy. There was a plastic lawn chair arranged next to a terra cotta pot full of orange flowers, and a row of orange pumpkins to match. Cigarette butts were scattered everywhere.

I knocked three times, and a woman swung the door wide open wearing a thin tank top and panties. She gasped when she saw me and put a hand over her chest that put to scale the size of her cartoonishly large, aggressively fake tits. She was not quite finished with her makeup. Her eyes looked bare and small comparatively.

"God you scared me. Jesus," she said. "Where the hell is Ryan?"

"I'm supposed to apologize on Diablo's behalf," I said, attempting to sound chivalrous, but the lady quickly shut the door until only a crack remained between us.

"Who the hell is Diablo?" she asked.

"Ryan. Sorry, Ryan. We call him Diablo around the restaurant. Steaks-2-Go. Mr. Leppich told me to make the delivery for him."

The door swung open again, and this time the lady took me by the arm and pulled me inside. "It's too cold for this," she said and shut the door behind me.

The little house was old and dark, but all the appliances in the tiny kitchen were brand new. The bedroom door was open, where the TV blared an episode of *Gilmore Girls*, and a suitcase was splayed open on the floor and covered in wrinkled clothes, curling irons, and prescription pill bottles. She reached for her purple purse that was thrown on the kitchen floor, boobs hanging down through the sides of her tiny top, and she began sifting through all the junk she kept in the purse. I knew she was looking for money, but I didn't want to stop her, because I enjoyed the view and wanted to see the transaction to its natural conclusion. The scene thus far was the beginning of every delivery driver's most unattainable dream.

She made sure I was watching her, before she stood up, and I covered myself with the sweet tea jug just in case. She had a roll of cash in her hand.

"Ryan must trust you if he sent you here," she said.

"I don't know anything about it, ma'am. I'm just a delivery guy."

"Have you seen him yet today?"

"No." I lied.

"Apparently, he got roughed up by his old girl. It seems I was found out."

"I'll make sure he takes some Advil if I see him."

She flipped through several $100 bills until she found a $20 and snapped it from the roll. "Are you okay?" she asked, taking another step toward me. I could smell her cinnamon flavored gum. "You seem nervous."

"Mr. Leppich will kill me if I take that."

She rolled her eyes and took the food and the jug of tea from me and placed it on her kitchen table next to a pile of glossy magazines. "I know how tips work, babe. This arrangement is between me and you. Forget Ryan and whatever he told you."

"Like you said, Mr. Leppich trusts me, so he trusts me not to take the money." This felt like a trap. A test. I needed to remain resolved.

She ripped apart the staples that held the brown bag shut, and she removed boxes of food. "Are you in school?" she asked.

I didn't want to get into the depths of my trials, so I simply answered, "Yes."

"What are you studying?"

"I'm in my first year at the Briscoe College of Law."

She raised her eyebrows. "That's just perfect," she said and smiled. "I'll make you a deal – I won't say a word to Ryan about you accepting my money as long as you spend it in the club."

"That's right, I almost forgot," I said and snapped my fingers. "Mr. Leppich also said that he would be there tonight. At the club."

"He better show up, and he better bring you with him," she said. There was a corded phone attached to the wall. She took the phone off the hook and dialed a number. "I'll be quick," she said when someone on the other end answered. "You owe me for missing out…I want you to bring your friend to the club tonight…the delivery driver…there's someone I want him to meet…I'll see you tonight, baby…" and she hung up.

She looked at me and asked, "You got a girlfriend?"

I didn't.

"Well then, it's a date," she said and clapped her hands together for a job well done, then she sat down at her little kitchen table and opened the small container holding the baked potato wrapped in foil.

"Ma'am, do you mind me asking what club we're talking about?" I asked, respectfully.

She smirked and repeated *ma'am* in the same hesitant way I had said it, then she answered. "The Panther."

The rest of my shift was tepid as Tuesdays often were. A couple of routine deliveries to apartment complexes, one to the crew at Bar PM, a few dice games against the cook in the back of the store, and a phone call from McClure who wanted to meet for dinner as soon as I was finished with work. At 8:30pm, I decided to take one last order for the night before calling it quits. The address was near the interstate and since McClure's place was along the way, I first stopped by his apartment to pick him up. His afternoon heater had cooled considerably, but he was still in no condition to drive.

"We're gonna smell terrible," McClure said after he hopped in the car and looked at the insulated black bag in the backseat.

"I've only got one more delivery to make tonight, and don't worry, the smell is a natural aphrodisiac," I told him.

"At the zoo?"

"Sure, it attracts a certain kind of woman, but they're still a woman, so it's an aphrodisiac nonetheless."

"I need specifics."

"Just wait. You might notice they'll be paying you some extra attention tonight."

"I will not return even a glance toward the certain kind of woman attracted to a steak cologne. If that has been your personal experience, I repeat, please offer specific details for my vicarious enjoyment."

"Honestly, I'm not sure if it was the steak cologne so much as the 50% off I gave her."

McClure looked at me for a long while, silently elaborating in his mind, then snapped out of it, and asked, "Can we at least keep the windows cracked?"

"Where we going tonight?" I asked.

"Mexico Border Grill?"

"Ok, what about after?"

"I could be talked into going out. What'd you have in mind?"

"Something new?"

"Like what?"

"The Panther."

"You're out of your mind. I heard somebody was murdered there last year. A bouncer or something."

"I met Diablo's new girlfriend. She works there." I debated telling McClure about the Corvette incident. Decided against.

"I didn't expect you to jump out of law school and immediately fall into the traps of hedonism," he said.

"It's been a weird Tuesday. Might as well keep it rolling."

There was another reason I wanted McClure in the car with me. The delivery location was just off the interstate frontage road in a dark and derelict warehouse surrounded by empty dirt lots littered with plastic bags and trash. I had been here before. I double-checked the name on the receipt. The order was made by someone named Silvia Winchester, but I knew that was either a fake name or a cohabitant. The guy I knew who lived somewhere in this dump was named Roger Todd. He worked odd jobs for Diablo around the restaurant. Cleaning vents. Detailing Diablo's cars. God knows what else. The staff gossiped about it around the store, but we never could figure out why Diablo kept him around. He was one of those rednecks with poorly spaced tattoos who smelled like Cool Water when he showed up and hot asphalt when he left from all the sweating he did. Diablo wouldn't allow him in the dining room unless it was after hours. My best guess was that Roger owed a debt, likely for betting football on Diablo's book, and he had to pay it off with hard labor.

However, Roger had recently stopped showing up, and we never heard a word about it from Diablo. The fact that he used a possible alias to place an order made me worried, so I wanted McClure with me as backup in case this yokel tried anything silly.

"You really go through with these things?" McClure asked. He had turned a shade whiter at the sight of the building. "This looks like a place where bodies are hacked up and melted in vats of acid."

"I go through with it because we are bearers of good news, McClure. The only thing getting chopped up is the steak."

"You go spread the good news then. I think I'll just sit in the car," McClure said, matter of fact. He crossed one leg over the other and tapped his knuckles on the window. "Depravity unnerves me," he added.

"This is nothing," I reassured him, "I once had a delivery so deep in the bewitched woods of a trailer park I found a place where children run around in wild packs, naked but for their dirty diapers, and coated in Cheeto dust."

"Did their leader carry a conch?" McClure asked.

"Yeah, but it wasn't a conch. It was a broken TV remote, and he was the one who paid me!" I said, which got a laugh from McClure. "Look, I've been here before. This guy has done some work for Diablo around the restaurant."

McClure pointed to a second-story window, partially covered with a blue towel. Peering through the grimy glass was a manikin wearing a faded Austin 3:16 t-shirt. "This shit here is where I draw the line, Shep," McClure said. "Call me a little bitch if you want, but I'm staying right here to cover your six."

"If you join me, you can have half the tip."

"I hope you're talking about money."

"He gave me a $20 last time." This wasn't entirely a lie. Last time I saw Roger, he gave me a $20 to buy him scratch off tickets while I was out on a delivery.

"$20? That's it?"

"That's it? Twenty is a lot. Hell, sometimes I get stiffed."

"I'm still not positive you're talking about money here," McClure said.

"You get half of whatever money we make inside, plus I'll buy two buckets of beer when we get to the bar."

McClure wobbled his head as he debated, then agreed. "Okay, it's a deal," he said.

I grabbed the bank pouch that held my spare cash and handed it to McClure, then I got the stapled paper sack full of food from inside the insulated bag. We knocked on the front door, and the whole building shook and echoed. When the aluminum siding stopped rattling, we heard footsteps on stairs, then the door creaked open and jammed against the broken concrete on the stoop. A skinny woman with stringy red hair and severely cracked lips greeted us with a mutated smile short of several teeth.

Her voice scraped against the back of her throat when she asked, "Why's there two of you?"

"Ma'am, this is my trainee, I'm showing him the ropes today," I answered, then gently pushed McClure ahead of me.

"How hard could it be?" she asked.

"You'd be surprised," I replied.

"Come on, my boyfriend has the money upstairs."

Reluctantly, we followed the woman to the second story, where dust particles floated in the air between blue tarps and soiled sheets that hung from low rafters on the ceiling. It was a labyrinth of construction and debris. The concrete floors were covered in beer cans, random tools, rolls of flashing, and stacks of slate tile. All of it a potential weapon. We reached a bedroom of sorts, with a mattress on the floor that was wrapped in floral bedsheets topped with drug paraphernalia.

"Roger!" the woman shouted with what appeared to be every last shred of energy she had. She crawled under a blanket on a pleather recliner and stared at Wheel of Fortune on a 19" TV balanced on a bench. "Roger!" she shouted again then coughed several times. It sounded like a chunk of her lung detached.

Someone approached us while cloaked behind one of the dusty blue tarps. I could see his two cracked work boots. There was an annoying scratch against the blue material. High to low. Then low to high. Four long blades wrapped around the edge of the tarp and slowly began to pull it back. The blades were plastic, attached to a black glove as part of a costume. The man also wore a Freddy Krueger mask and fedora that covered his head and face. Otherwise, he was in a wife beater, grey sweatpants, and he carried a liter of Mountain Dew in his free hand.

"Roger," I said calmly, "take off the mask, please, you're scaring my trainee."

"He's just messing with you two!" the woman screeched, as she struggled to light a cigarette. She pulled the lever on the recliner and propped her feet up once the Virginia Slim lit.

Roger lifted the mask just enough to expose his mouth and nose and the bottom of his eyes. "I remember you," he sneered in his growling accent that made McClure recoil.

"Your total is $64.11," I said, trying my best to sound assertive, confident, safe. Roger had ordered two pricey signature steaks, two loaded baked potatoes, two side salads, and two pieces of strawberry cheesecake; a big tab for a man with a porta-potty in the corner of his domicile.

Roger reset the mask over his face. "No, no," he said angrily, though muffled behind the mask. "That boss of yours fucked me over pretty good and I think it's time I fucked him back..." he said and started to creep toward us, clicking the plastic blades together.

After a short, panicked wheeze left his mouth, McClure bolted, slipping on sawdust as he ran for the stairs. I dropped the bag of food and grabbed a two-by-four that was lying on the ground. The board had two rusty nails dangling through the end of it, and I held it up and swung it to show I wasn't scared to use it, but one of the bent nails caught against a curtain behind me, tipping over a VHS camcorder that tumbled to the floor.

Roger's woman struggled out of the recliner and lunged toward him, holding him back and screaming at him while he staggered forward with one leg dragging behind him like he had an injury. I dropped the beam and ran down the staircase and all the way outside. I hopped into the car where McClure was already buckled.

"Not worth the $20!" he shouted. "Let's go…let's go…let's go," he repeated, looking back toward the warehouse to see if anyone had followed us.

"Didn't get the money," I said as I sped away. "I didn't get anything."

"Oh shit, where's the food?"

"Left behind."

"Those creeps stole it! Let's call the cops!"

I looked at McClure like he was crazy.

"What?" he asked. "Were you just fucking with me in there? Did you put them up to that?"

"Absolutely not. No cops, though. There's a procedure."

"What procedure?"

"A work procedure."

"A work procedure? This isn't even a real job." McClure shouted. His eyes popped as I zoomed to the next intersection along the Frontage Road, waited for traffic to clear, then I ran a red light to make a left turn, and hid in an alley behind an abandoned used car lot. From there, I dialed Diablo's cell.

"Yeah," Diablo answered.

"Got a problem."

"Corvette?"

"Your car is fine. You remember how you said to call if I ever had an issue on a delivery?"

"Are you okay?" Diablo asked. He sounded concerned and angry.

"I'm okay."

"What happened? Who was it?"

"It was Roger."

"Roger Todd? I thought we took him off the delivery list?"

"Guess not."

"Where are you?"

"An abandoned lot on 34th and L."

"That idiot still living in the warehouse near the Interstate?"

I gave him the address, then with deliberate contrition, I added, "Diablo, I dropped the food. Didn't get any money."

"Stay where you are," he growled, then he hung up, before I was able to explain exactly what happened.

For the next 30 minutes, McClure and I sat in the parking lot debating a variety of alternatives. What should we have done differently? Was Roger capable of doing anything to us? Would I really have smacked him with a board of rusty nails? Were they living there? What were all the tarps for? Could we have stepped on any meth needles? Is Diablo coming here first, or is he going to the warehouse, then coming here? Should we drive back around the block and spy?

McClure had his right leg balanced over his left and his foot was shaking with nervous energy. "I was giving it some thought today," he said. "Your decision. I'm sure my knee-jerk reaction was familiar. Parental, even."

"Honestly, that's probably what I need."

"If I can modify my advice, I'll add this: Ultimately, it's your journey and I don't want anything I said to get in the way of that. Just promise me, whatever you choose, it won't include the aroma of cheap steak."

A matte black Suburban rumbled into the parking lot and stopped in the alley behind my car. I got out and approached the driver's side. Diablo kept the Suburban running and rolled the window down.

"Who's that in the car with you?" Diablo asked.

"Friend of mine. This was my last delivery then we were headed to the bars."

"Shep, you have too many friends who know too much about me."

"You're hard to miss, Diablo, but I'm not worried about them. They're future lawyers. They'll keep their mouths shut."

"What happened with the delivery?"

"Roger and his scraggly girlfriend lured me inside their drug den. He was wearing a Freddy Krueger mask when…"

"Roger Todd was wearing a Freddy Krueger mask?"

"And a costume glove with blades. He was trying real hard to creep me out. He said he was going to fuck you for fucking him, those were his words, and he started to chase me, so I swung a wood plank at him and ran. That's when I dropped the food."

"I don't care about the fucking food, man, are you all right?"

"I'm good," I said.

I had been on several shaky deliveries before. Once, I delivered to a wrong address in the hood. When the front door opened, four Mexican gangsters jumped out and were not happy I had interrupted their meeting. The Roger incident wasn't that scary, really, but I noticed that Diablo noticed that my hands were shaking anyway.

Diablo reached into the glove compartment. He handed me a rolled wad of cash held together with a rubber band.

"What is this?" I asked. I held it lightly in my hands. These weren't like the crisp bills he gave Duck earlier. This money felt dirty.

"Consider it a settlement," he answered. "On the condition that there are no more questions asked about this incident. You got lucky. That's a good bankroll for The Panther, where a dollar goes a long way on a Tuesday night."

"What time are we going?"

"I'll pick you up at 11. At your place?"

"At my place."

"Does he want to go?" Diablo asked, referring to McClure.

"I doubt it. Who's this girl your dancer friend wants me to meet?"

"Don't know anything about it," Diablo said, and that was it. He nodded and rolled the window up, then he casually drove away.

"What did he say?" McClure asked when I got back in my car.

"He said he took care of it."

"How did he take care of it?"

"He wouldn't say. He handed me this on the condition I

wouldn't ask how he got it. The same applies to you. I vouched for you."

I tossed the wad of cash at McClure, who caught it, and immediately began counting the money. When he finished he said, "Two things. No, wait, three things."

"Three things," I repeated as I turned back onto 34th Street.

"Number one. We *are* considering this a tip, correct? In which case, as your trainee and per the terms of our agreement, we go 50/50 on it. There's a lot more singles than I would have liked but it's still $521 total. Is this their drug money or your boss's money?"

"Why would he give us his own money?"

"To keep us quiet? I don't know."

"Quiet about what?"

"What do you think happened back there?"

"I don't know. He told me it was a bankroll for the strip club tonight. You sure you don't want to go?"

"Are you kidding? I'm not going. Which brings me to the second thing I wanted to mention: I need the home base, Shep. Some place safe. Let's go straight to Rocky's, so we can recount this incident in friendly confines."

"Rocky's it is," I said. "As long as I'm home by 11. What was the third thing?"

"Number three," McClure said, disgusted now and holding the cash away from him, "There's actual blood on this money."

A FEW HOURS LATER, I found myself riding in a Cadillac with Diablo. Navigating the industrial roads, he had to slow the car to a near standstill in order to carefully dodge gigantic potholes on roads that crossed over a labyrinth of railroad tracks and acre-lots full of abandoned oilfield equipment. The soft purple light on the horizon grew brighter, until we finally crept beneath a sign worthy of the Las Vegas Strip. Outlined in bright violet neon and adorned with radiant yellow light bulbs, it boldly advertised "The Panther." The parking lot, nearly empty, contained only three nearly identical work trucks, each with matching ladders and orange jugs chained to aluminum toolboxes. A separate, secured lot showcased the usual suspects: a Mitsubishi Eclipse, a green Camaro without a spoiler, and a maroon Ford Escort.

"I have a confession to make," I said as Diablo checked his teeth in the mirror.

"Don't tell me you've never been to a titter before."

"No, but I usually only last half an hour in these places before I run out of money. Either because I don't have money to begin with, or because I fall in love immediately and lose what money I did bring."

"See if you can last until about 1:30 in the morning," Diablo said. "This place gets too fucking Spanish for me at 1:30. I'll back you until then," he said.

"What about all that money you already gave me?"

"Oh, you'll spend that in here, too. I promise."

"I still have a confession to make," I added.

"You aren't a homo, are you?"

"Nope. But, I did accept a $20 tip from your girl when I delivered her food earlier today. She wouldn't take no for an answer."

Diablo's temperament remained the same. "You two share a camaraderie working in the service industry. I'm sure she felt obligated. It's fine."

"She did tell me I had to spend it in here," I said and nodded toward the club.

"Sounds like you got trick-fucked to me, kid, so what the hell are we waiting on? Let's go spend it," Diablo said, and he got out of the Caddy.

A cold wind whistled through the covered driveway and whipped the slashed purple awning overhead like a gym towel. I followed Diablo inside into a small holding room where a middle-aged woman with greying braids sat on an office chair behind a caged counter. She held a grocery store romance novel marked with an orange 99¢ sticker and looked at us over reading glasses outlined with bright pink frames.

"Hey baby," she said casually, as if she had just seen Diablo 30 minutes ago. She returned her eyes to the paperback and said, "Y'all go on in."

Being part of Diablo's crew allowed me to bypass the cover charge. Nevertheless, Diablo tapped his hand on a plastic candy jar wrapped in paper, displaying TIPS in faded black marker. Above the jar hung a vivid orange sign advertising Taco Tuesday from 2-4:00am, coinciding with the club's closing time. It featured a half-priced cover charge and $2 tacos from Brown's Taco Truck.

Diablo glanced at me and said, "This one's on you. For the karma."

I reached into my back pocket for my wallet and got the $20 that Lexi F. gave me earlier. I knew exactly which one it was. I folded the bill neatly and slid it into the hole cut through the sealed plastic jar.

"Thank 'ya, baby!" the hostess said without looking up from her novel.

Diablo adjusted his collar and folded it high on his neck. He had traded his usual jeans and boots in for grey slacks and leather loafers. He headed for the club entrance where a fat man in an ill-fit suit stood in front of a black curtain. The bottom of the guy's turquoise tie ended in the dead center of his giant belly. He held a metal detector in his hand and stepped in front of Diablo. "Just a moment, sir," the fat man said and raised his doughy paw.

Diablo sidestepped him. "We ain't here for Taco Tuesday," he snarled and stepped through the curtain.

The fat man's crooked smile faded into annoyance and disbelief.

"Hey you big idiot! Let them boys through," the woman at the front hollered. "Stupid ass," she mumbled.

The fat man let me pass through without a pat down. He only wiggled the handheld metal detector in my general direction as I followed Diablo inside.

The mirrors lining the exterior walls rattled as the bass thumped from an Akon song vibrating through the dark room. A spinning disco ball cast twinkling silver light over the showcase area. Leaning over the edge of the stage, a heavyset girl reached for her cell phone that was plugged into an outlet near the floor. Her face glowed electric blue as her thumbs furiously typed a text. Behind her, a fog machine hissed, filling the empty stage with a smoky haze.

"Hey there handsome," a girl said and ran her hand down my arm. She was seated behind me on a tall chair at the end of the bar. She had platinum blonde hair, pasty skin, and gaps in her teeth. There was a paper plate in front of her covered in scrambled eggs and ketchup. "You want to have some fun tonight?" she asked, bad breath and all, then winked.

Diablo saved me when he called my name. He was near a set of elevated purple couches marked off by a red velvet rope. He faced the whole room up there where he could spot girls or trouble, and I headed quickly for him.

"Ignore the Tuesday talent," Diablo told me when I reached him.

I sat down next to him and adjusted my weight on the couch, careful to avoid any cracks in the fabric. A tear in a piece of duct tape on the cushion next to me revealed a Petri dish of bacterial horror.

Our perky waitress said hello in a Panther t-shirt, green stockings, with a red wig shaped into a bob haircut. She introduced herself to Diablo, or Mr. Leppich as she called him, and mentioned she was new. "What can I get you guys?" she asked.

Diablo ordered a bottle of Grey Goose and several setups, plus a bucket of Coors Light.

"Don't bring that bottle with any fucking sparklers and bullshit," he said. "Just bring the goddamn thing, okay sweetie?"

"Sure thing, Mr. Leppich," she said.

He handed the waitress a credit card for the tab and folded a $100 bill tightly into his hand and palmed it to her. "Keep the ugly ones away from us," he said, and nodded toward the egg eater at the bar, who was now joined by several sequined cohorts. "And please tell Lexi that I'm here if you see her," he added.

"Which Lexi?"

"Lexi F."

The waitress broke the news to the murder of strippers gawking at us, and they skulked back into the darkness. She returned with a bartender who helped setup a mini bar on the small table next to our couch, sans any fireworks, and poured two vodka sodas with lime. Over the club's deafening speaker system, the DJ shouted, "Danielle! Danielle, now on Stage Two. Danielle!"

A redneck wearing a cowboy hat and FR jeans tucked into Red Wings with untied laces followed Danielle to the pole on Stage Two. He pulled a chair close to the small platform and fed $2 bills into Danielle's panties when she bent over.

Diablo opened a bottle of Coors Light and alternated between sips of beer and vodka. "Given our romantic surroundings," he said, "I don't have much patience for a sob story about the path less traveled or any of that nonsense. But I did want to talk to you, briefly, about your decision on school. Did I ever tell you what I was doing when I was your age?"

This was Diablo's favorite late-night topic of conversation, when he was good and drunk and tired, when he easily forgot the stories that had already been told a dozen times. When Diablo was my age, he was twiddling his thumbs in Kuwait during the first Gulf War as part of a unit designed for the urban warfare that didn't really break out until the second war versus Saddam Hussein, long after Diablo was discharged.

I answered jokingly. "Yeah, you were jerking off in the desert in a 120° porta-potty, right?"

Diablo leaned back in his seat and reached into his pocket for a cigarillo. "That's really funny," he said with the brown cigarette dangling from his lips. "I wasn't always stuck over there, little boy. But when I was back home, I wasn't lucky enough to have somebody offer me advice in a dark bar with no windows and exotics walking around half-naked."

"I'm not sure it's advice I need."

"Have you made up your mind? Or are you stuck on decided to quit?"

"I suppose it's decided until it's official."

"Well, decided doesn't mean shit until it's done, does it?"

"Suppose not."

"That's the only advice I've got. But, there is somebody else that's supposed to meet us here later on, and I think he'll have something better to say."

"Who?"

"My lawyer. We've got some briefcase business to discuss."

"We?"

"Me and him and nobody else. You'll be preoccupied, I'm quite certain, but I'll make sure you're properly introduced."

"Well, if there's a menu for my preoccupation, I like tits, tit-for-tat, and teases who remind me of the one who got away, but I suppose I'm at the mercy of Lexi F.'s taste tonight."

"That's the best part of these clubs, man, you can always say no. What did you think of Lexi F.?"

I raised my eyebrows. "If her friend is in the same ballpark, maybe a little younger, I'll be plenty preoccupied."

"Just turn your cool on and leave all the law school bullshit for the sunlight tomorrow."

"That's a problem. There is something about a strip club that turns me philosophical," I admitted, "I'm not sure what it is. Need to conduct more research."

"That's tough when you don't last long."

"Unfortunately, you're right. My intimacy and my intellect are both fast fleeting."

"Don't forget about your money," Diablo said. He considered the embers on the tip of his cigarillo, and asked, "If Socrates walked in here right now, you think he'd want to loosen his mind? Or his zipper?"

"If he saw the Tuesday talent…"

"Granted. But you get my point."

"The great ones can do both, Diablo, the zipper and the mind."

He raised a beer bottle and said, "I'll drink to that." Then he asked, "How much was in that bankroll?"

"Five hundred and change. I split it with McClure for the trouble."

"You paid him off, huh?"

"I wouldn't put it that way. We had a deal. I'll see it again in return."

"That's what friends are for," Diablo said. He studied me and chuckled to himself. He checked his watch and looked toward the back of the room where a closed door blocked the girls' dressing room. He didn't see Lexi F., so he looked back at me and asked, "Tell me Shep, is it opportunity you're worried about?"

"An opportunity for what?"

"For work. As a lawyer."

"Frankly, I haven't thought that far ahead. It seems lightyears away and completely irrelevant."

"If you think you're ready for real work in the real world right now, I'll sell you a 49% stake in the restaurant."

"Was that a steak pun?"

"Hell no, I hate puns."

"As of right now, I'm $20,000 in debt to the government or Fannie Mae or to tell you the truth, I have no idea how my student loans work, so I can barely afford even a cheap steak, much less a financial one."

"It's a bad time to invest anyway."

"That sounds ominous."

"It's all ominous, kid. It's a big bad world. How many more years of law school do you take before graduating?"

"It's three total."

"Three years? Are you serious?"

"Does that sound too long or too short?"

"Way too long. What do you learn in all that time?"

"The common advertisement will tell you law school is where you learn to think like a lawyer. Guess it takes a while."

"What does that even mean? Think like a lawyer?"

"I don't know. Might never."

"Sounds like a scam," Diablo agreed. He surveyed the room from left to right and placed the remnant of his cigarillo on an ash tray. "Shep, I'm about to make the bloodsuckers at McGowan, Hall, & Kornegay LLC even richer than they already are. They'll be pumping up my legal defense for however long it takes. Years. Why don't you go work for them? Maybe you'll like all the money they make."

"Is it criminal legal trouble or like the tax man?" I asked.

"Aren't they one and the same?"

"Inherently, I suppose they are."

There had been several nightshifts I worked where, after closing the restaurant, Diablo would scoop the cash out of the register and pocket it. He would invite me to O Bar and there we'd drink until the cash was gone. Essentially, it was his money, but it also might have been a technical crime. What did I know? I wasn't a lawyer. I repeated this obvious fact to Diablo.

He smirked and said, "No shit? You're so green that if I buy you an hour in the backroom it'll take you 30 seconds before you've got an archipelago stained on your pants. That is if you ever quit talking long enough to give your girl some air to work with."

"I'll take that bet. What do I get if I win?"

"Look around, my friend. You're winning either way."

"I know. I'm grateful, even on a Taco Tuesday. I was trying to trap you into a bet."

Diablo just shook his head. "Okay, we'll get the bet right. What are we playing for?"

"There's a competition at the law school. Thursday evening at five o'clock. Duck is my partner and we have to pretend to be lawyers and we have to pretend to interview a potential client."

"So? I thought you were quitting."

"It'll be my last hurrah."

"Why are you telling me?"

"We need somebody to pretend to be our client."

The recognition finally appeared. "Shep, are you fucking kidding me?"

"It was a shot in the dark," I said. I knew there was a 0% chance Diablo would have agreed to this, but I owed it to Duck to at least make an attempt, so our deal was complete. "Here's another shot in the dark," I continued, "What I really want to know is, what do you see in me that would make a good lawyer?"

"What a stupid fucking question."

"Fine, then don't answer it."

"You people are always trying to attach words where they don't belong," Diablo said. "Why does something obvious have to have a name? When I know something, I just know it."

"There's a Constitutional Law case about that actually. The dispute was about defining what constituted--"

"I don't give one flying fuck about Constitutional Law," he said and pointed across the room. "Look at what we've got coming this way."

Lexi F's shoulders slumped forward from the hulking weight of her chest, but once she made eyes with Diablo, she straightened her back and thrust her moneymakers out. She wore classic red lingerie with a red feather sash draped over her neck, and she had a girl with her, following a step behind.

The girl was shorter, younger, less robust than Lexi F. Her jet-black hair had purple streaks that flashed in the popping strobe lights. She was in a narrow tank top with strategic cut outs, tight black shorts, and high heels with long laces that wrapped around her muscular legs. She had a sleeve of tattoos on one arm that were densely compact around her wrist and forearm, overlapping several mistakes, but along her elbow and upper-arm, over her shoulder and down one side, the quality of the work improved into a cluster of trees, some with skeletal branches, some with colored leaves – red, yellow, orange, brown. Her exotic makeup exaggerated the contour of her eyes that measured me with a stone-cold glance.

This was her home turf, and she had seen it all before, so whatever I was, I was nothing new. But because I'd receive her undivided attention and hopefully, her undivided affection, the nature of our impending although abbreviated relationship was at once intimidating but was also one of the sexiest thrills I knew.

Diablo stood up to hug Lexi F., and he whispered something dirty into her ear. She laughed at him and grabbed a handful of his crotch, then gently touched his face where he had been bruised.

Lexi introduced me to her friend, April. When I reached my hand out, like an idiot, to shake April's hand, she laughed at me, swooped to my side and eased me back onto the couch, where she sat with her leg pressed against mine.

April was very clearly not from around here. She was egregiously attractive, edgy, and just the right amount of trashy.

"You want a drink?" I started off simply.

"Here, let me," she said. First, she refreshed my cocktail, then she made her own.

"Where are you from?" I asked. "Because I know it's not anywhere around here."

"Why do you say that?"

"The way you talk."

"Do I have an accent? I don't think I have an accent."

"Around here if you don't have an accent, then you have an accent."

"I'm from California. Ohio, really. But I've been in San Francisco."

"How does one get from San Francisco to here?"

"I was headed for Atlanta. Or maybe Tampa."

"Is The Panther a known club? Like, on the way?"

April laughed. "You're asking if there's a stripper circuit that makes a stop here? No, I stopped here because some of us need work to get from one side of the country to the other. It's a big place."

"Atlanta. Tampa. Those are the Big Leagues, aren't they?"

"You think I'm good enough?" she asked. She arched her back and delicately ran her fingers down her neck and over her chest.

"There isn't any doubt about it at all. The sooner you get there the better. Just maybe wait until tomorrow before you leave."

"Enough about me," she said and put her hand on my knee, "what do you do here? Is there a special occasion we're celebrating?"

Diablo interrupted us.

"Shep, get over here," he said, shaking his head. I leaned toward him, and he put his arm around me and grabbed the back of my neck. "Are you blowing this already? You're talking an awful lot."

"She seems into it."

"She gets paid to seem into it. Do you like her?"

"Am I drunk already or is she way too hot to be working in this place?" I asked.

"You're goddamn right she's too hot. She's a universal eight! Why don't you take her into the back?"

"Universal eights charge $100 just to take a peek," I whispered, as loud as I could so that only Diablo could hear the urgency in my voice.

"I don't think you understand, Shep. I told you. It's all on me." He stared at me, jaw clenched, serious as though I had challenged the reputation of his family name. "But if she's any good, you better tip her extra."

There was nothing else I could say, so I didn't say anything at all. I only took April by the hand and waited, because the housekeeping that followed was a complete whirlwind. Diablo called our waitress over, issued instructions, then briefly debated an arbitrary security fee. Once April realized she stood to make some real money, she couldn't keep her hands off me. I had to focus all my concentration tampering an erection that made a nuisance of the walk across the strip club to the Champagne Room, as Diablo called out to us, "Take it easy on him! He's a rookie!"

The waitress walked us right by the fat man who now guarded the back room. She led us all the way to a red couch surrounded by a purple curtain and complete darkness otherwise. The last thing she told us was, "Mr. Leppich got you an hour," before she pulled a rope and closed the drapes around us but for a sliver of purple electric light.

I sat down and April rolled on top of me in a graceful motion, leaning forward so that I could see straight down her shirt. "You're cute," she said, lifting my chin so that I would meet her eyes. "And I get you for a whole hour? Whatever are we going to do for an hour?"

But when she crossed her arms and began to lift her shirt, I hesitated. It wasn't much, a skipped breath, but I still hadn't overcome the shock of being in the back room in the first place. April, who was designed to sense the vibrational changes in men, recognized the pause. She lowered her arms. Kept her shirt on.

"You know," I said and rattled the ice around in my empty glass, "I thought I'd be drunker by now."

April slid off my lap and snuggled next to me on the couch. "I bet we can sneak back into the VIP and steal that bottle from Mr. Leppich. He won't see us coming behind Lexi's gigantic rack."

Right on cue, the fat man cleared his throat and said, "Excuse me," as he pulled the curtain back and fat fingered a fresh bottle of Tito's, some glasses, a canister of soda, and a cup full of sliced limes, and placed them on the table beside our couch. He almost passed out when he straightened back up, then he wheezed several times and said, "Compliments of Mr. Leppich." He waddled off, still gasping as he left, and we were alone again in our purple-accented cave.

"Does this all feel like a production to you?" I asked.

"What do you mean production?" she asked as she got to work on my cocktail.

"Today has been one of those surreal ones. You weren't put up to this, were you?"

She flipped her hands in the air. "Of course I was put up to this. I'm working."

"That's not exactly what I mean. What did Lexi F. tell you about me?"

"That there was a cute boy who was going to be with her regular guy."

"That's it?"

"My guess is you tend to overthink things," she said. She took the old drink out of my hand, and gave me a new one, much stiffer than the one before. I took two big sips of it and held back a shudder each time. "Do you work for Mr. Leppich or something?" she asked and sat next to me.

I laughed. "I'm a delivery driver at his restaurant. Not exactly corner office problems."

"Maybe he needs you to be his getaway driver?" she said.

"I don't think so. I've seen Mr. Leppich drive 120mph through University Terrace."

"I don't understand that reference."

"It means he doesn't need a getaway driver."

"I hate to break it to you, but if I was in on your surreal scheme, and if the money was right, I wouldn't say a peep anyway," she said and inched closer to me. "From the looks of Mr. Leppich, I don't think money would be a problem."

"In your line of work, I bet you're pretty good at pinning people, aren't you?"

"Pretty good," she agreed.

"Would you guess that Mr. Leppich is wealthy? Rich? Or maybe he just has money?"

"I don't know. What's the difference?"

"Earlier today, a friend of mine told me there was a significant difference between each of those categories but the reasoning doesn't necessarily have anything to do with money."

"Is it a riddle?"

"I think his point was that people who just have money don't often have it for long. People who are rich spend money like flashy assholes. But being wealthy implies a certain way of life, not just a social status. Something like that anyway. He's kind of a crazy old man with a drinking problem." I faded off.

"Those types are a dime a dozen, trust me, and that's how I treat their advice, too."

"Fair enough."

"But if I had to guess, I'd say Mr. Leppich is rich. Just a little flashy. Definitely rich."

"For now he is anyway."

"What would a delivery driver know about it?"

"What little I do know I won't repeat, except to acknowledge the lawyers will be expensive."

She took my hand and placed it high on her leg, and I gently massaged her thigh. Her skin was smooth and tan. She was skinny but muscular. "Are you in school here?" she asked.

"What gave it away?"

"You look too clean cut to only be a delivery driver. What do you study?"

"I'm at the law school."

With a slight pitch of excitement, she asked, "There's a law school here?"

"Yeah, it's not exactly prominent."

"I'm not from around here, remember? I knew it was a big college town. That's it."

"Right, California by way of Ohio."

"People used to tell me I should go to law school."

"Let me guess, they said you were good at arguing?" I asked. This is the same advice people used to tell me, as if it were a relevant metric for law school.

She smiled and said, "Yeah, people told me that, but really, I was just good at being a bitch."

"Trust me, you'll find plenty of those in law school, too."

April stared through the sliver of light in the curtain, and in between small sips of her drink, she said, "I worked part-time at a bar while I was taking Juco classes, and met a lawyer who did criminal defense. He's the one who tried to get me to actually go to law school. I always thought he was dumb though, which was kind of a motivating factor for me. I mean if he could do it, why not me? You know?"

"What made him believe in your potential?" I asked.

"He hired me to be his secretary just so the other lawyers in town would want to do business in his office. It was crazy in there and hard work dealing with the people, the files…the people. I was just good at handling the insanity, and he told me my persistence would see me through."

"But you never made it?"

"That lawyer was full of shit for one thing. He was only persistent about a type of relationship I wasn't interested in having. I ended up leaving school because of all the drama it caused. Between that and a few other things, it just didn't work out."

"What other things?"

"Family stuff. Money stuff. LSAT stuff."

"Jesus, the LSAT. You took it? How'd you do?"

"You know," she said and innocently tapped her cheek, "I thought I'd be drunker by now."

"I'll do the honors this round," I said, and proceeded to mix us each a strong cocktail.

She drank much of hers quickly, then placed it back on the table. When I sat back down, she pulled my legs a little lower on the velvet cushion, then climbed on top of me and slowly began grinding to the rhythm of an electronic dance beat.

"I've always wanted to know," she began, taking my hands and moving them until they each held a handful of ass cheek, "do people at your law school know what everyone else made on the LSAT? Did you, like, talk about it?"

"Law students will tell you a score, but whether it's their real score?" I shrugged. "Who knows? Doubtful. It isn't really that important once you're all in the same school together anyway. You just assume there is a range and you fell somewhere within it."

"What did you make?" she asked.

"I got a 158."

"So that means you really got a one…forty…?" She looked hard at me without blinking and I knew I couldn't bluff.

"I made a 151. What'd you make?"

She kept the penetrating look squarely on me with her knock-dead stripper eyes, but then broke character, and exhaled. "Less than," she said.

"Remember those guys in the Logic Puzzles that were sitting around each other in a circle?"

"You mean A, B, and C? Or P, Q, R, and S? I hated those assholes."

"Yeah well, instead of a circle, now they're just lined up in rows studying in law school."

She thought about my comment then slowly nodded her head, repeating. "Assholes." And she smiled at me and laughed, and I don't know what kind of stripper pixy dust she had either blown in my face or mixed into my drink, but her laugh sounded genuine. Her smile looked real. I squeezed tighter, and she moved harder against me.

"If you're not going to tell me your score," I said, "then you owe me something else, since I told you mine."

"If your 151 is to be believed," she said and moved the hair out of her eyes. "What do you want from me? A truth or a dare?"

"For now? I want a truth."

"Really?"

"I said for now."

"What's the truth you want?"

"I want your real name."

She forced a small laugh. "What isn't real about April?" she asked, and her hips stopped moving.

"Is April supposed to be a contradiction?" I asked. I pointed to the autumn scene tattooed above her elbow.

"Why would it be a contradiction?"

"April is a month that occurs in the spring, but the ink on your arm depicts the fall."

"Now you really won't believe me when I tell you."

"So, April isn't your name?" I asked, proudly.

"Why do you want to know so bad?"

"Because if I know your real name, I'll know I'm talking to the real you."

"My real name is Autumn.

"For real?"

"It's as real as your 151."

"Makes more sense why you'd dive into the theme," I said, pointing to her arm again.

"It'd take a whole long story to explain it all."

"You ever have anybody ask to do weird shit back here?"

She purred, then coyly stated, "Absolutely."

"You want to spill any tea?" I asked. I wanted to know for the entertainment value, but more for clues about what I could get away with in the Champagne Room.

"Secrets. All," she replied, matter of fact, and shut down my curiosity.

"I want to hear about your name and your tattoos. Where would that rank on your scale of weird things men have asked for?"

"Not even in the top-100."

"Well, that's the second truth I want."

"So when do I get a turn?"

"How about we go two for two?"

She started sliding again, sexy and rhythmic, and without any other introduction, she began, "I left home when I was 16." I knew right away, just by the tone of her voice, that her story was true, and her name was really Autumn. "We were in West Virginia then. Had trees all along the hilltops and there was nothing prettier than when the leaves turned colors."

"I thought you were from California by way of Ohio?"

"There and everywhere in between," she said. "I used to watch those trees all day long sitting on the porch, and I swear I saw the colors change in real time. But my name was merely a coincidence. We were in the Florida Panhandle when I was born, but my daddy liked the way the name Autumn Jean Thompson rolled off his tongue. He was too mean and too stupid to appreciate anything other than the sound of his own voice."

"What about the tattoos then?"

"Before I left West Virginia, before things really got fucked up, I wanted to capture a feeling of home," she said, and considered her tattoos for a moment, then snapped out of it. "Here, drink up," she added and handed me my cocktail. She put her hand on the bottom of my glass and tipped it up, so I drank a good amount. When I was finished, she put the glass back on the side table.

"I've never been to West Virginia. Will you take me one day?" I asked.

"Wouldn't that ruin it? Seeing it again?" she said with a whisper in my ear. Her shirt came off. Then the shorts covering her thong. She recentered herself on my lap, and I wrapped my hands around her.

"I'm going to quit law school," I said.

"What! Why?" She stood up and turned around. She climbed on top of me again and turned her head sideways to listen, while I played with her thong and lost my breath.

"I don't know," was all I could think of, now that I was finally preoccupied.

"Don't be a fool. You have this amazing opportunity, and you want to throw it all away?"

"Amazing for some. Not for me."

"I'm not convinced."

"About what?"

"That that's what you want to do - quit."

"How can you tell?"

"It's a part of the job. And now it's my turn for one from you. Truth or dare?"

"Dare."

She smiled and winked. "I knew you'd say dare."

"How'd you know?"

"Because you're scared of the truth I'm going to ask about."

"Or, I'm just ready for the dare."

"Okay. I dare you to have an argument with me."

I had never been more aroused in my entire life. "Okay," I mumbled.

"You argue in favor of quitting law school," Autumn said.

"Okay."

"I'll argue in favor of you staying in law school."

"Okay."

"But here's the thing..."

"Okay."

"We can't use any words."

What occurred for the rest of our allotment in the Champagne Room was a cosmic blur, and measuring the passing minutes was like counting time on the precipice of a blackhole. The seconds that ticked by expanded and slowed down, allowing brief intervals of searing neon clarity, then it all contracted rapidly. Space and time vanished with inexplicable quickness. Entire rap songs I knew and loved played, but I never heard them. The vodka in the bottle emptied but I don't remember tasting it. One hour of wild conversation and dramatic foreplay, gone in a blink, but when I pieced it all together, the connecting thread was Autumn's eyes stuck on mine for those 60 minutes until I saw sparks and lightning bolts and supernovas in them.

The fat man appeared in the curtain and grunted.

Autumn whispered, "Time's up." She remained only lightly sweaty and composed, while I was blue-balled and nervous about what was to happen next. She climbed off me and reached for the mirror and makeup in her clutch. I heard the buzz from the club. It sounded crowded out there, and I worried for the strangers' hands that would soon grasp at Autumn. I wanted her all to myself, but the strip club protocol called for separation now that the money was spent. Autumn was on to the next sucker while her first mark of the night would have to find some other place to expend the overwhelming, pent-up desire created during the session alone together in the dark. All that work. All those hints. We never crossed the line.

After Autumn readied her face and straightened her hair, she looked at me, with a modicum of vulnerability evident in her own hardened eyes, and she asked, "So, who won the argument?"

"I did. But you sure as hell got close."

"Sorry I couldn't do better. Will you at least take me back out there and make me feel pretty?" she asked, and she pressed against me and kissed me delicately on the cheek.

I walked out of the Champagne Room ten feet tall with the equipment to match and the hottest girl in the place by a wide margin clung to my arm. This is how men get trapped, isn't it? Made to feel special by a professional and lured back every Tuesday night for $500 a pop. At least it was free this time.

Lexi F. still had her arms wrapped around Diablo in the VIP area. They were joined by a man. He wore a white dress shirt with his initials on the French cuffs and a Hermes tie with a loosened knot. Seated next to him was a tall black girl with long black braids.

The rest of the club hummed with people and activity, and it was a rough looking crowd, but Diablo didn't seem to care. He was drunk and happy and still enamored over Lexi F. When he saw me walking up the VIP steps, he looked like a proud father greeting his son behind the dugout after a Little League game. Diablo knocked the man next to him on the shoulder and pointed at me, then said something, and they both laughed.

"You get any extras?" Diablo asked me.

"Time of my life," I said and sat down.

Diablo watched Autumn closely and looked at her for a long time after she curled into me. He winked at me, then said, "Shep, I want you to meet somebody. My attorney. One of them anyway. Jason Kornegay."

We shook hands. He introduced me to the girl who went by Jamaica, and Jamaica could tell there was meant to be a conversation, so she pulled Autumn to the couch with her, and they talked about whatever it is strippers talk about to kill the time.

"I understand you're in law school?" Mr. Kornegay said.

"For the time being."

"What does that mean?" he asked.

"It means I intend to quit."

"Why?"

"It's not for me."

"You're going to have to do better than that. Surely you had words to get you into law school. Use them now."

"Maybe that's the problem."

The man studied Jamaica up and down. His intentions with her were clear. "Mr. Leppich mentioned you were going through a dilemma, though he did not specify beyond that. It will be much more difficult for me to hire you as a clerk, or an intern, or as an associate, if you are not first an active law student."

"And if I stay in school?"

"We'd want to review your resume, of course, make sure you are who you say you are. Why don't you stop by the office next week and I'll show you around to everybody."

"Seems too good to be true."

"We respect Mr. Leppich, and so we respect his opinion of you."

"And I respect the opportunity, but Mr. Leppich told me earlier tonight to keep law school far away from this place. That's the only advice I think I'm able to accept tonight, respectfully."

"Well earned, Shep. I heard it has been quite a trying day. But let me ask you this first: what kind of law did you intend to practice?"

"No clue," I admitted.

"Did you have any experience around lawyers at all?"

"I worked for one. Friend of the family. He did insurance defense."

"How was it?"

"Mostly unremarkable. I fell asleep during a deposition they let me observe."

"At least we can rule out insurance defense. I don't blame you. Do you even know if you'd rather be a litigator or a transactional attorney?"

I didn't have an answer. "No clue," I repeated.

"That's my point, Shep. Before you decide, you need to know. In the meantime, the offer stands. Stay in school, come by on Monday or anytime after. Leave school, I already gave you my best advice and that's all I can offer. Good luck either way."

Diablo motioned to Mr. Kornegay and gave an obvious little nod. The lawyer stood up and asked for Jamaica's hand. She gave it to him, and they walked away toward the Champagne Room.

Autumn returned to me on the couch, then I leaned into Diablo, and I thanked him. "I don't know what I did to deserve this," I said after reiterating my thanks.

"You were in the right place at the right time."

"Is everything going to be okay? The briefcase?" I asked in a way that Autumn could not hear.

"Short term, yes. Long term…" Diablo shrugged. "Wouldn't mind having an ally within the firm to monitor how they're spending all the money I'm paying them." He nodded at Autumn and asked, "Think you've got a shot with her?"

"A shot to do what?"

Diablo took a sip of champagne from a flute, then tilted it toward Autumn. "Sweetie, I took care of your exit fees, if you two lovebirds want to get out of here and paint the town red."

Autumn perked up. "What time is it?" she asked.

I checked my phone. "It's 1:00 in the morning? How?"

"What is today, again?" Autumn asked.

"Tuesday," I said, "Technically Wednesday."

"No, it's still Taco Tuesday," Autumn said, solemnly, eyes to the floor at first, before I watched a sudden transformation. Her shoulders rounded. Her eyes softened. The fuck or fight stripper mechanism evaporated and, in its place, relief, the rarest emotion in the stripper's arsenal. Autumn ran her hand along my leg and interlaced her fingers into mine. I held her hand. She felt 20 pounds lighter.

"You want to get out of here?" she asked.

I looked at her. I mean, really looked at her, to see if she would tip her pitches, but her poker face was back on and unbreakable. I looked at Diablo next to see if he'd break down in laughter, give the game away, but he stonewalled me. I looked at Autumn again. I looked at Lexi F. Nothing. They all looked at me, then each other, then me again.

"Okay!" I said, finally, and must have looked embarrassingly boyish saying it, overcome as I was with a faint headed torrent of excitement mixed with lingering suspicion.

Diablo said, "Good, I've got E.T. on standby. She's in a blue taxi van waiting outside."

The whole operation felt so entirely staged, made worse by Autumn who grabbed me by the arm, and said, "I'll meet you in the car. Out front," as though she already knew the rest of the plan. She ran off to the dressing room to retrieve her things.

The skeptic in me believed I was the patsy in a club-wide conspiracy, but the drunk in me? The drunk in me overruled the skeptic, and argued that this was it, that I was about to experience the real deal stripper jackhammer to the head, the heart, and soon the... Furthermore, the drunk continued, even if I was the patsy and she the actress in an overwrought scheme to gain leverage, to keep me in school perhaps, to groom me into a con artist, or a dirty lawyer, then at least get her back to the apartment before the conspiratorial reveal. Oh no, the drunk and the skeptic both realized, the apartment hadn't been cleaned in over a week. There was dirty laundry piled on the floor, old pizza boxes on the counter, and if it was a flat surface, it needed to be wiped.

Like clockwork, another dilemma disappeared.

"Shep, take her to my place," Diablo said, unprompted. "There's a bottle opener on the pool house wall and a cap collector underneath it. Spare key is buried in the caps. Security code inside is 2-7-2-0. Say it back to me."

"2-7-2-0," I repeated.

"There's a rolltop desk next to the bed with a Montblanc pen box in the top right drawer. The box has a baggie of cocaine in it. Can't remember how much. Certainly, enough to have fun with. Probably not enough to kill you," he said and waited for my reaction, adding. "I mean if you want any."

"I don't understand," I said.

"The stripper will understand. Trust me."

"I mean I don't understand why you're doing all of this for me."

"I take care of my people, Shep, because for now, I still can. You proved yourself today. That's a good sign." Diablo stepped back and looked at me. "I don't see Hawaii down there. Did you spend the whole time talking about your law school business?"

"Not the whole time."

"Probably best you saved some conversation for whatever is coming next," he said and winked. "What are you going to do?"

"With her? Or with the law school?"

"I know what you're going to do with her."

"I'll sleep on it," I said and winked.

"I don't think you're going to get much sleep, Shep, but I still consider that a victory," Diablo said. "Whatever you do decide," he added, "don't be a bitch about whichever choice you *didn't* make. More importantly, remember this: 2-7-2-0,"and he pushed me away.

I had another theory about him. In a fraternal way, I think I reminded him of someone he used to know. An old Army friend, perhaps. I made him laugh without really trying, so he always brought me around. But he treated me like an equal. He could sit down and have a beer with me, see eye-to-eye on one thing or another without patronizing me. My input was listened to. My opinion mattered. My points taken. Not many adults had treated me like that. But I also knew I shouldn't admire Diablo just because he offered me this respect. He cut too many corners. He might have been mobbed up. But if a fight ever broke out, I knew he'd be on my side no matter what, and in return, that put me on his side, too.

"Wrap it up!" Diablo called out to me as I left the VIP area. I wanted to call back, *Good luck!, You're gonna beat 'em!,* or *Fuck 'em!,* but clichés would be of little consolation. The sober people were after Diablo, and hot on his tail, dragging their dollies stacked with law books and bankers' boxes full of cases and files to be used against him. In that flickering moment in The Panther, between the bass beats and the sparkling lights, I wished I possessed the quality of determination like what Autumn described, now that I recognized a faint reason to be determined, and I wished I had the ability to help my friend, whatever his legal troubles, with the full force of the knowledge I should've learned already regarding the law.

Alas, I walked back into the cold November night, where a beat-up blue van covered in taxi stamps waited beneath the ripped, purple awning outside The Panther. A short woman wearing a driver's cap and a denim shirt with Looney Tunes characters on the sleeve leaned against the hood and puffed on an unfiltered cigarette.

I gave a little whistle first, so that I didn't startle her. "E.T., I presume?"

"That's me. Phone home?" she asked, her voice as rough as the cigarette she inhaled.

"Waiting on one more."

"She's already here," E.T. announced, sliding the door open to reveal Autumn seated in the middle row of the van. She had changed into yoga pants and a sleek black leather jacket. Holding a wipe, she diligently toned down the makeup on her face. She didn't have much left on. She didn't need any.

E.T. slammed the door shut when I got in, stomped her cigarette out, and walked around to the driver's side. She sped away from The Panther down the dusty back roads.

"Headed to Mr. Leppich's, correct?" she asked, and smiled at me in the rearview mirror.

"Do you know where his house is?"

"Upside down, butt naked, left-handed," she answered.

Autumn snapped her clutch shut and threw it in her gym bag.

She put her hand on her stomach and moaned. She sounded uncomfortable.

"You okay?" I asked.

"Can you hear my stomach growling?"

"What's wrong?"

"I haven't eaten anything all day."

"That's perfect, because I'm starving, too. Burritos?" I asked.

"Oh…my…God." Autumn closed her eyes and inhaled slowly through her nose. She looked like she had known burritos in another life and only just now recalled their existence. "A burrito sounds so good right now," she said.

"E.T., did you hear that?" I asked. "Do you mind if we make a pit stop."

"Burritos? You want Josey's?" she blurted out. "Only if I get a chicken, rice, and cheese out of the deal."

"To Josey's then, posthaste, please."

"Yessir!" E.T. said and flipped her blinker on to make a left turn.

"You ever see any weird shit go down in Josey's?" I asked E.T.

E.T. glared at me in the mirror again and asked, "Are you kidding me?" She turned out to be quite the talker. She regaled us with a longwinded story that should have been a lot shorter, and funnier, but for several stutter steps that included one wrong turn and an unexpected detour due to road construction that really tormented her.

Josey's resembled an eclectic club after midnight. College kids. Drunks. Stoners. Scary people. But one thing every customer had in common, if they visited Josey's with any regularity, was a crazy story to tell about the restaurant. E.T. was eating a chimichanga one night when a drunk frat boy turned into Josey's drive-thru entrance, failed to veer, and smacked into the front of the building, only to realize he was staring down a hungry taxi driver and four police officers seated inside at the table next to her. The cops rushed outside while the driver tried to reverse and speed away, but he backed into 19th Street and clipped a speeding truck of drunk locals, who all hopped out and dragged the drunk kid out of his car, until the cops ran onto the scene, tasers drawn.

By the time she finished the story, E.T. had reached the center of town, not too far from campus, when her phone on the dash rang. She answered and loudly berated the potential fare that had called her, then caught the red light at the intersection in front of Hannagan Hall.

When the light turned green, I nudged Autumn and said, "There's the law school."

She perked up and watched the boxy brown building pass by in the night. "Really! That's it? It's ugly," Autumn said. "Can we go inside!?"

"Are you serious?"

"Serious as your 151."

"E.T., did you hear that?"

"What do you want me to do?" E.T. asked.

"Turn around and go back to the law school. Just make a left at the next light," I said.

I directed E.T. through a couple more turns on campus, and then we reached the circle drive in front of three tall flag poles at the law school. It was only then that I worried about my ability to gain access. The school issued students security cards at the beginning of the year, because the doors locked at some point, but I had never been at school that late, and so I had no clue if I still had the key in my wallet. I searched and found it stuck to an expired gift card.

E.T. checked the time. "I've got to get back to The Panther to get Mr. Leppich at some point. How long you gonna be in there?"

I shrugged. "How long we got?"

E.T. did some math in her head. "I'm gonna take a 15-minute cat nap. That good?"

"That's fine."

"We'll have to go through the drive-thru at Josey's," E.T. added, as she reclined her chair and got comfortable.

For the second time that day, I exited a taxi at the entrance to the law school. My hand shook with cold when I tested the security card against the black box mounted to the wall next to the front doors, but it worked. The red light on the box switched green, and the locks unlatched with a loud click, followed by an audible splat at our feet. I jumped and instinctively checked my shoulders, hair, and shoes for splatter. Found none.

"What was that?" Autumn asked.

"A close call," I said. There was a fresh splotch of bird shit on the sidewalk. "Let's get inside before they let fly anymore."

The foyer was dark, so too were the hallways, and the classrooms hidden behind closed doors. A dim light from the forum shined through an archway in the middle of the building, where Autumn headed at once.

"This place is all bricks and windows, isn't it?" she said while looking at the oil-paint portraits hung on the wall that depicted former deans and distinguished professors. She faced the empty forum and looked disappointed. "But where is everyone?" she asked. "I thought law school students were supposed to study late into the night."

"Not this late. If anybody is here, they're in the library and probably asleep."

Autumn walked around empty couches, and between cleared tables to the far wall where there hung a huge mural – 30' high, 50' wide. The mural had pop culture references and legal symbols, all made of various mediums, glued or otherwise suspended and scattered around the wall in dubious patterns. There was a small canvas painted with a scene from Pac-Man, near a Wonder Woman action figure dangling from a thin piece of rope, next to a computer printout of a judicial scale, a headshot of Sandra Day O'Connor, the word PEACE spelled with magazine cutouts, and on and on. Each piece within the mural was connected to other pieces via colored string or yarn. Where there was a great deal of overlap, the connected material created an opaque backdrop, while in other areas, where there were fewer connections, the exposed brick was still visible. But if the number of connections had anything to do with the statement being made by the mural, no one could figure out why the broken bowling pin had the fewest connections, or the small, taxidermied fox the most. The mural was widely considered artistic gibberish, and even became a target during campaigns for first-year student offices, with candidates who claimed the mural's lack of artistic merit demeaned the pursuit of our legal education. They vowed to have it removed, so far to no avail.

Autumn agreed with the consensus, stating, "What the hell is this ugly piece of shit?"

"Nobody knows."

"What is it supposed to mean?"

"Probably nothing."

Autumn pointed to the top corner of the mural where Snoopy, wearing his flying cap and goggles, sat atop his red doghouse and steered toward an opening high in the room. "I think Snoopy is trying to escape," she said.

"Then he is the only rational thing about the entire mural. My theory is that a rich alumnus of this school has a kid with an unsophisticated palette, and that alum offered the school a donation with one big requirement," I said and spread my arms wide to cover the mural.

"What's the artwork look like in the library?" Autumn asked.

"You want to see the library? Or you want to see if there are people in the library?"

"Are you embarrassed?" she asked. "Are you ashamed of me?" she asked again, raising her voice louder.

I knew I couldn't defeat a stripper in a test of wills, even in my own law school, so I didn't put up a fight. We walked through the forum and across a dark hallway to another set of secured double-doors where I had to use the access card again. We entered the library's reception area where normally there were librarians and student assistants working behind the counter. At this hour, the room was dark, empty, and silent, which made the footsteps that echoed on the stairs that much louder.

I closed my eyes and prayed for a janitor, but when I opened them, Mary Khong appeared, taking an exhausted breath when she had cleared the last step. She wore two straps of a Jansport backpack jammed with heavy books, and a grey hooded sweatshirt emblazoned with the St. Louis Cardinals' logo. Her jet-black hair was tied in a simple ponytail that had undone and left several grey hairs frazzled above her face. She was a few years older than most of us in Section Two, but as Duck often reminded me, she didn't look it save the few stray greys. Her tired eyes grew to life once she saw me, and then really grew to life when she saw Autumn.

Mary shrugged the backpack off her shoulders until it thudded against the brick floor. She thrust her hand toward Autumn with unexpected enthusiasm. "Hi, I'm Mary," she said, and she didn't blink once, fearing that her gaze might slip into a judgmental once-over.

Autumn used her apparently fake name. "Hi, I'm April," she said, smiling.

Mary then quickly turned to me, and shouted "Are you kidding me? Here? Of all places!"

I stepped in front of Autumn like I needed to protect her. "What's going on?" I asked, confused about Mary's sudden aggression.

"I've been looking for you all day," Mary said. She unzipped the backpack and grabbed a spiral notebook. She opened it to a page that included three columns of names with a letter written next to each. Mary continued, "I went to Duck's house. He said you were working. I went to the steak place. Ordered a steak salad. You weren't even there, and the salad wasn't that good."

"I was at both of those places at one point or another," I told her. "You must have just missed me. Please tell me you didn't search anywhere else."

"I didn't. Why?"

"Oh, no reason."

A quick laugh snorted through Autumn's nose, and when I heard her, I nearly lost it too. I was trying to be upright and proper with Mary Khong, but there was an unavoidable and extreme imbalance between her astute sobriety, my inebriation, and Autumn's gravitational pull. I can only imagine what we smelled like – a perfume of vanilla and cranberry and smoke.

"What are you doing here so late, Mary?" I asked, with a dumb smile stuck on my face.

"I'm studying. What are *you* doing here so late?" she shot right back. Her eyes darted back-and-forth between me and Autumn, who was still listening but had opened a casebook she found on a rolling cart.

"What's with the notebook?" I asked Mary.

"I'm keeping a tally of everyone's grades," she said.

"Excuse me? You're what?"

"Becker's practice exam. He said there were four A's. I'm trying to find them."

"That's a tad crazy, don't you think? How many have you accounted for?"

"All but one."

"Were they obvious?"

"I wouldn't consider them obvious, no," Mary said, then she named them. David McDaniel. Monica Reed. Cally Johns.

"How many more people do you have left to poll?"

"Five."

"Five people!? You already found out the grade for 60 of them?" I asked.

"You sound curious, Shep," Mary said, smiling. "You want to go over it with me?"

Autumn cut in like a scornful mother. "There isn't any reason he should sound curious," she said suddenly, so that Mary and I both jumped. "Why don't you tell her about what you've decided to do, Shep."

"What's this about?" Mary asked. "What have you decided to do?"

"He's going to quit school," Autumn answered on my behalf.

Mary's lips pursed, and she shook her head. "He's lying to you. Who quits because of a practice exam?" she asked.

Autumn looked confused. "Wait, this is about a practice exam?"

I glared at Autumn and tried like hell to hold another laugh back. "It's not because of the practice…" I wanted to explain, but Mary still had more left to say.

"I guess that means you got the last F?" Mary asked.

"To be fair, I think Becker said 'other,' so it could be a D, right?"

"Sure. Is that what you got?"

"Wait, what did you mean when you said the last F?"

"There were four people who failed. I found three of them easy."

"I figured those would be the most difficult to account for," I said.

"I'm friends with her. She told me about him. He told me about the other one," Mary said. She couldn't bring herself to say the names out loud, so she pointed to each of them. "I didn't really care about the failures though," she added and snatched the notebook away before I could explore any further. "I was only after the A's, and now, of the five people left, there is one A and one F that elude me. Fantuzzo is down here, too, you know, but he's hiding in his carrel to avoid me. He's one of the five unknowns."

"Why is he hiding? I pinned him for an A."

"Did you not hear?"

"Hear what?"

"He was shat on when he arrived at school this morning."

"He was what?" Autumn asked immediately.

"One of the birds outside pooped on him. It's bad luck around here. It means an F is imminent."

"Oh, Mary…" I said and shook my head. "Tell me, were you one of the A's?" I already knew from Duck what she made, so this was something of a test.

"No, I got a B+," she admitted.

"Well done."

"It's nothing. That's the point. It needs to be better. I want to see who did well, because I want to size them up. See what they look like. See what it takes, you know? So, let's cut to the chase. What did you make, Shep? Was it the other? You'll find no judgement from me."

"You mean Duck didn't tell you about my dilemma?" I asked.

"Duck only talked about his party. So, here we are. What will it be, Shep?"

"Mary, why don't you go look for Fantuzzo and the others. Eventually, you'll know what I got by the process of elimination."

"Fantuzzo," Mary said, putting her hand over her face. "He's been hiding from me all night. He must not have much of a social life."

"All the more reason he's the odds-on favorite for that last A. Despite the bird shit."

Mary smiled and yawned. "At least the stakeout gave me some time to study. Can you believe freaking Becker pulled my card again?"

"How many times is that for you?"

"Fourth time already."

"What was your card?"

"The three of spades."

"Must be unlucky."

"What's yours?"

"Seven of diamonds."

"How many times have you got it?"

"Just the once."

"Must be nice," Mary said. She shoved the spiral notebook between the books in her backpack.

"Random question for you, Mary - what did you do before law school? You didn't come straight from another college, did you?"

"No, I worked in advertising for a few years. It was awful, and it's what motivated me to apply to law school. Why?"

"Just curious."

"That's all beside the point though, isn't it Shep?"

"If I give up Fantuzzo, will you leave me alone?"

"What do you mean?"

"You know I'm his carrel-mate, right?"

"Fantuzzo's?"

"The one and only, but I don't know if I can get into my carrel to find him."

"Why don't you make this a two-for-one deal and tell me what you got, Shep. I don't want to have to haunt you all day tomorrow."

"I can't tell you what I made, unfortunately, because I threw my test away before I looked at my grade."

Mary tapped her foot for a few beats, then stopped, and frowned, frozen by her disbelief, waiting on the punchline that didn't come. She gasped and looked at me like I had instigated a major political scandal. "You did what?" she asked, flatly.

"I threw it away," I repeated. "I never looked at it. I've decided I'm going to quit law school."

"No, you can't do that. Wasn't there a movie about this?"

I sighed. "No, that guy didn't quit."

Mary looked irritated. "Where did you throw it away?"

"You'll never find it."

"Where!?" She held her hands in front of her and squeezed like she was going to strangle my neck.

"Not anywhere around here."

"Where!!?" She was joking now, but the sense of humor faded, replaced by yet another yawn. "You really didn't look, did you?"

"No."

"I just don't understand how you can be that confident in yourself," Mary said.

"It has nothing to do with confidence. I told you. I'm quitting."

"Shep, you're a mess, but I don't have time for this nonsense," Mary said, shaking her head quickly to knock the sleep out of her eyes. "I'll assume you're telling the truth, for now, because I'll be able to figure it out soon enough. Can you at least take me to your carrel? Maybe Fantuzzo fell asleep. I'll snatch his Blue Book."

"Let me see if I even have the key," I said, searching through the keychain in my pocket.

Autumn walked behind me and ran her hand along my back. "What's a carrel?" she asked.

Mary answered, "A carrel is basically a closet to study in."

I found the silver key for Carrel 15b. I had only visited it once near the beginning of the semester, but after meeting the person assigned to share the space with me, I never used the key again. Fortuitously, I saved it in case of an emergency, and my God, did this ever apply. We went down to the basement where there were tables, cordoned off desks, and glass encased rooms where study groups held sessions, but to Autumn's disappointment, there were no other law students to gawk at. Mary marched us through several stacks of law books until we reached a row of carrel doors and found 15b. She moved aside to allow me to insert the key, and the moment I did, she jumped in front of me and burst through the door.

The narrow desk inside was cluttered with schoolbooks and legal pads. Fantuzzo's Torts book lay open to a case, its pages a mosaic of highlighted text in yellow, green, pink, or blue. On the wall, a pegboard displayed a meticulously organized calendar, every square filled to the brim with detailed plans down to the hour: reading, classes, study groups, reminders, and tactics. Next to the calendar he'd pinned a black and white photo of Johnny Cash flipping the bird. But, Phillip Fantuzzo was not inside.

"He escaped!" Mary Khong shouted. She buckled her backpack straps together over her chest, and ran as fast as she could, which wasn't more than a shuffle due to the weight of her bag. She headed toward the staircase and disappeared around the stacks.

Autumn barely reacted to Mary's bizarre departure. "Is it true you threw it away without looking at your grade?" she asked.

"It's true," I answered.

"You weren't curious?"

"A little," I admitted. "But it was just a practice exam, so who cares?"

"She certainly does," Autumn said, nodding in the direction Mary ran.

"Whatever that gene is, I don't have it."

Autumn was finished talking. She took me by the arm and jerked me into the carrel, then closed the door gently behind her. She swept her arm across the narrow desk space and knocked to the floor Mr. Fantuzzo's precious color-coded books, his neatly arranged highlighters, E&E guides, case briefs, and his stacks of yellow legal pads. She grabbed the back of my neck with one hand and pulled me tight and kissed me. She pressed against me until I sat atop the cleared table, knocking a cup of pens over in the process, and for the second time that night, she took her clothes off. No rules. No money. No stopping us this time.

. . .

An unfamiliar ringtone jostled me awake. I was alert but unable to open my eyes. The phone blared a repeating jingle five times, paused, then whoever it was called back, and the obnoxious jingle began again. Autumn answered this time. I cracked my eyes wide enough to recognize the morning time. It was light, but not bright, and a steady rain pelted against a window. I ran my hand along my stomach and sides, felt for my intestines, and did the same to my junk. Despite everything being accounted for, the relentless headache and nausea had me wishing for the final reprieve.

"Yes…yes…yes," Autumn repeated in the same hushed way. She was naked and entangled in navy blue sheets and a plaid bedspread, surrounded by the blue-gray walls of my tiny little bedroom in my awful apartment. It smelled like vanilla, burritos, and marijuana, and there were underwear and condoms on the floor.

"You alive?" she asked. She had finished her mysterious answers and hung up the phone.

"I wish I wasn't. Was that your boyfriend coming over to kick my ass?"

Autumn laughed. "No."

"How did we get here?" I asked. "And why does it smell like drugs?"

"You don't remember?" She was clearly surprised. She rolled over and faced me in the bed. "You look terrible."

"How do you not look terrible?"

"I'm used to these hours," she said. "Tell me, what's the last thing you do remember?"

"The carrel incident."

"The carrel incident? If that's the *last* thing you remember, then you forgot a lot."

Consuming a certain amount of drinks inevitably led to my unpleasant curse of forgetfulness. Sometimes the memory lapses lasted forever, sometimes they trickled back. I tried assembling a few details. I remembered the beginning of the carrel scene vividly, but I couldn't remember finishing, and worse yet, the more I concentrated on piecing the puzzle back together, the more my head hurt.

"Was it bad?" I asked.

"It wasn't bad," Autumn said. "I promise."

"All right, spill it, and please spare no detail. What did we do?"

Autumn sat up casually and reached for a Bic lighter and the remainder of the joint left on the bedside table. She lit it, hit it, and offered it to me, but I declined. It would've made me puke immediately.

"We found, uh, what was his name? The guy you share the carrel with?"

"We found Fantuzzo?"

"No, we knocked one of the cabinet doors open and found his bottle of Crown."

"What did that carrel look like when we left it?"

"We tried to put it back together. Wasn't good," she said, shaking her head and scrunching her face in embarrassment.

"Did we finish the booze or something?"

"We might have left a shot or two. We found the cab driver asleep in the taxi. Mr. Leppich had called her and said he didn't need a ride, so we left with her and got burritos."

"Oh God, did we go inside Josey's?"

"We went to the drive-thru."

"Good."

"But when we got to the window, you recognized the guy working, and he recognized you."

"Oh, no."

"They told you to get your ass inside, so we went in, and took a few Polaroids with the staff. They hung them on a wall in the kitchen, and we had a beer with one of the waiters in the alley."

"I delivered food there one day. Made friends," I explained. "But here's what I don't understand - how did I black out after I ate a Josey's burrito?"

Usually, a Josey's burrito was like finding an extra life in a video game, a second wind, batteries fully recharged for nightcaps and late-night hookups.

"You never ate it," Autumn said. "I think it's still on the counter."

"That explains it. But if we never got to Diablo's, then where did the weed come from?" I asked.

"We were headed to Mr. Leppich's place, but the cab driver started complaining about her foot problems, from diabetes or something, and how she couldn't afford the medicine, so we went to your friend's house to get her some. Duck, right? He was so happy to see you. Like, ecstatic," Autumn said. "He gave the cab driver a bunch of weed just because. Had these joints already pre-rolled, and gave them to us," she added.

My headache rotated in shifts from major to extreme pain, and I laid down again and closed my eyes. "I'm going to get evicted," I said.

Autumn laughed. "You think you're the only person smoking a little dope in this complex? I wouldn't worry about it."

"I still don't understand why we came here instead of Diablo's," I said.

"You told me you wanted to show me a movie."

"A movie? How pathetic. Which one?"

"Some surfer movie."

"Did we watch it?"

"No. Plans changed."

"Thank goodness."

"There was an incident on the couch. An incident in here," she said, referring to my messy bedroom. "You really don't remember?"

"Pieces will come back to me, eventually. Like a brownout. Not a complete blackout. Hopefully," I said.

Autumn unwrapped herself from the covers and rolled out of bed naked and without a concern in the world for it. The sight of her body, tight little muscles from her ankles to her chin, was like taking three ibuprofens and drinking a bottle of Pedialyte. I watched her closely, as she walked across my bedroom and into the kitchen. She opened doors until she found a plastic cup, the last clean cup, and poured lukewarm tap water from the faucet above a pile of dirty dishes. She chugged the water in one go, then strolled back into the bedroom and picked up her athletic bag and took it into the bathroom. She turned the shower on and ran the sink and brushed her teeth. After she finished brushing, a fog of steam followed her, and she reappeared in the doorway.

"Come on," she said, her hand resting high on the door frame, "if we hurry, you can still make class."

"What is today?" I asked. I was confident it was Wednesday. I had already missed Civil Procedure, but I could still make Contracts if we booked it.

"It's definitely Wednesday."

"I can't go to class."

"Why not?"

"Because it's raining? Besides, I thought I quit school. How much did I talk about that last night?" I asked while rubbing my head.

"Quite a bit."

"I'm going back to sleep," I said, ashamed, and I begged her to join me.

"I can't."

"Why not?"

"Because you're coming in here for this shower incident," she said and disappeared into the steam.

The remnants of hard alcohol still coursing through my veins must have all gathered at once, creating an effect akin to taking one more shot of whiskey, and like the hair of the dog, my hangover receded, and the fun drunk I had been the night before made a final appearance, and gave one last performance, careful this time to remember every detail, certain I had shattered multiple personal milestones in the process.

From the moment Autumn introduced herself to me as April, to the moment I stepped out of that shower and dried off, we had not experienced an awkward second together. But when the shower incident ended, and the euphoric traces of lust and booze wore off again, we faced the full breadth of the day's ordinary schedule in our ordinary lives. But what was ordinary to me was extraordinary to Autumn, ten-fold in reverse, and we were both aware of the 500lb gorilla grunting in the middle of the bedroom. I found a t-shirt, a coat, and a pair of old sweatpants that I wore with fur lined house slippers and insulated socks. I sat on the end of the bed, twiddling my thumbs, while Autumn finished gathering her things. When she was ready, she slung her athletic bag over her shoulder and followed me outside into the gentle rain. She was inside the passenger door of the 4-Runner before I could open it. When I started it up, she curled away from me and embraced her bag tightly like a teddy bear.

I pulled out of the apartment complex and made a right turn. I had no clue where I needed to go to get her home.

"Where are we going?" I asked.

"Do you know the Planet Fitness?" Autumn replied. She sat up and looked through the windshield.

"Of course," I answered, reminding her I knew this town better than the back of my hand. The Planet Fitness was near the high school next to a row of townhomes where an S2G regular ordered food twice a week and never tipped.

Autumn wasn't impressed. She rolled over again and silently watched the rain falling.

I reached for a CD from the case attached to the sun visor, and I pressed a customized disc into the CD slot on the dash, a Radiohead mix. I turned the volume up to a comfortable level, enough sound that it was obvious I wanted to hear it, but not so loud that it would discourage conversation should Autumn decide to speak up.

Speed was essential for this journey, and there was a simple route on the main streets to reach our destination quickly, but I wasn't operating anywhere near 100%. The bitterness pulsated through my body in waves like flashes from a fever. I needed to avoid morning traffic, left turns, and I wanted to catch as many stop signs as possible, because slowing down kept my head from spinning and kept my empty stomach from churning violently with the poison swirling around inside of it.

The heater kicked on and burned hot. I turned off the vents on my side and cracked open a window. The cold air that seeped in felt soothing on my hot face, as were the flecks of rain that sneaked through, and the therapeutic sound of tires splashing along the wet roads. The quiet neighborhood began to stir. I reached a four-way stop behind a short line of cars. Nearby, people sat inside a little coffee shop, watching the rain. Across the street, a grocery store manager held an umbrella for an old woman walking to her Buick. These simple details that contrasted wildly against the unholy, smoking hot stripper seated next to me, who hid her face from the outside world, burying it in her bag. Or, maybe it was me she hid from. Me, who represented the seemingly unattainable dream she longed for, a dream I nonchalantly intended to quit out of spite, or apathy, or boredom, or confusion. Whatever it was, it amounted to nothing in Autumn's quest for Atlanta or Tampa or at least one more shitty town along the way. If, by some strange chance, we crossed paths somewhere down the line, all that would remain is the inexplicable connection we shared one fateful Tuesday night.

I reached the little shopping center that housed the Planet Fitness and turned in. "Where to?" I asked.

"I told you. Planet Fitness," she said, indignantly.

"Are you going to work out?" She had only slept a couple hours, max, and no telling what sleep she had missed the night before.

"Don't worry about me," she said.

But I was worried about her. I think that bag contained every possession she had left. A few clothes and toiletries. Some wadded up cash. An ID. Membership cards to gyms, where she worked out, caught a nap on a couch or a bench, worked out again just to kill more time before she needed to be back at The Panther. At least that life, the Planet Fitness life, was better than living with half a dozen crazy strippers crammed into a two-bedroom apartment.

I waited on a car to back out from a spot on the front row and parked there so Autumn wouldn't have to walk through the rain. She unbuckled her seatbelt, jutted her eyes at me quickly, and asked, "You are going to class, right?"

"Certainly not with this headache."

"Does that mean you're still quitting?"

I didn't answer her question, instead asking one of my own. "What are you going to do?" I asked. "I mean other than work out."

"I'll figure it out," she said without a trace of self-pity. She took a deep breath, and she gripped the door handle.

"I had fun," I told her, because it was the only thing I could think to say. I wanted her to keep talking, but I didn't know how to reconnect with her now. Whether to hug her. Walk her inside. Whether to ask her out or find out if I could help her in some way. She'd probably laugh in the face of my schoolboy chivalry, so whatever was to happen next, she'd have to be the one to show me the way. She was the professional.

Autumn smiled dismissively. "Here's what I think, Shep. I think you regret throwing that test away. I watched you last night. When you were talking to your friend Mary. You wanted that last F, didn't you?"

I just smirked and shook my head, no. I didn't yet understand her point.

"At least if you got an F, it would make the decision easier. Like you weren't deciding for yourself at all. An F would tell you to leave."

"I know law school was your dream, Autumn, and I know I've been flippant about that," I said, trying to take some of the heat off of me. "I'm sorry."

"You don't understand, Shep. It's not law school. The difference between me and you, the difference I care about, is that you have the choice to begin with. Your problem is you have no confidence to act on it. You want somebody to tell you what to do. I'm the opposite, Shep. I have all the confidence in the world, but I don't have any choice, and the choice is all I've ever wanted."

She opened the door and got out of the car, holding the bag over her head, her whole world, to block the rain, then she leaned back into the car, and told me one last thing. "If you were half as confident as you were with me all night, you'd have it made, no matter what you decide to do."

She shut the door behind her and skipped beneath the overhang in front of the Planet Fitness. Shoulders back. Head up. Ready to face the next hardship like she had already moved on from me and my petty problems. But in between the rain drops, and the wipers that squeaked against the windshield, I saw something familiar from Autumn. It wasn't a complete stop and turn. It wasn't a heartfelt gaze. It was a only a tiny pause, the slightest look, but it was intentional, and so she might as well have been handing me her phone number, an address, or asking me out on another date, when she subtly glanced back at me.

I turned the ignition off and jumped out of the 4-Runner and called out her name before she walked inside. Autumn stopped and turned around, shivering and cold with her arms still folded across her gym bag. A giant man in a sleeveless t-shirt with hulking pink biceps reached the entrance at the same time I did. Autumn held the door open for the musclebound man, who briefly stopped between us, considered her, then me, and shook his head in disbelief before he walked inside.

Autumn took my hands and wrapped hers around them, squeezing them, massaging them for comfort and warmth, and said, "What's the matter?"

I looked at her dead in her hardened stripper eyes until I saw through April all the way to back to Autumn, and I asked, "What are you doing Thursday evening around five o'clock?"

# An Elaborate and Fantastic Golf Swing

The annual two-man tournament received its nickname, The Stickup, after masked bandits raided the Calcutta and took off with $50,000 in cash. The thieves were armed with revolvers and compromising photos of prominent members taken during a private charity event that itself turned Western. I was there. Saw the whole thing go down from a seat at the blackjack table in the Men's Grill. Those were the glory days at Sendero Country Club. Back when I could stay up drinking until 4:00am, make my early tee time, and still break 80 every once in a while.

I waited by the four-sided, gold-rimmed clock near the first tee, and looked for my teammate. It was 8:35am and we were due on the box in eight minutes. I found him leaning against a portable bar that overlooked the practice putting green. A waiter wearing a black bow tie poured vodka, club soda, a splash of cranberry, more vodka, then added four lime wedges, and a little more vodka, into a 32oz Styrofoam cup. Trip took the drink and a pouch of Redman chewing tobacco, then stuffed money in a tip jar, and gingerly climbed back into the driver's seat of his empty golf cart. He tapped the accelerator, careful that the cart didn't lurch forward, and slowly wheeled around to me.

"Final swing thought?" Trip asked and nodded toward the plaque next to me that was buried in purple irises at the base of the green clock tower. The inscription on the plaque read, *God hates a coward. Dedicated March 28, 2015. In honor of Dr. J.J. Fontaine.*

"My only thought right now is how we're going to get this over with as quickly as possible," I said and strapped my bag onto the back of the cart, then slumped into the seat next to Trip.

"I hope you consider five hours quick."

"Whereas withdrawing would be the easiest and quickest solution."

"Nobody would blame you." Trip angled forward, careful to keep his body rigid, and removed his drink from the cupholder. He took a long sip through the straw and slowly leaned back. His eyes teared up either from tasting the full force of all that vodka or from feeling yet another pain shoot up his spine.

The first text I received from Trip was at 4:30 in the morning and it simply said, "you're gonna kill me." When I replied to him two hours later, he unraveled the absurd tale of his late-night misadventure. The Whataburger he'd devoured on the way home had mutinied, and he'd spent the night imprisoned in the bathroom. When the ordeal was over with and he finally attempted to stand, a searing twinge wrecked his back. He yelped for his wife, who gave him a Vicodin, and now, reduced to a stupor, the only service Trip could provide as a teammate was as my intoxicated chauffeur.

We owed our current placement in the rankings to a classic ham and egg tandem during the first two days of the tournament. Trip strung pars together, while I made a lot of bogeys and a few crucial pars. In the Blue Flight, the fifth flight overall, our 74-75 start was good enough to put us three shots behind the leaders, two shots out of second place. We were currently tied for third with the Woodberrys, the pair we were grouped with in the final round, whom I would face alone.

All morning, I thought about withdrawing and the sudden relief that would occur from having done so. Trip might claim to understand, but had the roles been reversed, and had I been the one who was injured and unable to swing, the idea of quitting wouldn't have crossed Trip's mind.

So, I reassured him. "I once accidentally shot a 77 with this ugly swing. If I get lucky like that today and put a little pressure on these Baptists, they may lose their faith yet."

"77, huh? Mind telling me the course where that occurred? And was there a witness?"

I smirked at him. "You don't need to try to lighten the mood today. I'm locked in." Hollow words stated confidently.

Trip's lip snarled and he nodded his head. "I might as well write 76 down right now."

"Unless…" I began.

"Unless what?"

"How many shanks do I get before I'm allowed to quit without any judgment?"

"I told you, withdraw now if that's what you're worried about."

"So, like, three shanks?"

"Why do you put yourself through this? Most people don't even like saying that word. Let alone saying it right before they tee off."

"I've got an addictive personality, Trip, you know that. These days, I'm addicted to self-loathing."

"I know, Justin. I know. How many yesterday?"

"Three."

"Then make it three today. You hit three shanks, and I'll drive you right off the golf course."

"Three and I can just get in the cart and we'll go?"

"Absolutely. Three. If you really think that's the number, I'll take the under." Trip said.

"How much?"

"Can't be too high otherwise you're incentivized to hit the hosel."

"$100?"

"It's a deal," Trip said, his eyes darting to mine, "You sure you're okay if I, uh…?" He shook the cup in his hand and waited for my answer with the straw pinched between his teeth. This marked the third consecutive day he had asked a version of this question, and after all this time, it still required a great deal of hesitancy on his part. My old drinking buddies never figured out how to act in my presence after my stint in rehab six years ago. They have remained tentative in their interactions with me, and our conversations have often been burdened by awkward tension and dramatic silences once they remembered I was no longer in on the big joke.

"Six years of sobriety and the only thing that will make it worse is if you refuse to have a good time because of me," I told him.

Trip sucked vodka through the straw. "Has it really been that long?"

Six years sober and four years since I moved away from the place that was, in many ways, a catalyst for my drinking problem. Time had granted me this clarity, though I was still drawn to the heart of my past struggles to prove I could confront the demon and either triumph over it or find the strength to walk away entirely. So far, I had been triumphant. I arrived late on Wednesday night, deliberately missing the practice round, the Horse Race, the Stag Night, and the Calcutta. Since I had no date, I skipped the Thursday night party that was thrown for wives and girlfriends as a token of gratitude, and apology, for whatever transpired at the Stag Night. With no Friday night event, the tournament committee focused on the Saturday night bash, featuring a huge party tent, stage, and Robert Earl Keen. Temptations, all, and temptations I knew I must avoid.

Here's to the next six years then," Trip said and raised his cup. "Why don't you go out there and give us something else to cheer about."

"I want a good story to take home from this round other than whatever comedy ends up on my scorecard, so promise me you'll chirp at the Woodberrys. Make it entertaining."

Trip slushed the ice around in his cup. "I'll drink to that," he said. He pressed the accelerator on the cart, but only succeeded in popping the parking brake. We didn't move. "I want you to know how much this hurts," he said.

"I can see the pain that you're in," I told him. "You want me to drive? I'll go slow."

"You know the hurt I'm talking about. Ever since the flights were announced, I've been dreaming about this matchup."

"I'm doing this for the both of us," I assured him, "and if I can get off this first hole without blowing up, I'm going to beat their ass."

"Just let the clubhead go," he reminded me. "Let everything else go, too. Be an athlete."

We arrived at the opening hole, a par-4 that doglegged left, framed by a few scattered trees and the native habitat of low lying, thorny mesquite bushes packed onto hard baked Earth, replete with rat holes and rattlesnake dens. Members referred to that awful shit as the Gunch.

"Tees are forward," Trip said, trying his best to perform like a good caddie given his limited viewpoint and range. "You still going to hit driver?" he asked.

"I need the largest face possible," I said and stretched my own back reflexively, as though Trip's injury might be contagious.

"I'd get out of the cart to hand you your club, but I don't think I'd make it back in."

"I don't need a caddie, just a driver, and maybe offer a few psychological points every once in a while."

"You don't need a psychologist. You need a lobotomist."

"You got a pill for that in the Mexican pharmacy you call your closet?" I asked.

The genesis of all his injuries was his D1 college football career playing linebacker. He had vitamins, Viagra, Vicodin, Adderall, HGH, deer antler spray, and whatever else would fit in his medicine closet. They all helped. None of them really worked.

"I think the kind of lobotomy I'm talking about still requires a drill," Trip replied, then he asked, "You think the Woodberrys will give us any action?"

"Action? Only if you mean Christ in action." I took the head-cover off my driver and tossed it in the basket on the back of the cart then unzipped a pouch on the side of my golf bag and opened a new sleeve of ProV-1's.

"I'll go find a mustard seed," Trip said, "and I'll bet them whether it grows into a mighty tree by the time this round is over with."

"What are you going to put up for the wager?"

"Sunday prayers."

"Good, because I need all the miracles I can get."

I used a Sharpie to add Trip's usual three stripes above the T in Titleist on each golf ball. "In your honor…" I added and showed him the marked balls.

"Do you know how many of those are hidden in the Gunch all over this golf course?"

"Exactly. Improves the chances of finding my ball."

Trip nodded several times in agreement, then said, "Okay, here's the bet I'll make with you: I'll take Mr. Woodberry straight up versus Austin."

"In number of strokes? Or number of fist pumps."

Trip chuckled. "Which side are you on with fist pumps?"

"I'll take Austin all day. Both ways."

"Another $100 on each bet?"

"That's a deal," I said.

I climbed the steps up to the first tee box where the Woodberrys talked with Callum Blair, the Scottish assistant pro who was seated underneath a popup tent nursing a hangover. Austin Woodberry held two clubs in his hands and alternated focus between each – holding one, lifting it, testing its weight before trying out the next. Austin was a geologist about my age, 35 or so, completely and unforgivably dull, and an Aggie, but he was also extravagantly rich having been born into a family with vast oil money. He always dressed like a Peter Millar model on the back cover of Golf Digest, and today, he wore tailored white shorts, a navy-blue needlepoint belt with repeating Pebble Beach logos, a light green Polo with thin stripes, a fresh set of all-white Club Professionals that the locker room attendant had cleaned and buffed that very morning, with a high-profile Titleist visor to top it off. But the similarities to a typical country club snob ended there. Austin was an usher at the First Baptist Church where his father, and playing partner, gave a sermon once a month. They didn't smoke. They didn't drink. They didn't cuss. And neither of them possessed the slightest aptitude for good golf course bullshit. But worst of all, even when they played inconsequential, non-tournament rounds, they putted everything out.

We exchanged curt hellos, then Mr. Woodberry quickly resumed a strategy conversation with his son. "Austin, after you sliced one into the deep rough yesterday, I think the 3-wood is too much club." He talked with a slight country accent that made him sound moralistic and demeaning. His facial features remained still when he spoke, stuck in a perpetual frown. He took a few steps backward and removed a khaki bucket hat from his bald, freckled head, and sprayed SPF 100 over his face, arms, then face again until he coughed from the aerosol. He held a hand over his mouth and waved the bucket hat to displace the sunscreen particles floating in the air. "You can hit your 3-iron as far as I hit my driver," he added. "You'll have nothing but an 8-iron left. It's a lot safer shot."

The Stickup was a stroke play event. Each golfer on a team of two played his own ball, and the team's best score was recorded for each hole. Because the average golfer is legitimately terrible at golf, this was a nerve inducing format compared to match play or the usual scramble – formats where the failures of the individual golfer are less extreme. I am better than the average golfer by a few shots, but not good enough to be confident playing solo versus a couple of strategic golf nerds. And for me, there was nothing more annoying on the golf course than the slow playing, hyper critical grinder scratching and clawing his way to an 82. I needed Trip for his ability to make pars and a couple birdies, because birdies were very important in this flight, but more than that, I wished Trip could be with me at the back of the tee box and around the greens to talk about anything other than golf.

"I'm more concerned about the second shot, Dad," Austin said. "Even after a bad first tee shot, it was still the greenside bunker that got the best of me yesterday. I don't want back in the sand. The closer I can get to the green on the tee shot, the better."

"Hey, Pro," Mr. Woodberry said to Callum, who hated being called Pro, "where's the pin today?"

Callum double-checked a pin sheet with only one eye open. "Back left," he answered.

The Woodberrys waited for more specificity.

Callum sighed, opened his other eye, and squinted. "Six off the left. Four from the back," he added.

Mr. Woodberry looked at Austin and continued his advice, "Play that beautiful little natural draw you've got and play it twice," he said. "Once with the 3-iron. Once on the approach. Birdie putt. Sounds like a pretty terrific start to me, Son."

"This hole just doesn't suit my eye, Dad" Austin complained.

Mercifully, the fairway cleared, and it was time to tee off. Callum carefully stood up to perform his sad, ceremonial duty. Despite the lack of any onlookers at all, he introduced the groups formally. With a raised voice, he said, "Gentlemen, welcome to Sendero Country Club's 2017 Autumn Invitational Tournament. We'd like to take a moment to thank our sponsors - FergCo International and Tiger Cat Oil Company. First on the tee in the 8:43 grouping, Mr. Austin Woodberry."

Austin raised his hand and pretended to accept applause from the nonexistent crowd, then used a short tee to rest his ball atop the low-cut grass. He had chosen the 3-iron after all.

Meanwhile, Trip was still in the cart, hunched over and chugging his vodka cocktail, shaking his head in disgust. He had gone completely unnoticed. He waited for Austin to finish his customary two full practice swings before he interrupted the routine.

"Hey, you boys want any side action today?" Trip asked. "There's only one of us playing, but I'm sure we can find a way to get the bet right."

Mr. Woodberry angrily cleared his throat. "I am quite confident you are aware of my position on gambling at Sendero. I decline your bet. In fact, I discourage it," he said, frowning per usual. "Ignore their gamesmanship, Son. Let's go get 'em!" he said to Austin, and then the father and son duo exchanged short but enthusiastic fist pumps.

Trip raised both of his index fingers to indicate a score of 1-1.

The Woodberrys resumed their laser focus on the task ahead.

Austin took one more practice swing, then he stood a few feet behind his ball and aligned his target by holding the 3-iron in front of him, parallel to the ground. He squinted and aimed down the shaft line, then took a long, deep breath and strode toward the ball, assertively planted his feet into the ground, shook the tension out of his hips and shoulders, performed two pump fakes to rehearse the first half of his backswing while he deliberately monitored the placement of his hands, made several rapid-fire glances at his target, then swung. It was a short move but strong and athletic. The momentum of the swing carried his arms three-quarters of the way through a full finish, but he manually forced his arms around his head and posed until the ball descended onto the fairway. He clenched his hand into another fist, pumped it, and quietly complimented himself with a "Yessss."

"Perfect shot, Son. A real beauty."

"You were right, Dad. I'm really pleased with that," Austin said.

Callum performed another introduction. "Next on the box… Mr. Robert Woodberry," he said and applauded softly.

Where Austin was meticulous in his pre-shot approach, Mr. Woodberry's process and swing were comparatively pithy. He teed the ball high, took a wide stance, and checked his target only once. He immediately set his wrists in the backswing, lifted his arms, stood nearly straight up, then whipped the club face perfectly on plane. The ball flew low and slow but with a slight hook that rolled for half of its total distance and nearly slammed into Austin's ball before it stopped in the fairway.

"Great shot, Dad!" Austin exclaimed. They slapped their hands together and gathered themselves on the back of the tee box, grinning, and relieved now that the first tee jitters were behind them.

I still faced mine. Each breath felt shorter than the one that preceded it. The oxygen that made it into my lungs felt insufficient. My heart rate increased, and I became acutely aware of things completely unrelated to hitting the first tee shot. An itch behind my ear. The tightness of the athletic tape wrapped around the blister on my left thumb. The squeaking straw in Trip's drink that sucked up the vodka. I tasted the cranberry and lime. I squinted into the glare of the morning sun shining against the fairway, and the remnants of dew that sparkled atop the thick rough. Black spots floated around my eyeballs.

"Now on the tee box," Callum Blair shouted, making sure Trip could hear him in the golf cart, "Mr. Trip Pierce!"

"I was serious, Callum. I'm not playing," Trip groaned from the cart. "Threw my back out this morning."

Callum shrugged, too hungover to worry much about it. "Okay then, next on the tee box…Mr. Justin Peterson," he said, then out of the side of his mouth he whispered, "Go beat these assholes." The pros knew the country club politics as good as any member. They also had side bets with each other and multiple wagers on every Flight.

I labored to the center of the box, leaned over, and pushed a wooden tee in the ground, but my trembling fingers struggled to balance the ball atop the tee. I nearly fainted when I stood up. After I lined the shot up and addressed the ball, I sensed Mr. Woodberry craning his neck for a better view of my ball's placement. From my vantage point, the ball was teed perfectly, an inch or two behind the drill bits painted blue and used as markers, but I was cautious of Mr. Woodberry's apparent skepticism. He was the type of person who would wait until I hit the shot before he'd protest with a rule violation, arguing my ball was teed in front of the markers, a two-stroke penalty, on shot number one, against a shorthanded team. I erred on the side of caution, leaned over again, and removed the ball and tee from the ground, shifting the setup back a foot or so. When I addressed the ball again, my stomach churned with nausea. My vision constricted into a narrow tunnel, and every time I blinked, a black void lingered longer than the previous blink, worsening my sense of unease.

This was my favorite moment in golf. The mild shock that ensued was a welcomed relief from my typical golf neurosis, in which my brain overreacted to every thought, labored over every doubt, and obsessed over every distraction. Not here though. Not this shot. This was pure instinct. A physical reaction. Nothing but muscle memory.

My shoulders felt a little closed. I tried to shuffle my feet but was only able to wiggle my toes. I waggled the club once. Waggled it twice. Double-checked my target. I checked my line to my aiming point, the left side of a fairway bunker on the right side of the dogleg. Waggled a third time. I started to pull the club back and that's when I noticed my left shoelaces were coming untied…I should probably tie them.

At impact I knew that the club head had swung too far from the inside, but I still smashed the ball against the toe of the driver and sent a line drive speeding into the morning light. The ball started sharply right but hooked across the fairway, then bounced several times and ran harmlessly into the first cut of rough well down the left side and well ahead of the Woodberrys.

I strode confidently back to the cart, slid the driver into my bag, and sat down next to Trip, who had his fist out for a dap.

"How'd that look?" I asked.

"It went pretty far."

"The swing though - did it look okay?"

"Elaborate," he said. "Otherwise, fantastic."

Mr. Woodberry insisted on walking to his golf ball, claiming his left ankle felt stiff. As Austin drove down the cart path, leaving his father behind, Trip attempted to do the same. However, his path was abruptly blocked by Mr. Woodberry, who stood in the way, impeding our progress.

Whispers had always circulated around the club about Woodberry's gambling problem. A hypocrisy easily believed given his flair for the political and his part time gig in the ministry. Neither me or Trip were all that surprised when, after halting us, Mr. Woodberry snarled with irritation, "All right listen here, you little shits, we'll play you a Nassau. One large on each side. Two on the total. How many strokes are you going to ask for?"

Trip did the talking on my behalf. "Is he playing against your individual scores or against the team bet?"

"This is a team tournament. It's a team bet."

"We want five a side."

"Five strokes a side?" he laughed.

"Did you not see that swing?"

"He's 40 yards by us."

Unwilling to deal with any added pressure, I jumped out of the cart, and started walking. "Figure it out without me," I told them.

About halfway to my ball, Trip pulled up next to me in the golf cart, and I got back in.

"Get it settled?" I asked.

"We did."

"How many strokes am I getting?"

"Not telling you," Trip said, sharply.

"Why not?"

"Same reason you jumped out of the golf cart and started walking. You don't really want to know, so let's put it this way, it's a good deal. Pressure is off. Just go play golf and we'll be fine."

"That's too big of a bet to argue that the pressure is off."

"I'm not worried about it. Woodberry is, though. He said if we bring it up around Austin or any other member, he'd revoke my membership and ban us both."

"He can't do that."

"I mean, not on the spot, but eventually, he would. The bet's made. You just go play a decent round of golf and we'll have fun with it."

"I'll take 50% of it, if you need me to."

"I got you covered. There's a bounty on the Woodberrys though. You win, it's worth 25%."

"You mean 35%?" I asked, and we shook on it.

Austin and Mr. Woodberry were first to play from the fairway, both hitting the middle of the green. I had 130-yards left, a fluffy lie, and residual nerves lingering from my shaky tee shot. It only took a pinhole, though, for the lightness of pessimism to creep through the fog. Suddenly, I felt vulnerable and alone. I took a pitching wedge, addressed the ball, and shuffled my feet. I waggled the wedge once. Waggled twice. Double-checked the target line. First, a yellow spot in the rough in front of me, and behind that, the middle of the green. Waggled a third time. I began my swing, and as soon as I did, a sharp burst of breeze blew through the Gunch line and put goosebumps on my arms, reminding me of the coldest round of golf Trip and I had ever played together.

We were invited to participate in the Wednesday pro-am for the annual Web.com tournament that Sendero hosted. We warmed-up on the range as the first light of dawn peeked through the clouds. Despite the early hour, the temperature for the day reached its peak at 33 degrees, with bitter gusts of wind over 20mph, making the chill even worse.

Nobody in our group wanted to play the round except for a business associate of mine whose company had paid our team's $8,000 entry fee, plus the pro assigned to us who was contractually obligated to play. Since Trip and I had already raided the Swag Room and taken several bags of complimentary merchandise, we both felt somewhat obligated, too, and decided to play.

The pro assigned to our group was a Swede who had never seen the course before and would go on to make 17 pars and one birdie for the coldest, most casual 71 I had ever witnessed. His caddie was a gruff old man from Idaho named Smitty, who had a one-liner for everything. Though the pro golfers rushed through the round and treated it like practice, for the pro caddies, the pro-am was a chance to earn a decent gratuity to help sustain their travel expenses plus all the cigarettes it took to make an 18-hole loop. Before the round, Smitty watched us carefully on the range while we hacked away. He cleaned our clubs, arranged them properly in our bags, and observed our swings to dial-in yardages.

At that point in the devolution of my golf swing, I had unconsciously added several hitches in the takeaway. On my first swing in front of Smitty, despite the stutters and jerks, I hit a 5-iron moderately flush, though who could really tell in that awful weather.

"How'd it look?" I asked Smitty, as a gust of wind smacked tiny sleet pellets against my face, like needles pricking my frozen cheeks.

"That's an elaborate backswing you have there," Smitty said with an excess of enthusiasm that fell just short of mockery. "Otherwise, it was fantastic."

. . .

I HIT the pitching wedge thin, off the bottom groove. The ball flew low, landed short, and limped to the collar of the green. From there, I lagged a putt near the hole and felt good about my chances at par until I stood over the four-footer. The putter shook when I took it back and a white flash popped in my eyes when I made contact, but the ball snuck inside the right lip and curled in for a four. The Woodberrys parred the hole, too, so we remained tied after number one. A minor victory.

The par-5 second hole played 549 yards from the blue tees. Normally a prevailing wind made reaching in two shots an impossibility, but because the cold morning breeze had not yet stiffened to its maximum velocity, many of the 10.0 handicappers in our flight maintained the impossible hope of an eagle. Thus, we waited for a quiet eternity on the group ahead of us, who waited for a group on the green to clear, who themselves waited while the worst player in their foursome plumb bobbed a short putt for bogey.

"I saw the flash when I hit my short putt back there," I told Trip while I waited in the cart. "Glad that's over with."

"What color was the flash this time?"

"White."

"I played in the Club Championship a few weeks ago. Four putted the first hole from nine feet. My flash wasn't white though. Mine was like an electric blue."

"Maybe it's like a mood ring trying to predict the outcome of the round."

"Maybe white means white hot. It's a good luck color. You're going to make everything now."

"I only have one good luck charm on this golf course," I said. "Seen any lately?"

"Not in a long time. I think they all got shot or learned their lesson and moved on."

"A real shame."

The fairway finally cleared, and it was time for the Woodberrys to hit. Instead of joining them on the tee box, I stayed by the cart and made bets with Trip.

"I'll take Austin hitting it in the fairway. Mr. Woodberry out of the fairway."

"That's a bet. How much?" Trip asked.

"Twenty on each?"

"Deal."

Both Woodberrys hit it square in the middle of the fairway and nullified the bet. When it was my turn again, I teed it up, addressed the ball, and shuffled my feet. Waggled the driver once. Waggled twice. Double-checked the target. First a broken tee in front of me, then the middle of the fairway behind it. Waggled a third time, and I felt good. Confident and good. I looked down at the ball, wide-eyed, ready to smash it into ten thousand pieces, but as I pulled the club back, I felt the first jerk take the clubhead way too far inside. I was about to lose control, and oh shit, I thought, in Japanese.

I REMEMBER the Patient Zero swing. The swing that began my downfall. It happened at Whistling Straits in Sheboygan County, Wisconsin. I was playing as a solo, and the starter matched me with three Japanese people who were traveling across the US to mark courses off their bucket list. Only two of them actually played. The male player was decked out in Mizuno's traditional blue. Hat. Shirt. Shoes. Bag. Clubs. The woman, his wife I presumed, looked identical except in canary yellow. Neither spoke English. The third person, an older gentleman with white hair, was mostly there for the walk, the views, and the simple translations he was capable of. It was like watching two colorful orbs float around the course with their Sensei on a dreary, gray morning.

When we reached the par-3, 17th hole, an ominous cloud hovered over Lake Michigan just off the shoreline to our left. Normally I would've been content with a lightning bolt and an airhorn calling us to more Spotted Cow inside the warm clubhouse, but I had a decent round going and a bet with my caddie, a fellow named Bender. The 17th green was perched on the side of a hill covered in wispy yellow grass. A prominent bunker ramped out of a dune and guarded the right side of the hole, while a series of bunkers sunk below the green on the left-side provided a last-ditch safety net from the rocky, narrow beach below.

While we waited to hit, I noticed a row of divots near the back of the tee box that all pointed in the direction of choppy Lake Michigan where water white capped over a large rock near the shore.

"What's this about?" I asked Bender.

"No idea what you're talking about," he said. He raised a rangefinder to his face. "But the tip of that rock in the water may or may not be 172-yards from where you're standing right now."

"Ever seen anybody hit the rock?" I asked.

"Nope."

"What's the secret? What happens if I hit it?"

Bender shrugged and pulled a 6-iron from my bag and handed it to me. "Don't worry. You'll miss."

"Am I hitting all of this?" I asked, referring to the 6-iron.

"It's way downhill but it's also into the wind," he said and tossed me an old Titleist he kept in his caddie bib.

I placed the ball next to the row of divots, addressed it, and looked at the rock. Waggled. Did the whole thing. At the top of the backswing, I felt the club in the slot. I knew I could swing as hard as I wanted to, but I also knew I didn't need to. My swing sequence unwound, and I struck it pure. That old Titleist golf ball cut through the wind and floated into a high, beautiful draw.

"Great swing," Bender muttered under his breath and watched the path of the ball as it hovered over the water and gently drifted downward. It splashed 10 feet in front of the rock. A miss but so close that even the Japanese people flinched and said "ohhhhh… awwww" and bowed and clapped.

"Never a doubt you'd miss," Bender said.

"What was the prize? You'd have to buy me drinks for a change?"

Bender shrugged again. "Guess you'll have to play another round and try again. The good news is you get to hit that same shot for real." He turned his attention to the flag on the 17$^{th}$ green, where the group ahead of us had cleared. Bender continued, "Winds blowing from left to right. Hurting a little. With the pin tucked front right, I'd play the same shot you just hit to the middle of the green. Start it at the flag. The wind will hold up the draw."

This time I shoved a tee into the ground with a pearly Pro-V on top of it. Waggled. Did the whole thing again. At the top of the backswing, I felt the club in the slot. Same as before. I knew I could swing as hard as I wanted to, but I also knew I didn't need to. My swing sequence unwound, and...

Clank.

The air rushed from my lungs.

The sound of the hosel echoed in my head.

A piercing, stinging sensation shot through my abdomen, spit gathered in the back of my mouth, and the muscles in my arms contracted, painfully.

The ball whizzed straight to the right and spun wickedly through the grass and sandy hillside, and time briefly stood still, until the Sensei said, "Ohhh, kuso!"

Using every ounce of athleticism I possessed, I managed to save the swing, and proceeded to block my drive on Number 2 so far to the right that it soared over the Gunch and landed safely in the adjacent fairway of Hole 6. Good thing it's near impossible to shank a driver.

We parked in a shaded spot near where the ball landed. After I stepped out of the cart and leaned against its side, I noticed the Woodberrys just beyond the Gunch, eyeing what we were up to.

"You guys need something?" Trip called out. Their shots had landed nowhere near where they had stopped.

"Did you find your ball alright?" Mr. Woodberry asked, his tone laced with skepticism.

"I did," I said, and gestured towards it.

Mr. Woodberry squinted, not entirely convinced, as his view was obstructed by mesquite thicket. With a final, lingering glance, he drove toward their own tee shots to do more waiting, just like we were doing.

Trip stared at him in disbelief as he drove away. The blatant disrespect left him momentarily speechless. Then he said, "You know how people like to argue about how they'd travel back in time to kill Hitler? I'd like to travel back in time to meet the guy who created the first golf course, and around the time he finished his 12th hole, I'd tell him 'Hey man, that's good. You're done here.' And if he tried to keep going, I'd strangle him."

"I wholeheartedly endorse it. Imagine how much easier a Front-6, Back-6, Emergency-6 would be."

"Those old-time guys must've really hated their wives."

"Was it the Scottish or the Irish who created the game?"

"Which ones have uglier wives?"

"I'm not discerning enough to appreciate the difference between them," I replied, chuckling. Standing on the side of the cart, I peered over the Gunch to check on the status of the group ahead of us. It was still going to be a while. "What if, instead of uppity British people," I continued, "the game had evolved from another source entirely. What if golf was invented by some stoner in Colorado who got tired of disc golf because his buddies were getting so damn serious about it, so he makes up a new game with a stick and a little white ball. What would golf become then?" I asked.

Trip thought about it. "Instead of using numbers to indicate scores, the scoring system would be based on pleasing generalizations. Today, I shot somewhere between One Heckuva Round and a What a Great Day to be Outdoors."

"Imagine the snacks," I said.

Nevertheless, I was aware that a game that laid-back wouldn't truly resonate with Trip's nature. His innate competitive spirit, fueled by a penchant for degenerate gambling, demanded a more intense challenge.

"Honestly, I probably wouldn't change much," Trip said, agreeing with me for different reasons. "I like the exclusivity of golf more than anything else. That's why I couldn't stand slackers eating cereal at 3:00 o'clock in the afternoon in the Men's Grill."

"You mean the Men's Chill."

Trip clicked his teeth. "No, I do not."

"You know, speaking of preferences," I continued. "Most people only like golf for reasons that don't have anything to do with golf. Exclusivity is a perfect example. I certainly wouldn't play this much if I had to fight for tee times over at Green Acres," I said, of the semi-private course on the other side of town, where golfers in jean shorts spent 4.5 hours shooting a 102.

Trip agreed.

"Nature is another good example," I continued. "Build a 110-yard par-3 amongst the trees of a $30 municipal course in rural East Texas and it evokes nothing. Build the same hole on the Pacific Ocean shoreline and weepy eyed people will pay $500 to play it, and they'll come away preaching the virtues of golf."

"At least golf is somewhat integrated with nature," Trip said, "Take the ocean front property in California, without the golf course there, Pebble Beach would be overrun with monotonous condominiums."

"And if not for Sendero Country Club, this entire native area that surrounds us would be overrun with single-story homes from the $250's."

"You'd think the Gunch that avoided such a tragic outcome, all because of our exclusive golf hobby, would be a lot more forgiving to the wayward drives we never can seem to find."

"No, no. Forgiveness is a sin in golf, for people like the Woodberrys anyway, who play this game because they think it's a fair representation of real life."

"Not me. I get enough real life in my real life," Trip said.

"What would this moment represent, in real life?"

"We're literally waiting in traffic."

"If we were stuck in actual traffic, at least we could listen to music."

"Rule 14-3 strikes again," Trip said. He knew the letter by heart and kept a framed copy of it in his home office.

---

*ATTN: GOLF COMMITTEE*

*Gentlemen, after researching rule interpretations and consulting with a PGA rule official, we have determined speakers and other listening devices amplifying music during a round of golf are in violation of USGA Rule 14-3. The rule states a player may not use equipment that "might assist him making a stroke or in his play." In addition to aiding a player's swing tempo and potentially improving a player's concentration, music is an unnecessary, artificial nuisance and a distraction.*

*The Committee should vote to disallow the playing of music on the course immediately.*

*Should this simple request be denied, we will seek appropriate changes to Committee leadership per the various warnings stated in our previous correspondence regarding general course etiquette, the annual CCA banquet, and tournament performance.*

*Concerned SCC Members*

Thus commenced Mr. Woodberry's crafty takeover of the President's seat on the Golf Committee, adeptly forging alliances with the old money members and his fellow golf pedants. When they took over, fun was officially suspended at Sendero. Music was banned. The dress code was strictly enforced. The initiation fee skyrocketed. Worst of all, given my current predicament, because Mr. Woodberry was embarrassed about SCC losing the annual Ryder Cup style match versus the club across town, his cabal decided to make The Stickup a true stroke play event bound by the complete and penal USGA Rules of Golf. This applied from the Championship Flight through the bottom flight where pars were rare enough. Mr. Woodberry argued that playing to a more strenuous standard would strengthen the club's competitive resolve and would finally end the back-to-back-to-back-to-back-to-back losing streak.

Mr. Woodberry whistled loudly from the second hole, and he

impatiently waved the bucket hat over his head. We had not noticed the group in front of us had advanced to the green.

"I guess they think I'm laying up," I joked. I had 300 yards left, so like I had done 100 times before from nearly this very position, I needed to hit a 5-iron safely back onto the appropriate fairway, and then I'd have a comfortable wedge left to get home. A pumpjack in the distance made the perfect aiming point. I addressed the ball, waggled once, waggled twice, and found the discolored piece of grass I selected as my close target. I waggled a third time, then I pulled the club back, and when I did, my body flinched, like it sensed an imminent emergency, and I was suddenly reminded of the first of the two times I saw an ambulance at Sendero Country Club.

TWO DOZEN GOLF carts navigated the shortcuts through the course to reach the isolated 17th fairway, far away from the squares where we could enjoy our privacy and make ludicrous bets. Earlier in the day, Trip had a shot from 150 yards and missed the green, then got into an argument about how many times he could hit that very shot onto the putting surface if given 50 golf balls to do so. Since it was one of those summer days where the sun stayed in the air forever and bidding hadn't yet begun in the Calcutta, we decided to take Trip up on his bet. Fifty shots from the same spot. At Trip's request, the over/under was set at 30 balls and Trip was on the Over, so I was on the Over. We were the only two.

I don't remember much more than that.

I don't remember the exact number of balls Trip successfully hit onto the green.

I don't remember driving toward the green to count them up.

I don't remember who told the joke in the cart next to me, or what was said, but I remember I laughed and laughed at the punchline. It was such a comfortable feeling, the warmth that enveloped me from the revelry and camaraderie, that I did not recognize my inebriated state or the dangerous turn it was about to take.

The rest of the story was filled in later by Trip and those who witnessed the crash. After I passed out, I kept my foot on the accelerator, but I slung the wheel hard to the right, and steered the golf cart directly into the pond along the right side of the hole. The force from the sudden impact with the water flung my body through the frame of the cart, and I smacked my head against the vertical support bar as I was ejected out.

They said Trip reached me first and pulled me out of the water like I didn't weigh anything at all, and laid me down in the grass, soaking wet, where I made some god-awful snoring sound as I struggled to breathe. Someone called 911. Had no choice. Someone else texted Callum Blair, who arrived with the GM to investigate around the time I came to, dazed, confused.

When it was clear I was at least going to be okay, Trip pulled the GM to the side, and they conspired to keep things hush-hush. This proved a difficult task once the ambulance that arrived hopped the curb in the parking lot and drove down the 18th fairway with the siren still blaring. He parked right on top of the tee box as there were trees and other obstacles in the way, then the paramedics disembarked, rolling out the gurney and a big red medical kit.

By the time they reached me, they surely knew the score. A bunch of drunk golfers standing around, 50 golf balls scattered all over the green complex, 31 of them on paydirt, a cart upturned in the water, and then they took one look at me.

"Sir, have you had a lot to drink today?" one of the medics asked.

"Sir, that depends on what you consider a lot," I am said to have answered, then I blinked heavily, smiled, and my eyes rolled back in my head.

I HIT my second shot on Hole 2 dead in the screws. The ball compressed and screamed over the Gunch line as a divot flipped over in front of me. Soaring high in the sky with a buttery little fade, it disappeared behind the mesquite trees, and if I had to guess, I'd call it perfectly in the middle of the fairway.

"Beautiful," Trip commented.

"Swing look any better?"

"Same," he said.

"More elaborate? Or more fantastic?"

"Same," he repeated.

We cruised down the fairway, breeze in our face, and golf briefly felt grand, until we reached my intended landing spot where there was no sign of my ball. We circled around. We checked the nearby fairway bunkers. I got out of the cart and walked through the thick rough, hacking away with a club, to no avail. I searched the Gunch line just in case. I retraced the ball flight. I walked its path. Never found it. The only evidence I could find was a sprinkler head near the area where I wanted the ball to land, and my best guess was that my shot landed on top of it and bounced far enough to reach the Gunch. It was lost.

Meanwhile, over on the opposite side of the fairway, Austin had sliced his second shot deep into the rough. It took the Woodberrys longer than usual to talk themselves through their pre-shot strategy, and after Austin hit his shot onto the back fringe of the green, they drove toward us.

"Can't find it?" Mr. Woodberry asked.

It took restraint not to reply with an obvious quip for his obvious question. Worse yet was the glee I detected in his voice.

"Guess not," I said. "We were sure it would be in the middle of the fairway."

"By rule, I think your search time is probably up," Mr. Woodberry stated.

Trip gripped the steering wheel like he was about to rip it into two pieces and eat it. He tilted his sunglasses down the bridge of his nose and stared down Mr. Woodberry like a predator hunting a tiny slot receiver running a route over the middle. "How long is the search time?" he asked.

"Five minutes."

It sure didn't feel like five minutes had elapsed yet, but I couldn't be sure.

Trip was pissed. "You need to take it easy," he said, making sure Mr. Woodberry knew he meant it, too. "My playing partner is doing this alone, and I don't need you up his ass about the stupid rulebook."

Mr. Woodberry's cheeks flushed red, and his bottom lip quivered in a rage. We weren't going to win this battle, and I didn't want Trip's good standing jeopardized on my account, so I tried to cool things off before Mr. Woodberry fired back.

"I'm tired of looking anyway," I said and got back in the cart, and quietly told Trip to forget it.

Austin tried to play peacemaker, too. He added, "I'll keep searching just in case. There might be a few more seconds yet." He half-heartedly poked his club around in a couple of mesquite bushes.

"Don't worry about it," I called out and waited for Trip to accelerate, but the cart didn't budge an inch, while he stared bullets into the back of Mr. Woodberry's head.

"What are we doing?" Trip finally asked me. He was clueless. Normally, using the local rules, we would play this as a lateral hazard. I could drop a ball where I thought it entered the Gunch, take a penalty stroke, and be done with it, but because we were playing by the official Rules of Golf, my punishment was more severe.

I explained to Trip, "We repeat the shot I just hit as close to the previous spot as possible. With a penalty stroke."

"So, you're dropping three, hitting four from way back there?"

That was correct but I was too nervous to acknowledge it.

"Damn," Trip said solemnly, then he drove us back down the fairway toward the tee box, around the Gunch line, and onto the adjacent sixth hole, where we waited for a group to hit their approach shots. It was impossible to ignore the math. Hit the fourth into the fairway, hopefully hit the fifth onto the green, hopefully two-putt for a seven. That's a big number with a much bigger number lurking.

"Do I place a new ball down or drop it?" I asked and studied the area around my previous divot.

Trip laughed. He had no idea.

"Within two club lengths, right?" I asked. "Or does it have to be right next to it?"

"I'm still not positive why we drove back here in the first place," Trip said, then a lightbulb moment. He looked at me curiously, and said, "You don't think they'd…"

"Think they'd what?"

"That ball was headed for the dead middle of the fairway, right?"

"There's no way."

"Lot of scratch riding on this match. If he's got a weird gambling compulsion, maybe he's got the same kind of problem with cheating?"

"Not with Austin around. There is no way."

I made sure the Woodberrys couldn't see me through the Gunch, just in case, and placed a new ball on a fluffy bit of grass next to my original divot. Once again, I grabbed my 5-iron, and once again, I aimed for the pumpjack rising in the background. I waggled once. Waggled twice. Rechecked the target line. The pumpjack creaked when it tilted up and down. But this time when I pulled the club back, I noticed the three red stripes on the shaded side of my new ball. These stripes looked a darker shade of red. A familiar hue I hadn't seen in a long time. The color of many late nights alone when my mind refused to rest.

She wasted no time launching a smear campaign against me. The most damaging attacks included chapter length Facebook posts revealing the intel she received from the private investigator she'd hired to tail me. She controlled the narrative from the very beginning of our separation, and so the story she spun was that she'd kicked me out of the house, and I slinked away like a beaten dog. In reality, I left the house without a fuss, leaving her everything but what little money I needed to last me through the year. I packed my essentials into a suitcase and left so abruptly that it didn't satisfy her need for drama. She wanted fireworks, and so she popped a few in my direction, hurling verbal M80s as I nonchalantly walked away.

I knew there was a place I could find respite, and I knew I didn't have to ask permission to go. I drove to Trip's house and found him on the porch with an air rifle across his lap, smoking a cigar, gazing at the deep red leaves fluttering on the towering maple tree in his backyard. I opened the suitcase and removed the bottle of 25-year-old Laphroaig I had smuggled out of my house. Her father had given it to me on the wedding night, told me to save it for a special occasion. So, I got two plastic cocktail cups from a cabinet in Trip's kitchen and poured heavily into each. I placed his cup on the patio table next to him, then sat down in a chair and watched the red leaves blowing in the wind.

"Mind if I stay here long enough to watch all the leaves fall out of that tree?" I asked.

Trip slowly leaned forward. His eyes narrowed on a squirrel bounding atop the power line hanging over the alley behind his fence. He trained the air rifle on the squirrel, but it ran behind the maple tree before he could get a shot off. He replaced the gun on his lap and picked up the bottle to read the label.

"As long as you provide provisions like this," he said, "you can stay as long as you like. She finally kick you out?"

"She finally did."

For the remainder of the night and well into the early morning, neither of us moved except to relieve ourselves in the yard. We drained the good stuff and moved on to the cheap stuff, and eventually I wanted to pass out. I moved my belongings into the guest bedroom, took some of my clothes off, and collapsed in the bed. Looking around, head spinning, the bedroom's walls were painted a deep red - red like a vintage cabernet, red as the leaves on the maple tree in the backyard.

I didn't sleep that night, and never slept well in that room any night after. When I did manage to drift off, my sleep was restless and insufficient, and any dreams that dared appear were shaded the same ruddy hue as the walls that surrounded me.

. . .

"Instant replay," Trip said after I contacted what was now my fourth shot on Number 2. The ball shot high into the air with another buttery little fade on the exact same line as my first attempt. Even the divots looked identical and parallel. But this time when Trip and I made it back to the Number 2 fairway, we found my second attempt atop the most luscious piece of center-cut fairway, 130-yards away from the pin, exactly where I thought the first one had landed.

The Woodberrys were still near the Gunch where we left them. Curiously, they both had their hands in the air and waved us over. When we reached them, Mr. Woodberry put a shit eating grin on his face.

"Found your ball," he said proudly.

"Which ball?" I asked.

"Your first ball, but I don't think you're going to like it."

Austin squatted down to the ground at the edge of the Gunch and pointed beneath several thorny branches where, balanced on a clump of entangled weeds, my original golf ball had stopped inside a rotted mesquite stump covered in swarms of ants. The three red stripes were easily identifiable.

"Well as you can see," I said and turned toward my ball in the middle of the fairway, "I already hit my replacement, so this is a moot point, right?"

"I am not sure you are using that word correctly," Mr. Woodberry said. I had no idea if he was referring to the word *replacement* or *moot*, because I had no idea if I used either correctly. "The rules state you must play the original as it lies," Mr. Woodberry said, firmly, like he was the author of the original rule and was offended I did not immediately comply.

"No," I said, "I don't think that's right. Once I put the second ball in play, the original was, uhhh," I struggled for the word again. "Replaced?" I said, still uncertain.

Trip's jaw dropped but his hands tightened into clenched fists. "Woodberry, you had already declared our search time was expired anyway," he said.

This inflamed Mr. Woodberry who shot right back, "And you

argued time wasn't up! And! I didn't hear you declare anything when you drove off!"

"Where'd you think we were going?" Trip barked. "Choir practice?"

Mr. Woodberry instinctively reached for the cell phone he usually kept clipped to his belt loop. "I'm calling the pro shop!" he shouted, "We'll get to the bottom of this." He dug through the compartments inside the golf cart until he found his phone.

The last thing I wanted to do was argue with the asshole, so I sat back down in the cart next to Trip, who winked at me and smiled. He mocked Mr. Woodberry by quoting the only movie he ever quoted. "Okay sir, you're a Lebowski, I'm a Lewbowski. That's terrific," he said like a grumpy old man.

Austin remained squatted by my first ball, deliberating. "Even if the original had to be played, I think you would get two club lengths of relief from this position," he said. "There are ants all over the ball. Don't you get relief from ant hills, Dad?"

"An ant is an insect not a burrowing animal. Ants build hills, not holes. No relief," Mr. Woodberry said as if these things were obvious. Somebody in the pro shop finally picked up and Mr. Woodberry switched gears. "Bethany," he said into the phone, "get me the Head Pro, please. I have a rules violation on Number 2." As if Bethany cared. Mr. Woodberry then screeched, "What do you mean he's not there!?...Where's Callum?...Send a cart boy to fetch him."

"No! I'm not waiting," I shouted from the cart. "Just hang up the phone. I'll make you a deal."

"I don't do deals," Mr. Woodberry said. "The rules are the rules."

"Look, I don't even know the rules."

"Then you have no business playing in this tournament."

"We're in the fifth flight!" Trip said and laughed at Mr. Woodberry's projected superiority.

"I'm going to play my ball in the fairway," I said. "When the round is over, I'll disqualify myself out of last place if that's what's required, and I don't give a shit if that's a dangerous anthill or not, Austin, you can keep the fucking thing as a souvenir."

"Watch your language!" Mr. Woodberry yelled.

Austin grabbed him by the arm and said something quietly, causing Mr. Woodberry to sneer. I think he realized how much he liked the idea of watching me struggle through the next 17 holes with the possibility of disqualification lingering over my head. So, they let me be, and Trip drove me to the provisional I hit into the fairway.

"I think that all but guarantees another letter," I told Trip.

"We really took it out on Austin, didn't we?"

I finished checking the distance, then said, "He needs to find better friends. Why else would he want to play with his awful father?"

"Justin, let's be honest, we all know why you're mad at Austin."

Not that it mattered, but two years ago, my ex-wife remarried. Austin. They're perfect together. He's too nice, a pushover, wealthy, and most importantly, he won't ever betray her.

"How confident are you, by the way, about the rules?" Trip asked.

"About 15%," I answered and lifted the 52* wedge out of my bag, my face flushed with a hint of anger, determined to hit for a change. I took dead aim at the flag stick. Waggled once. Waggled twice. Double-checked the pin. Waggled a third time. Just as I pulled the club back, I felt a sudden and violent urge to pee.

It was the same red-hued dream, and it always began in the same way.

I'm on an international flight. In India. I've never been to India. I'm seated in a window seat next to two sleeping strangers. The pilot makes an announcement in a language I do not recognize. I check my watch. One hour of flight time left.

I have an urge to pee. It is light and easily ignored.

Later, another announcement is made. I sense a slight inertia. The plane has initiated its descent.

The urge to pee increases. I should go to the bathroom while I have a chance. My seat neighbors are asleep. I'll be okay.

The flight attendants begin their work. The fasten seat belt lights turn on. It smells like curry.

A sharp pain pokes my bladder, and I can feel urine near the tip. I put my hand in the pocket of my jeans and squeeze to help hold it in.

It is torture until the wheels touch down. This excitement allows for a moment of relief, but soon after, an even greater urge arises.

The plane taxis forever. I look outside the window for a distraction, but I only see smog. The plane stops and the people in the rear jam their way forward into the aisle. Minding my manners, I am one of the last to deboard.

I stand up from my seat and the urge completely vanishes, so I walk down the aisle of the plane, past the lavatory, and it's not until I'm into the jetway that the urge returns, worse than before. Much worse. I walk fast but the faster I go, the longer the tunnel appears, and the more people clog the exit. Once I make it to the terminal, the gate is crowded with Indian men yelling at a gate agent. Their native language interspersed with English. Though surrounded by a hundred angry men, the gate agent has only contempt on his face. Somehow people argue with him one at a time. I push through the crowd.

I begin to run.

There isn't so much a line when I reach the men's restroom as there is general congestion. I wait.

When I reach an open urinal, I am bouncing off my left foot, right foot, left foot, right foot, as I try to unzip my pants.

I'm ready to burst.

Finally, I aim at porcelain, except, cymbals crash, and nothing happens. I have forgotten how to pee. I am left standing there, same pain, same inflamed bladder, same urge, with no way to relent. First, I try to recall how to relax, how to let go, like a swing thought, but when that doesn't work, I focus acutely on the specific muscles it takes to pee. Since I don't really know which muscles those are, I obsess over each of them, how to work them individually, how to contract them and open them, so that I can find the muscle that needs to be repaired. I never do. The more I focus, the further away the solution seems.

Then I wake up. More than once, I've peed my pants.

I SHANKED IT. My fifth counted stroke on the second hole was a shank. It came out of nowhere as random shanks always do, and the ball flew wickedly to the right and buzzed like a hornet as it spun into the thick rough. The air hissed as it escaped from my lungs. An anxious pit formed in my stomach. My knees wobbled. My face burned red with shame.

"That's one," I said to Trip, who knew not to say anything in return, less I fly off the handle.

I placed the tainted 52° wedge back into my bag, careful that it didn't strike any of the other clubs and infect them with treachery, and I got the 56° wedge this time and walked to my ball in the rough. Clusters of black stars filled my peripheral vision like I had just donated blood and was about to pass out.

The pin was tucked on the back-right-side of the green, but I wanted nothing to do with right, so I aimed at the center, then center left, then a little further left, where one piece of a wide green-side bunker was now in play. There was a light wheeze in my chest before my mind slipped into a golf coma reminiscent of the first tee. I had swung without realizing it. The ball flew as low as a shank, but it went straight, jumped into the bunker, climbed to the upper lip like it might escape, but then fell back into the middle of the sand.

I climbed into the trap and shuffled my feet until they were locked in place. As I always did in the sand, I opened the face a degree or two, but when I placed it behind the ball, ever so slightly above the sand, a ray of sunlight reflected off the shiny silver hosel and blinded me with terror. I closed the face and swung fast. I bladed it again, but the ball ramped up the side of the bunker, landed on the green, and rolled to a stop 20 feet from the hole. From there, I three-putted and successfully manifested the big number. A 10.

I pulled my ball from the hole, feeling disoriented and disappointed. Austin hovered next to me with the flagstick in his hand. "You okay?" he asked.

"How many was that?" I asked. It was a lot of strokes. I wanted to be certain, and if anybody knew for sure, it was the Woodberrys.

"A 10," Mr. Woodberry responded quickly, satisfaction in his voice, and I knew it was written in stone.

Austin watched me curiously for a moment, then replaced the flagstick in the hole, and he and his father followed me as I slowly trudged off the green, weighed down by disgrace, and the amount of money Trip had placed on me.

Mr. Woodberry tightened the screw. "As the great Bobby Jones once said, golf is the closest game to the game we call life," he proclaimed loudly, "You get bad breaks from good shots; you get good breaks from bad shots – but you have to play the ball where it lies." With that, he took a banana route back to his golf cart, passing by Trip along the way. In a hushed voice he said, "I'll let you out for half, if you want it." Trip shook his head in decline, and Mr. Woodberry continued on his way.

I wanted to hit my tee shot on the par-3 third hole and I wanted it over with as quickly as possible. Should I shank the shot into the Gunch, I'd re-tee as fast as I could, and if I shanked another, I'd hop back into the golf cart and I'd vow never to step foot on any golf course ever again. But I didn't have Honors on the tee box, because not only had I carded a 10, but the Woodberrys made another efficient par on Number 2. I had to wait on them, and while I waited, I couldn't bear to be near Trip, so I stood at random between cart path and tee box, like a lost child.

The Woodberrys huddled next to the water cooler, refilling their paper cups, silently watching the group ahead of us like hawks trying to gain as much intel about the green as possible. It wasn't until all four putts were holed and the pin replaced that Austin walked to the center of the tee box and used his rangefinder to shoot the flagstick. "186 to the pin," he said. He reached into his back pocket, then flipped open a custom-made, leather-bound Sendero yardage book. He had decorated each page with intricate details and Google Earth overlays, yardages, break lines in the greens, with notes and reminders in tiny print.

I had been so focused on the Woodberrys that I hadn't noticed Trip had stepped out of the cart. After downing a giant cocktail along with the lingering numb from the pills, his back was as loose as it was going to get. He cautiously took an iron from my bag, stretched his back with a wince, then made two gentle practice swings, each with just enough force to hit a 50-yard punch. With each follow-through, his face twisted as if a bullet tore through a muscle in his back. He returned my club, climbed back into the cart, and resumed his static position, frustrated that he had doubted the severity of his injury because of my dismal performance.

"How far is it to carry the water?" Mr. Woodberry asked Austin. There was a small pond protecting the front right of the green. Though the pressure of losing to a solo player had vanished after only the second hole, the pair of them still mimicked the deliberate conversational pace between the tour caddie and the tour pro. They were in striking range of the leaders in our flight, and they really wanted to win this thing, again.

A long pause followed while Austin lifted his rangefinder to his eye and double-checked his manual calculation.

"179 to carry the water," Austin answered. He detached then reattached the Velcro strip on his glove several times until the fit was just right.

Mr. Woodberry put his hand on his thigh for balance and slowly bent over. He reached down and pulled a few tufts from the higher cut grass surrounding the tee box, then tossed the pieces of grass in the air and watched until the very last blade tumbled away. "Breeze is helping slightly," he told Austin. "What's the distance to the back?"

Austin raised the rangefinder again. "212," he said after pressing the finder's button multiple times and consulting his book again. Though Austin had listened to his father, watched him perform the wind check, and could also feel the wind direction standing casually on the tee box, he repeated the experiment anyway. He lifted a tuft of grass and watched it blow out of his hands much like his father had done. "Don't forget it plays about eight yards downhill," he said. I wanted to kill him.

"What club are you thinking?" Mr. Woodberry asked.

Austin strolled toward the cart where the volume of their conversation lowered and they spoke to each other discreetly, like I was going to choose my own club based on their overwrought pre-shot process. Eventually they each decided on a club to hit, and after all the planning, the yardages, wind gauging, and the club selection talk, Austin cut an iron that bounced once before it splashed in the pond, followed by Mr. Woodberry, who hit a line drive with his hybrid that ran into the bunker on the left side of the green.

Before his ball even hopped in the sand, I had already moved to the opposite side of the tee box. I fumbled through my pocket, but my fingers couldn't grasp a tee, so I picked up the first discarded one I found on the ground. I tried to press it into the ground, but my fingers tensed into mangled curls. I knocked the ball off the tee two, three, four times. Couldn't get it. Blood rushed to my head. I felt dizzy again. I tossed the broken tee to the side and simply rolled the ball onto grass between several divots. I stood up and took my stance. My shoulders were so taut they crowded my neck. My arms dangled an inch or two higher than usual, and my weight pressed against the tips of my toes. The slightest increase in the breeze would have blown me over. Better go quick. I aimed left. Way left. Left of the green. I waggled once. Waggled twice. Double-checked the target and shifted a little further left. It looked good. It felt good. Waggled a third time, and I wanted to begin the swing, I wanted to get it over with, but I couldn't, because the thoughts gripping my mind were stuck on Eddie Murphy and Dan Aykroyd.

SHE NEVER SAID hello when I called. She only answered and waited for me get straight to the business at hand.

"I'm about to go in and sign," I said.

"It was much less surreal than I imagined," she replied. "What have you been up to?" By this, she wanted me to confess my latest sins, many of which she had probably heard in elaborate detail down the rumor mill.

I answered her by saying, "Something has happened to my golf swing."

I could hear the oxygen rushing into her nose and I could visualize her nostrils thinning, her usual, natural reaction when she was slowly inflating with rage. These passions of hers were wild and uncontrollable while we were married, but now that we were about 15 minutes and one more signature away from being unmarried, her emotions were tempered by the redeeming fact that it was all about to be over.

She composed herself and said, dully, "How fascinating." She had always been completely bored with my golf game. "Developed any guilt yet?" she asked. She possessed this destructive ability to increase the importance of any conversation through a sudden shift in pace, guilt being her weapon of choice.

"I stand over the ball, and I just...can't...move," I continued, playing my own games, not hers.

"Save it for your solo sessions, Juh-stin." I hated the way she said my name when she mocked me. "You are still seeing the therapist, right?"

My position since the breakup was to remain mum about everything. True, she'd find out one way or another, but the fact she worked at it made her appear desperate, and that comforted my petty, broken heart. I didn't talk about therapy or rehab or any of it. I did, however, fess up to one thing. "I'm not sleeping," I said. "When I do fall asleep, I have a very strange, reoccurring dream that's haunting me, and I wake up in the middle of the night. Stir crazy. Can't go back to sleep."

"Your ego may be able to dodge accountability, but your body remains a prisoner to the truth."

"I think you may be right. Have you ever forgotten how to pee?" I asked.

"Are you drunk right now? Or high? Or both?" she asked.

"I'm tired," I said. "And my swing is just...broken."

"Never once have I cared about your bullshit swing."

"I am fully aware of that. At least I tried to keep you involved."

"Are you really being serious right now? About your golf swing? You sound serious."

"I am."

She sighed. "Well, as a token of respect, and as my last official act being married to you, why don't you go ahead and state your piece. I've had just the right number of margaritas to listen."

"The golf club's basic construction is simple," I began, "There is the shaft and there is the clubface, and where the two pieces meet is the infamous hosel. Its literal meaning has little importance compared to its symbolic meaning. If the hosel strikes the golf ball instead of the club face, a shank will occur, and the ball will ricochet straight to the right and maim anything in its path. You following?"

"Uh-huh."

"There is such a thing as the stray shank. Usually, they happen during warmups with zero consequence, save a little embarrassment if anyone sees it flying across the range. Even if that kind of shank occurs on the actual golf course, it's still harmless, because it's isolated. The Shanks are something else entirely. The Shanks have a foreign origin, created as best I can tell by aliens small enough to corrupt a golfer at the chromosomal level. Once infected with them, the aliens procreate and spread, first in the mind, then through the body…" I said and waited for her to say something.

"Aliens?" she said.

"Yes, aliens. Think of them like a conduit. The brain doesn't comprehend the negative. So, if you think *don't* shank it, the brain will only know that a shank was called to attention. This is merely a byproduct of the mind. The aliens, though, they take the same formula, and they apply this corruption to different parts of the body. On one swing, it will be felt in the hands. On the next swing, the feet. Then the elbow, and so on. Next thing you know, the whole body has been invaded and snatched."

"These aliens sound pretty mean."

"They're more like mischievous aliens. The type who likes to laugh at people who trip and fall."

"Is that what happened to you? They infected your whole body and you fell down?"

"Do you remember when I want to Whistling Straits? Near Milwaukee?"

"And you bailed on my entire family to go golfing? How could I forget?"

"I hit a shank there. When we got back from that trip, I needed to know if they had followed me home, so I went out to the club and tried a little three-quarter swing with a wedge. Shanked it. Then another. And another. One hosel rocket after another. I filled a soft cooler full of beer, and I hauled it with me to the far end of the range. By the time I finished that practice session it was dusk, the beer was all gone, and I was seated barefoot and cross-legged on the grass, next to the empty trays where there had been balls stacked up, and my shoes and socks, one of which was stained with blood from a cut that had somehow developed behind the toenail on my big toe. I was dazed and I had blisters in new places on my hands, but I thought I had made a vital discovery. The initial part of my backswing, the takeaway, that was the culprit. I had been taking the club back too far to the inside the entire time, and in doing so it changed the position of my arms, and hands, leading to The Shanks. Reversing this trend and mastering the takeaway would be like replacing one broken bulb in a long string of lights that, once fixed, would illuminate the path to my true swing."

"Did it work?"

"Of course not. I avoided the golf course and instead I rehearsed. Back-and-forth, back-and-forth. I practiced the beginning of the backswing until the move turned into a nervous tick. Back-and-forth, back-and-forth. I repeated the motion in the mirror, standing in the shower, waiting for a coffee, in empty grocery store aisles, back-and-forth, over-and-over, until I returned to the mirror, and I saw what might as well have been the first quarter of Ben Hogan's very own backswing in the reflection."

"I remember that move now. I kept having to apologize to people."

"The problem wasn't my takeaway. It was only the first of

many problems. The next one was my grip. It was too strong for the new takeaway positions. So, I changed my grip. Next, it was my…

“Okay. I get it. My patience is wearing thin here.”

“Each new problem paralyzed my swing in unique ways, and every time I addressed a ball, whether it was on the course, on the practice range, or in my mind’s eye, I felt every single kink, and as if it were an instinctual, perverse mindfuck, I exaggerated each kink, until my backswing was full of stutters. Instead of back-and-forth, one-two, Ala---Bama, my backswing felt like going back…up…around…weight shifted all over the place…a complete loss of power…no compression at impact. A—A—A—A---La……… La……..Bama. At my lowest point, I couldn’t even hold onto the club with my right hand. It would hover over the grip until I reached the top of the modified backswing, and I would regrip the club at the top, then pray that this would be the swing to break the chain. It never happened. And through all of the lessons and books and advice, and after being so scared of shanking it that my swing had become a Rube Goldberg machine, I learned something valuable.”

“That you suck at golf?”

“Exactly,” I said. There was more to it than that, sure, but she was right in her mocking simplicity, too.

“Maybe our split will be the catalyst your golf game needs,” she said, and this time I heard her yawn. “I think I’ve shown you just about all the respect I can handle right now.”

“Thanks for listening.”

“One day you won’t live here anymore, Justin. I can just tell you’re going to move away. Just as soon as you’re the one not at the center of it, the gossip will be good again. Maybe we can even be friends and commiserate together.”

“I’d like that,” I said, and just as soon as I did, she hung up the phone.

She was right about one thing, because the moment wasn’t strange at all. I walked into my attorney’s office and signed the divorce papers without a second thought. There were no nerves, no regrets, or any sense of time lingering slowly by offering a last-ditch moment to change my mind.

I texted her to let her know the official deed was done, and she replied with one of the few endearing traditions in our relationship, a quote from the first movie we ever watched together.

"The document is fully executed. You were right. Wasn't surreal," I text.

"Thanks for letting me know," she replied, "Don't drink yourself to death.

"I won't."

"Looking good, Billy Ray."

"Feeling good, Louis."

My hands felt frozen to the grip. Wrists tight. Arms stiff. I started a fourth waggle, but the only reason I realized I moved at all was because I saw my shadow flinch, and then my perspective flattened, and I witnessed myself from the shadow's point-of-view, as though I could hide from what had to be done. Sweat dripped down my nose and recalibrated my attention, inflated me back into the dimension where I needed to swing the golf club.

Had the Woodberrys noticed? How long had I been standing over the ball? An extra second? An extra ten seconds? That's a lifetime. Oh my God. I made a 10. Pull the club back. Hit the shot. Just hit the shot…and don't shank it!

The clubhead jerked way too far to the inside. I lifted my hands. My shoulder popped. My left arm bent sharply at the elbow. My weight tilted forward. I saw the clubhead pointing way over the line out of my peripheral vision. I was stuck. I couldn't transition. Then came another sudden gust of wind. It was cold and strong, and though it did not knock me completely over, it shifted my balance ever so slightly. Merciful wind. Early and cold. The wind that signified the end of the golf season, maybe only two swings away, but for the time being it gave me the perfect excuse to shut that awful swing sequence down and back away.

After I stepped out of the shot, my shoulders shook so hard that the left one popped out of socket, then popped right back into place.

"Sorry about that," I said quietly, and shivered.

"Do you need some water?" Mr. Woodberry asked.

"The wind picked up. Did you feel it? Nearly knocked me over."

"Was there wind?"

I addressed the ball again. Waggled once. Waggled twice. Double-checked the target. The left side of the green was still down there somewhere. Waggled a third time. The silence was so oppressive it allowed me to hear Mr. Woodberry mumbling to himself, still enraged by their performance off the tee. I missed the days when a gentle country tune could effortlessly wash away Woodberry's annoying peculiarities and the furious voice in my own head, urging me to scream, "Shut the fuck up!" Instead, I took a deep breath, holding it as long as I could, and at the peak of my inhalation, I thought of the first lyrics that came to mind before I swung: Carlos Zaragoza left his home in Casas Grandes when the moon was full.

THE HOUSE WAS ALWAYS in disarray with guns, golf gear, and our married friends hiding from their wives, drinking beer, watching football. The thought of advancing my newfound life beyond this simple, bachelor's routine was a distant responsibility I didn't care to entertain. We played a lot of golf, too. Trip and I often snuck out to Sendero for a quick 18 holes during the work week. On one of these morning rounds, we made the turn tipsier than usual. I was hungover, playing terrible, and pushing it to get drunk again. Trip was riled up because his ex-girlfriend had traveled down from Brooklyn to attend a film festival in Marfa, and per usual, he was consumed with the idea of winning her back. This despite the tumultuous nature of their three-year, on again, off again relationship, but he wanted to try the knight in shining armor routine one last time. After we ordered a cocktail at the turn shack, he convinced me to be his navigator on the drive down. We left the course right away and drove to Fort Stockton before we needed supplies – gas, tobacco, a case of beer, half a dozen tacos. We made it all the way to Alpine before Trip got cold feet.

The twin peaks of the two mountains hovered over the bristling little town as the sun set on the edge of Big Bend. The orange and purple hues in the sky painted soft edges on that hard old country and gave it an ethereal quality.

We pulled off Highway 90 into the Railroad Blues where we sat at the bar, ordered shots of homemade Sangria, drank Fat Tires, and talked it over. There were several teams of locals competing in the bar's Trivia Night behind us. The emcee was a brunette in a Sul Ross State sweatshirt. She had an olive complexion, dark hair, and dark eyes that, when they crossed Trip's, must have sensed his desperation for love that had grown in excess on the flat stretches of highway we took to get there. When the trivia ended and the bartender turned the music back on, Tom Russell's "Gallo del Cielo" was the first song that played, and though it wasn't much of a two-stepping song, Trip asked that girl to dance, and we never made it to Marfa.

It wasn't long before I lost my running mate to the very thing that caused me to seek shelter with him in the first place. I resented him for it, and the change that I would have to endure as a result, and so I selfishly revolted. I hooked up with a Mexican waitress who worked at a shitty sports bar across town, and I stayed at her scary apartment for several weeks. It was there I learned how much I could really drink and drink without stopping. This catapulted me into a three-month bender that ended with an arrest for disorderly conduct and trespassing at a dive bar in Odessa. I played "Fancy" 11 times in a row on the jukebox and was asked to leave. When I tried to sneak back into the bar, one of the regulars wrestled me to the ground and held me there until the cops arrived. They hauled me to jail where I called Trip to bail me out the next morning. He was pissed he had to drive to Odessa to get me. He was pissed at my condition. He was still pissed at the way I had treated him since he met his girlfriend. Nay fiancé. After we found my car, I drove straight to Trip's house, and while hungover and wearing the same clothes I had worn to jail, I packed up the rest of my shit, and I finally, officially, moved out. I never thanked him for bailing me out of jail. I never thanked him for the sanctuary he provided. I said, 'It's been real,' then, I left.

THIS TIME my attempt on Hole 3 was so rigid, so deliberate, so disjointedly executed that striking the hosel was an impossibility. I connected with the golf ball way out on the toe of the club where the grooves ended. The shot flew weakly left, about half as high as I'd normally hit my 6-iron, and it immediately faded and faded back to the right and landed harmlessly 40 yards short of the green.

I returned to the cart, where Trip seemed happy that I had not yet reached my shank limit. "It's an improvement," he said. "You hit it like a little bitch, but it's an improvement."

"I'm just thrilled I pulled the club back," I admitted.

"I thought you were having a stroke there for a minute."

"Minor aneurism probably. It's over with. I think."

I took a wedge and my putter out of the bag and walked to my ball. I was first to play and casually hit a shot that bounced twice, threatened the hole, and stopped two feet next to the cup. Austin dropped near the pond and chunked his pitch back into the water. It took Mr. Woodberry two swings to get out of the bunker, and he was lucky to make a long putt for bogey. With a tap-in par, I gained one stroke back after losing five on the second hole.

On Number 4, a par-5, I thinned a driver that flew for 70 yards and rolled for another 170, then I thinned a 3-wood that rolled another 200, hit a pitch shot to ten feet, the birdie putt lipped out, but I tapped in for par.

On Number 5, I hit a towering fade with my driver that curved perfectly with the shape of the dogleg right, landed in the middle of the fairway, and left me with an 8-iron that I skulled to the fringe of the green. I got up-and-down from 60 feet for par, and watched Austin pull a four-footer. Another bogey for the Woodberrys.

On Number 6, I hit my drive pure, but straight, and into a tough jigsaw bunker. I had a decent lie but chunked a 6-iron, then hit a line drive of a 7-iron to the front of the green, and drained a 25-footer for par.

After nearly whiffing my drive on Number 7, I rolled a 5-iron all the way to the back of the green, left a lag putt seven feet short, jammed it in for par.

On Number 8, a par 3, I hit a tee shot that was debatably a shank. Trip and I went back and forth as to whether it counted, but on the second shot, I hit it 100 yards to eight feet. I missed the putt on the low side and tapped in for bogey, and the argument was never resolved.

My drive went well right on Number 9, but landed in a clearing where I chopped a 7-iron into a bunker, blasted out, and made a dead-straight, seven-foot par putt.

I had finished the front-nine with one quintuple bogey, one regular bogey, and seven pars. A six-over, 42, which was only three shots back of the Woodberrys' 39. Of course, I promptly hit a drive on Number 10 that nearly crashed into a windmill and landed so deep in the Gunch I didn't bother looking for it. Made double bogey to Austin's birdie. He sank a long winding putt and viciously jabbed his sixth fist pump into the air. His joy didn't last long though. They both hit it in the water on 11 and carded a double bogey themselves, while I began a new streak of unlikely pars. I made one on 11, 12, 13, and 14. On the par-5 15th, I hit a tee shot into the bunker, a long iron into another bunker, a short iron to the middle of the green, and made my first birdie of the entire tournament with a 20-foot putt. After a par on 16, I hit an approach on the 17$^{th}$ green that came to a rest on the crest of a hill, rolled a half-revolution, gained steam, and trickled to six feet. I missed the short putt but tapped in for par, so, when we reached the tee box on the final hole, I was still +7 for the round. The Woodberrys were +6.

The last tee box was always a refreshing place, like the feel of the air conditioning in the Men's Grill after a hot summer round, or a dive into the country club's swimming pool. My enthusiasm to finish briefly turned to camaraderie and I threw a dumb line at the Woodberrys when they joined me on the tee box.

"Well guys, we made it this far; might as well finish now," I said.

Mr. Woodberry was having none of it. "Don't forget," he told me plainly, "we've still got to discuss the rules violation with the pros. The Committee. Whatever it takes."

I glared at him, but his judgmental, drooping eyes could not bother to meet mine. He just stared down the fairway with his jaw slightly clenched. Behind the smug veil, I sniffed the tang of defeat in Mr. Woodberry, and his subtle admission filled me with confidence. I took a deep breath and addressed the ball. Waggled once. Waggled twice. Checked the target line. A slight discoloration in the grass two feet in front me, and behind that, the bunkers down the left side that were out of reach. Looked good. Waggled a third time. I started the swing, and when I did, a gust whistled through the Gunch and emitted a slight howl, reminiscent of a distant coyote.

One year it didn't rain from September to September. The course burned out. The water in the ponds dried up, and all the little critters around Sendero started disappearing. Their absence forced the larger predators to stretch their hunting grounds to the limit, so instead of rabbits we saw foxes, instead of road runners, there were vultures. A bobcat hung out on Number 15 for several days. I saw him twice, majestic and curious despite his desperation. One of the course maintenance guys claimed to have seen a mountain lion's footprint in a bunker, but it was the coyotes that became the most visible nuisance around the golf course.

I had just hit a weak tee shot off Hole 2 and walked to my ball. It had barely reached the fairway. I took the headcover off my three-wood and tossed it on the ground, and that's when I saw the coyote resting in the shade of a dead tree. He was sprawled out on his belly with his tongue dangling out the side of his mouth, and he had crossed one of his front paws over the other. He barely paid me any mind, even when I topped a 3-wood and loudly cursed it. I strapped my bag on my shoulder and started walking, and when I looked back, the coyote had done the same. He followed me, staying about 100 feet behind, until I reached my ball. He stopped along with me and sat and waited.

"Well, Mr. Coyote," I said, "You can follow along if you want, but I wouldn't stand immediately to my right if I were you."

I was forever and a day away from the green, so I grabbed a 4-iron and swung hard. Shanked it into the Gunch. Put another ball down and this time I hit it straight but chunky. The ball trickled back into the fairway where I still had 190 yards to go.

I gathered my bag and counted my strokes while I walked. Driver, topped 3-wood, shanked it out-bounds, penalty stroke, shank. The coyote trotted along 50 yards behind me. I had a chicken salad sandwich in my bag. I took the sandwich out of its Styrofoam container and left it in the grass. The coyote waited for me to reach my ball, then he snatched the food, ate it, and trotted to a shady spot nearby. Instead of hitting the next shot, I scooped my ball up, and walked to the green.

The troubles that began in Whistling Straits eventually produced so many worrisome kinks in my backswing, that it turned me into a golfing leper at the club. I withdrew from my usual schedule of money games, and instead, I tried to work on my swing, to figure it out on my own.

When that didn't work, I sought help through private lessons with pros. I studied video of my swing from every angle. I bought training aids. I read awful books about golf. I found a Korean guru on YouTube and binged his entire channel. None of it helped in the slightest.

Over time, I realized there were some things about my game that were not going to change, so I began to practice accordingly, to negotiate with my problems rather than trying to defeat them outright. If I couldn't break 80 anymore because my backswing was so disjointed, then I'd learn how to break 80 by adapting to my neurosis.

I waited to practice when it was especially hot, rainy, or cold enough to keep the regular players away from the course. I didn't want anyone to witness what I was going through, both the ugly swings and the number of drinks it took to get through them. At its worst, I played a five-hole loop. Number 1, 2, 3, 4, and 9. That route brought me back to either the parking lot or the bar. If I was playing okay, I'd play the full nine. If I thought I could break 90, I'd continue through 18, but that didn't happen very often.

Most of the time I accumulated so many strokes on a single hole before I sniffed the putting surface, that I would simply quit. I'd pick the ball up wherever it lay and move on to the next tee box. I eventually learned, especially on those rare occasions when I played a full 18 holes, that my good rounds were dictated by the performance of my short game. I was going to hit some drives out-of-bounds. I was going to shank an iron or two. But if I was inside 50 yards, requiring shots that did not engage my backswing mania, I had to take advantage. I needed to finish every hole, even when I had a bad case of The Shanks, especially when I had a bad case of The Shanks. So, I developed my own rules to compensate. On a par 5, for example, I had five shots to reach the green or somewhere very near it. If the ball was not within the boundary of the green complex within five strokes, I picked up, moved it to the green, and placed the ball either on the putting surface at the farthest possible location from the hole, or somewhere for a chip, depending on what I wanted to practice. From the placed location I had a maximum of three shots to get the ball in the hole. This limited my score to a maximum of triple-bogey and placed a premium on the ability to get up-and-down in two shots, whether it was for par or double bogey.

These modified rules never improved my swing, but over time my skills within 40 yards sharpened to the point that my scores lowered significantly. I was the C player on a team of four, often the D player, and the A golfers refused to look at my swing for fear it might infect them, but in my return to the Money Game, I shot 88, a score that felt worthy of a green jacket. Every round I played, some wise guy brought up Charles Barkley's erratic swing, but it only took a couple of weeks to overcome the embarrassment, and all the ridicule, none louder than my own, faded into the background like the gentle rustle of leaves along the cart path.

After taking a quick survey of the green on Number 2, I decided to try an exceptionally long putt to impress my coyote friend. Since the hole location was in the far back of the green, I placed the ball on the front left edge, took a quick second to study the 80' putt, the hill, and the break I had to decipher, and then I casually put it to three feet and scooped it up for a seven. Still a big score, but a seven is one better than the maximum of eight, and a whole lot better than a 10.

The coyote was waiting for me when I walked up to the Number 3 tee box. He had laid down in a sliver of shade near the pond by the green. The water had all but evaporated through the drought, save a tiny pool of sludge in the center of the pond that was surrounded by dozens of golf balls plugged in the mud or baked into the pond's hardened edges. The coyote tucked his head into his paws like a puppy and waited for me to hit. So, I took a 6-iron, waggled, did the whole thing. The backswing felt the usual, Mr. Barkley would be proud, but at the top of the swing I felt unusually balanced. Peaceful, even. I could have swung as hard as I wanted to, but I knew I didn't need to swing all that hard. The club dropped in the slot. My swing sequence unwound on time, and I struck it pure. The ball compressed, ripped through the air, then floated high, and never left the flag. I have no idea how it didn't strike against fiberglass or polyester or the plastic cup in the hole. It flew right over the top of the flagstick, landed two inches behind the hole, and stopped dead on the spot.

The ball's impact created a loud thud that startled the coyote. The animal sprung to its feet, shook its head wildly, as if in pain, and then he trotted away without further ceremony and vanished into the desolate native area behind the golf course.

Two days later, one of the club's members posted a picture on his Facebook page showing he had killed a couple dozen coyotes around a neighborhood near the course. The coyotes had been sneaking into backyards, taking cats, and they severely wounded a family's dog. They were dealt with. I never saw another coyote on the course after that, and just assumed the loner that day was one of the purged. But I think he took from me my extraterrestrial curse. The shot he witnessed was the end of one long battle versus The Shanks, and after that day, I never had a drink again.

• • •

My drive on Number 18 soared high and true, landed in the fairway, and bounced in a friendly direction. The Woodberrys both hit and sounded giddy as they walked off the tee box, but after observing them all day, I could no longer bear the sight of the outcome of their shots. Trip, however, remained deeply invested. Not only did he closely watch where the Woodberrys' tee shots landed, but he also scrutinized their every move as they returned to their cart, attempting to detect hints in their psychological makeup.

"Another elaborate fist pump for Austin," Trip said. "And on the same note, your tempo looked a lot better there."

"Fantastic," I said, not believing his compliment in the slightest. "It's a lot easier knowing it's the last drive I have to hit."

"I think it's going to take a birdie from here to beat these guys."

"What if we tie?"

"Scorecard playoff, right?"

"Think so."

"Would the scorecard review begin on Number 1?"

"Sometimes they do it in reverse, I think? Start on 18 and go backward?"

"I have no idea."

"If they begin with Number 1, it's a quick L. Par then quintuple bogey wasn't exactly a world class way to begin the round."

"Hell of a recovery though."

"I wouldn't have done it had you not pried yourself off the toilet. If I squint hard enough it feels like the old times."

"Unfortunately, I do care about the result."

"Am I still in the bet?"

"Oh yeah."

"Down to the wire?"

"You've done okay without having to worry about the bet. Let's not change that now."

We arrived at my ball. I shot the distance with my rangefinder from the cart.

"You want to take this one seriously?" Trip asked. "Argue about the wind direction, the lie, the trajectory?"

"It's 155, what should I hit?"

"An 8-iron?" Trip guessed.

"That's good enough for the girls I go out with these days," I joked.

"No matter what happens, we're still following the same protocol after the round, right?"

"This will be, what, the fifth time we've done it?"

"That makes it a tradition," Trip said and nodded. "Come on now, remember, get of your own way. Be an athlete."

I eagerly addressed the ball. Shuffled my feet. Waggled once. Waggled twice. Checked the target. Pin was front left, a few paces over a bunker, but I was aimed toward the center of the green. It felt right. Waggled a third time. I've got this, I thought as I pulled the club back, then, God hates a coward.

Trip had missed our standing lunch in the Men's Grill for several consecutive weeks. I knew something was amiss when he was adamant about meeting on a Wednesday when the weather was awful. It had rained early in the morning, then the temperatures dipped and formed ice over the roads. I drove 25mph all the way to the club and found the whole place empty except for a skeleton work crew, Trip, and four players in Dr. Fontaine's daily gin game, including the doctor himself. Snow and ice were no deterrents for those old boys. They had played so much gin over the years that their assigned chairs carved custom grooves into the Men's Grill's tartan green carpet. A little weather wasn't going to keep them down. Most of them anyway.

The phone rang behind the bar and one of the waiters answered. He reported the news to the room. It was Mr. Patterson calling in to let everyone know he was laid up with gout again and wouldn't make the game, and he had just heard from Mr. Mitchell, who spent the night at his ranch and was iced in. The gin game might have gone on with only four players, but since I and Trip were the only other members in the entire building, and since we must have looked like two harmless minnows to the sharks at the table, we were invited to join the game.

Dr. Fontaine motioned for me to sit against him, and once Trip and I admitted we were at least competent at gin, he casually set the bet at a dime a point. I decided that if I escaped the game losing anything less than $500, it should be considered a generous blessing.

Dr. Fontaine offered to cut, then dealt, and as he arranged his cards in his hands he leaned back, favoring one side of the chair, crossed one leg over the top of the other, and lightly puffed from an old brown pipe that produced a silvery white smoke matching the color of his slicked hair. Then he ginned after three discards.

In between hands he remained in the same pose, same gentle puffs on his pipe, and he asked harmless questions about my background using his old man's locker room slang. Harsh as the questions sounded, legitimate answers were legitimately sought, and Dr. Fontaine listened with meaningful attention. It was both polite, endearing, and probably a tactic because I lost hand after hand.

Though I had never been formally introduced to the doctor, I was always around him because he was always around. Like many of the other younger members, I mostly knew him by the slogan he shouted from his usual seat at the gin table. He used it as an adage for everything.

Should you go for the green or lay-up?

God hates a coward.

Difficulty closing a deal?

God hates a coward.

Nervous about the girl from the bar last night?

God hates a coward.

One box of gin ended, and another began, and as the session wore on, and as I got drunker, I chased too much paint and got caught with my pants down a few times. After holding onto two kings and losing 20 more points than I should have, I tried Dr. Fontaine's line on for size.

"I should've gone smaller there," I told him after losing the hand, "but then again, I heard a man say one time that God hates a coward."

"I might've said that a time or two," he admitted. He swept the cards up, stacked them into a neat pile, and neatly shuffled, first by cutting the deck in his hands, then with three quick snaps when he shuffled them against the table. "Truth is, should've never coined it. I give the same advice about giving a good speech or wearing a bow tie – do it once and they expect it of you every time."

He waited for a quiet moment in our next hand before he explained himself at a deeper level.

"Everyone assumes the coward is the person who declines the adventure, who calls it a night, who misses the party," Dr. Fontaine said, as though to himself. "If he is called the coward, who then is the god?"

I wasn't sure if he had something specific in mind, but I never got the chance to ask for clarity. Mr. Campbell fell asleep next to an empty bottle of wine, and it was decided we should call it quits. I had to settle first with the rickety old ATM the club kept hidden in a closet with its $7 transaction fees, and then I paid Dr. Fontaine the $185 I owed him.

Dr. Fontaine's friends left the club, but since he stuck around, I invited the doctor to sit with us for another drink. He declined, saying, "Those rotten sons of bitches that left are my last friends in the whole entire world and they're the only friends I need. When another one of them dies, maybe I'll start accepting invitations again." He cleared his pipe into an ash tray and said, "Oy," as he grunted and rose from his chair. "And remember this, too, boys, sometimes friendship is the place, not necessarily the people in it." He folded the money he'd won and put it in his pocket and left the room after promising to order a nice bottle of cab, on me.

Trip and I decided to make a day of it, like the old times, and so we stayed at the club until dinner, when Trip got drunk enough to reveal the truth. He was going to marry the girl from Alpine. I listened to Trip pour his heart out about the whole matter, then in a quiet, defensive rage, I left alone, and as I drove away, I saw the second ambulance I ever witnessed at Sendero pulling into the drive. Dr. Fontaine never made his dinner reservation. They found him dead in the sauna.

. . .

Trailing the Woodberrys by a single shot with 165 yards left to the middle of the green, disaster struck again, and I shanked a 7-iron. The ball initially seemed destined for the Gunch, but a fortunate patch of thick grass grabbed it like a claw and halted its wayward path. Although I felt relieved to have avoided another catastrophe, the weight of Trip's expectations troubled me, and I couldn't bring myself to look him in the face after such a drastic mistake. Instead of riding with him, I took two clubs and a putter out of my bag and walked. Along the way, I noticed the Woodberrys celebratory gestures, another two fist pumps, as I made my way to my ball, which sat atop a patch of rough. I was directly on the boundary between the full swing and a long pitch, but it didn't really matter anymore. I addressed the ball, shuffled my feet, waggled once, waggled twice, double-checked the target, the pin, waggled a third time, and I just hit it, and I hit it crisp. The ball landed precariously atop the bunker, checked perfectly, and rolled toward the cup. It dropped into the hole without a single revolution to spare, as if the shank had somehow programmed that Titleist to travel the precise distance to safety.

I don't have a lot in common with pro golfers. Their victories, their jubilation, and certainly their prize money is all exponentially more dramatic than anything I'm capable of accomplishing in golf. But The Stickup was my Major. It was my US Open. My British Open. My Masters. And so, when I watched that pitch shot creep in for a birdie, I thought that of any time in my golfing career, it would be the time to experience a professional rush of excitement, adulation, and joy with such potency that it would curl my hand into a fist and the adrenaline burst would pump the arm with a dramatic thrust of Woodsian elation. A celebration to put the Woodberrys and Tiger to shame. But when the ball wedged against the pin and fell into the hole, no such reaction occurred. Instead, I experienced the same stoic feeling that I had after sinking a putt on the last hole on Day 1 for bogey, on Day 2 for double bogey, and now on Day 3 for birdie. It was simply relief. The round was complete. At least for the day, I didn't have to swing anymore. I didn't have to worry.

The Woodberrys were both on the green in regulation. They

needed to make one of their putts to beat me, and they needed to two-putt to tie. Austin missed his birdie putt by two feet. He tapped in for par, and the match came down to Mr. Woodberry, who methodically read his 30' putt from several angles, then several more, and after one last discussion with his son about the break and speed, he left the putt six feet short.

There was no handshake after I replaced the flag in the hole. Mr. Woodberry's face turned deep red, and his bottom lip puffed out in a furious pout. He motioned for Austin to quickly join him in the golf cart, and they sped off, nearly crashing into onlookers grouped around the leaderboard behind the green. When Woodberry slammed the brakes, the tires screeched so loudly that Callum Blair, now updating scores in neat calligraphy despite his condition, added an unintended squiggle to a 7.

Though Trip wore a smile on his face, his restraint suggested that his bet with Mr. Woodberry might have ended in a draw. Nevertheless, we adhered to our five-year old tradition – no discussions, no fond farewells, no leftover joy or anger. We didn't speak a word. Trip drove past the commotion at the scoreboard, past my erstwhile friends, and delivered me to my car. No consolation or salutation. I transferred my gear into the trunk, and I told him, "Let me know how the bets turned out."

"It's been real," he said, and drove back to the scoreboard, back to the bar and all the excitement that used to get me into so much trouble.

Freed from the allure of these temptations, a coward no longer, I cruised down Sendero's winding entryway, feeling as though I was floating on a cloud. Once I reached the highway for the long drive home, I recited my familiar autumn prayer, "Lord, let me return next year with a beautiful golf swing." Then, I tucked away the elaborate and fantastic thing into a remote chamber of my heart. A sacred place, bordered by mesquite thicket and Gunch that keeps our secrets hidden, under the watchful eyes of rattlesnakes, bobcats, and occasionally, a coyote.

# The Chapel Bells

Narrow trenches in the fields stretched until they curved into the horizon, where a swirling haze danced around a stand of trees. To the eyes of Doug Garcia, it could have been a Comanche war party kicking up dust out there in the wild days, instead of the harmless green tractor trudging for the shelter of a solitary barn. Engaging in this adventurous daydream, where he was the lone cowboy running from painted warriors on paint horses, provided a surge of adrenaline, helping Doug remain alert. The burst of excitement also diverted his attention away from the very real and imminent danger upon him: a looming snowstorm and the fuel gauge where the needle had been flirting with E for the previous ten, flat miles that looked identical to the ten, flat miles of highway ahead of him, an endless trail of asphalt, straight as an arrow.

The last remnants of daylight disappeared behind the encroaching clouds, and darkness covered the landscape except the cones of light illuminated by Doug's headlights and the anxious expression on Doug's face, highlighted by a glowing display screen on the dash. He pressed the AM button and used the tuning knob on his steering wheel to find a station in range. There was a weak signal on 1020 AM, and through the static, a weatherman predicted six inches of snow for parts of Vernon County.

Doug drifted into the shoulder and ran over a pothole that jostled the Tahoe. The engine sputtered but kept running, as sweat dripped on his face. He wiped it away, then gasped with relief when he saw in front of him a beacon shining bright. It was only a small light at first, still miles away, but as he approached it, Doug made out a water tower draped with red and green lights, capped with a bright white Christmas star that hovered over the silhouette of a tiny speck of a town. He ran his shaking fingers through his hair, grateful that his scalp was safe.

The speed limit lowered from 75mph to 35mph in quick succession. The wind picked up and whistled over his windshield as a green city limit sign announced Dewbre, Texas, Population: 1,029. A pickup truck zoomed by headed in the opposite direction, the first Doug had seen in more than 20 miles. He flicked two fingers above the steering wheel, a custom he had noticed along these desolate stretches, but it was too dark to see the driver except for the outline of a cowboy hat.

The outer limits of town were junkyards packed full of rusted farm equipment, derelict auto shops, and a neighborhood mixed with small ranch houses and single-wide trailers. Nearly all were lined with neat strands of Christmas lights. Lawns were covered in plastic reindeer, Nativity scenes, and blowup Santa Clauses. Doug stopped at the first gas station he saw, a tiny one with two old fashioned pumps out front, a wreath on the door, and Christmas music playing inside.

He handed the cashier two twenties. "How's the weather look?" he asked.

"Not good," the cashier said quietly. "Using all $40?"

"All $40."

The cashier pressed a button on the register and the cash drawer opened. "Merry Christmas," he said as he put Doug's money in a slot and closed it. "You need a receipt?"

Doug shook his head and looked confused. "A little early, isn't it?"

Now the cashier looked confused too. "Early for what?"

"For saying Merry Christmas."

"Not in Dewbre it's not. Not on December the 1st. So, I'll say it again - Merry Christmas."

Doug just nodded and went back outside to the pump. He sat in his car as it filled up, then he drove to the center of town. The streetlamps were mounted with steel rod decorations shaped into bells, candles, and poinsettias, each covered in red and green tinsel, each intertwined with Christmas lights that shined with an old-fashioned yellow glow. Dewbre's sole traffic light blinked red in all directions, and nearby, a wire-framed Christmas tree covered in red bows towered over the yellow lawn in front of the Vernon County Courthouse, a drab, three-story box surrounded by a vacated town square. The only businesses that remained were the Sheppard Title & Abstract, a Farmers Insurance agent, and Baker's General Store. The abandoned buildings had forgotten names on their faded facades like the St. Clair's Depot and the Chicago Junction, but even these unused places had rooflines with rows of white lights and windowpanes featuring puff paint depictions of Christmas icons.

There was a restaurant across from the courthouse under a familiar red shingled roof. The sign out front was shaped like an ellipsis, but it had been hollowed out and left bare. A poster board pinned to the front door advertised Connie Jo's Diner.

"If a Dairy Queen can't make it," Doug thought out loud, "what could possibly be left behind?"

He spotted the Estacado Inn and its buzzing red vacancy light half a mile down the road. Since the diner was right next to him, he turned off the highway and pulled into the parking lot. He hadn't eaten all day. When he walked inside, silver bells jingled on the Cyprus garland tied to the door frame. Nutcrackers in glass display cases filled the shelves and counter tops. A waitress in a red Santa hat stood next to the register with her back to the front door. She didn't pay Doug any mind at all. She stared at a muted TV tuned to Wheel of Fortune. On a low corner of the television screen, a pixelated radar displayed the purple and blue features of the storm boring its way toward town.

"Have a seat wherever," the waitress said, waving her hand, her accent a country mile wide, when the door jingled to a close. She never turned her attention away from the television.

Doug sat in a cracked leather seat at a small booth with a linoleum top. The faux brick floors smelled of fresh Pine Sol that mixed with the cinnamon Yankee candle burning near a Coca-Cola dispenser. There was a tray full of sugar and sweeteners on the table with a glass bottle of ketchup and a tri-fold menu tucked underneath a silver napkin dispenser. The entire back page was dedicated to pricing info and ordering instructions for ice box pies.

When the waitress finally turned around, she put her hand over her chest, embarrassed, and said. "I am so, so sorry, sir! I thought you were one of my regulars sneaking in." She had short, platinum blonde hair beneath the Santa hat, and she wore a white V-neck shirt with a nametag that glittered silver and gold. Kaylee. Her skin was tan for this time of the year and her face held sharp angles that cut deep into her cheeks when she flashed her wide smile. She was enchanting, a captivating presence in a dusty little place like Dewbre.

"Can I get 'ya somethin' to drink?" she asked. "Coffee? Tea?"

"I'll have a coffee."

"How do you take it?"

"A little of both."

Doug watched Kaylee walk away, his eyes round with curiosity at the sight of the waitress' golden glimmer. She returned carrying a red tumbler of water and a green mug that said Merry Christmas in candy cane font. She reached into a tartan apron folded and tied around her waist and laid a plastic straw next to Doug's water. She smiled at him, and her eyes twinkled.

"Sure hope you're headed south," she said.

"I was headed into the teeth of the storm, actually," Doug replied. "Somewhat by mistake."

"You take a wrong turn?"

"Left my phone in Fort Worth and didn't realize it until Sweetwater. I thought I'd do it the old-fashioned way, so I got off the interstate, tried my best heading north and west using nothing but intuition. Didn't expect the storm."

"Your intuition was a reliable compass to get you this far. Lord knows where I'd end up if I tried something like that. Frozen in a ditch, maybe."

"I'm actually quite excited about the whole thing."

"I don't think I understand why you would be."

"Well, I like to think we can trigger unexpected fate when we put ourselves in unexpected places, so, I intend to make the most of it."

"Where were you expecting to wind up?"

"New Mexico."

"Whereabouts?

"Ruidoso."

"Well, you're not doing too bad. You probably wanted to get yourself to Roswell tonight, but you can't chance it now. The edge of the storm is right on top of us."

"Radio said up to six inches."

"Yeah, but it's starting to turn ever so slightly. I don't think we'll see the worst of it."

"When's it supposed to clear up?"

"Looks like it'll be warm enough tomorrow afternoon for the roads to clear, so if you're stuck, it shouldn't be for very long."

"I saw the Estacado Inn up the road. That my only option for a motel?"

"There's only the one, and there's never anybody there except on Christmas Eve. I will *not* vouch for its quality. I doubt Belinda has changed a thing in there since the mid-90's, including the sheets, so my advice is to sleep with your socks on."

"I saw they're still advertising free HBO out front. Maybe I'll get lucky, and they'll show a Christmas movie in the rotation. Your little town all lit up is threatening to put me in the spirit of things," Doug said, then he peeled the menu open and looked it over. "Anything good I should know about?" he asked.

"What are you up for?"

"You got anything festive?"

"We've got festive covered," she said and sat down in the chair across from Doug. His cheeks flushed once he was face to face with her. "Let me qualify. I'm responsible for the festive desserts, but as for the dinner menu," she said and nodded toward the kitchen, where the cook wiped his sweaty face with the soiled sleeve of his t-shirt, "Miguel doesn't really have much panache for the holidays. I'd go with the chicken fried steak if I was you and save room for my cranberry-apple pie that came out of the oven an hour ago."

Doug straightened his back against his chair and met the waitress's eyes. "Let's give it a shot," he said.

"I can crank the festive up a notch if you'd like. You like eggnog? It's not on the menu, but I brought some for the show tonight and I've got it chilling in the fridge."

"What show?" Doug asked, leaning forward again.

"Every December 1st in Dewbre, we turn all the Christmas lights on for the first time, and then there's a Christmas pageant at the high school gym. With the snow coming in, I thought I'd start the night over at Gaylene's with a little eggnog and brandy. Get in the mood myself."

"Gaylene's?" he asked. "That a bar?"

"Gaylene runs it anyway. Everybody calls it The Bar because we've got only the one."

"I wouldn't mind riding this storm out from a barstool. Where do I find this place?"

"It's just under the water tower. Can't miss it."

"Mixed with brandy, you said?"

"That's right."

"If I see you there, I'll buy you one."

"It's a deal," she said and smiled. "Let me get your order in. We're shutting down early and I know Miguel is ready to pack the kitchen up."

She hustled into the back and pinned the paper receipt onto a metal order wheel. She said something in Spanish, then hurried back into the dining room and refilled Doug's coffee, though he had barely touched it.

"Ma'am," Doug began, voice expressing curiosity, "this may

sound a little strange, but this seat I'm sitting in is the farthest west I've ever been in my entire life, and yet I feel like I've been here before."

"How do you mean?"

"It's like an inexplicable familiarity."

"Like déjà vu?" Kaylee asked.

"No. I don't think so. It's more profound than that. It's like nostalgia, but…"

"One thing is for sure," Kaylee interrupted, "it can't be remotely related to nostalgia. Not for Dewbre anyway."

"Why not? It's very charming here."

"Put it this way," she began and slid back into the seat across from Doug, "on the census when I was born, there were 4,300 people in town. It's only 1,029 now, and I'm certain it's less than that. When people leave Dewbre, they don't hardly ever want to come back. So, I'm telling you, it can't be nostalgia."

Doug countered, "What about on Christmas Eve when the motel is full?"

Kaylee shrugged, idly spinning her thumbs, "Even in Dewbre, people are obligated to visit granny and grandpa," she said. "Trust me, it's just the lights. Christmas lights can make even a crime scene look charming."

"I disagree. The jaded local isn't allowed to judge these things anyhow. Let your town's guest be the critic, and I say the way Dewbre is lit up tonight makes it worthy of a setting for a Christmas movie."

"A Christmas movie?" she laughed. "In Dewbre? You better see this place in the daylight before you book that production. We ain't exactly Evergreen, Vermont."

"Evergreen, Vermont? That can't be a real place, can it?"

"It's the setting in several Hallmark Christmas movies, but I think you're right, it's fictional."

"Don't forget there's a snowstorm coming through here. That's production value worthy of Hallmark."

"Don't forget there's a lot of disaster movies that involve snow, too."

"Can't be a disaster. I already avoided disaster out on the highway. This is now my safe haven."

"And how do you figure that?"

"I was driving blind headed straight for that snowstorm, and I was just about out of gas, but then I saw your water tower lit up like the Christmas Star. Way I see it, I might as well be in Bethlehem."

"Oh yeah?" Kaylee said and looked around. "So, where's the two other wise men?"

Doug laughed. "I'm no wise man. I'm just Doug."

"Hi, Doug," she said and looked down at her nametag. "I'm Kaylee."

The cook slid a hot plate on the order window and tapped a call bell. Kaylee left Doug alone to eat, while she helped Miguel prep for close. After he had finished, she brought out a dessert plate with a huge piece of pie topped with vanilla ice cream.

"I was thinking about something," Kaylee said while Doug began to eat his pie, "you wouldn't happen to be a high-powered corporate executive who's lost his way and needs to rekindle the Christmas Spirit, would you?"

"That's oddly specific, but no, I am not."

"What about a food critic from a glossy magazine based in New York City who lost his fiancé two Christmas seasons ago and now he's on a mission to find the next great American baker…and the true meaning of the season?"

Doug nodded as recognition set in. "I see. Did you recently breakup with your boyfriend who hates Christmas?" Doug asked and winked. "Was your city job unfulfilling during the holidays, so you had to move to the country?"

"The plots are a little predictable, aren't they?"

"They are. I've seen a few of those movies, too."

Kaylee's eyes grew wide. "Wait!" she said, "please tell me you're some kind of royalty from a far-off country I've never heard of."

"Unfortunately, no. I did have an ex who called me a royal pain in the ass, but that's as close as I ever got to a crown. Sorry."

"Uh-huh, how many times you tried that line, your Highness?"

"Lines like that usually come off a little better over a glass of wine. Or an eggnog and brandy. Maybe we can workshop the plot a little further over at The Bar?"

"If I see you in there, it's a deal," she said, and placed the check upside down on the table.

Doug drove to the Estacado Inn and paid $50 cash for a room. The bed had a floral print bedspread not much thicker than the matching curtains draped over the window. There was a Bible on the bedside table and a miniature Christmas tree lighted atop a wooden desk. He reviewed himself in a foggy mirror in the bathroom, reapplied deodorant, brushed his teeth, then hurried back to the Tahoe.

The outer reaches of the water tower's light fell over a cinderblock building, stained yellow over the years by the barrage of sediment whipped up each time an 18-wheeler drove by. BAR had been spray painted on a side wall in red block letters. A cold wind blew against The Bar's heavy front door, and Doug struggled to pull it open. He was greeted by a cigarette machine and a coat rack in the corner, where he hung his parka on a knob then turned the corner to find the place was empty. The room had a low hanging tiled ceiling with several empty light fixtures missing bulbs. The lights that did work cast a dim yellow hue that, when combined with the pink and blue neon that buzzed from vintage beer advertisements hung on the wall, created a smoky, reddish glow. There was a coin op, bar box pool table next to a Christmas tree stuffed into a corner. Pulsating lights blinked in the tree's branches and illuminated the dust on the ornaments that had gathered for a dozen Decembers.

A woman burst through a flimsy, swinging door behind the bar. She was tall with jet black hair tied up in a messy bun, and she wore a black sweatshirt with a ripped collar.

"Can I help you?" she asked, perplexed.

"Are you open?" Doug asked.

"I'm open." She checked her wristwatch. "Who are you, mister? There's a snowstorm coming, didn't you know?"

"Yes ma'am. I'm aware."

"If I was you, I'd hit the road. Save the drink for some other town."

"It's too late," Doug said. He threw up his hands, then sat down at a barstool. "I have already been advised that I cannot make it to Roswell."

"Who advised you?" the bartender asked and looked around the room.

"A waitress at the diner. Plus, I have already secured a room at the Estacado Inn. Cost me a $50 bill, but I wanted to get rid of that thing anyway. Fifties are bad luck, you know?"

"Fifty is fifty, if you ask me, but either way that's easy money to leave behind, especially if it's got bad luck on it."

"I think I'll stay. Now, what about that drink?"

She rolled her eyes. "What do you want?" she asked.

"I'll have a bourbon, neat, and a Budweiser, please."

The woman shook her head and got to work. "Preference on the bourbon?" she asked with an empty lowball glass in her hand.

"The well is fine."

"Double?"

"Sure. I've got nowhere to be but right here."

She reached into a bucket below the bar and twisted the cap off a bottle of Wild Turkey. She eyeballed a generous double. "We don't get many out-of-towners. Where you coming from?"

"East."

"Like, East Texas?"

"Much farther."

"You get far enough east of Abilene and it might as well be another planet. All them trees make me claustrophobic. I like to see where it is I'm going at all times."

"Then Dewbre must be paradise," Doug said.

Her laughter was low and gravely, and it seemed to catch halfway up, like there were dust and dated secrets lodged in her throat. "Report back to me about paradise after your stay at the Estacado Inn." She reached into a small refrigerator, removed a bottle of Budwesier, and popped the cap using a tool she kept in her waistband. She put the beer bottle in front of Doug on a cocktail napkin that she sprinkled with salt. "That'll be $8.50, please."

"Mind if I start a tab?"

"I don't mind." She made a notation on a small white pad next to the register.

"Need a card?"

"I know where to find you," she said. "She put you in the honeymoon suite?"

"Room number four," Doug said and winked.

Gaylene grumbled. "Don't get any ideas, mister, you're 30 years too young for me. Not my type either."

"It wasn't an invitation. Just a location. But while we're on the subject of types," Doug began, "that pretty waitress over at the diner, what's her story?"

"Careful, mister," the bartender said. "She calls me Auntie."

"I'll have you know, I was nothing but gracious and I remain respectfully complimentary."

"Before you say anything ignorant, I happen to know that she has recently sworn off men entirely."

Doug lifted his glass of bourbon and said, "Then here's to what must be little Dewbre's most attractive lesbian."

The bartender clicked her tongue and glared at Doug.

"I better warn you," Doug added, nervously, "I have invited your niece here for a drink, and she has tentatively accepted."

"You were lied to. Probably out of pity."

"I'll believe it when I see it myself. Reminds me - do you happen to have any brandy back there?" Doug asked and looked to the rows of sooty bottles on display behind the bar.

"I've got cognac somewhere. Why?"

"Is there a difference?"

"Cognac comes from a particular part of France, I believe."

"Where does brandy come from?"

"Somewhere other than Cognac."

The front door burst open and raked against the loose concrete outside. The noise alarmed both Doug and Gaylene, who each flinched, made eyes at the other, then looked to see who had arrived.

Cold air rushed inside, followed by an old man who poked his head around the corner. "Hello!" he hollered, then he removed a grey Kangal and a brown, waxed jacket that he hung on the rack next to Doug's parka. He wore a white button up shirt that fit 20lbs ago, loose slacks, and Redwing boots. He had a red and green striped Christmas tie around his neck, worn during so many Christmases the edges around the knot had frayed.

"How goes it, Luther?" Gaylene asked, her mood dramatically improved. She started mixing a gin and tonic. "You look flat worn out," she added after Luther sat down a few spots away from Doug.

Luther sighed. "There's another damned Chinaman at it again, Gaylene."

"Uh-oh," she replied, disinterested. She had heard it all before. She finished his drink and placed it on a cocktail napkin in front of him, then added two lime wedges.

Luther tried it and nodded his thanks. "This time they bought surface rights way out in the county," he continued. "They doctored a picture to make it appear like a whole fictitious subdivision was out there. Had it promoted in Asia on some real estate website with pictures of a beautiful sunset and pumpjacks in the foreground." He painted the picture as he wiped his hand in front of him and stared longingly toward one corner of the room. "I logged 45 deeds today from The Golden Sunset Land Company to names I cannot pronounce with addresses in places I've never heard of, and there are a hundred more to go. I decided we're not logging another one, so if anybody named Yoo Ji Ho from Go-yang shows up looking for a sake or whatever it is they drink, holler and let me know. Or is it Ji Ho Yoo? Hell, I'll worry about it if I ever see him. Or her. Can you believe it? There ain't water or roads or nothing out there!"

"You sure it wasn't a regular gringo doing the swindling?" Gaylene asked. She pointed to Doug with her thumb. "This fella here at the bar with you just referred to Dewbre as paradise. Seems suspicious to me."

Doug raised his hands in innocence. "Sir, my name is simple to pronounce. It's Doug Garcia, and I don't know nothing about nothing."

"Gaylene is just being prickly with you, Mr. Garcia. She's a real badger this time of the year, which is why I've come to put her in the Spirit. I could use a little bit myself after today," he said. He swooped his drink off the table and carried it with him to an elevated platform in the corner. He placed the glass next to a small karaoke machine and two speakers.

Gaylene leaned over the bar and whispered to Doug. "You wouldn't know it by the look of him, but Luther Thompson can flat out croon."

"Check one…check two…" Mr. Thompson said into a microphone. The speakers popped so he adjusted knobs and settings until the static backed down to a quiet hum. "Check one…check two," he repeated.

"That's got it," Gaylene told him. "Say, how about a request?"

"No chance, Gay."

"I will pick up your tab for the entire evening if you sing some Dwight for me. Just no Christmas music until the shows over. I beg you."

"Can't do it, Gay. I've been holding off the Christmas tunes for as long as I could stand it." He pressed a button, and a familiar tune played, then he serenaded Doug and Gaylene in a high baritone. *"Chestnuts roasting on an open fire…"*

Goosebumps covered Doug's arms and he immediately swiveled around in his chair and looked at Gaylene with wide-eyed disbelief. Her eyes were covered with a thin layer of tears, though none dropped against her cheek.

*"Jack frost nipping at your nose…"*

"Are you kidding me!?" Doug asked Gaylene.

"Got-dammit," she muttered and wiped her eyes with the bar towel she had slung over her shoulder. "I hate this time of year," she added, and replaced the forlorn look on her face with a gruff bartender's scowl.

"I don't know if I believe you," Doug said.

"Mister, I hate positive people so don't you dare start preaching to me about Christmas."

"A harmless guess. I bet you have to deal with a fair amount of Christmas cheer, huh?"

"Loads."

"I feel like I'm in a snow globe."

"Don't mistake the fleeting warmth for more than it is, mister. This place is cold, hard reality."

The Bar's front door jerked open and cold air swept through the room once again. This time, Kaylee turned the corner. She removed a white coat and a green scarf and hung them on the coat rack. Underneath, she wore a sweater with a bejeweled brooch attached below the shoulder. It was shaped like a Christmas tree. Tight red leather pants clung to her calves, a color that matched her rouge lipstick. She carried a carton of eggnog in one hand and a pie plate wrapped in foil in the other, and she stopped dead in her tracks when she heard the singing. She closed her eyes and waited in the entryway until Mr. Thompson finished the last lyric…*Merry Christmas to you.*

Kaylee breezed toward Doug like she had known him his entire life. As Doug began to rise in acknowledgment, Gaylene's sharp, pointed voice froze him mid-action.

"Kaylee, what in God's name are you wearing?" she asked.

"Oh hush, Aunt Gay." Kaylee said. She placed her things on the bar top and sat down casually. "Can you make me two eggnog cocktails, please? On him." She pointed at Doug.

"With Cognac," Doug added and smiled.

Gaylene didn't budge an inch. She stood in the same pose and stared daggers at Kaylee, who glared right back with steely eyes of her own, rhythmically tapping her fingernails on the bar rail.

Gaylene finally caved. "I don't have any fancy snifters, so don't ask." She put the pie in the fridge, then grabbed the carton of eggnog, made the drinks, and set them on the bar.

Kaylee indulged in long sip of her drink before settling comfortably into her seat, shifting her attention to Doug. "Did Aunt Gay give you the history lesson yet?" she asked.

"We more or less skipped over the pleasantries."

"Not surprised. She's the only Scrooge around."

"So, what's the history lesson?"

"It's a pretty good story, but, hmm…" Kaylee frowned and thought for a second. "If this script is fit for a family Christmas movie, I better keep quiet about some of the details that might get us rated PG-13 or worse."

"We're really leaning into this movie script idea, aren't we?"

"You're the one that told me you wanted to workshop it."

"All right, I'm on board. And we can always edit the mature stuff out later."

"Let me remind you, Doug, this is Dewbre. Not Evergreen. We're on a tight budget around here. We've got two actors, a few unwitting extras, and a location, but I don't think we can afford an editor."

"Especially not after we pay our company bar tab. Better get it right in one shot then."

Kaylee laughed and made eyes at her aunt. "One shot you say? That brings us back to Gaylene, who was the bartender here back when the place was owned by a mean old lady named Betty. It went by Betty's Place then, though I don't think she ever did have a sign or anything, did she Aunt Gay?"

Gaylene ignored the question and instead snapped her fingers at Mr. Thompson, who had finished his song and gone silent. "Hey Luther," Gaylene called out, "at least sing something that Elvis covered. Would you, please? And turn it up!" she called out.

Mr. Thompson began "Blue Christmas." Kaylee scooted her stool an inch or two nearer Doug and said, "One day, Betty keeled over dead right over there. Heart failure." She pointed to a spot on the floor behind the bar near a drain. "Betty's mean old husband took over running the place, but he didn't know nothing about the bar business other than how to drink it all up. He'd get hammered on Old Crow and turn into a rattlesnake. One night he's on a bender so bad that Gaylene kicked him out of here. Had no choice," Kaylee said. The memory brought a wry twist to her lips - one of those darkly humorous moments that become local lore. "Well, that idiot left but he came back armed with an old pistol that hadn't been cleaned or fired in ages," she continued. "He aimed it at her head, pulled the trigger, but the gun jammed. Dummy lost his grip and only then did the gun fire." This time Kaylee pointed to a spot on the wall where there hung a wooden frame centered around a single bullet hole. Pinned next to the frame was a black and white mug shot of a bearded man with a black eye and a bruise covering half his face.

Doug asked, "Gaylene did that to him?"

"He got so distracted by his pistol that he didn't see Gaylene swinging a shovel at his head."

"A *shovel*?"

"Why was there a shovel, Aunt Gay?" Kaylee asked.

"Leave me out of this," Gaylene said tersely. "You know exactly what I'm talking about. Coming in here looking like that."

"Looking like what?" Kaylee shot back.

"Like you're trying too hard. That's all it will take to set somebody off and you know it." Gaylene said, then she hurried through the floppy door into the kitchen.

Doug narrowed his eyes. "Be honest - are you married or something?"

"Divorced."

"Officially?"

"Officially."

"For how long."

"A year…and a month."

Doug sat back and took a sip of the beer he had in front of him. "I don't think that story is too harsh for the censors as long as the rest of the movie sticks to the traditional whimsy."

"Visions of sugar plums."

"And while not a creature is stirring," Doug whispered, "how come your Aunt Gaylene is so hostile?"

"Is she acting hostile?"

"She is," Doug said. He took another drink and straightened up. "You look fantastic, by the way. Not like you're trying at all."

Kaylee tried hard to contain her smile, but she couldn't help it, and smiled wide enough to flash her dazzling teeth, an expression potent enough to etch itself into any man's memory. When she had her composure under control, she said, "In a boring little town like Dewbre, it doesn't take much to get the church people gossiping. Even Aunt Gay has to worry about those pecking hens." She paused. "And she really does hate Christmas."

"Maybe," Doug said, "But I was in here when this man first started singing, and I can report that I saw a tear form on her eyes when he hit the very first note."

Kaylee angled toward Doug and lightly placed her hand on his forearm. "What song?"

"*Chestnuts roasting on an open fire*…That one."

"Duly noted," Kaylee said. "But I have a feeling her attention was more on the singer than the song."

Doug balanced his feet on the bottom dowel of the stool. He leaned forward and peeked over the counter and searched along the floor.

"What are you looking for?" Kaylee asked.

"A shovel," Doug told her.

Kaylee laughed. "She's harmless unless you point a gun at her. Don't worry."

Doug sat back down. "Maybe that's the point of our plot. Our mission is to warm your aunt's cold heart with Christmas cheer, and that song is the first clue."

"If that's the point of our movie, it's going to be a looong one," Kaylee said.

"A trilogy, perhaps?"

"I'm up for it," she said.

Doug checked his watch. "It seems obvious that the Christmas Pageant is integral to the plot, so what time will you need to leave for that?"

"I figure we've got time to finish another round before we head that way." Her leather pants stretched and creaked when she uncrossed and then re-crossed her legs.

"What do you mean we? You and Gaylene?" Doug asked.

Kaylee gently shook her head. "Gaylene would never."

"You want me to go?"

"You up for it?"

"We should definitely get another round of drinks first. Where's Aunt Gay?" Doug snapped his fingers.

"You better watch it," Kaylee said. She held Doug's hand, so he'd stop snapping, and she called out for her aunt. "Bar wench!" she shouted. "Where you at?"

Gaylene pushed through the swinging doors. Behind her there were four big silver pots steaming with something. "What do you want?" she asked.

"Can we get two more? I'll make them if you want."

"I can handle it," she said and reached into a small fridge where she had stored the carton of eggnog. "Hell, he's probably TABC." She made the drinks and dropped them down in front of Doug and Kaylee.

"It sure smells good back there," Doug said.

"That's Aunt Gaylene's chili. It's the only reason a lot of people around here will tolerate her."

Gaylene gently rolled her eyes as she stirred their drinks.

Kaylee continued, "People who've never drank a drop of whiskey in their life will come in here, people who'd just as soon see this bar bulldozed with Gaylene sitting inside if it wasn't for her chili."

"Will I get to try some?" Doug asked.

"This batch won't be ready until the pageant is over with," Gaylene answered.

"How much have you already frozen?" Kaylee asked.

"I got no more space left in the freezer."

Kaylee shifted subtly, a gentle lean bringing her a fraction closer to Doug. "She sells it frozen by the Ziplock bag if you want to take a souvenir home. By the way, Aunt Gay, I got me a date to this year's show."

Gaylene stood there, grinding her teeth, and after a moment of tense contemplation, she allowed a slow, disbelieving shake of her head. "Don't you go poking that bear, kiddo," she said. "I have absolved myself, remember? If something happens, I will not come to your rescue and you damn sure better not bring trouble back to my bar, you hear me?"

"It's December 1st, Aunt Gay. The lights are on. We purge all our grudges tonight."

Gaylene didn't retreat into the back this time. She opened a drawer and grabbed a spray bottle with bright blue cleaner, then a handful of paper towels, and she set to work wiping the long mirror behind the bar, grumbling to herself.

"Don't worry, Doug," Kaylee said in a playful tone, "Gaylene's allergic to happiness, but she'll perk up when her register starts to fill up later. And you watch – the more they drink, the more expensive that chili will get."

Doug lowered his voice. "I think we've established that Aunt Gay is a Christmas curmudgeon, but if I recall, don't these cheesy holiday scripts usually reveal a heart-tugging backstory at this point? You got any wholesome Christmas exposition we can jam into this exchange?"

"Hmm, let me think," Kaylee said. She tilted her head upward and tapped her cheek curiously.

"You have the perfect anecdote, don't you?" Doug said.

"We may have to twist the lens a little bit, but yeah, I've got something we can work with." Kaylee looked at her aunt like she needed permission to continue, but Gaylene continued with her chores.

"You're in charge," Doug told her. "Follow the wholesome path and see where it takes you."

"I lived with my grandma in a tiny little house for a while. We didn't have much at all, so when one Christmas morning I found an extra envelope under the tree, it created quite the commotion for the two of us, because I had nothing to do with it and she claimed she didn't either."

"What was in it?"

"A postcard. Unsigned. And money."

"How much money we talking?"

"The first year? $150. Since then the range goes all the way up to $1500."

"So, you got more?"

"Every Christmas since."

"Where are they from?"

"The first one was from Miami, Florida."

"What's the significance of Miami?"

"Haven't figured it out."

"Are they always from Miami? Or different places?"

"Different places. Last year it was Copenhagen. The year before that it was Charleston, South Carolina. For a while I thought each place, each postcard, was like a clue, but if there was ever some kind of hidden message, I haven't figured it out."

Suddenly, a bottle of vermouth toppled from the edge of the counter, crashing into the ground and shattering into a scatter of glass shards. The abrupt noise cut through Doug and Kaylee's deep conversation, and caused Mr. Thompson to falter mid-song and lower the mic to his side.

Gaylene, not all that surprised by her apparent clumsiness, reached for a broom and dustpan. Her voice, though steady and casual, held an undeniable authority. "I'm going to need a moment alone with my niece. If you don't mind."

"Know what?" Doug replied, "I needed a quick bathroom break anyway." He slinked backward off the barstool and slowly walked to the restroom. He relieved himself in a broken trough, washed his hands, re-washed them, and stared at his reflection in the dirty, broken mirror, until he no longer heard the women's voices arguing in strained whispers. Doug walked back into the bar to find Kaylee was standing next to the coat rack, smiling, ready to go, while Gaylene had returned to the kitchen.

"You ready?" Kaylee asked.

"Actually, Kaylee, I'm having second thoughts."

"Please don't mind Gay for one bit. She's just a humbug who needs to mind her own business. When we come back later, she'll have had her allotment of wine and she'll be twirling around this place happy to have a crowd. Mr. Thompson will vouch," Kaylee said.

Luther Thompson shrugged. "Sure," he said, but before he could elaborate, Kaylee weaved her arm through Doug's and hustled him out of the bar and into the cold.

"You're driving!" she shouted.

Doug walked her around to the passenger side of his Tahoe. He held the door open for her while she climbed in and settled into her seat. He got in the car and started the engine and rubbed his hands together, then turned Kaylee's seat warmers on.

"Head to the intersection and take a left," she said. "We'll get there before the car is heated."

Doug drove slowly toward Dewbre's lone, blinking traffic light and took a left. They passed the gas station and a side street with more abandoned store fronts - an old TV repair shop, a dance hall with busted windows, the old theater with a hollowed-out ticket kiosk – and arrived at the high school.

"I don't exactly know how to put this…" Doug began.

"I'd prefer you'd be as blunt as you like, Doug, movie script notwithstanding. I'm sure that was all shades of weird back there at The Bar."

"It isn't anything like that, Kaylee. It's perfect, don't you see? A mysterious backstory. A stranger in town. A foreboding bartender. I think it's as easy as us putting one foot in front of the other, and this little movie of ours is going to turn out."

"If you're right," Kaylee said, "Act Two should get going any minute."

"What happens in Act Two?" Doug asked.

"The confrontation."

Doug pulled into a space and shut the car off. "It felt like we already had a confrontation with your Aunt Gaylene," he said.

"No, that was more of…what'd you call it before? Extra details…"

"Exposition."

"Right. Exposition."

Doug rushed around to Kaylee's side and opened the door for her again. He held her hand and helped her step out, and he didn't let go of it. They walked along the broken edges of pavement on the street in front of the high school building and reached the gymnasium where Kaylee's grip on Doug's hand tightened a fraction. People were trickling inside, and some of them had stopped to admire a group of old women wearing old-fashioned dresses and bonnets who serenaded the small queue with "Silent Night."

"So, here's the heart of it," Kaylee said, stopping to face Doug, "Gaylene is actually my first ex-husband's sister. She's my aunt by marriage, not blood, but we were always close, and she never had a daughter of her own, so…"

"Wait a second, your first ex-husband? Which ex was the one who became an ex a year and a month ago?"

"That was my second ex-husband."

"What happened to the first one?"

"To put it delicately, let's just say he's no longer with us."

"That's the best way to say that he's…dead?"

"Presumed dead."

"Presumed, huh" Doug said, "Might he be the one sending you the postcards every year?"

"Unlikely. He left Dewbre tormented by his personal demons. The consensus is that they got the better of him."

"Why was Gaylene so angry that you brought it up?"

"For a time, I thought it was her sending the postcards. We always talked about the places we wanted to see, and a lot of those postcards were from those places, but I don't think it's her."

"That still doesn't explain Gaylene's reaction, does it?"

"She just doesn't like gossip in her bar, Doug, especially when there's a stranger around. It's nothing more than that."

"It seems a little odd to me that, in a town so small, you can't figure it out."

"In small towns like these, people get good at keeping secrets. There's nowhere for them to hide."

"I, for one, remain optimistic about the postcard angle. We're going to figure it out."

"Wouldn't that be something," Kaylee said, her voice softening with melancholy. She looked down, self-consciously studying the pattern on her shoes, then she swept her fingers through her hair, pushing it away from her face. "Unfortunately," she continued, "I need to introduce you to a more pressing character who we may have to interact with soon."

"The confrontation?"

Kaylee gestured toward the foyer of the gymnasium where an imposing figure stood in the doorway greeting people. He wore a vintage Santa coat, colored so deeply and so warmly red that it must have been stitched by hand in the North Pole. The coat had Western lapels, shiny brass buttons, and a reindeer fur lining with a hemline that hit just above the knee. The man wearing it was tall with a strong jawline made to compliment his thick mustache, and he wore his hair slicked back fashionably over the nape of his neck. By his muscular build and the greys in his hair he could've been 50 but the creases around his eyes and the streaks of white in his hair made him look 70.

Doug took several steps, wandering toward the gym. "I want to get a closer look at this guy," he said. "He's so handsome he looks borderline creepy."

Kaylee grabbed Doug's arm and held him back. It was a subtle movement and far enough away from the light emanating out of the gym that it happened in the dark, but the man in the red coat noticed. His green eyes focused on Doug and formed into two shimmering emerald orbs, mesmerizing and clear, like they captured Doug's identity, scanned his entire history, all with a simple glance.

Kaylee ran her hand down Doug's back and sent a jolt of icy electricity through his spine that snapped him out of the brief trance. The man's bold green eyes shifted to her, and her steely irises glared right back without a trace of retreat. The tension mounted for several heavy heartbeats, until another Dewbre resident took the hand of the man in the red coat and shook it vigorously, and the green eyes turned away. The resident pointed to the red coat, and the man opened it and in doing so he exposed the badge on his chest and the pearl gripped revolver holstered on his hip.

"Kaylee, I think we need to clear up your definition of confrontation," Doug whispered, though Kaylee was the only person who could hear him.

"That's the Sheriff. The most handsome man who ever called Vernon County home. You were right to think he's a creep." Kaylee watched the Sheriff, who refit his felt hat atop his head and moved further inside.

"Do I want to know the whole creepy history?"

"Probably not."

"That was no ordinary look you two exchanged."

"How'd you interpret it?"

"Seemed intensely personal."

"Let's just say we have a little rivalry."

"A rivalry like who has the better decorated yard? Or more like a criminal rivalry?"

"Remember I said I had a second ex-husband?"

"You were married to him!?"

Kaylee forced a hollow chuckle. "No, I was married to his son."

Doug took a deep breath and adjusted his shirt collar. "Does the son look like his daddy?" he asked.

"Not really."

"One year and one month, right?"

"Feels like a lifetime in a town as small as Dewbre," Kaylee said. She grabbed both of Doug's hands and pulled him toward her. "That's long enough to mourn over a divorce, don't you think?"

"I don't really know how that works."

"You're lucky you've never been divorced."

"Never been married either."

"I suppose that makes you lucky, too."

There was a moment of silence shared between them, an interruption in their conversation. With fingers entwined, hearts in sync, they shared something more than words.

"Tell me," Doug said, when the moment passed, "is there something in the water in Dewbre that makes you people so attractive?"

"There's nothing in our water but sediment that turns your teeth gray," Kaylee said. She looked inside at her fellow townspeople, the last few of whom were making their way down a hallway to the basketball court. The men sported cowboy boots and Christmas ties. They had grime in their fingernails and sunburnt cheeks. Their wives wore colorful Christmas sweaters, holiday trinkets, and plain faces. "We're as dull and ordinary as they come," Kaylee continued, "but I think we look our best this time of the year, all of us, in all the light and excitement. That's all that matters to me right now," she said, and her voice cracked. She looked up into the dark night sky in search of snow but only saw the blackness of night.

"You remember what I told you in the diner? About unexpected fate?"

"This night already means a lot to me, Doug. I think it's going to be even more special to experience it with someone who hasn't been here before."

The lights inside the gym flickered on and off and the foyer emptied of people. Doug and Kaylee finally ventured inside where it was packed with foldout tables covered in holiday themed desserts, casseroles, punch. Kaylee stopped at one table and grabbed two Styrofoam cups from a stack, then poured hot chocolate from a large Thermos into them. She handed one to Doug and said, "Trust me."

Doug took the cup from her. "What else should I try? Dewbre's grandmothers have to be good at this, right?"

Kaylee rolled her eyes. "Are you kidding? There's a reason I don't have to give mine away for free."

Doug pocketed a sugar cookie covered in green glitter anyway. He took a candy cane from a jar and looped it through his front shirt pocket then added a gingerbread man, a large piece of fudge, and a baggie of Christmas trash to his pockets. He followed Kaylee, who opened one of the double doors leading onto the parquet basketball floor.

Metal foldout chairs, full of people, were arranged in neat rows. They faced a small stage assembled behind the baseline of the court, where the hoop had been raised into the rafters. Dewbre's modest marching band was organized on one side of the stage, struggling through "Here Comes Santa Claus" to begin the show. Doug followed Kaylee to a darkened back corner. They climbed into wooden bleachers, focused on the swishing hot chocolate delicately balancing in their cups, otherwise they might have noticed the prying eyes of Dewbre upon them.

Kaylee took a seat, then removed her clutch from under her

arm, unzipped it, and pulled out a silver flask. She wedged her hot chocolate between her legs and unscrewed the cap.

"I poured us a roadie while you were in the bathroom at the bar," she said. "Take a sip to make room."

"I thought you were arguing with the bartender."

"I was doing that, too."

"Probably never a good idea, generally speaking," Doug said, blowing cool air on the top of his cocoa. He took several small sips, then he placed the cup on the bleacher.

"Turn the movie cameras off," Kaylee said. She looked around and over her shoulder before she poured multiple glugs of peppermint Schnapps from the flask, and they both tried it.

Kaylee raised her eyebrows and asked, "Tastes like Christmas morning, doesn't it?"

Doug tried it and exhaled pure peppermint as the band finished their song. A black-haired woman in a sparkling silver dress approached the microphone stand. Her high heels clicked and echoed with each stride, and she smiled and waved.

"Merry Christmas, y'all!" she shouted. Despite the airy lilt to her voice, a subtle grit could not be disguised. "Welcome to our 21st Annual Christmas Extravaganza! Can you believe it!?" She raised her hands in praise of the people in attendance, who offered a rousing round of applause. "And if you can believe the weatherman, by the time our show has ended, there's liable to be snow on the ground. I remember the last time we had significant snow at this time of the year. It was 2004…"

Kaylee leaned into Doug and quietly said, "You'll never guess who that is."

"Hmm, let me see," Doug said, "Sleek. Elegant. Another supremely attractive citizen of Dewbre. Has a touch of sinister about her. That has to be your former mother-in-law," Doug finished confidently. "Am I right?"

"Sinister?" Kaylee asked. "You really think so?"

"There isn't any doubt. Does she have a sinister name to go with the look?"

"Veronica."

"Definitely sinister."

"I agree to an extent, but to truly be sinister, you have to be somewhat intelligent, and my former mother-in-law is dumber than a half-empty can of beige paint."

Doug held his hands in front of him and formed a square like a camera lens until the woman was centered. She was still giving her speech, praising the fundraiser that the town held for a Mennonite family with a sick child. He added, "She definitely looks like a villain."

Veronica finished her introductions, and the maroon curtains on the stage parted. Children filed in and assembled on several rows of choral risers. Behind them were large Christmas trees, each decorated with colored ornaments – one green, one red, blue, silver, and gold. The children hummed "Hark! The Herald Angels Sing," while a little boy dressed in an orange jacket and a green beanie carried a blue blanket to center stage where he stuttered a Linus monologue from *A Charlie Brown Christmas*.

When he finished, the Sheriff stood up from his seat in the front row, waved to the crowd with the big red coat still covering his wide shoulders, and as he walked to the microphone, their cheers exceeded the applause they had given to their own children. Their backs straightened. Their faces upturned. Their smiles brightened.

"Mighty fine job, children!" the Sheriff said. His voice matched his physical glamour. It was assertive and masculine, yet comforting. Attractive and somehow ominous. The Sheriff thanked several people, including his wife, and then he said, "Now, I've been looking forward to this part of the program for some time now. As you are well aware, since the Sheriff Department's Fourth Annual Thanksgiving Turkey Eating Competition, it is now my honor to introduce the last place finisher, who is going to add another yule log to the Christmas fire we've got burning now, first with his jazzy rendition of "Jingle Bells." The Sheriff removed his hat and pointed it near his seat on the front row and added, "Deputy Gonzalez, it's time, son."

Deputy Gonzalez, dressed in official Vernon County regalia – tan on tan with forest green accents, a badge, and a gun – climbed the steps onto the stage and wasted no time mangling the song from the very first jingle. When the second song in his set began, the crowd joined him in singing, Kaylee included, and they sang so loud that they drowned the poor deputy out, which just provoked him, and made him sing louder and even more offkey.

The song ended, and the crowd provided more rousing applause. When the noise died down, the Sheriff returned to the mic to highlight his office's accolades throughout the year. It was the secretary's 35th year in the department. He talked about the record drug bust out on Highway 74, and the illegal immigrants wanted for felonies that were apprehended on the Dickenson Ranch. Kaylee edged forward while the Sheriff spoke, attention straightening her posture, and caught the soft light from the stage against her face. Ever so slightly her lip quivered, her nostrils snarled, and sharp lines formed on her cheeks where she gnashed her teeth.

Doug asked, "Why can't my eyes look away from him?"

"Because he looks like what you'd want a sheriff to look like. Virile. Confident," and after a long pause, she added, "Fair."

"You don't seem like you mean that last one," Doug said.

"When you look like him, it doesn't matter what you do, Doug, people will call it fair."

The show continued with more locals introduced. The football team won their district. The old-fashioned carolers made an appearance in a Scrooge skit. Doug put his arm around Kaylee, and when he did, she said, "We have a problem."

"My arm?"

"No," she answered and wiggled the empty flask, adding, "You ready to get out of here?"

"Really? I thought this was your thing?"

"It is. But trust me, they frontload the talent in this show, and I don't think I can handle another year of Mayor Richards' rendition of "Twas' the Night Before Christmas."

"How much longer is the show?"

"It's not even intermission yet."

"Wow, ok, I'm ready when you are. I bet it's snowing outside," Doug added and winked.

"I keep forgetting about the snow! Do you think it's going to be romantic?"

"How could it not be?"

"The doesn't show signs of stopping kind of snow?" Kaylee asked.

"The what?"

"The brought some corn for popping kind of snow?"

It took Doug a second to place the reference. When he did, he winced. "I think we've finally crossed the line on the holiday sap."

"There's no such line, Doug. Not today. That's the whole point!"

Doug inhaled deeply and exhaled slowly. He closed his eyes and tried a line. "In that case, let's go outside and play in the lights are turned way down low kind of snow," he said.

Kaylee giggled. She gathered her clutch and coat, and together they climbed down the bleachers holding their heads low, trying their best to avoid drawing further attention to themselves. Doug gently opened the gym door, just enough to get skinny and squeeze through, and they were back in the light of the empty hallway. They hurried through the gymnasium's exit, and back out into the violet-blue night, where thousands of snowflakes fell so slowly toward the ground that they looked suspended in the piercing cold night sky.

Kaylee raised her arms to the heavens. "This is incredible!" she screamed.

"I cannot believe this," Doug said to himself. He put his palm out and before long he had snowflakes melting against his skin. "It's beautiful."

"It really is like a movie set, Doug! Please, please, please can we walk?" Kaylee pleaded.

"Where are we going?"

"Let's go back to Aunt Gay's."

"What about my car?"

"What about it?"

"I don't want to leave it here."

"Is it locked?"

"Yes."

"Is there something valuable in it?"

"No."

"Then you should be safe from Dewbre's roving gangs of car thieves. It's well known that they don't like to work in weather."

Doug smirked, then put his arm out and asked Kaylee to lead the way. She threaded her arm through his and led them on a shortcut across an open lot, then onto a dirt road. There were several open boxcars and half-full trash tailers and a single, abandoned house, but despite the bleak surroundings, the top layer of snow that had settled made even this modest vista in Dewbre appear charming. Kaylee twirled around in circles, catching snowflakes on her tongue, and soon they reached pavement again and workshops covered in Christmas lights behind the main square.

"I know you won't agree with me, but your little town really does look enchanting."

"Obviously, you're here on an unusual night."

"You always imply how bad things are, but if that was really the case, why did you never leave?"

Kaylee answered as she walked. "I did leave for a time, but I'm Dewbre right down to the homecoming crown on my mantle. I couldn't stay away for long."

"Where'd you go when you left?"

"My shining city on a hill. Tulsa, Oklahoma."

"Tulsa? Really?"

"Have you ever been there?"

"No. Why was it your shining city? What was there?"

"For one thing, my ex-husband."

"The first or second ex-husband?"

"Second."

"The Sheriff's son, right?"

"Right."

"Was he there tonight?"

"Might have been. I didn't see him. Anyway, he played ball in Tulsa. For the Drillers."

"Oh, wow, isn't that Double-A ball?"

"It is."

"He must have been good?"

"Yeah, he was a damn good high school pitcher. Got drafted in the 47$^{th}$ round, made it all the way to Tulsa, but his fastball topped out at 92. We could've bounced around through semi-pro leagues, but neither of us wanted that life."

"So, why'd you come back home?"

Kaylee sighed. "My husband wanted me home."

"But you didn't want to come back?"

"I had this dream of starting my own bake shop in Tulsa with the signing bonus and some money we had saved up. I found a space to lease in a little strip mall. Would've specialized in holiday-themed bakes, Christmas stuff, weddings…you know."

They had reached the back of the courthouse where Doug asked, "You should still do it, you know? Just go for it. The pie was that good. Really."

"Is that your secondary role in all of this, to convince me to pursue my dream?"

"Maybe so."

Kaylee smiled and winked at Doug. "Do you have $125,000 you could loan me? I'll need an incredibly low interest rate. I could probably get by with $75,000, truthfully."

"Unfortunately, I have my own debts to conquer first."

"That's why I was hoping you were royalty."

"Maybe I'll hit a jackpot in Ruidoso."

"Though I doubt that ideal location is still available in Tulsa."

"There are towns better than Tulsa. Remember, unexpected places and unexpected fates."

"I can already see the final scene, you know?"

"What final scene?"

"Of our movie. The snow clears and I'll be driving north to Tulsa, or someplace better than Tulsa, and they'll play some inspirational song, and I'll be full of hope and motivation, smiling and watching Dewbre disappear in my rearview mirror."

"Don't forget your longing memory for the stranger who inspired you to follow your dreams."

"If I'm going to be longing for your memory," Kaylee said, "we better get going out of the cold. But first, there's something special I want to show you."

She put her head down and braved the cold wind as she walked to the front of the courthouse. Doug trailed closely behind, shielding his face from the wind to avoid the chill of the air in his lungs. Kaylee skipped through a wooden Nativity scene and went right up to the wire framed Christmas tree on the front lawn. She looked up and pointed to something suspended high in the tree. Doug hurried over to her and followed her gaze, discovering a sprig of mistletoe concealed behind one of the tree's plush red velvet bows.

Doug wasted no time. He took Kaylee by the waist and spun her around. They looked deep into each other's eyes, and when Kaylee closed hers, Doug leaned in to kiss her, but just as he was about to, her eyes flung open, and wrinkles creased on her forehead.

"Wait," she said, pushing Doug away.

Doug looked around to see if anyone might be spying on them, but it was obvious the whole town was still watching the second half of the Christmas pageant.

"What's the matter?" he asked quietly.

"Shhh. Do you hear what I hear?" she asked. Tilting her head to the sky, she closed her eyes again and listened.

Doug's shoulders slumped and he frowned. "Ok, we already got one cheesy lyric into the script earlier, I don't think a second reference serves the…"

"Quiet!" Kaylee demanded.

Another gust of wind, cold and heavy, blew snow over them. A faint sound echoed in the distance, growing into a wail, a siren. The snowflakes refracted purple light, separating into red and blue in the light bar of a Vernon County Sheriff's cruiser. Kaylee ducked behind the tree and watched the car zoom beneath the blinking red lights at the intersection, lifting off asphalt, sparks flying. The car vanished down the highway and Kaylee leaped from her hiding spot, knees bent, ready to sprint after it. Her body was tense with anticipation, until the lights disappeared, then the siren, too, leaving only the whistling wind, a chain slapping against a flagpole, and the snow-covered silence between them. Their romantic moment had slipped away.

"That's Gonzalez's car," Kaylee said. "Where could he be going?"

"Something to do with the storm, maybe?"

"Maybe. He was driving awfully fast." Her posture slackened, and she looked up toward the sky, and let the snowflakes fall on her face.

"Is there anything in that direction?"

Kaylee wiped snow from her cheek and returned her attention to Doug. "Not for 30 miles and then it's Morton, but Morton is Cochran County's problem." She took a deep breath. "Sorry for the scare, Doug. We live in the middle of nowhere, so even a minor emergency is enough to completely tilt us."

"The way tonight is going," Doug said, "I wouldn't be surprised if Santa's own sleigh crashed somewhere in the countryside."

"I know where we can find out for sure."

"Where's that?"

"Gaylene's has a way of attracting Vernon County's breaking news."

"Then let's continue to Gaylene's?" Doug asked, extending his elbow for Kaylee to take once again.

"We need to hurry," she said after she weaved her arm through Doug's.

"Are you feeling okay?"

"I have to pee something awful."

They walked double-time together across the highway and hurried toward the water tower. At The Bar, they knocked the snow off each other and hung their coats on the rack.

Gaylene was in the kitchen. She poked her head through the floppy door and said, "Why the hell y'all back so soon?"

"Ran out of schnapps before intermission," Doug said.

Gaylene turned a knob that lowered the volume on the jukebox. She looked at Kaylee and immediately knew there was something wrong. "What's the matter, baby girl?" she asked, like a worried mother.

"Did you hear Deputy Gonzalez zip by here a second ago?" Kaylee asked.

Gaylene shook her head. "I had the juke playing on speakers back here. I didn't hear nothing. Where was he headed?"

"South."

Gaylene added, "Lights on?"

"Lights on. And siren." Kaylee answered. She shifted her weight from left foot to right foot, left and right. "Where'd Luther run off to?"

Gaylene looked worried. "Left a half hour ago to check on something at his house. I'll call him." She disappeared into the kitchen.

Kaylee started toward the ladies' restroom. "Excuse me right quick, Doug, I need to go powder my nose."

Suddenly alone, Doug investigated the shuffleboard along The Bar's longest wall. He sent one red puck down a sandy lane, but a severe lean caused the puck to veer left into the alley. So, he went back to the bar top and took the same stool he sat in before and waited. Gaylene was the first to return, through the kitchen.

"Did you get a hold of him?" Doug asked.

"No answer."

"What's south of here?"

"Cochran County."

"What's in Cochran County?"

"Damn near nothing. You want something to drink?"

"I'll take a Budweiser."

Gaylene put a bottle in front of Doug and popped the top. "Kaylee okay?" she asked.

"Yeah, bathroom. She looked awfully worried when we saw that sheriff's car fly by us."

Gaylene scoffed. "Stranger, in our provincial little town, this is what passes for excitement. Gives our local law enforcement a chance to stretch their legs. Drive wild for a change. They got all this pent-up energy from being bored and horny all the time," she said, and then her eyes doubled in size. She put her finger under her nose and turned still as a statue. It was the faint sound of another siren. A few seconds later and the noise screamed by The Bar, headed in the same direction as Gonzalez's car.

The bathroom door flung open and Kaylee stepped out. "Was that the Sheriff this time?" she asked in a panic.

"Can't say for certain," Gaylene answered. "Maybe Gonzalez is driving around in squares."

"You still have that police scanner?"

"Got confiscated."

"Should I call the Sheriff's office?"

"Won't do no good. They won't tell us nothing."

"I'm gonna drive out there," Kaylee said.

"Don't be crazy, girl. If they're where we're worried about, you're already outnumbered."

"What do you mean outnumbered!?" Doug asked.

The phone in Gaylene's kitchen rang, startling everyone.

"That's going to be Luther," Gaylene said and darted through the swinging door.

"Kaylee," Doug said, "What is the place we are worried about?"

"I'll explain everything in just a minute," Kaylee answered. "It's probably nothing," she added, eyes focused on the kitchen door, swinging in less of an arc until it nearly stopped, then it burst open again when Gaylene reappeared, pale faced and stunned.

"We got trouble," she said.

"What kind?" Kaylee asked.

"Carson."

"Carson?" Kaylee said, dismissive and demeaning, "What does he want?"

"He wanted to know if you were here."

"What'd you tell him?"

"Nothing. I hung up."

"Who's Carson?" Doug asked.

Kaylee sat down next to Doug. "Give me a shot of something," she said to Gaylene, then she looked at Doug and answered, "Carson is my ex-husband."

"First or second?"

"Second," she sighed.

"How much trouble are we talking? Is he also a deputy?"

Gaylene interrupted with an answer. "He's just a cattle hand with mailbox money," she said. "And an asshole who isn't welcome in here."

The sudden rumble of a truck engine reverberated through the room from outside. The brakes squealed, and as soon as the engine turned off, Gaylene squatted down and unlocked a cabinet door beneath the bar. She grabbed a 12-gauge, double-barreled shotgun, opened the break-action and inspected the red cartridge in each chamber, then closed the break and concealed the gun beneath the counter in a hidden compartment.

"I thought you said no trouble?" Doug asked, terrified from the mere sight of the gun.

The Bar's front door burst open and thudded to a close. Heavy footsteps followed. Doug couldn't bring himself to look, so he peeked through the mirror behind the bar and saw the man's reflection as he walked inside. Carson wasn't as big as his father, or as handsome, and by his narrow frame he didn't appear to be all that athletic either, but he had long arms and giant hands that were wrapped in thick work gloves. His jeans were starched and folded over his custom boots and his cowboy hat sat high and wide on his head. His intense green eyes had a color that looked familiar, but they lacked any magical glow, and instead conveyed a narrow, suspicious stare.

"I apologize for the intrusion," he said, voice quivering. "But I bring bad news." He widened his stance and opened the buttons on his jacket, revealing the black butt of a pistol tucked into his waistband.

The moment Gaylene recognized his gun, she snapped her trap door open, and before he could blink, Gaylene had pumped her shotgun, aimed it between his eyes, and with her lip snarled she said, "Carson, your dumb ass standing in my bar is bad news enough."

Carson raised his hands to eye level, grinning uncomfortably like a mad man, like it wasn't the first time Gaylene had trained a gun barrel on his forehead. "You sure you want to play it that way, Aunt Gay? Think mine will misfire, too?"

"Reach for it and let's find out," Gaylene said, still without an atom of hesitation in her breath.

"Don't miss, Aunt Gay. If you miss, and I get one round off, I'll get them all off," Carson said. "I assure you."

An eternity of silence followed, until Kaylee spun around on her stool and spread one arm wide along the bar top. She gently laid her other hand on Doug's leg and said, "We saw that idiot friend of yours driving like a stunt double through town. What happened? Did he flip it over trying to bust John Samuel's boy with pot again?"

"Who's we?" Carson seethed through his teeth.

"Me and the guy I'm trying to get laid with tonight. So, can we get on with whatever tragedy you came here to bother us about?" Her voice cracked through the murky room like a whip and knocked the tightness out of Carson's shoulders and nearly caused Doug's eyes to burst from their sockets.

Carson sunk his elbows to his side and relaxed. His hands dangled loosely in the air. His cheek began to twitch, and his lip trembled. "Luther Thompson is dead," he said, solemnly. "Shot in the back of the head," he added, while his eyes never left Doug's reflection in the mirror behind the bar. "Executed."

Gaylene's breathing intensified. Deep, violent breaths. "Who did it?" she asked.

"Don't know. Got a pretty good guess."

"Then why are you here? We didn't have nothing to do with it!" Gaylene said.

"You know why I'm here. Put the shotgun down, please," he said, stretching his neck, reassuming an athletic posture.

"I don't know who you think you're scaring."

"He looks scared," Carson growled and nodded at Doug.

A small splotch of urine formed on Doug's corduroys. He shifted his weight, tugged his shirttail, and tried to hide the coward's mark. He looked at Kaylee to see if she'd noticed, but her eyes were on the ground, staring into the void.

"We need to find out who this man is and why he's in Dewbre," Carson said. "Considering Luther has been murdered, I don't think that's too much to ask."

Gaylene shook the barrel of the gun to remind Carson who was in charge, as she barked, "He's my customer, so he's vouched for."

"Vouched for?" Carson said sarcastically, "By Gaylene Carter? Not exactly a character witness, are you, Aunt Gay?"

"Up yours, Carson," Gaylene said and steadied her aim.

Kaylee finally blinked. She steadied herself, and spoke up, "What about me? Am I a good witness, Carson? Because I'm his alibi. We've been together since he pulled into town."

"You ever going to speak up for yourself, mister?" Carson sneered. "Or you gonna let these women protect you all night long?"

Doug finally spoke, trying to sound sympathetic. "Carson, if I may…I'm nobody from nowhere," he said, shaking his head dramatically. "I was headed to New Mexico but got caught in the storm." He stopped talking after Kaylee squeezed his leg.

"Where'd it happen?" she asked. "Where did Luther get shot?"

Carson ignored her. "Mr. Doug Garcia, we already know that much. You need to go back to the Estacado Inn, room number four, and you need to stay there. If you don't, then consider yourself a fugitive to Vernon County."

Kale came to Doug's defense, "If you know who he is, you already know he's nothing to worry about."

"We may know who he is, but we don't know what he's capable of. I'm here to find out and protect you if that's what it takes."

Gaylene shouted, "You ain't got no authority to tell this man what to do, child. Not him or anyone else around here neither, so why don't you run home now, and hide behind your daddy, before whatever it was that got Luther comes looking for you."

Carson looked at Kaylee, and his eyes softened with tears. The sorrowful look they exchanged told a story that only they could understand. He slowly held one hand out to Kaylee, and quietly said, "I need you to come with me, Kay. Gonzalez is dead, too. And the chapel bells were ringing."

This time, there was no quick retort from either Gaylene or Kaylee. Their eyes met, a mirror of disbelief, bracing themselves for what was to come.

"Kaylee," Carson repeated in the same sympathetic way, "I need you to come with me. We don't have much time, so I won't ask nicely again."

Kaylee firmly sucked in air until her whole demeanor intensified. "Aren't you a gentleman," she said. "Only thing is, you're the one that needs protection. You're on your own, Carson."

"We talked about this, Kay, in good times and in bad. Remember? We have a plan. We need to stick to it."

Kaylee stood up. "Aunt Gay, will you do me a quick favor?" she asked.

As gruff as ever, Gaylene answered, "I'll do anything for you, sweetie. Just tell me to pull the trigger and I'll do it."

"Hold Carson here for me, will you?"

"We don't have time for this!" Carson yelled.

"How long do you want me to hold him?" Gaylene responded.

"I'll call you in the next 30 minutes or so," Kaylee answered, looking at her watch. "If you haven't heard from me by then…"

Gaylene finished the sentence. "I'll shoot him through the heart," she said. "After I've blown his dick off." Gaylene darted her eyes toward Doug. "But what do you want me to do with this one?"

"He's coming with me," Kaylee said. She grabbed Doug's hand and pulled him away from the barstool.

"You're making a mistake, Kay!" Carson said. "You don't know him. You don't know what he has to do with this."

Kaylee marched Doug over to the coat rack where they put their jackets back on, and before Doug could even contemplate which direction he needed to run, they were walking through the door as Carson shouted, "And what do you mean 30 minutes? Or so!?"

She walked to a beat-up maroon Silverado and jumped in. A peppermint scented air freshener dangled from the truck's rearview mirror, but it failed to mask the stench of a cigarette habit. There were 20 or more used Styrofoam cups from a Stripes convenience store scattered on the floor and dash. Taco Bell receipts piled everywhere. Kaylee reached under her seat and grabbed a keychain full of colorful trinkets and keys. She found one wrapped in green rubber and jammed it into the ignition. The cold engine churned through several startup attempts before it turned over, then roared to a start. She made sure the heat was all the way up but left the car in park.

Doug was breathing heavily. He couldn't control it. "I can't go back to the motel, can I?"

"Better not."

"What about my Tahoe?"

"Wouldn't risk it."

"What do they want with me? I didn't have anything to do with this."

"I know that. But to them, you're a stranger in town, and they're scared. Hell, I imagine the whole town was deputized at the pageant once the news came in." She pointed toward the glove compartment. "You'll have to excuse me, but I need a smoke."

"Who killed Luther Thompson? That poor man," Doug said.

"Don't know."

"What are we going to do about the situation inside?"

"If they were going to shoot each other, they'd have done it by now."

"What plan was Carson talking about?"

Kaylee snapped her fingers and pointed toward the glove compartment again. "The plan is no different than the other naïve vows we exchanged, shattered by abuse and betrayal."

Doug pulled the latch on the compartment door and opened it. Underneath a stack of crinkled papers, he found a small hunting knife in a leather sheath, a hard pack of Marlboro Lights, and a Sig P320 Compact 9mm handgun. He handed Kaylee the cigarettes and a pink Bic lighter.

"Thank you," Kaylee said, "I need the gun, too," she added, coolly, as if the gun was equal in danger to the cigarettes.

Doug handed the gun to Kaylee, then wiped his sweaty palms against his pants. She dropped the magazine out, checked her ammunition, then snapped the clip back into place, pulled the slide, turned the safety off, and placed the gun in her lap. She moved the hot air vent away from her face and pressed her thumb against the pink lighter to ignite a flame, taking several puffs through the cigarette without exhaling. She tossed the lighter into a cup holder, and held her breath while she cracked the window then exhaled a long stream of smoke.

A shotgun blasted inside The Bar. The noise was muffled through the wall, but its source was obvious, even to Doug, who leapt back in his seat and gasped, "Oh shit!"

A succession of smaller pops followed. Pistol shots. Quick ones. Emptied the whole clip. Then another loud shotgun blast.

"Oh shit!" Doug gasped again.

Kaylee shifted into reverse. The tires spun out on the gravel and the truck hopped over a cement parking block. She jerked the stick shift into drive and crept forward until all four wheels were level and ready to fly out of the parking lot.

"What are we doing!?" Doug screamed. "Let's go!"

"Gotta see who won," Kaylee said, as if she was watching a scene unfold on television. She angled the gun to double-check that the safety was off, and kept her trigger hand over the gun, ready to use it.

The Bar's door flew open and slammed against the wall. Carson stood in the frame hunched over with the pistol dangling in his fingertips. His jacket and shirt were torn open at the left shoulder, flesh blackened with tiny holes stained with deep red blood.

"Kay!" Carson screamed with all his might, and he collapsed over a cement bollard and struggled to regain his footing. "She shot first!"

Kaylee mashed the accelerator and the Silverado tumbled onto the street.

"Oh my God, did he kill her?" Doug wheezed.

Kaylee didn't answer.

"We need to call someone! We need to get her help!"

"There isn't anyone to call," Kaylee said.

Her eyes were unblinking and enraged with terrifying focus while she sped toward the main intersection. She yanked the steering wheel hard right, and the tires lost their grip on the slippery highway and screeched until they regained traction. The truck skidded and drifted through a turn, then roared by Connie Jo's

Diner and the yellow courthouse with the Christmas tree on the lawn that still hid unused mistletoe. The snowfall had collected in a layer over the untraveled pavement, but it wasn't thick enough or slick enough to slow her down. Within three blocks, Kaylee hit 70mph. The truck jumped and jolted all over the road as they zoomed by the Estacado Inn, and Doug watched room number four fly by. He pressed his head against the cold window and closed his eyes, then deliberately counted six deep breaths, in through his nose, out through his mouth.

When he opened his eyes, he saw Kaylee looking back and forth between the snow-covered road and something that caught her attention in the rearview mirror.

"You buckled?" Kaylee asked, staring through the rearview. She finally took the cigarette out of her mouth and extinguished it in a Styrofoam cup half full of flat Dr. Pepper.

Doug spun around in his seat and peered through the back windshield, spotting a pair of headlights. He pulled the seatbelt strap and tightened it over his chest, then he watched the truck gain on them until the King Ranch came into clear view, with a lighted Christmas wreath attached to the grill guard.

"Is that him?" Doug asked, panicked.

"It's Carson," Kaylee said, pistol still in her lap.

"What will he do when he catches us?"

"He looked crippled to me, so probably not much."

"Then you might as well slow down before this truck wobbles off the road and falls apart."

The shrill ring of a cell phone echoed from the center console, but it was locked away and went unanswered after five rings. Carson flashed his bright lights several times, but Kaylee pressed on, accelerating until her truck couldn't go any faster. The visibility dropped to a car length, yet Carson crossed over the center line and drove in the opposite lane of the two-lane highway. He pulled up next to Kaylee, and when he did, Doug cowered behind her in the passenger seat.

Despite his wounded arm, Carson rolled his window down and held his phone aloft, yelling for Kaylee, but his words were lost amidst the roar of the engines and the wind whipping past them.

Kaylee jammed the brakes and spun the wheel, veering her front bumper against the back-right panel of Carson's pickup. The jarring impact spun Kaylee's Silverado that fishtailed and stopped in the middle of the road, facing the direction they had come. Meanwhile, Carson swerved off the highway, careening over a roadside embankment capped with the skeletons of dormant mesquite trees. The King Ranch went airborne several inches and landed awkwardly in an empty field. Turning sideways, it rolled twice and teetered to a halt, reduced to a mess of flying metal and shattered glass. The lights in the truck flickered and went dark, and smoke from the engine block slithered upward, intertwining with the falling snow.

Kaylee quickly reversed. She turned around along the shoulder of the highway, then slammed the accelerator and they sped away.

Stunned and shaken, Doug wrapped his arms around himself. "We have to call him an ambulance. Give him a chance," he implored.

Kaylee opened the center console and rummaged for her cell phone. She rolled the window down and casually tossed it into the air. The phone clacked off the asphalt and broke into pieces.

"Just turn around. Just turn around," Doug repeated, anxious, speaking fast. "Take me to my car, please!"

"You think it's a good idea to go back into town for your damn Tahoe that's not even four-wheel drive?" Kaylee replied, calm as ever.

The realization slowly sunk in. Doug curled into the corner of his seat and closed his eyes, teeth chattering, his back hurting now that the adrenaline had died down. Every mile they traversed, Doug opened his eyes and checked the mirrors in search of more headlights, more Christmas wreaths, but he saw none, mile after mile, as Kaylee drove them farther into the blackness and snow. Finally, her headlights reflected off a yellow marker in a snow-covered trench beside the road. Kaylee shook the tension out of her shoulders and tensely moved her fingers, causing her knuckles to crackle. She slowed the truck down and tapped her finger against the window to get Doug's attention. He squinted and made out what appeared to be a tiny flame in the distance between the falling snowflakes.

"That's where we're headed," Kaylee said.

"What is it? A bonfire?"

"It's a tree."

"A tree on fire?"

"It's covered in Christmas lights."

The fear that consumed Doug gave way briefly to anger. "We have to abandon this Christmas shit, Kaylee!" he yelled. "We were wrong. This is a goddamn nightmare."

"Watch your mouth, Doug."

"Watch my mouth? Murders just happened. Multiple!"

"All I'm asking is that you please watch your language, Doug. I won't tolerate it. And what I had to do was clearly self-defense, do you understand me?"

"Yes, I understand the gravity. I'm just scared. I need to know where we're going."

"A safe place. I promise," she said, and she slowed to make a sharp left turn off the highway onto a gravel path. She stopped in front of a locked gate over a cattle guard.

"How do you know it's safe?" Doug asked.

"Because it's always protected me before."

"From what?"

No answer.

"Who's out here?" Doug asked.

"A ghost," Kaylee said, delicately.

Doug let out a disbelieving scoff. "Listen. I'm going to say one more cuss word. Just one more. Are you ready?"

Again, no answer.

"What the fuck are you talking about?" Doug asked.

She turned the ignition off and removed her overloaded keychain, fumbling through it until she found a small one that she removed from the loop.

"I'll answer your questions inside," she said. "Right now, I need you to get out of the truck and get the gate open." She handed him the freed key and restarted the engine. Doug took it but only looked at it and didn't move, so Kaylee continued, "If they find us on the road, they'll kill us both and they'll feed us to the pigs on a Mennonite's farm. No one's left to shed a tear for me, and they'll make it look like you never came through here, you understand that right? If you need any more motivation than that, you are deadweight to me. You might as well get out and walk naked into the thick of the storm."

There was no choice for Doug. As soon as he stepped out of the vehicle, the biting cold stiffened his fingers and his arms trembled with fear. He carefully cradled the key in both hands, mindful of the slick road, until he reached the locked gate. He unraveled a thick chain wrapped through vertical fence posts and found the padlock, but it took several stabs before his icy fingers inserted the key into the slot. He unlatched the hook and unwrapped the chain, then walked the creaking gate open.

Kaylee crept the truck over the corroded cattleguard, her tires crunching over the snow where the road turned to caliche. When she stopped, Doug closed the gate behind her, then threaded the chain through the fence posts. He tried to latch the padlock, but his frozen fingers had difficulty, so he gave up, and balanced the lock so it appeared fastened.

He ambled toward the Silverado, where he got a better look at the shining tree beyond the truck. A towering silhouette, the tree stood stark and prominent, its bare branches covered with the delicate glow of white Christmas lights. The tree's sturdy trunk was wrapped so tightly with strands of bulbs that no piece of bark was left exposed. Nearby, a single wide trailer was affixed with floodlights positioned on all corners, blaring bright light that illuminated the trash in the yard - an assortment of truck parts and scraps of random metal, a drastic contrast against the backdrop of the snowy night.

Kaylee reached a narrower gravel path that curved toward the trailer. She turned onto it and parked next to the back end of an empty trash trailer.

"Stay behind me while I clear the place out," Kaylee said.

Doug studied Kaylee, then asked, "What do you mean clear the place out? Clear it of what?"

"I don't know. That's why I have to clear it out."

"I'm tired of being dragged through this like I got a chain wrapped around my neck. I'm not going anywhere until you tell me…" Doug began, but Kaylee snapped at him.

"Then you can freeze in the truck," she said, turning the engine off and grabbing the 9mm from her lap. She dumped the keychain under the seat and hopped out, slamming the door behind her without a second glance at Doug.

Doug's eyes strayed toward the keychain under the driver's seat, but he reconsidered any idea of an escape plan when he saw Kaylee handling the pistol like a professional. The gun conformed to her hand like it was molded solely for her, and so, Doug joined her near the front door and watched her work.

She lifted a blue pot half-full of dirt and found a key in an envelope underneath. She unlocked the trailer door and slowly turned the knob and raised the pistol chest high. With a forceful kick she pushed the door open, then she thrust her arms forward and swept the gun from right to left, disappearing to search the rest of the trailer. It was dark inside except for a small white Christmas tree on a Formica table in the kitchen area. The tree had blue lights that cast an eerie glow. Moments later the overhead lights flicked on, and Kaylee reappeared, the handgun casually at her side.

"It'll be warm soon," she said calmly, and beckoned Doug inside. She moved to the corner of the room where a Liberty gun safe stood in the corner. Kaylee rotated the dial on a mechanical lock, and cranked the heavy door until it opened, then removed an AR-15 and two additional magazines that were already loaded with ammunition. She leaned the rifle against a back window that was covered by a light blue bed sheet. Pointing toward the kitchen, she said, "There's some wine in the cabinet by the refrigerator. It's cheap but it'll do." Kneeling next to the window, she lifted one corner of the sheet and peeked through the windowpane, but saw nothing, then repeated the process at each window. Nothing aroused suspicion, so she walked into the kitchen where there was a cordless phone near the sink. She dialed a number. Nobody answered, so Kaylee ripped the phone off the wall, cutting the cord in the process.

"Why'd you do that?" Doug asked. "I could've called somebody."

"Who would you call right now, Doug?"

"The police. Good police. From somewhere else."

"You call any county in the entire state, first thing they'll do is radio our dispatch, and what do you think Carol down at the Sheriff's office is gonna say when she answers their call?"

"Then I could've called someone I know personally."

"Who do you know that can break through a snowstorm to get here?"

"Nobody," Doug admitted. He opened the refrigerator. It was empty but for several Styrofoam boxes, a case of Busch Light, two bottles of ranch dressing, and several packages of venison wrapped in butcher's paper. In the adjacent cabinet he found the wine and a corkscrew with a wide handle. He opened the bottle, sniffed it, then poured as much cab as he could fit into a clear plastic cup. He drank heavily from it, wiped the wine from his top lip, then poured one for Kaylee.

She tried the wine, turned her nose up, then drank some more. "I'm going to put on a movie," she said at last.

Doug's mouth hung open. "Excuse me? A movie? Are you kidding me?" he asked.

"No, I'm not. I want to watch a movie, and I want to drink wine until I'm nice and warm."

Doug put his fist against the counter and clenched his jaw. "There's a maniac, who is obviously madly in love with you, bleeding out in a field after he killed your aunt, and his goddamn green-eyed father is the fucking law around here, and the whole town his posse, and that may be the least of our problems, and you want to watch a fucking movie?"

Kaylee took Doug's hand and reassured him, gently caressing his skin. "We're safe now," she said. "I promise. But please watch your language."

"If we're safe then why are you patrolling around with an automatic rifle?"

"You don't know anything about guns, do you?"

"What gave it away?" Doug said. Drinking more wine, he added, "Gaylene couldn't deal with the danger standing ten feet in front of her, and you expect me to believe we're safe out here in the middle of the dark?"

"I'll protect you, Doug."

"From the law? You just ran the Sheriff's son off the road."

"But you haven't done anything wrong, have you?"

"Then who will protect you from the Sheriff?"

"I told you. The ghost."

"Isn't it a blessing that I've got your protection, because I don't believe in ghosts."

"I don't believe in them either. But the Sheriff…" she began, and after a long pause, added, "He believes in one ghost in particular. It's what has always kept him away from here."

She walked to the couch and removed a cushion and found the remote. Turning the TV on, she leaned over a cardboard box marked Christmas and flipped through a jumble of DVD's.

"You in the mood for anything in particular?" she asked.

Doug folded his arms and leaned against the counter. "I'm in the mood for staying alive."

Kaylee lifted a DVD out of the box and looked at Doug. "I'm either going to watch a movie to calm my nerves, or I'm going to sit on the couch and sob until I pass out. Which would you prefer?"

Doug walked to the front window and looked outside himself, but all he saw was falling snow that gathered atop busted pickup trucks and the other junk illuminated by the limited range of the floodlights. He moved to the couch and kept his arms crossed over his chest after he sat down.

"Why does the Sheriff believe in this ghost?" he asked.

"Because he turned my mother into one," Kaylee said. She looked toward the box and added, "I'll give you a few options," as she flipped through DVDs again. She placed two on the coffee table and continued searching.

"He killed her?" Doug asked.

"She's buried under the tree outside."

"Why that tree?"

"They used to meet out here. To hideout together."

"How romantic," Doug said, noticing the moldy water stains that pockmarked the ceiling. "So, why'd he do it?"

"He loved her."

"Please, just give it to me straight."

"Their affair was found out, and the Sheriff decided to end it, even though he was still in love with her. Momma didn't want to leave him, and in the end, she turned her sorrow into anger, then turned her anger upon herself. Allegedly." Kaylee placed a third and fourth DVD on the table and said, "I need you to pick one."

"You don't believe she killed herself?"

"I didn't see her do it with my own eyes, but I readily admit she was in a bad way at the end. She probably did, but I occasionally slip up and hold out hope that she didn't have that in her."

Doug looked over the movies Kaylee had prepared for him. *Home Alone*. The 1994 version of *Miracle on 34$^{th}$ Street*. *Christmas Vacation*. Bing Crosby's *White Christmas*.

"Did your mother love Christmas, too?" Doug asked. "Is that why you keep the lights on the tree?"

"No, I put the lights on the tree to remind everyone for miles around who's buried underneath it, and for the Sheriff, what's lurking behind it. Pick one, Doug, I made it easy for you."

Doug took one deep breath then another. "Christmas Vacation," he said.

Kaylee tossed the other three movies back into the box, then she took the *Christmas Vacation* disc out of its case and slid it into the DVD player beneath the TV. She drank her wine and took both of their cups back into the kitchen where she split the rest of the bottle between each one, then opened another bottle in a futile attempt to let the wine breathe. She excused herself and disappeared into the trailer, and returned wearing tight black pants and a bright green sweatshirt with a white-lettered quote on the front of it that read "You serious, Clark?"

She plopped down next to Doug, pressed play on the remote, slouched into a comfortable position, and asked, "So, what's in Ruidoso?"

Doug thought carefully about his answer, then said, "Safety. Reality. Decency."

Kaylee's composure failed her. Tears welled in her eyes, but none fell down her cheek. She grasped Doug's hands with her own, and held them, then brought them to her face and gently kissed his fingers.

"Doug, I'm trying my best to keep it together here," she said. "Please don't make it any worse, okay?"

"In Ruidoso," he said, softly, "there was the mountain and skiing and a girl named Valerie."

"Won't Valerie be missing you tonight?"

Doug's own voice cracked as he revealed, "She didn't know I was coming."

"I'm so sorry, Doug. What were you going to do when you saw her?"

"Not really sure. Say hello for the first time in a long time. See if I could detect anything."

"That sounds awfully romantic. I'm certain it would have worked."

"I'm not in the mood for romance anymore. How am I going to get out of here tomorrow?"

"To Ruidoso?"

"No, God no. I'm turning around. If ever there was a sign from God that I should absolutely not continue on to Ruidoso…"

"You'll get out of here tomorrow. In your own car. You'll be fine."

"How?"

"For one thing, you didn't do anything wrong."

"You already said that. You also said that they'd feed me to a pen of pigs if they found me."

"I didn't want to be alone," she said, her voice revealing disappointment. "I just needed time, and I really wanted to get here, and be with you."

"I'm worried I'm implicated in something I don't even know about."

"Tomorrow, you can go to the Sheriff. Explain everything. Just as you saw it happen. We'll arrange for me to come in, and soon, this will all be over with. For you anyway. For me, it's only just getting started," she said and paused, then clarified, "A continuation, really, of what's always been going on in Dewbre."

As the toy soldier ornament fired a cannonball at a cartoon Santa Claus during the opening credits of Christmas Vacation, Kaylee tried like hell to fight a smile but couldn't resist. "My first time watching it this year," she said. "It was my mother's favorite. We watched it every year."

"Help me understand something - if the Sheriff loved your mother, as you say, then why does he hate you so much?"

"He blames me for Carson's downward spiral. The loss of velocity. The pills. The divorce."

"Were you bad luck or was it something intentional?"

"Everybody's got a bad luck streak, Doug. Mine and Carson's happened to coincide at the same time. Though the intentional and final nail in our coffin was when I fucked one of his teammates in the visitor's bullpen during batting practice before a game."

"Yeah, that'll do it."

"To make matters worse, the guy that busted us was a former teammate who held a grudge against Carson for this, that, and the other. Carson was pitching that night, and the guy made sure to break the news to him slowly as the game progressed, yelling at him from the dugout."

"Are any of those sordid details pertinent to the mortal predicament I am stuck in?" Doug asked.

"No. But you asked why the Sheriff hated me, and so I told you the source of the story."

"There has to be more to it than that."

"As I've grown older, I look more and more like Momma, and I think he resents the fact I'm me and not her."

"He's going to blame you for Carson's death, too."

"If Carson dies."

"Then he'll blame you for trying."

"You saw how crazy he was driving. We were pushing 100. My truck was bouncing all over the road. Not to mention he had just killed..." but Kaylee's head fell and she was not able to say the name.

"I know you're innocent, Kaylee. I know what I must say to the Sheriff. But we still don't know about Luther. Or the deputy. Who did it?"

"Probably Nolan."

"Who is Nolan?"

"My first ex-husband, but let me just tell you right now, we weren't ever properly married. It was common law." She pointed at the TV where the Griswolds were loaded in a Ford Taurus station wagon driving along a snow-covered highway. "Fa la la la la, la la, la, la," Kaylee sang, then snorted.

"What do the chapel bells have to do with Nolan?"

"Fa la la la la, la la, la, la," Kaylee sang again.

"You are insane," Doug said, with anger in his voice this time.

She slowly turned her head and faced Doug. Her eyes locked on him, cold, dark, glassy. "No, I am not insane. I am drunk. Delirious and drunk."

"I wish you'd sober up. Whoever the actual bad guy is around here, should he show up, you're the one with the weapon."

"You want one? There's plenty more."

"I wouldn't know the first thing of what to do with it."

"Good thing for you, I have no problem being the heroine in this story. I am in control, remember? And I am sick of people treating me like I'm helpless."

"I don't think you're helpless, Kaylee, not one bit. I just need to know what I've gotten myself into here. I need to know about Nolan, and I don't want the Hallmark parts either, I want to know it all."

Kaylee shifted her position on the couch. She crossed her legs, facing Doug, and said, "My birth father went to the penitentiary before I was ever born. The rest is all so...typical. I was a young girl when the preacher started showing me special attention. It was

Nolan. By the time I was 16 I was in love. By the time I was 18, we were living together. That's about when he started to turn. He got more aggressive with the way he treated me and with the way he treated his faith, the way he thought about God's use for him." Kaylee put her fist to her mouth and wiped a lingering tear from her eye. "He was also a terrible drug addict, and a horrible drunk. Mean. Pentecostal and mean. He had been forced out of the church in town, but one of his followers loaned him an acre of land, gave him money that he used to build a chapel complete with a little bell tower. That follower was the man you met earlier," Kaylee said and again her head fell as she closed her eyes in grief.

"Luther Thompson?"

"May he rest in peace."

"Why would Nolan kill one of his own like that?" Doug asked.

"You mean if it really is Nolan?"

"I think it's safe to say it really is Nolan, don't you?"

Kaylee didn't answer him. She looked away, staring at the TV, then she gritted her teeth and finished her story. "Around the same time I moved out of his house, the Sheriff's nephew made a charge against Nolan. The kid was six years old at the time. Said something inappropriate happened."

"Did it?"

"No. No way. Nolan was obviously into younger girls, but that's it. The whole thing felt very rehearsed, and even though I had nothing to do with it, I was so happy for it, because I could finally break free of his evil. I was seated with Carson and the Sheriff the day that Nolan showed up to the big church, the Sunday after the accusations were made, and he interrupted the choir, drunk and shaking from drug withdrawals, hair all slick and nasty, and he tried to clear his name. The Sheriff wasn't having it, but he made him a deal. He told Nolan he had 24 hours to leave Dewbre, and if he ever came back, the Sheriff promised to hang him from the tree right outside, where my Momma is buried, so he'd hover over her in shame."

"I don't understand why everyone is so scared of an alleged pederast."

"He already killed two people, Doug."

"I know, but, is he just insane? Or is there something else that we should be worried about?"

"There was an incident years ago…" she began.

"Oh, Christ. Hold on. Is there any wine left?" And so first, Doug drank more wine. "Okay, what incident?" he asked after he drank enough to numb his tongue.

"A truckload of Mexicans broke down on a highway out in the county. They were drug mules. Sheriff happened upon them, and a gun fight broke out. He was shot up, but barricaded himself, and called for help. Not just any help though. He asked for Nolan."

"Why?"

"Because after Nolan showed up, not a Mexican survived. He got them with a long rifle first. Then he drove up on 'em and finished 'em off. Five total."

"But that was justified, right? Why isn't he a hero for saving the Sheriff? What am I missing?"

"He was hailed as a hero, but he'd always been a loose cannon so people around here, especially the Sheriff, were weary of his heroic status."

"And how did your mother feel about him?"

"She and Nolan grew up together, in Dewbre, but she held a deep-seated hatred towards him. I think she had always been tuned into his madness, even when it was buried deep below the surface. So in my stupid, tyrannical, teenaged mind, that's what attracted me to him. The Sheriff was aware of Momma's intuitions, too, and he viewed his stand against Nolan as a final act of devotion after Momma died – defending, protecting, and reassuring the whole town of his worthiness in comparison to him. That's why he issued the ultimatum should Nolan ever return."

"And now he's back and we're sitting right next to the tree he's supposed to hang from?"

"Isn't that the last place you'd go poking your head?"

"Unless he thinks he can hide out here, too."

"I don't think he has any intent to hide."

"Why do you say that?"

"That day at the church, when the Sheriff exiled him, Nolan vowed he'd return one day, and said he'd ring the chapel bells when he arrived to let the whole town know that he was back, and that he'd brought all hell with him."

Doug sat intently, unblinking for a prolonged moment, then asked, "Would he apply that hell against you?"

"The fact he killed Luther, it's not a good sign. Hey kids, look, a deer," Kaylee said and raised her middle finger at the television.

The cheap wine and Kaylee's random quotes gradually took hold of Doug. What began as a quiet snicker turned to shared laughter as their eyes met, and by the time the attractive department store clerk showed Russ her panty line, Kaylee discarded her sweater and set to work undressing Doug. By the time Uncle Eddie showed up in his tenement on wheels, the pair had transformed Kaylee's trailer into the set of a hardcore pornography, having drunkenly reclaimed the illusion that they were still in control, still directing their ideal movie, occasionally pausing their carnal escapades to quote their favorite lines in the movie. But by the time the cast on screen prepared to sing the National Anthem, Kaylee and Doug succumbed to exhaustion and collapsed in each other's arms amid the icy darkness of night.

THREE RED STOCKINGS dangled from brass hooks on a mantle adorned with flickering candles and snow globes. The electricity had failed so the room was cast in darkness, leaving only the glow from the fireplace to offer warmth and illumination in the ramshackle house. Deputy Gonzalez's mother sat slumped over in a chair near the hearth, surrounded by her family. She had tear tracks stained on her cheeks and her eyes were crazed with fatigue. Her sorrowful gaze moved from the framed photo her trembling fingers held in her lap - her son's first official Vernon County portrait – to the shadowy figure in the corner next to the unlit Christmas tree. She sobbed loudly, as she had done throughout the night, and repeated the same desperate plea. *Encuentra al hombre. Quiera una bala entre sus ojos.* Find the man. I want a bullet between his eyes. Then she fell into the cold, shaking arms of the Gonzalez sisters.

Amidst the dim yellow glow cast by the fire, the Sheriff's crimson coat still clung to him. His green eyes met the mournful stares of the grieving family, exuding an unsettling calm that had persisted for hours. In that silent exchange, he acknowledged their anxiety, contempt, and anguish, without uttering a single word.

The somber scene was interrupted by headlights shining through the window as a pickup truck pulled into the driveway with a single horse trailer dragging behind it. The Sheriff's wife entered the house. Veronica still wore her elegant makeup but had changed into a Carhartt jacket. Two men bundled up in winter gear followed her inside, each holding a large silver pot simmering with chili. They placed the pots on the stove under the candlelight and then returned to the porch where they remained as sentinels.

"One final gift from the bartender," Veronica said to the family in the kitchen, adding, "We saw the power company men on the highway. It won't be but another hour before the electricity is back on."

She walked into the living room and hugged several more Gonzalez family members, and she kneeled next to the deputy's mother and offered teary-eyed condolences before she joined the Sheriff and embraced him.

"Why aren't you headed to the hospital?" he asked.

"I won't leave you. I wouldn't think I'd have to explain that part."

He rubbed her arms and hugged her once more. "What's the last we've heard?"

"Ambulance met them at the edge of Levelland. Carson is stable. Punctured lung. Broken bones. Lost a lot of blood."

"Going to make it?"

"Couldn't say," she said, and nodded toward the saddened crowd. "How are they holding up?"

"Not good. Some of them are angry with me. I can feel it even if I can't understand a word of it."

"You said anything to them yet?"

"Not particularly."

"I think it's time."

The Sheriff agreed. He moved past his wife and stood in front of the huddled family, hat in his hands, his piercing eyes shared their sorrow, and his voice cut through the heavy stillness in the room, breaking the silence. "Anybody have anything they want off their chest?" he asked in an assertive timbre, "Go ahead and state your piece right now."

There wasn't any hesitation from the man sitting in the darkened kitchen, the deputy's father, who spoke English in a heavy accent, and had everything but peace on his mind. "Where is he hiding?"

"Can't say."

"Where's he going?"

"We've got a pretty good idea."

"What does the girl have to do with this? And the stranger who's with her?"

"We're investigating. Doesn't look connected."

"They say you're scared of him, Sheriff, because of what happened out on the highway. They say you're scared of her because you're haunted by her mother's ghost…"

The Sheriff stopped him before he continued, forcefully stating, "I will not tolerate any talk of ghosts, do you understand? That myth was started by one person, exaggerated by another, and for some reason, believed by everyone since. I wonder why that is?" He scanned the room, and when nobody answered, the Sheriff said under his breath, "It's because you're all so goddamned scared you'll believe anything." He stepped to the mantel and picked up a snow globe and shook it and watched the snowy Christmas scene unfold inside the glass dome, then put it back in its place.

"Your deputy, our son, was also our protector," the father said and sniffled, "and benefactor and friend. Now he is gone, and his killer roams in the night while you lecture us about ghosts."

"You forget," the Sheriff said sternly, "my son fights for his own life, and until his very last breath, I treated *your* son like my own.

When this is over with, should Carson succumb, I'll mourn him just as deeply as I'll mourn for Romero."

Romero Gonzalez's father slowly stood from the kitchen table and let the blanket that covered him slip off his shoulders. He had a bottle of tequila in his hand, and he carried it with him to the Sheriff, and handed it over. The Sheriff took one long slug and handed it back.

"How will you handle this?" the father asked.

"Do you remember, when I was a boy, Daddy put a bounty on the coyotes on our land?"

"I remember. Twenty dollars a head."

"One day I got 13 of them, and he strung them up on the fence outside the ranch house. I always thought he had me do that because he wanted a receipt for the bounties, but he admitted there was a trace of superstition in the practice, and he did it so all the other coyotes would see their fate, if they dared trespass. *That's* how I'm going to handle this," the Sheriff said.

He took his wife by the hand and led her through the front door, then stepped back inside. After a moment of reflection, the Sheriff added, "It was never a ghost. It was my foolish heart clinging to the possibility of redemption. I won't be haunted by second chances any longer," he said, shaking his head methodically. "You have my word."

The Sheriff climbed into the pickup truck, and let his wife drive him. She turned onto the highway and headed slowly toward the Birch property. When she had reached a manageable speed in the snow, she looked at her husband and asked, "What about the preacher? Tell me what happened."

"Luther saw something at the chapel on his way home from the bar, heard the bells ringing. He called 911, hung up, and was executed right there in his truck. When Gonzalez arrived on scene, he was ambushed."

After a long exhale, Veronica said, "I'm sure he was hoping it would be you."

"I have no doubt."

"You have a plan?"

"What do you mean a plan?"

"Well, for one, do you know for certain it's Nolan who did it?"

"I just know, and I think you just know, too."

"After all this time, why now?"

"Can't say for certain."

"How do you know he's going to Kaylee's trailer?"

"For one, he knows there's a cache of weapons there. I also think he's after her, and I think she thinks that tree will keep us both away."

"How do you know he hasn't already gotten to her, and now he's waiting to ambush you?"

"I've had eyes on the place. I know Kaylee's there with the stranger."

"Then why don't we drive right up to it? I got my rifle in the back seat."

"Because I'm not after her. She's the bait."

"Not after her? After what she did to Carson?"

"I have a feeling there's a lot more to that story than what we know."

"You really think Nolan would kill her?"

"I'm assuming that if Nolan would kill Luther Thompson, he'd kill Kaylee. I think the best policy is to assume he's got a hit list, and I'm guessing, me and her are at the top."

The Sheriff's wife re-gripped the steering wheel with her white knuckles and popped her neck. "What if Nolan doesn't show at all?"

"Then I'll take care of Kaylee and the stranger."

"What do you mean take care of?"

"I'll take them in. If they'll go."

"And if they don't?"

The Sheriff didn't answer.

"What did we find out about the stranger? He can't be a confederate, can he?" she asked.

"Best I can tell? Wrong place at the wrong time. Doug Garcia is his name. He's a useful distraction because I'm quite sure Nolan doesn't know him, and that mystery might be keeping him at bay for now."

"I saw him at the show with her. Doug Garcia, you say? He didn't strike me as dangerous."

"Like I said – a useful distraction," then he gestured for his wife to turn. "Take a right up here on Telephone Pole Road. Drive down for one mile and that's where I'll get off."

The Sheriff's wife deliberately made the right turn, and about half a mile down the road hit the brakes when she saw a truck parked on the side of the road, engine running, lights off.

"Don't worry," the Sheriff said, "it's just Ted. I told him to meet us here."

"He's your eyes?" she asked, lifting her foot off the brake and creeping forward.

"He's going to escort you back to the courthouse. Bunker there until it's all over with."

"Is it safe?"

"The rooftops are manned around the square. They're expecting you. The mayor will be waiting by the Christmas tree. If you don't see him, don't stop."

They pulled behind Ted's truck on the side of the road. Ted greeted and hugged them both, then helped unload the Sheriff's brown mare, Elmira, down the short ramp and into the snow. The Sheriff patted her on her white snip, then ran his hand over her rump and smoothed out her winter coat. He checked the saddlebags and pouches to make sure all that he had requested was packed up. The magnum flashlight he needed right away, but his favorite rifle, a Marlin 1895 with custom gold and nickel inlayed across the stock, receiver, and barrel in an old West design, could wait.

The Sheriff put one foot in a stirrup and whipped his leg over Elmira. The eager horse lunged forward and back, sensing the urgency. The Sheriff adjusted his weight in the saddle and eased her steady with the reins.

"Adios," he called out to Ted, then he turned to his wife, and he told her how much he loved her.

"You listen to me, Sheriff," his wife said after she blew him a kiss, "You lie. You cheat. You steal. You do whatever it takes to end this here and now, you understand?"

"He doesn't deserve nothing except for what he's about to get."

The Sheriff guided Elmira through a break in the fence line then into a snow-covered field. He had ridden all the trails that were ever trod in Vernon County. Surveyed every fence line. He'd driven across every stretch of pavement, and he'd flown his Cessna over the far reaches of the county. He knew shortcuts and he knew where there'd be openings in gates, and if they were locked, he had keys and codes.

The Sheriff steered Elmira along a pipeline easement that was barely visible on a clear day, but he knew it was there, under the snow. When the ground beneath him was free of impediment, the Sheriff let Elmira gallop, and she was the fastest horse in Vernon County. By the time they reached the perimeter of the Birch property, it was still an hour before dawn.

They entered an old scrapyard that was mostly farm equipment, and the Sheriff tied Elmira to a rusted tractor. He searched through a saddle pocket and found the apples his wife had packed. He fed the food to his horse and reassured her that it would be over with soon and she'd be warm again in her stable. Then he unloaded several necessities: a wool blanket, a rucksack, a second pistol that he loaded onto his left hip, the Marlin rifle, a standalone scope, and a tobacco-colored field jacket. He took off his red coat and laid it over Elmira, then he put the field jacket on, folded the Christmas coat, and tucked it under his arm.

He left Elmira behind and carried the necessities with him through a tractor cemetery and nearer Kaylee's hideout where the floodlights blared in all directions. Next to an empty oil tank and a disassembled pumpjack, he found a wood planked flatbed trailer with the hitch balanced on multiple tires that were stacked in a small column. The ground beneath the trailer was dry and the slant provided adequate cover and a vantage point between the front of Kaylee's house trailer and the caliche road off the main highway, both sunken down a few feet in a depression created by a former creek bed.

After several minutes of studying and watching, the Sheriff took the red coat and stalked the back of the trailer, arcing around the security light, while monitoring the trailer windows that were covered and dark. He could see the blue light of a TV screen, but it wasn't flickering. There were no signs of lookouts, cameras, or trip wires. He made it to the opposite side of the property where a generator hummed and kept Mary Beth's tree lit. He made no ceremony of it all and unfurled the red coat that he had kept tucked under his arm, then he balanced the coat around a low hanging branch on the tree and collapsed on his knees next to her gravestone, where he remained for a silent minute.

"Mary Beth," he whispered at last, his voice low and deliberate, "Another Christmas is upon us. All the lights came on tonight. I just know you'd hate it," he sighed, "another autumn snuffed out, a whisper on the wind. But I want you to know, I still smell it, the scent from the leaves in far off places, a perfume that will always remind me of you." The Sheriff stopped, his instincts uncertain of the danger that lurked in the blackness behind him, and he checked his surroundings with a wary eye. "Forgive me, sweet Mary Beth, for what must come to pass, but I know you would understand. I know you would want it this way. She never changed. She's kept all that hatred inside of her," he sighed. "I changed too, Mary Beth. All that's left of the man you once knew is the score I'm about to settle. I'll show you the trophy when I'm finished." He stood up and looked over her grave one last time and added, "They thought you were a ghost. For a long time, I wished you were."

The Sheriff retraced his steps until he was back under cover of the flatbed, where he shimmied and maneuvered underneath the overhang and arranged the blanket over himself. He practiced aiming the rifle through the cover of the blanket, first by laying on his stomach, then by crouching. He tested the angles and learned his blind spots, and when he was satisfied, he waited. He reached into his rucksack and found a small can of ground coffee. He pinched a wad between his fingers and wedged it between his bottom lip and gums like chewing tobacco. Since it was always windy in Dewbre, the town smelled like the top layer of dust that blew all over everything, but the snow had covered the dust and dirt, and there wasn't a hint of a breeze to speak of, so the morning smelled unfamiliar. It was this unfamiliarity that heightened every sense the Sheriff had, and all his senses were tuned for revenge.

When the sun lifted over the horizon the clouds glowed into pillowy white pockets, and a truck approached on the highway. The Sheriff watched the headlights dim before the black Chevy turned and idled, then the gate swung open, and the truck crawled along the caliche road. It stopped at the gravel turnoff and grumbled.

The Sheriff took his handheld scope and carefully raised it over his eye, but the tinted windows obscured his view. Setting the handheld one aside, he trained his eyes through the scope of his Marlin rifle, poised for whatever lay ahead.

Doug stirred awake suddenly, gasping on an air mattress flung on the floor in a tangle of thin blankets and Kaylee's naked body. Morning light crashed through the window and lit the room in cold blue. Kaylee's blonde hair looked darker than it had the night before and Doug could see through to her black roots. Her tan skin was covered in freckles, and she had a butterfly tattoo on the small of her back. Groggy, Doug rolled off the mattress, threw some clothes on, and stepped outside, having mistaken the trailer's front door for a bathroom.

Low-lying clouds drifted overhead, and a foot of snow blanketed the ground. Doug shielded his eyes to block the overbearing brightness of dawn, then he tripped over the leg of an upturned charcoal grill that was buried in the snow. Falling on his knees and palms, Doug hurled a burgundy concoction of gas station wine that spoiled the snow. He grabbed a handful of cold slush and wiped his mouth. The stench was awful, so he stood up, scooted a few feet away, unzipped, and relieved himself.

The bitter cold felt good upon his flushed face and numbed his aching head. He surveyed the property with one eye open, a line of yellow urine forming in the snow, until his gaze became fixated upon the gravestone nestled beneath the illuminated tree, where a deep red coat hung from a leafless branch. The stream of piss halted abruptly.

A car door creaked open somewhere behind him, and Doug's eyes widened with fear. He looked in the direction of the highway where a black truck idled on the caliche road. A black boot emerged and crunched into the snow as the driver stepped out. He had a black beard and a black cowboy hat, and he carried in his arm a black rifle that he wedged through the crease in the door. Doug just stood there, frozen, with his shriveled pecker in his hand.

The sound of a rifle shot shattered the morning air and dropped Doug back to his knees. The black cowboy hat fell of the man's head, and the barrel of the rifle that he carried pointed to the sky. His body turned limp then slumped into the snow beneath the truck door. Another shot echoed and thudded against the man's crumpled body. A third shot followed, sealing the man's fate, if there was any doubt left.

Doug zipped up quickly. He intended to run inside to the safety of Kaylee and her AR-15, but his terrified feet wouldn't work properly, and he stumbled over into the snow. The trailer door flew open, revealing Kaylee wearing a stained turquoise bathrobe. She carried the rifle at her side and raised it when she saw the black truck, but before the gun was waist high, a fourth shot rang out, and a bullet ripped through Kaylee's chest. Her arms flailed backward, and her gun clanked off a wooden handrail. She dropped to the ground and fell flat on her back as blood pulsated from her torso. Her last breaths were terrible gasps, then there was complete silence.

"Doug Garcia!" a voice echoed from the junk scattered in the property. "Don't you dare move, boy! Keep your hands up where I can see 'em!"

Doug's arms shook so violently that he clutched his own hair, desperate to keep his hands on top of his head. He endured this, his skin agonizingly cold, his body convulsing involuntarily, until the Sheriff appeared from behind a trash tailer. He slung a satchel over his shoulder and cradled the rifle in his hand. He disappeared again, briefly, and reappeared astride a magnificent brown mare. He rode with a regal air, chin high, rifle slung triumphantly over his shoulder. He trotted to the brightly lit tree, where the Sheriff dismounted, removed the Santa coat from the branch, and exchanged jackets once again, preferring the bright red. Then he walked his horse back to Doug and loomed over top of him.

"Mr. Garcia," the Sheriff said, "you're in the jackpot."

Doug took quick, deep breaths and regained enough composure to stammer a few words. "How…How…do I get out?"

"That depends, Mr. Garcia. Are you a good person, or a bad one?"

"Which one are you?"

The Sheriff laughed deep in his belly. "Among the scholars here in Dewbre, I'd say there isn't a consensus. I'm sure Miss Kaylee had an opinion one way or another." He brought the rifle down to his side and slid the gun into a tasseled leather slot on the saddle. "There isn't anybody else around, is there, Mr. Garcia?"

Doug's shoulders slumped. His eyes were downcast. His predicament was obvious, so he didn't have to say anything, and he didn't. He just shook his head, no.

"Now, I'm going to hop off Elmira and walk over to that black truck to admire my shot. You want to walk with me?" the Sheriff asked.

"Do I have a choice?"

"Well, no, but it's a lot more polite if I ask, so why don't you please get out of the snow and walk in front of me. And Doug, I'm going to give you a warning right here and now: Don't you dare try anything. Don't run. Don't reach. Don't get jumpy. You hear? You do any of those things and I'm going to treat you like an accomplice to the Birch Family, and today, there isn't a member of the Birch Family who I'd think twice about shooting in the back if presented with the slightest incentive."

"Just tell me what to do, and I'll do it," Doug said, resigned to whatever his fate might be. He stood up and kept his hands loosely raised near his head.

"You were told to stay at the Estacado Inn. Room number four," the Sheriff reminded him. "So as far as you following orders is concerned, you're not off to a great start," he said, as he tied Elmira's reins through a loop on a rusted water heater laying sideways in the yard.

"Kaylee told me that you would kill me. Who was I supposed to believe?"

"Let's begin with why you so readily believe her. How do you know her?"

"I got caught up in the snowstorm. Had no choice but to stop and I met her in the diner. We had a drink together at Gaylene's." Doug's voice faltered as he recalled the events, then he asked, "What about Gaylene? Is she alive?"

"She's dead."

"What about...your son?"

"Might survive. Might not."

The Sheriff stopped walking. He looked back toward the trash trailer where he'd been hiding, and he pointed to the spot where he fired his shots. He traced his finger in the air until it was directed at the truck.

"I'd say that's about 215 yards. What do you think, Doug?"

"I don't know shooting or distances."

"Whatever the number, I'm almost certain it went in around his eyebrow. Killed him dead instantly."

"Then what were the next shots for?" Doug asked, pale and in shock.

"Well damn, Mr. Garcia, are you critiquing my shooting?" the Sheriff said and shook his head in disbelief. "You see, people in this town like to believe in miracles and ghosts, and so I wanted to make sure this man was all the way dead. Come to think of it, wait here." He walked briskly back to Elmira, and he removed the rifle from its slot in the saddle. He added ammunition, pulled the lever action, then moved into a position where he had a clean shot at the front porch of the trailer. He pumped another round into Kaylee's lifeless body, frowned, then nodded his head for a job well done.

"Do I need to pat you down, Mr. Garcia?" the Sheriff asked when he rejoined Doug on the walk toward the black truck. "The protocol of course says I need to pat you down, check for weapons, but I don't think you need to be patted down, do you?"

"No. No, sir. I don't have anything on me."

"Where were you headed yesterday before you got caught in the storm?"

"New Mexico," Doug answered.

"Santa Fe?"

"Ruidoso."

"The Land of Enchantment." The Sheriff ticked his teeth and lifted his face toward the gray sky. "I bet the mountains look beautiful underneath all this snow. Were you headed to the casino to stick it to the Mescaleros?" the Sheriff asked, returning his intimidating stare to Doug.

"I'm sorry, I don't know what that means."

"The Indians run the casino up there. They're Apache."

"No, I was going to see about a girl."

"Excuse me? A girl? What would she say about…" the Sheriff asked, and he looked toward the trailer at Kaylee's bloody corpse.

Doug stood his ground, refused to look, and instead kept his eyes fixed on a patch of snow.

"All right, Mr. Garcia, all right. It's time I heard your side of the story," he said, his hand hovering around his hip. "Go ahead and tell me the whole truth and nothing but the truth and all that, since we're off the record right now."

"The truth about what?"

"Let's begin at Gaylene's."

Doug gave a decisive nod, clearly ready to sing. "Carson walked into The Bar and wanted to take Kaylee with him. Gaylene pulled a shotgun on him."

"Why would she do that? Was she provoked?"

"He opened his jacket, and he had a gun on him. Gaylene got spooked."

"Then what happened?"

"Kaylee asked Gaylene to hold Carson there, and me and her left. We heard the shots from outside."

"Who fired first?"

"Shotgun."

"You sure?"

"No, I'm not sure, but it sounded like it. There were a bunch of gun shots after. Like a pistol. Carson came to the door, screaming something, but me and Kaylee were already in the truck, and she sped away. He chased us down the highway, and…" Doug paused.

"Don't hesitate now, Mr. Garcia. Go ahead and finish."

"To be fair we had no idea why he was driving so fast, but I think Kaylee wrecked him on purpose. After the crash, I tried to get her to check on him, but she wouldn't do it. She tossed her cell phone from a speeding truck and she ripped the corded phone off the wall in the trailer."

After a prolonged silence, the Sheriff said, "I'm not surprised."

The Sheriff shifted his attention to the black truck, in which the fallen man in black had his legs crossed at uncomfortable angles beneath his tangled body. One arm was jammed in the door's map pocket that housed several folded brochures advertising the Golden Sunset Land Company. His neck was twisted unnaturally, his head marked by a lethal hole over his left eyebrow. The bullet exited the back of his head in a much messier fashion. The blood and brain matter stained the snow around the tire a deep crimson.

Doug doubled over and vomited once more. With no liquid left in his system, it was only bile and violent retches that the Sheriff watched with curious contempt.

"When you overcome the shock of it," he said, "you might offer me some thanks. From the angle I shot him it sure looked like his gun was aimed right at your face."

The Sheriff picked up the black rifle next to the dead man, ejected the magazine, and cleared the bullet out of the chamber, then he tossed the gun into the slush.

"Is that Nolan?" Doug asked.

"That's him."

"Kaylee thought he was dead," Doug said.

"He sure as hell is dead now."

A well of emotion turned Doug's face red, a tidal wave that threatened to spill over. He hid his face, his hands shaking as they shielded the tears shining in his eyes.

"Now, what's wrong, Doug? You can tell me," the Sheriff said, his captivating green eyes were alive.

Doug looked to the overcast sky, trying to block the gruesome scene in front of him. With disbelief and regret, he quietly said, "I can't believe we thought we were in a…" before trailing off.

"You thought you were in a what?" the Sheriff leaned in and asked.

"A Christmas movie," Doug mumbled.

The Sheriff threw his head back and laughed. "A Christmas movie!? In Dewbre? With her?" and the Sheriff looked back to the trailer and pointed at Kaylee's bloody body, but again, Doug refused to follow the path of the Sheriff's finger. The Sheriff continued, "You didn't stop to think that the handsome green-eyed lawman wearing the Santa coat was the hero?"

"Things were going so well. The pageant. The snow. All the lights. And she told the most compelling backstory about Christmas postcards – was it him? Was it Nolan who sent them?"

The Sheriff composed himself and wiped the look of astonishment from his face. "I suppose I have to give you some credit there," he said. "Of all the days to roll into Dewbre, I can see how you might be tricked into thinking this was a charming place. You still think that, Mr. Garcia?" the Sheriff asked and he offered a predatory grin.

Doug shook his head, no.

"As for the postcards," the Sheriff said, his expression tightening with disappointment, "that was always Carson, whose poor, broken heart has loved Kaylee since they were six years old. She always looked right past him until she needed him the most, and he always turned the other cheek." The Sheriff ran his fingers along his mustache and added, "I suppose I also owe you some slack regarding Miss Kaylee. By any man's standard, she was certainly a fine woman. Tell me, did you, uh…?" and the Sheriff raised his eyebrows and poked his finger through a hole he made with his left hand.

Doug didn't acknowledge the Sheriff's juvenile mockery.

"Here's the thing, Doug, if you began with Dewbre as the epicenter and drew an approximate circle with a radius that stretched from Muleshoe to Floydada, Post over to Denver City and all the way to Clovis," the Sheriff said and mimicked drawing a circle as wide as his arm would stretch, "I'd say, give or take, eight percent of the men inside that circumference have had relations with that woman. That's a lot of Eskimo brothers, Doug. Me included, I hate to admit, but that's another story for another day." The Sheriff took a deep breath and scratched an itch on his cheek, then his jaw suddenly clenched and the words snapped out of his mouth with disgust. "A Christmas movie," he said. "What a goddamned snake." He took another deep breath, then spoke directly to Doug. "Unfortunately, this ain't no Christmas movie, Mr. Garcia. Kaylee isn't innocent. She's no damsel in distress. She's not even a whore with a heart of gold or however they call it. She's just a plain old slut. But Nolan? He's been the baddy around here for a long time, and now that he's been dealt with, there's only one man left standing that's badder than him…" The Sheriff tilted his head upward, filled his chest with air, and said, "And that makes me good, you see?" He paused, then asked, "Did Kaylee tell you about the promise I made this man if he ever returned to town?"

"She said you would hang him from that tree."

"Do you know why I'm hanging him from that tree in particular?"

"I don't."

"Come on, she didn't tell you? You know who's buried underneath it?"

"Her mother."

"That's right. When Kaylee first started seeing the preacher, her momma came to me, desperate and seeking help. The more she intervened with Kaylee, the more Kaylee pushed her away. The further that mother and daughter grew from each other, the more Mary Beth hated the preacher, the closer I grew to Mary Beth."

"She said you killed her, because you loved her."

"I abandoned the relationship once my son declared he was going to marry Kaylee. That choice ultimately marked the end for Mary Beth." The Sheriff looked long and hard at the grave, then snarled, "I ought to string Kaylee up from that tree with him. Would be fitting…" The Sheriff snapped out of it, looking at Doug, he asked, "Well, I guess you know what comes next then, don't you, Mr. Garcia?"

Doug hung his head.

"You said you wanted out of the jackpot, right?" the Sheriff asked.

Doug nodded, yes.

"This is the only way," the Sheriff said, and he walked to the back of the black truck and waited there.

Doug gathered his wits and staggered to his feet. He blinked heavily and willed himself through another wave of nausea, then he set to work with a methodical, detached demeanor. He pulled the man's body backward by the shoulders and unfurled him from the inside of the door. With a firm grip on the man's legs, he dragged the lifeless body toward the back of the truck, leaving a trail of crimson smeared in the snow and staining Doug's clothes with blood.

The Sheriff opened the truck's tailgate, and said, "Trade sides with me and take him by the hands. I'll grab him by the boots and help you, but I'm not getting blood on my Santa coat."

Doug took the man by his arms and they both lifted, but the weight was more than Doug could handle. His bloody grip gave out and he fell backward. The dead man's head slammed against the tailgate and the limp body crumpled again into the snow.

"Slippery 'fella, ain't he?" the Sheriff said. "Let's swing him in an arc and heave him in this time like a big bag of fertilizer."

They tried again and swung him in a semicircle to gain momentum. "On three," the Sheriff said, "One…two…three…" and this time they gained enough momentum to swing the body over the edge of the tailgate, and it thudded into the bed of the pickup.

Doug clambered over the tailgate and dragged Nolan further into the truck. Meanwhile, the Sheriff followed the crimson trail back to the driver's side. He searched in the consoles and underneath the seats and found a black pistol that he wedged into the waistband of his pants. Once satisfied the truck was empty of weapons, he issued instructions to Doug. "Keys are still in the ignition. I want you to drive around to the other side of the property, and park beneath the branches of that tree. Back in and make sure the body is underneath that last big branch on the side." He pointed and stared at the tree, and whatever light reached them, gathered in the Sheriff's eyes and brightened them with excitement.

Doug complied, maneuvering the truck beneath the suggested branch as instructed. The Sheriff dismounted Elmira and moved toward her saddle. Over the worn leather cantle, a sturdy rope was looped, one end tied in a traditional hangman's knot, its chilling precision marking five perfect coils.

"You might find this fact a bit macabre," the Sheriff told Doug, "But the rest of this chore will be fairly easy. I've gone over this ten-thousand times in my head, so if it looks like I've done this before, I assure you it's only because of mental repetition." The Sheriff climbed into the back of the truck and tossed the rope over the thickest branch. A branch he had already chosen. One he knew the exact specifications of. Its height from the ground. How much weight it might support. He tossed the rope around the branch once and pulled the noose end toward him, then tossed it around the branch again, laying the business end next to Nolan's dead body in the back of the truck. "Okay Doug, you're up," he said and illustrated his instructions with the rope. "Put the rope around his neck. There'll be a little slack left in the handle. Cinch it tight. I'll take care of the rest."

Doug retrieved the rope from the Sheriff and climbed in the back of the truck, a sense of dread spreading through him as he confronted again the grim spectacle. Doug tightened the rope until the man's neck compressed. Once done, he raised his frozen, bloodied hands to acknowledge the grisly task he had completed as a fulfillment of their agreement. His voice shaky, yet resolute, broke the uneasy quiet, "What happens now?"

The Sheriff did not look impressed. "Me and Elmira here are going to hoist him up. You get behind the wheel and as soon as he's free of it, I want you to move forward a few yards, just far enough away that this truck won't interfere with our view."

Doug got into the diver's seat. Creeping forward, he watched in the rearview while the body moved slowly toward the rails on the side, thudded against the wheel arch, and then the head and torso began to lift. Doug moved forward a hundred feet or so, stopped, and never once looked toward the road he might have escaped to. Instead, he walked back to the Sheriff, who was tying the loose end of the rope around the base of the tree. He staked the rope into the ground with a hammer and spike, then he climbed back atop Elmira, and moved her a few paces away from the tree so he had ample space to admire his work. He had his arms folded over each other on the swell of the saddle, bodyweight slouched comfortably, eyes deadest on the man swinging from the tree.

"Hope can do strange things to a man, can't it, Mr. Garcia? It can break a man's will, destroy his ambition, when the expectation realized doesn't match the potency of the hope for it. Isn't that usually how it works?"

The Sheriff waited on Doug to answer, and so Doug simply said, "I suppose so."

"This is not one of those moments, Doug. You are witnessing a man whose reality has finally matched the expectation. Ten thousand times I dreamed this, and no dream did it justice. Hell, maybe this is a Christmas movie after all, Mr. Garcia."

Doug refused to role play further, so he remained silent.

"Or does it depend on the protagonist?" the Sheriff continued, smiling. "I'm being selfish here, aren't I? I know our agreement has succeeded. You completed every task I asked of you, but, there is just one more thing: I need to ask a friendly favor, is that okay?"

Doug knew he had no choice but to agree.

The Sheriff put his hand inside his coat and covered his heart. "Have I told you about this beautiful coat yet?"

"Only that you didn't want to get any blood on it."

"My wife claims it came custom made all the way from Norway. I never could figure out what Norway had to do with anything, other than it's cold there, but now this coat is synonymous with me, and I'd like to enshrine its legend permanently." The Sheriff reached further into the coat, to an interior pocket, where he kept a small digital camera. "Would you mind taking a picture, Doug?"

Doug accepted the camera from the Sheriff, who pointed to the spot where he wanted Doug to stand.

"Make sure you get as much of the tree as possible. Maybe take one sort of up close, then zoom out for another angle, so we can see the whole thing," the Sheriff said, trying but failing to contain his glee.

The Sheriff led Elmira back under the tree. She snarled and scooted away from the hanging man, but the Sheriff calmed her, and she became still, with her nose facing the dangling corpse. He removed the Marlin rifle from its sliver on the saddle and put it back on his triumphant shoulder.

"How's this?" he asked.

Doug pressed the camera's shutter button several times, capturing the Sheriff in a variety of poses, pausing to review the images on the digital display. When he was assured of a satisfactory portrait, Doug retreated a few paces, adjusting his vantage point to encompass the shining tree in its entirety.

"Did you get it?" the Sheriff called out. "How's it look? Come, let me see!" He dismounted from Elmira and holstered the rifle in the saddle. He removed the glove from his hand and took the camera from Doug, scrolling through each picture, then scrolling back through them the other way. The smile never left his face.

"Not a bad picture taken, Doug. You've really got an eye for the scene," he said, sliding the camera back into his coat pocket. His hand lingered there a moment longer, as though the fabric reminded him of something, then, impulsively, his fingers lowered and grazed the cool, pearl handle of his pistol.

Doug recoiled after he caught a frightened glimpse of the Christmas tree engraving on the grip, his breath hitching in his chest, when suddenly, the tree behind them crackled ominously. As they turned, a bright branch snapped with a resounding crack, and both limb and body tumbled into the snow.

# Dino

The Waffle House in Batesville, Mississippi looked like any other Waffle House; a yellow shoebox surrounded by an entangled mess of power lines, gas stations, and budget motels. Though an outsider, it seemed to me the South had traded the uniqueness of its charm for the monotony of convenience, making it difficult to identify the subtle yet crucial distinctions within the deeply revered and equally monotonous restaurant chain. I placed my trust in my friend Caleb, who had lived throughout the Deep South and was well-versed to Waffle House culture. He was able to distinguish the good ones from the bad ones from the scary ones. I followed him into the bustling diner and watched him casually approach an empty stool along the countertop, where he sat down like a Saturday morning regular. I couldn't match Caleb's composure because I was struck by several surprising observations. When I grabbed the handle on the front door and held it open, no syrupy gunk clung to my hand, and as I walked inside, the soles of my shoes did not cling to any mysterious spills. Instead of the anticipated greasy aroma mixed with traces of body odor, the Waffle House in Batesville smelled of bacon, waffles, and coffee. Also, Caleb and I happened to be the only two white people in the place.

In this regard, I must ask for understanding. I was raised on a remote ranch and graduated high school with 14 other people who looked just like me. My first meaningful conversation with an African American didn't occur until I attended a small college, where I played baseball with a politically minded African American teammate. He introduced me to politics, and we joined the campus Democrats together. Though there were only seven of us total, it was an enlightening experience that taught me the value of diversity and of equity and of my whiteness within these contexts.

So, I was ashamed of my visceral reaction to the demographics inside the Batesville Waffle House, but again, forgive me, I am simply not used to such environments. Until we crossed the state line earlier this morning, I had never stepped foot in the state of Mississippi. Therefore, my understanding of the state was shaped by its history, racial, and political infamy. The legacy of figures like Medgar Evers and James Meredith, and *Mississippi Burning* weighed heavy on my mind, standing in the foyer of the Waffle House, where I became hyperaware of this privilege and saddened for reasons I cannot fully explain.

Despite my inner turmoil, none of the black patrons in the Waffle House paid me any attention. Quickly, I took a seat next to Caleb at the countertop and awkwardly studied a menu.

The front door opened and shut behind us and someone gently said, "War Eagle." A family of Auburn fans had walked in and huddled together near the doorway. The man of the family looked about my age, 30-something, but he was dressed in Under Armour branded Auburn gear from his orange and blue shoes right up to the low-rise visor on his head. His son wore a #2 Cam Newton jersey and his young daughter dressed like a cheerleader with temporary Auburn tattoos on her face. His wife removed an orange and blue pom-pom from her purse and shook it when our eyes met. "War Eagle!" she repeated, louder this time.

Caleb remained inconspicuous and pretended like he didn't see them. His gameday outfit – blue jeans, plain navy-blue sweater, and a navy-blue interlocking AU cap - were understated in comparison. He thought wearing three or more pieces of Auburn flare was tasteless, which was a truly absurd standard on the road versus a rival from the West division within the Southeastern Conference. To counteract his snobbish fashion ideals and his discreet Auburn fanfare, I liked to embarrass my friend with exuberance for all things Auburn, most especially the ubiquitous War Eagle exchanged on this occasion as a greeting between Auburn people.

"War Eagle!" I shouted back, matching the family's sartorial enthusiasm, and I smiled and tipped my own Auburn cap.

"War Eagle!" the family replied in cloying unison before a passing waitress cut them off.

"It'll be just a minute," the waitress said, "We really busy and most of 'em just sat down."

The Auburn man smiled wide and nodded and apologized like it was his fault the restaurant was full. He kindly indicated they were in a hurry and would have to try a drive-thru. Though polite, his accent sounded coarse, more country than Southern, more straight ticket Republican than folksy or poignant. I was always in search of that elusive, soft accent, and always disappointed when I heard generic redneck instead.

But before he left, the Auburn man approached us. "The food here tasted better when they only accepted cash," he said.

I had no clue what he meant, so I just smiled and laughed cordially.

"You boys headed to the ball game?" the man asked.

"Wouldn't miss it," I answered enthusiastically.

The man raised his eyebrows. "I sure hope Gus is ready to go today."

SEC fans always referred to their head coaches in this manner, as if Auburn's Gus Malzahn was a demigod through which the outcome of the game would be solely decided.

"That's a hot seat he's sitting on," I added. "But he's used to it by now. He'll have the boys ready."

"Say, do y'all need tickets to the game?" the man asked through another wide smile. "I had a buddy cancel and we've got two seats on our row. They ain't too good but they're in an Auburn section and they're on the house if you want them."

I spoke up quickly and rejected the offer before Caleb had time to contemplate the idea. "Awfully generous, sir, but we've already got tickets," I said.

This wasn't exactly true, because *we* didn't have tickets. Caleb's cousin had the actual tickets in his possession. We were scheduled to meet with him sometime before the game, but in all the years I had known Caleb, on the rare occasion he mentioned his extended family, it was always in a derogatory manner. 'Fractured, white trash, back dealing rednecks,' he called them. It seemed prudent to accept the Auburn stranger's gift of tickets in hand, just in case Caleb's cousin lived up to the family name and either let us down or tried charging us a fortune for them.

However, there was an extenuating circumstance that outweighed Caleb's usual impression of his family, introduced to me by his own mother. She called Caleb first, telling him that she had secured tickets on our behalf. All we had to do was meetup with the cousin. Then, she called me and revealed the truth after I swore on Caleb's father's grave to take the conversation to my own final resting place.

The cousin indeed had the tickets and agreed to let us have them, but he also had vital news about the family. The details remained a mystery, as Caleb's mother either would not or could not divulge them, other than to suggest that the secret would be a revelation for her son. She insisted that I steer Caleb toward the cousin because she believed that if Caleb knew there was more than just football tickets involved, he would avoid the cousin at all costs. I agreed with her assessment. It was my opinion that Caleb should donate his body to science, because if his chest was opened and examined during an autopsy, they'd find a circuit board and wires before they ever found a beating heart. So, I accepted this mission from Caleb's mother, and intended to carry it out with commitment and fervor.

"War Eagle!" the Auburn Man added after we thanked him for the offer.

"War Eagle," Caleb mumbled.

"War Eagle!" I said.

When I spun back around in the stool, a waitress hovered over us. She had thin braids pulled taut against her head, and she wore bright eye shadow that matched the neon green fingernails clicking against each other when she tossed the yellow order pad on the counter and wrapped her chubby fingers around a pen.

"Mornin'" she said. She leaned against the counter with her attention on us generally, but with her eyes elsewhere. "We havin' coffee?"

"Yes ma'am," Caleb answered. His own mutt of a Southern accent drawled a little more when he was back in this part of the world, but as always, he spoke low, just enough volume to be heard by his audience, and not a tick louder.

I nodded, yes.

"Y'all want cream?"

"Yes ma'am," Caleb repeated.

I nodded again.

"I'm gonna bring y'all a water, too," she said and finally trained her eyes on me, then my Auburn windbreaker. "I can tell by that ugly orange y'all are up to no good today."

"Yes ma'am, it is an obnoxious color," Caleb said without skipping a beat.

The waitress pulled two ceramic mugs from a drying rack and set them down, then poured coffee out of a glass pot. She placed the mugs in front of us along with a small dish of Half & Half pods, then poured ice water into two clear cups. When she returned to us, she had a twisted, confused look on her face.

"I got a question for y'all."

"Let's hear it," I said.

"I get that Ole Miss people have a reputation for being kind of snobby. You know, preppy. And I get that Mississippi State people are more like the country type, but what are Auburn people supposed to be?"

I laughed, knowing I was incapable of defining it, so I let Caleb take a stab at it.

"Take 60% of a State person," he began, "Forty percent of an Ole Miss person, add 10% extra credit to account for Alabama, and that's what an Auburn person is supposed to be. Make sense?"

It certainly didn't make much sense to me, but our waitress seemed to understand. She nodded, then said, "Makes sense. 'Cept for the part about Alabama. But, why do Auburn folks say War Eagle? Ain't y'all the Tigers?"

I looked at Caleb and grinned. "Remind me, why *do* the Auburn Tigers say War Eagle, Caleb?" Of all Auburn fans, especially Auburn fans who graduated from the university, Caleb was in the running for least inspired when it came to the school's traditions.

"You want the long, corny version? Or the short answer?" Caleb asked, dry as ever.

"Short answer," the waitress shot back, then quickly added, "Y'all know what you want to eat?"

Caleb answered instinctually. "All-Star. Over-easy. Grits. Add hash browns - smothered, covered, diced. Bacon times two. Wheat toast, please."

I scanned over the menu, same as it ever was, but for once I felt the urge to try something new. I just couldn't seem to zero in on anything. Steak & Eggs, maybe. I sensed an impatient frown from the waitress, so I pointed at Caleb with my thumb. "Tell the War Eagle story," I said without averting my eyes from the menu. I wanted to hear him struggle through an explanation in the meantime.

Caleb took a quick breath and spoke fast. "A long time ago, one Auburn person said War Eagle to another Auburn person. Who the hell knows why? But the second person said War Eagle back to the first person and a third person heard it, and so on. Now it's like shaking hands and saying 'peace be with' you in church. You have to say it. You don't always mean it."

That amount of cynicism, so thickly applied, made me burst out loud with laughter. The waitress, too. Saucy and bobbing her head, she cackled and said, "Don't always mean it, huh? Kinda like me saying 'Go Rebels!'" She looked back to see if anyone in the kitchen heard her, and she shared a laugh with a waiter.

I found her humor confusing. The University of Mississippi's awful, racist Rebel nickname was certainly no joking matter for me. It was a cruel, offensive reference, and though my only physical connection to Mississippi was this very seat in this very Waffle House, I despised any Mississippian that accepted this traitorous rally cry, and I despised them for reasons far more essential than football colors. I inferred that the waitress was disguising some unfathomable truth within her joke, and laughter was the only solace she had left to deal with it.

I tossed the menu on the counter and said, "I'll have the same as him, but now I have a question for you, ma'am, because I know precisely what you mean when you mock the expression Go Rebels."

The waitress evidently recognized my seriousness, as her laughter halted, and her face resumed the static expression with which she first greeted us.

I asked her, "How can the state University of Mississippi continue to associate itself with such an offensive nickname? It's appalling. Embarrassing, really. And worst of all oppressive, don't you think?"

She angled her head so both me and the kitchen could hear her, and a little smile broke on the corner of her mouth when she said, "It could always be worse, mister. We could have to say Roll Tide!" and this time the cackle turned into a belly laugh and she slapped a cook on the shoulder.

When she caught her breath, she called out the necessary parts of our order, shouting over the metal spatulas that clinked against sizzling flattops, and the murmur of morning chatter, and the timers that beeped on the waffle makers, and the Otis Redding lyric sung from the jukebox in the corner, the familiar Waffle House symphony. The waitress then dipped away, back into her Waffle House realm where the staff carried on as if I did not exist, even though I sat right in front of them, as if the conversation I initiated had never happened. Not an attempt to reconcile a racist nickname, not even a common rival in the SEC West like the University of Alabama could penetrate the barrier that separated the Waffle House's dining area from the Waffle House's kitchen. Only the employees were allowed to pass back and forth between this mythical obstacle, and once the banter transferred into the kitchen, the conversation belonged to the staff and the semi-intelligible code they spoke to each other with. According to Caleb, this custom was no different at any Waffle House and so that included the cleanest Waffle House I had ever stepped foot in.

"Was it me, or did that Auburn mommy wink at me on her way out?" I asked.

"I think that was your overactive mom thing firing up again. Besides, that whole family was dressed like manikins at the team store in the Birmingham mall," Caleb said. "Why do people think they need to dress so preposterously? To prove their loyalty?"

"Yes. Of course. How else are they going to differentiate themselves from miserable Auburn grouches like you, Caleb. And she winked at me precisely because of my overactive mom thing. They can sense it."

"Or she was merely saying War Eagle when she winked."

"Can you wink a War Eagle?" I asked.

"You can fill in any blank with a War Eagle. It's an incantation for everything."

"An incantation for 'call me?'"

"She had an 11-year-old with her, man, I don't think she winked at you like the kind of wink you're talking about. And even if she did, once you get into the whiskey and start screaming at the referees from 110 rows up, she'd change her mind."

"Maybe she has a thing for informed fans with excellent eyesight."

"I'll give you the eyesight."

"You think I'll need it today? Are your cousin's tickets up in the nose bleeds? Is it too much to hope for seats in a section that looks like a sorority composite?"

"I haven't the slightest idea where they'll be."

"When was the last time you saw this guy anyway? What's his deal?" I asked, prying for information without alerting him to the reason for my curiosity.

"Probably at my grandmother's funeral in the mid-90's. My

mom told me he's married now," Caleb said, blinking dramatically while he cleared his throat, "...to a woman," he added. "She also said that he's in Mississippi politics, but she used finger quotes when she said politics."

While I tapped my chin I said, "So, your cousin is a bi-sexual swinger in an open relationship, who uses his bizarre sexual preferences to catch legislators in honey traps?"

"That's what was implied," Caleb said, subtly mimicking the finger quotes. Then, he shuddered. "God, I hate these 11:00 am kickoffs. It's too early for all that Auburn Family bullshit."

"Early kickoffs are punishment for losing to Tennessee," I reminded him. "And you should be careful, you know. We're within the circumference of the Family. You have to say War Eagle back to people or the ghost that lives in the Auburn University Chapel will find you and confiscate your diploma."

"I'd happily give them my diploma back if it somehow led to us winning a few more ballgames."

"Good thing you've got Auburn's good luck charm with you, Caleb. When I attend an Auburn game, not only do we win, but we also go on to win a National Championship."

"I think we need a few more data points before we declare you the impetus of Auburn's success."

"I'm eager to conduct more research, because if my presence delivers a title to Auburn once a decade, they'll build a shrine in honor of me outside of Jordan-Hare Stadium bigger than Pat Sullivan's, Cam Newton's, even Bo Jackson's, combined, and Auburn fans will make it a tradition to worship at my altar the Friday night before every home game."

It was Caleb who introduced me to what became my college football fanaticism when he took me to my first Auburn game seven years ago. That day spent in Auburn, Alabama was amped with an excitement so palpable all I had to do was breathe in, and the collective Auburn spirit flowed through me, shading my soul orange and blue hours before we even entered the stadium. Campus was a giant, moveable tailgate, part culinary show, Jimmy Buffett concert, and church revival, where pork barbeque and whiskey mixed with Toomer's Lemonade was communion.

We joined our adopted family inside Jordan-Hare Stadium, and as the Auburn faithful, we fired each up in our devotion. We screamed it in every cheer, sang it in every note of the fight song, and in doing so, I was called to the faith. We sat. We stood. We yelled. We prayed. When I thought the pregame ceremony had peaked, Caleb pointed to one corner of the upper deck, where they let fly a golden eagle that circled the stadium in a majestic arc. The magnificent bird swirled overhead, right above me, before it glided to midfield and pounced on its prey, completing the sacrament to thunderous cheer.

Auburn beat LSU that day, and they kept winning until they reached the National Championship. We wanted to attend but tickets were $2000 each, and neither of us could afford it. Throughout the following offseason, we discussed Auburn's schedule and the games we were going to attend in 2011, but we never made it back, a trend that continued. We blamed scheduling problems and work. Caleb was laid off, his father died, he was laid off again, then he and his wife miscarried. There was plenty going on, but money was usually the true culprit. It was just too expensive. Too time consuming and expensive.

Instead, every Saturday since that LSU game, no matter what, Caleb has walked through the alley that separates our homes and knocked on my back door just before ESPN's College Gameday. Together, we indulge in Bloody Mary's and eat imitation Momma Goldberg's nachos for breakfast, drink beer for hours on end, watch every game until Auburn comes on, then we get serious.

Caleb was critical of everything, most especially the things he loved the most, and I think that's why he remained so dedicated to our shared Saturday tradition. Through the reflection of Auburn's spirit in my eyes, he sought renewed validation for the divine magic of Auburn that he once knew, the same magic that bounded us together as friends.

The waitress walked up; arms stacked with plates full of food. "Y'all good?" she asked and spread our breakfast in front of us.

"Yes ma'am," Caleb said.

"Ma'am, you think Auburn has a chance today?" I asked her.

The waitress rolled her eyes at my question and clicked her tongue. "I saw what happened to y'all last week. Ole Miss is fixin' to blow you boys out," she said, then walked away.

Caleb paid her no mind, and focused on his breakfast, using his fork and knife to lift an over-easy egg onto a triangle shaped piece of buttered wheat toast, then he crumbled strips of bacon into small pieces that he mixed into his bowl of grits with a scoop of butter, and he stirred it with a spoon until it melted, and he topped it off with several dashes of pepper from a shaker. He didn't blink once. When he was done, instead of eating it, he balanced the spoon in the grits, put his hands on his lap and stared at the food.

Something larger than hunger was eating away at him. I wanted to understand what it was and why, but I also knew that confronting Caleb with even a scintilla of vulnerability would trigger his emotional flight. Pinning him down was like trying to catch a wild hare with your bare hands.

"I know I don't have to tell you, of all people, that the food in front you is a work of art, but you might recall, it's even better when you eat it," I said.

Caleb didn't acknowledge me in the slightest.

"You going to snap out of it sometime before kickoff?" I asked.

"Snap out of what?"

"Whatever funk you're in."

He sighed and slouched forward and tapped the yolk on the egg lightly with the side of his fork, but not firm enough to break it. "I think the funk might be the whole of Mississippi."

"There's no funk in this Waffle House. That's for sure. This must be the cleanest one in the whole country."

Caleb finally broke the egg and watched the yolk soak into his toast. "Kind of wish we'd taken the free tickets."

I had to be careful here. I didn't want to fail my mission before we even reached Oxford, so I knew I couldn't appear unduly attentive. "I wouldn't worry about the tickets," I said. "People are literally giving them away at this point. Let's go get the tickets from your cousin, and if they suck, we'll see if we can find someone else giving them away for free."

"That's not a bad idea."

"Do you have something against this guy? Your cousin?"

"Not really. My mom is the only reason I'd remain loyal to many of the people in my extended family. She insisted I find my cousin to get these tickets, so I'm sure he'll have one piece of gossip or another to pass back to her. I'm just wary about it. That's all."

"Why?"

"When any of us get together it feels like a bad omen, like the hammer will drop on one of us at any moment." Caleb let his fork hover over his plate for a few seconds, then added, "You were right about one thing," he began and took a bite of the grits.

"What's that?" I asked.

"This is the cleanest Waffle House I've ever been in," he said, and I let him finish his breakfast in peace.

Throughout the week, the weather forecasts for gameday had been grim, but the system blew through earlier than expected, resulting in an overnight deluge. It rained steady for an hour on the journey from Memphis, but softened by the time we reached Batesville. As we departed, headed east toward Oxford, the clouds lightened one more shade of gray and the rain reduced to mist. Through this perfect football weather an electrical current sparked a level of excitement inside of me that intensified with every mile traversed, with every flag mounted atop the cars we passed, with every favorable prediction called from Rod Bramblett on the Auburn Radio Network pregame show.

We arrived in Oxford and found a Baptist church, where we paid a $20 donation to park in their secured lot. Caleb popped the trunk, and we stretched our legs, and prepared our provisions. In the old days, people would park their trucks near football stadiums and quite literally party around the tailgate. But since vehicles had been forced to the outer edges of most college campuses to preserve green space, anything that involved a drink before the game was considered a tailgate. Big party in a tent – tailgate. Large crowd gathered around a grill in a parking lot –

tailgate. A couple of buddies holding beers and walking around – tailgate.

Without a particular destination in mind, our plan was to meander from one party to the next, seeking conversation and libation. Caleb had a fifth of Jim Beam wrapped in a brown paper bag that he stuffed into his back pocket, while I put several mini bottles of vodka in my Auburn jacket and grabbed a 12-pack of Michelob Ultra I had stored on ice in a Styrofoam cooler. The parking lot attendant, a gray headed woman in an Ole Miss poncho, stared at us with beady, judgmental eyes while we prepped ourselves. I offered her a mini bottle of Fireball, but she declined, so I shot it myself, then cracked a beer open and drank it until the cold stung the back of my mouth. The best tasting beer I knew: the Auburn football Saturday beer.

"You sure you want to lug those around all morning?" Caleb asked while he looked at my case of beer.

"Why? Is there a tyrannical open container law I should be worried about?"

"I think liquor is allowed here if you aren't openly consuming it, maybe, but beer and wine are illegal to be seen with in public. Don't take my word for any of it, though, it's been so long since I was here."

"You mean to tell me that Mississippi has backward laws on the books?" I said sarcastically. "Good thing two handsome white men like us won't have to worry about racist cops stomping out our good time, huh?"

"Careful. These days in Oxford, you're only profiled if you're ugly, so you better hope your self-description holds up."

"I'm handsome enough that I've got us both covered, Caleb," I said and smirked at him. "Anyway, if the police approach me about the beer, I'll just play dumb, which won't be difficult at all in this Auburn jacket."

"You can play dumb about the city code all you like, but please don't turn dumb into aggressive. I know how you get when you begin your day with shots," he said and slammed the trunk shut.

We followed several Ole Miss fans through a sleepy neighborhood full of collegiate cottages and homes styled in Greek or Colonial Revival, some Victorian, all of them decorated with Ole Miss flags and accoutrements. The leaves on the extravagant trees had just begun to turn. Their edges were warm shades of yellow and gold, a mild contrast to the electric orange on the occasional Auburn fan or the vibrant, cardinal red worn by the Ole Miss people. As we approached University Avenue at the edge of campus, the air grew cooler and filled with tension. The trickle of people around us had increased, and we crossed a bridge over train tracks to get our first glimpse of the Ole Miss football stadium. Compared to other SEC venues, it was on the small side, but the lights shining through the mist and the blaring music still gave me an adrenalin burst and tingles through my fingertips.

A short walk into campus and we reached The Grove, a tree lined, ten-acre lot that was checkerboarded with hundreds of tailgating tents colored red, white, and blue, all tightly packed together and bustling with activity. Well-dressed people in their Ole Miss coordinated Saturday best gathered under the canopies of tents and tree limbs, and they carried on in the muddied slop as though conditions were perfect. Fraternity pledges wore blue blazers and striped ties with mud caked over their penny loafers. The girls wore sleek dresses, impossibly short hemlines despite the chill in the air, with tall boots or designer shoes that some had wrapped in plastic bags to protect from mud.

Caleb wanted to cross the street and enter the madness of The Grove right away, but what he didn't know was that I had been online all week reading stories about the Ole Miss campus. Its layout, its violent political history, and an infamous landmark that I wanted to see before, God willing, it was gone forever. In fact, the statue's heralded location on campus was so prominently displayed that it only took me a few seconds searching before I spotted a building in the distance with elegant white columns, where there arose a pillar and statue framed by an array of grand oak trees.

I convinced Caleb that we should walk the full perimeter of The Grove first, scope it out, before diving in, and so we followed a sidewalk until I easily navigated us toward the statue. The grey sculpture depicted a mustached soldier in his uniform. He balanced the butt of his rifle against the ground with one hand. His other hand shielded the sun from his eyes that gazed into the distance in search of his lost cause. A large inscription read, "To Our Confederate Dead."

Surely there were many Southern towns that still bore their share of monuments - even Auburn, I presumed, though I could not recall seeing one on its campus. But this statue before us represented more than just itself. It stood as a symbol of every unremarked monument I had missed, a troubled emblem of the South's tumultuous past. Here, in the heart of Mississippi, where the essence of Southern identity was intensified, this figure served as a dark reminder, a distillation of a history that echoed across every Southern town.

Maybe this reaction was unfair to the state Mississippi, or maybe it was punishment, but the nausea that overcame me in the presence of that statue, and the boiling contempt simmering beneath my skin, was a pittance compared to the torment that every African American student must feel when they are forced to walk past the statue. This was not some objective, historical waypoint, left here as an innocent reminder. This was an active symbol of supremacy and racism, those grim ideals that lurked around every corner. And yet, all around us, life went on. Passing fans, students, faculty, none of them seemed to notice the statue's arrogant gaze. It was as though its ugliness, its crude crafting, its enduring legacy, were all invisible to them.

Caleb, who had so far ignored my sighs attempting to direct his attention to the statue, finally said, "You can be mad at that inanimate stone for as long as you'd like, and as long as you don't get dizzy and fall over, it won't hurt you at all."

"The power lies in its symbolism, Caleb, which I know you understand, yet again you choose a form of cynicism, the laziest way to conduct a life."

Caleb exaggerated a yawn. "I prefer the Auburn football fanatic to the moralizing political pundit," he said. "Why don't you finish your beer, pause for a moment of silence, and let's weave through The Grove a couple times until we're nice and tight?"

I jabbed a furious finger at him and said, "Oh, there's plenty of time for the angry football fan, don't worry. In the meantime, allow me to reflect and express my contempt. If you don't feel the same, then quietly experience my pain vicariously."

"As you experience pain vicariously," Caleb mumbled. "Wait, I do feel something. I feel like I could take a leak right now. We should find the Hotty Toddy Porta Potties."

"How long have we been best friends? Ten years? In all that time, all I've wanted from you, just once, is your legitimate participation in this movement that is very important to me, or at the very least your respect, but you can't hide your instinct for ridicule, can you? You can't, or you won't."

Caleb ever so subtly nodded his head, in apparent, shocking agreement, until he had raised his eyes completely and faced the statue, stating, "It's too bad you never saw this place when I first came here in the 90's. There were battle flags everywhere back then. Everywhere."

"I suppose you think the fact those battle flags are gone is proof of progress?"

"I suppose in some ways it is."

"You think they threw all those flags away? Or did they just fold them up, hide them in a drawer to be passed down to their handsome sons the day they pledge KA?"

"When the statues are gone, they'll be forgotten like the flags, and we'll move onto the next Southern tradition to be condemned. Pray God, not the Waffle House."

"You can't hide yourself from this forever, Caleb. Look how these people rally around a football field. Imagine if their rage was in defense of your heritage instead."

"My heritage?"

"Your heritage."

"My last name is Orlando."

"So?"

"So, I don't think there were any Italians running around in white hoods, though I'm sure numbers are down these days. They'll probably accept anyone for the dues."

"Let me ask you one question, Caleb…"

"Just one?"

"If the fight broke out tomorrow. The big one. Whose side would you be on?"

"Depends. Is there a Sherman equivalent burning his way from one Waffle House to another?"

I glared at him until, unfortunately, he answered.

"I'd be on this guy's side," he said, and to my complete dismay, he slowly nodded toward the statue of the Confederate soldier, hands in his pockets like his defensive posture could lessen the blow.

"Your politics remain a disgrace. I am ashamed I have taught you nothing."

"Do you notice how diminutive the soldier is?" he asked.

"Diminutive?"

"Diminutive," he repeated. "It means small. Disproportionately so. Think diminished."

"I know what diminu…I know what it means."

"That is the most telling criticism regarding this statue, if I may speak from a position of Art Appreciation 101, which is a class I attended at Auburn. Got an A."

"Be honest with me - did you eat a weed gummy this morning?"

Caleb droned on, "The setting also minimizes the stature of the soldier. The trees dwarf his proportion. The location is meaningful, sure, but shouldn't the individual represented here be the major focus? And so, shouldn't *he* be emphasized? And disproportionally so, instead of the opposite, as it stands now?"

"Caleb, I wouldn't trust your Auburn Art Appreciation bullshit on a third graders' self-portrait. Let alone this awful thing. The statue was intended to last forever. The symbolism, the art, lies within the act of its placement and now of its removal, pray God, to commemorate the traitors one last time, and to remind them who won and who lost."

"The mustache looks stupid," Caleb continued, eyes still focused on the face of the statue. "But I bet it looked stupid on the kid wearing it, too. Nineteen years old, married, new baby at home, and no clue what world existed twenty-five miles beyond his own back porch."

"What are you talking about? Was this guy an actual person?"

"I have no idea, but isn't that the point?" Caleb answered. "Maybe he was a clerk in his family's store, where every day the next customer brought some new paper or flyer or rumor claiming the enemy is the aggressor, and the enemy is coming for him and his family any day now."

"He should have known better," I stated defiantly.

"He did know better. There was a more immediate threat. His friends and neighbors, hell, his own wife, who should he dissent, would issue a death sentence just the same. So, he fought to save his family, and his reputation, and his livelihood, and he died in some forest in some far-off state he didn't care about, and all he got out of the deal was a shit statue for people to bitch about 150 years later."

"Sure, Caleb. You're a real fine person. A real fine person."

"Bring it down, people forget it was ever here. Let it stay, let it glorify nothing except to commemorate the foolishness of our neighbors and the lengths they will go to feed their insanity." Caleb snapped out of his political interlude and asked, "How many times did you watch *Ghosts of Mississippi* before this trip?"

"It was *A Time to Kill*," I replied. "Seven times. Maybe eight."

"That movie is terrible. Objectively terrible."

"I don't care. I won't tolerate any appeasement on this subject."

"You wanted my opinion," he sighed. "The fact is, no matter how it is honored, I prefer the historical timeline that, by a fantastic amount of luck, has deposited me in a beautiful college football town on a beautiful autumn morning to watch one of the few things in the world that truly…"

My attention was momentarily diverted by two individuals strolling behind Caleb, catching my eye as the perfect candidates to add to the conversation. They were African American men, near our age, wearing all black everything. Black Nikes. Black jeans. Black jackets. Their timing was impeccable, and because I wanted to rub this in Caleb's face, I didn't feel shy about it at all. The Fireball helped.

"Excuse me, sir?" I called out, then put my hand up and said, "Hold on, Caleb, let's see what these guys think."

Caleb turned around to see who I was talking to, his expression shifting from slight annoyance to extreme discomfort. From the way his body tensed up, I thought for a moment he might internally combust, reducing himself to an embarrassed poof of dust. The only thing Caleb hated worse than large crowds were confrontations with strangers.

"Excuse me, sir?" I called out again. The two men either didn't hear me or refused to believe I was speaking to them. "Wearing the all black?"

"What's up?" the bigger of the two said.

"You two wouldn't happen to be local activists, would you? With Black Lives Matter, possibly?"

Caleb buried his face in his hands and said, "Oh, Jesus Christ."

The smaller guy answered. "Naw, we're catering a tailgate..."

"Hold on just a minute!" the big guy jumped in. "My black life matters, and I'm taking donations today. Cash. PayPal. Venmo. Bitcoin."

"I'm sorry to have bothered you, but my friend here was trying to *both sides* this Confederate statue, and I thought you might have an opinion about it."

"So?"

"So? He needs to be educated by someone truly affected by its presence on campus."

"Is this for the internet or something? Where's the camera?" the smaller guy asked, looking around.

"It isn't anything like that," I told him. "We were just talking. I wanted to make a point."

"I'll talk for $5 a word," the big guy added. "It's a ugly ass statue. That's five words already," he said, using his fingers to count. "That'll be $25."

Well, this had backfired, and now Caleb was enjoying every second of it.

The smaller guy nodded his head at something behind us and made it worse. "Y'all want to know what it's like to be black around here? You about to find out," he said and looked behind me, wide eyes indicating something noteworthy.

I spun around to see two police officers approaching us. They were in black uniforms with yellow reflective material on the sleeves and shoulders. The male officer was tall and athletic with a high and tight haircut, who looked like someone who made political Facebook monologues from his pickup truck in Wal-Mart parking lots. The female cop was petite with her hair in a ponytail. She shined a lot brighter than some of the former homecoming queens tailgating nearby.

I looked at the African American guys and quietly asked, "Is this some racist shit or what? What is going on?" I was confused why the police would be bothered by two white Auburn fans speaking with two grown men just trying to get back to their work.

"Naw man, they don't give a shit about us this time," the shorter one said, as they walked away. "It's the beer you got out."

As quickly as the two African American gentlemen left, they were replaced by the cops, who stopped in front of me and Caleb and flashed very brief, disingenuous grins.

"First time in Oxford?" the woman cop asked.

"It sure is," Caleb lied. "How can you tell?"

The big cop spoke next in a polite monotone. "You're in breach of an ordinance. The beer needs to be consumed from an opaque cup." He stuck his oversized chin out and looked around, drawing our attention to the crowds of people who all drank from red plastic cups, not a single exposed beer can in plain view.

Caleb and I both blinked at each other.

"Do you know what opaque means?" the woman cop asked. Her demeanor was so intensely curt that I could not decide whether this was an attempt at humor or not.

"Opaque…hmm," Caleb said and stared into the big oak trees while he rubbed the temple of his head with his fingertips. "That's got to be a Latin etymology, right?"

I started to spell the word. "O-P-A…" but I honestly had no idea how to finish it.

Caleb did. "Q-U…"

The female cop stopped Caleb short. "We get it, you're like a comedy team," she said.

"Were they trying to be funny?" her partner asked, then with all five of his fingers straightened, he pointed toward a random spot in The Grove. "There's plenty of nice people around. I'm sure they'll lend you a cup if you ask nicely."

"Help me understand," I said and looked at my beer, "it's against the law to drink this beer from the can, but if I pour the same beer into an opaque cup, it transforms into a legal substance for consumption?"

The lady cop exhaled loudly through pursed lips. "Sure," she said.

I lowered my eyelids and peered at her. "Does the color of the cup matter?" I asked.

The big cop was swaying now, shifting his weight from his heels to his toes. "You may think it's absurd," he stated, "but some cocky Auburn fan coming to Oxford once every two years and complaining about the way we do things around here isn't going to change a thing."

"No kidding," I said, and gestured toward the statue, but they didn't catch my drift, or they didn't care.

The lady cop put her hands out and scooted us toward The Grove. "We're trying to do you nice Auburn people a solid here. We're hospitable. To a point," she added, forcefully.

Caleb knocked his elbow against my arm and said, "Thank you for your leniency, Officers. We'll go find a couple of cups."

"Wait a second," I said as the realization hit me, "did you profile me because I'm ugly?" I asked the cops. They were already over it, shaking their heads, they turned and walked away. They had better things to do while it was still relatively tame. Their job would become a great deal more difficult later in the day when everyone was good and drunk and hopefully enraged that Auburn had rolled into town and beaten the brakes off Ole Miss.

I followed Caleb away from the statue, back toward The Grove, then finally we made it into the thick of the party, where people were crowded together shoulder-to-shoulder along the narrow sidewalks. The scant pavement was the only relief from the mud and the wet, slippery grass.

"See any friendly faces?" I asked as we wandered deeper into the trees, unsure of which tent to disturb.

There was no uncertainty in Caleb. "We're going to that one," he said and pointed to a cluster of tents neatly formed together.

A decorative placard hung over one tent and announced the name of the tailgate space: The Pine's Box. Each tent panel alternated red and blue and featured the cartoonish image of Ole Miss' defunct mascot - Colonel Reb. The school had officially abandoned the image, but he was still plenty visible around The Grove, dressed like an old cotton planter on his way to a formal Sunday supper. Red suit. Ribbon tie. Cane. Wide brimmed hat cocked atop his head. One arm hidden behind his back, probably holding a coiled whip.

The foldout tables in the tent were covered in white linen cloths and topped with silver serving trays full of wrapped Chick-Fil-A sandwiches, waffle fries, chicken biscuits, and there must have been 2,000 chicken nuggets arranged on silver platters. There were black ribbons tied into bows around the tent poles, black cocktail napkins, and authentic Ole Miss football helmets displayed upside down holding bouquets of black roses. In the corner they had a full-sized wooden casket propped up. It held a realistic skeleton wearing a blue sweater vest, a red Ole Miss cap, and a coach's headset over its skull. Its bony fingers held a cluster of white lilies. A framed, black-and-white headshot of Tommy Tuberville, Auburn's former football coach, graced an adjacent table.

The instant Caleb and I crossed over the tailgate threshold, a man stepped out of a conversation and greeted us abruptly like he was a part of a security detail. He wore duck boots and khaki pants with a white button down and plaid suspenders in Ole Miss colors. He had dirty blonde hair slicked back under a navy-blue ball cap with a big red M, and he wore a slightly damp, out-of-season, seersucker jacket.

"You boys lost?" he asked, assertively, and took another confident step toward us.

Caleb nodded his head upward at the guy. "Sorry to bother you. We were just accosted by a couple of cops about my friend's beer."

The man looked down at my case of Ultras and in his own authoritative way he said, "That's right, can't have an open container on campus."

"We were told to drink from opaque cups," Caleb finished, "and since we didn't bring any, we find ourselves at the mercy of your hospitality."

"First time in Oxford?" the man asked.

"First time," Caleb lied again.

"Well, it's no problem at all," the man said somewhat tersely, his jaw noticeably clenched. He was bound by his Southern upbringing to act neighborly toward us, but it was clear the presence of even modest Auburn fandom in his tailgate space made it difficult. He reached into a big tote and handed us two red cups from a stack of several dozen. He gave me a plastic grocery sack that I used to hide the case of beer, for which I thanked him profusely. Caleb did, too.

"Help yourself to some nuggets," he added, in an equally uninviting tone, looking for backup from his cohorts as he said it.

"No thank you," I said and tapped my stomach, "I'm still full of Waffle House. They've got a real nice one over in Batesville." Then I placed my bag of beer on the table, picked out a fresh can of Ultra, opened it, and casually poured it into my new plastic cup. After I took a long drink of it, I looked at the cup and said, "Ahhh, now I fit in."

"And no one the wiser," Caleb added.

Our speechless host watched us with utter bewilderment, as if he had just witnessed me and Caleb stripping down to our underwear while belting the "Battle Hymn of the Republic."

"Can I trouble you with one more question?" I asked him, "What's with the guy in the coffin? Is it a Halloween thing? I don't get it."

Caleb pointed at me with his thumb and apologized on my behalf. "He's relatively new to the SEC, so I'll let the home team take the honors explaining this one."

The man laughed to himself and shook his head in disbelief that two Auburn dupes had fallen directly into his trap. "Funny you should ask," he said, speaking louder than before to gather everyone's attention. "That story begins with my Daddy – Mr. Thomas Pine." This guy didn't have much of an accent but when he said that word, Daddy, it sounded as thick as sludge in a Mississippi riverbank.

Caleb looked at me, eyes widened with mocking interest. He quickly turned to the nuggets and used a set of silver tongs to grab several pieces of chicken that he placed on a clear plastic dish, adding one packet of Polynesian sauce. I knew Caleb wouldn't tolerate a paternalistic Southern trope with anything more than passing ridicule, but because of the nuggets combined with Ole Miss tailgate guy's bravado, he leaned in, ready to hear more.

The Ole Miss guy obliged. "Daddy hated Auburn worse than any other school in the Southeastern Conference." Now the man was preaching. He had one hand out, palm upturned, the other hand was behind the lapel of his jacket, and he angled himself to project his booming voice to the people behind him as he made his case against the Auburn Man.

But before he worked up to a crescendo, I interrupted again and untimed his cadence. "He hated Auburn worse than Mississippi State?" I asked, feigning disbelief.

"Worse."

"Worse than Alabama?" I asked, really pouring on the disbelief this time.

"Much worse. You must understand, Daddy respected Mississippi State," the man said in a tone of voice worthy of a politician. "We knew good people who chose to go to school in Starkville. Engineers and farmers and people fulfilling family legacies. And Daddy always revered Bear Bryant. No sir, he reserved all his hate for Auburn University. The red bricked armpit of Lower East Alabama. So crooked they can't keep their mascot straight. No honest man ever came out of Auburn, Daddy always told me."

Caleb, who chomped on his nuggets with an amused look of suspicion on his face, butted in. "Wait, I'm sorry," he said and swallowed the chicken, "is it that dishonest men attend Auburn in the first place, or is it Auburn that turns them into dishonest men?"

The man didn't have to consider this one long at all. "50-50," he said, smirking.

"Fair enough," Caleb replied.

"Which one were you, Caleb?" I asked.

"I went in as a fair skinned virgin," Caleb said, "but I sure didn't come out that way."

The man continued, louder this time. "As I was saying, there were three people who Daddy used as Exhibit A, B, and C in his argument against Auburn. The first person you will not know. My father's cousin on his mother's side, Campbell Cooper, a known cheat and liar, and to be fair to Auburn he flunked out after three semesters on the Plains, then disappeared to the Florida panhandle. Second," he proclaimed, "there was David Langer, a football player from Mom's hometown of Birmingham, who played ball for Auburn at the same time my Daddy was a respected walk-on lineman for the 1972 Rebel squad. Where is Mom? Is she in here?" And the man looked around the tent but did not see his mom, so he continued. "David Langer played the game violently and recklessly and showed no class before, during, or after the game, as Daddy told me, repeatedly, when I was learning to play this great game myself." Then he grabbed the framed photo of Tommy Tuberville and raised it over his head, "And finally, the third, here is Coach Iscariot himself, who was the head man at the University of Mississippi and famously said the only way he'd ever leave Oxford was if he was carried out in a pine box, only to prove his treachery days later when he abandoned his team in the dead of night and took the job at Auburn! And for what?"

"Thirty pieces of silver!" someone shouted from the tent.

"We have commemorated his betrayal ever since." The man replaced the framed photo near the coffin, then he removed his Ole

Miss cap and held it over his heart as he looked toward the prop skeleton. "This little pun and the decor for the Auburn game was all Daddy's idea, but he passed from this Earth shortly after the Egg Bowl in 1999, and never got to see Ole Miss' redemption against that scoundrel, Tuberville."

Caleb gently raised his hand, and said, "I was at that game when Tuberville first returned to Oxford. It was the 2000 season, wasn't it?"

"I believe that's correct. Yes." the man answered, perturbed that Caleb had interrupted his sermon.

"My freshman year," Caleb continued, "Deuce McAlister was Ole Miss' running back, and Tuberville had bumper stickers placed everywhere on Auburn's campus that said 'Deuce For Heisman', trying to motivate our defense during game week. I'll never forget those boos when Coach Tuberville ran out of the tunnel."

"And I was among the loudest," the man said, proudly.

"Didn't work though, did it?" Caleb replied behind a wry smirk of his own. "Auburn won that game."

"But what about Deuce McAlister?" I asked. "Did he at least win the Heisman?"

"Nope. I think 2000 was Chris Weinke."

"Who?"

"Exactly," Caleb said, then he turned to the Ole Miss guy. "Your father must have really loved Chick-Fil-A, too," he said, respectfully. Then he dunked his nugget into the sauce and ate it.

"Well, actually, I own several Chick-Fil-A restaurants in the greater Jackson area. War Chicken is on the menu today." He pointed to a marker board on a linen topped table that read MENU: WAR CHICKEN. Just above it, hanging from a red chandelier, was a plush Aubie doll, Auburn's Tiger mascot, dangling from a piece of string. "What was I saying before I was interrupted? Oh yes, I remember." The man furiously raised his own red Solo Cup and his eyes sharpened on something outside the tent, over the heads of the fans passing by on the sidewalk, high up in an old oak tree, as though he saw a ghost perched on a limb. "To my Daddy. And to Ole Miss, where we honor those no longer with us, whose spirits we summon when we gather together here in The Grove. These elegant trees unworthy of single ply toilet paper. The hallowed soil beneath us, impenetrable to Spike 80DF."

Finally, he had reached the punchline. Toomer's Corner is where Magnolia Avenue intersects College Street in the heart of Auburn, Alabama, where downtown meets campus at a spot famous for its oak trees. Following Auburn's 2010 National Championship season, a crazed Alabama fan poisoned the 130-year-old live oaks with an herbicide called Spike 80DF. The trees slowly shriveled to brittle trunk and blackened, shortened limbs, before they were removed and eventually replaced by substitute oaks that won't feel the same for at least 130 more years. It was very much a sad ordeal for Auburn people, and I was offended at his remark, made worse by the people in the tent who laughed.

"I still don't get it," Caleb said, dryly.

The Ole Miss guy, who was triumphantly grinning and nodding at his friends around him, looked at Caleb, confused, and asked, "What don't you get?"

"Tommy Tuberville is still alive, so why is there a skeleton in the coffin?"

The man chuckled and pointed his thumb at Caleb. "Yeah, he has his sights on the United States Senate, I hear. Thank the Lord in Heaven I don't live in your dreadful state, otherwise I'd have to vote for a Democrat in a federal election for the first time in my life."

After the laughter died down, Caleb said, "It still doesn't make any sense."

"It's a joke," he said, and examined Caleb.

"Jokes are funnier if they make sense," Caleb said.

"Okay, okay," the guy waved us on. "You got your cups. You got your nuggets. Needless to say: you've worn out your welcome."

Caleb wasn't quite done. "Maybe the bones represent the honor that Tuberville left behind?" he pondered.

"Sure," the man said, standing a little too close to Caleb now, for my comfort, and he added, "Now why don't you two get the fuck out of here."

"Whoa!" I shouted. "Why you trying to escalate it like that?"

"Because I want you out of here!" the man shouted, eyes suddenly furious with rage. This entire time, I thought he was play-acting, but I think he truly hated Auburn, and therefore, truly hated us.

That's when Caleb pressed the button to initiate the nuclear option, "Come on, let's go," he told me, "You'd be mad at Auburn, too, if David Langer made a cuckhold of your dead dad."

The guttural noise revealed the Ole Miss guy's intent. When he lunged at Caleb, I put my chest out and held him back. I had three inches on the guy and 50 pounds at least. I shoved him and he fell into the arms of his tailgate friends. The harder they pulled him away, the more frantic he got. "I will fuck you up you Auburn assholes," he mouthed at us, his eyes bulging out of his head.

I casually grabbed the handles on the plastic bag holding my case of beer while the entire Pine's Box tailgate complex reiterated their hosts demands for the Auburn trash to leave their tent. I put my arm around Caleb, and I shouted, "War Damn Eagle!" before we fled into the steady stream of fans pouring through the sidewalk.

Even while wearing electric orange, it didn't take long before we were immersed in The Grove and hidden from further reprisal. We reached a fountain where the crowd thinned. I sat on the ledge of it and carefully poured another beer. I watched the head of the Ultra rise to the brim, then I took a sip before it spilled over.

"Opaque cups, secured," I said.

"I knew I had found the perfect tent the moment I laid eyes on that coffin setup."

"I wonder, were we the assholes there?" I asked.

"They definitely had us in the first half. Not gonna lie."

"I thought we were just messing with the guy. Did it not come off that way?"

"No, he was serious the whole time. I think he actually hates Auburn."

"And who the hell is David Langer?"

"I have no idea," Caleb answered.

"That comment was obviously off the top rope," I said and raised my cup, "Anyway, to our Daddy's."

"The living and the dead."

We walked through The Grove so many times that the tents eventually fused into a singular, fantastic party, and I could no longer distinguish the tailgates we had already seen from the parties yet discovered. Random Ole Miss fans flagged us down, said hello, offered us breakfast and booze, proving our earlier interaction an outlier. We stopped at one tent for Bloody Mary's when Caleb recognized an old Auburn classmate. It was there where Caleb's phone buzzed with a text message from his cousin that included his pinned location on the opposite side of The Grove. We crossed to the other side and reached Sorority Row near an orange bricked building capped with white rotundas, where it didn't take long for Caleb to spot his cousin.

"Jesus," Caleb said when he saw him, "what is he wearing?"

His cousin stood in front of a blue historical marker with a heading titled "Documenting the Blues." He wore navy blue pants covered with repeating Ole Miss script logos, a grey Patagonia vest over an oxford button down, and a striped bow tie. He had graying hair, neatly parted, neatly compact, with swooping Mississippi bangs that swept over the full length of his forehead. He held a champagne flute with his pinky stuck straight out.

"That's an awful lot of look," I said.

"You're wearing a look," Caleb remarked of my orange getup. Speaking of his cousin, he added, "That is a costume."

"There isn't any doubt that he works in politics, right?" I asked.

"No doubt about it. If he starts jabbering too much, here's the getaway story: I've got an old Auburn roommate that we have to meet near the stadium. Oh, that reminds me, if my cousin asks about the extra two tickets, just tell him that my old Auburn roommate and his wife will be the ones using them."

"We have two extra tickets?"

"Yeah, and he thinks we're using all four. I want empty seats as a buffer from the crowd."

Caleb's cousin spotted us. He waved us over and smiled when we reached him. He had big, white, flashy teeth, and he stuck his hand out and said, "What are old cousins supposed to do? Shake hands? Hug? Half and half?" He had an understated lisp and carried an extra note at the end of every sentence. He also slurred his S's because he was quite drunk.

"How about a fist bump?" Caleb said coldly.

"Maybe you're right. I don't want to be seen consorting with the enemy." He stuck his hand out toward me and said, "I'm Aaron. Nice to meet you."

"Jeremy," I said and shook his hand. It was soft and delicate, and he barely applied pressure to his grip at all.

"I'm sorry Eloise couldn't be here," Aaron said. "Her little country club group has a tent somewhere in all this madness. I'd invite you over there but frankly I needed a little breather. It's a hot mess in all that mud." When there was only air in the conversation, Aaron continued, "Listen boys, I do have another little soiree to attend, so I must be brief. It's always one party to another. You know how it is on a big gameday." He reached into the pocket of a sport coat slung over his arm and found an envelope. "I'll be watching on the club level for the game today, so you'll be using my season tickets. I must therefore add a quick warning," he said and put the envelope over one side of his mouth like he was about to spill some big secret. "These people are nuts about Ole Miss football. And I mean truly mad. But you must remember, even the loud ones might be influential people around Oxford or in Jackson, so I'd appreciate it if you guys minded your manners inside. I'm not trying to say Auburn people are known to be rowdy, but my seat neighbors keep a close eye on visitors, and so any infraction will be noted and gossiped about. If you'll be so understanding, I'd appreciate it greatly."

Caleb glanced at me, then said, "We won't be a problem. I can assure you."

Just to make certain we were truly in the clear, I asked, "Aaron, you wouldn't happen to know any Chick-Fil-A peddlers in the greater Jackson area, would you?"

"Not off-hand, no. Why do you ask?"

"Forget it," Caleb interrupted. "We have to meet a friend of mine near the stadium, so we've got to get going, too. Thanks for the…"

"Wait, didn't your mother explain to you…about our grandfather?" Aaron asked, looking puzzled.

"Our grandfather? You mean Dino?" Caleb asked, equally perplexed.

"Yes, Dino. She didn't say *anything?*"

"No. Did he die or something?"

"He's alive. Eloise and I attended a wedding in Greenville a few weeks ago, and I had some time, so I decided to drive over to visit with him. Eloise and I host themed parties at our house, and we've got one coming up we're calling 'America Before the War.' I knew MeeMee kept several jewelry boxes full of old broaches, bracelets, necklaces, perfect for the theme, so I dropped in to see if I could take some of them off Dino's hands."

"How's he look?"

"Like he hadn't budged an inch in 20 years. Painfully alive but like death was creeping around the veranda biding its time, you know what I mean?"

"Last time I saw him was at Father's funeral, but it was only for a minute."

"I heard what happened," Aaron said. He looked down and used his right foot to knock some mud off the back of his left shoe. "I'm sorry I didn't attend. Your father was always kind to me. He was my favorite of the uncles."

I was at the funeral and heard the story about Dino, though I never laid eyes on the man. Dino hired a driver and traveled in for the ceremony, but he got so drunk after his arrival that he peed his pants at the Hampton Inn. He had to be helped by several relatives, including Caleb, who left Dino passed out on top of the bed after they hosed him down in the shower. Nobody could blame him, having to bury his own son, but Caleb later informed me that Dino had been completely sober for over two decades, until that hotel room, and the family was worried what devil he might unleash during the relapse.

Aaron continued, "I must warn you that Dino doesn't smoke

anymore. He got bad emphysema. Said it was affecting his stamina at the casino in Tunica, so he quit, cold turkey." Aaron turned up his nose. "I miss the smell of that pipe smoke. It masked quite a bit."

"Why would you have to warn me about that?"

"Because you need to go to Clarksdale."

"Why?"

"He has something for you."

"More costume jewelry?"

"Dino told me there was a family secret nobody knew about. He said it involved your father and that your father was the only one who deserved to know. Since he's gone, Dino wanted you to be the first to know. You and you alone."

"If it's so important, why couldn't he pick up a phone?"

"Laziness. Insanity. Spite. Who knows?"

"Could be money," I added.

"Oh, I'm certain it's not money," Aaron said, laughing, "because if it were money, it would already have been lost to a slot machine." He instinctively sipped from the empty champagne flute, then twirled the glass and frowned. "Dino had a box with him," he continued. "Sitting on the little table next to his chair. He kept his hand over it the whole time we were talking about it. It was about yea big, wrapped in brown paper, tied with twine," Aaron said and formed his hands into a slender rectangle. "Dino claimed he didn't know what was inside of it. He told me he hadn't opened it, but he knew who it was from, and he knew why it was sent."

"About the size of a check," I said.

"Dino knows who the box is from," Caleb stated, "and that's why he knows it isn't money. The sender is either poor now or was poor whenever he sent it."

Aaron contemplated Caleb's point, then said, "There was a moment after Dino struggled out of his chair and took three forevers to relieve himself, when I wanted to investigate, to at least test the weight of the box, but I couldn't bring myself to do even that. I'm not sure if it was because I feared Dino would catch me, because I'm still scared of that man to this day, but I also worried about the implications in the box independent of Dino. You know how it is with the family. It's rarely good news. So I left it alone. I didn't touch it. I barely looked at it. Then, after my first time seeing Dino in a blue moon, not three days later I've got your mama contacting me on Facebook, out of the blue, asking about tickets to the Auburn game of all things." Aaron's head shook with disbelief, then he asked, "How long are y'all here for?"

"We're headed back to Memphis after the game," Caleb said. "Have to catch a flight."

Our presence at the game was serendipitous: Caleb had a work obligation in Little Rock earlier in the week, and since I had come into a modest bonus I'd yet to blow through, I persuaded him to attend this game with me. My second Auburn game ever. Despite his lack of enthusiasm for Oxford, he agreed. But since we both had work on Sunday, unfortunately, our time here would be brief.

"How far away is Clarksdale?" I asked.

"Oh, I'm not going to Clarksdale," Caleb said, forcefully, before Aaron could answer my question.

Aaron handed over the envelope with the tickets, then he put the empty champagne flute under his arm and clapped his hands together, displaying his empty palms to Caleb. "Very well. I've done my part," he said, "and now I've really got to find more champagne."

We both thanked him for the tickets, but each of us avoided shaking his hand. As he walked away, Aaron added one more thing. "If you beat traffic, it's an hour to Clarksdale from here," he said then he made a cross over his heart. "Let's pray a triumphant Ole Miss gives you reason to leave early." He smiled, then he sashayed across the street and blended into the people and trees like preppy camouflage.

Caleb had a skeptical look on his face as he watched his cousin waltz away.

"Okay, so...what's in the box?" I asked.

"Nothing valuable," Caleb said.

"Any idea who it could be from?"

"No."

"Maybe it's something sentimental? There's value in that."

No answer.

"That was really bizarre, right?" I asked.

"I was expecting worse, honestly."

"Caleb, be straight with me. Do we need to go to Clarksdale?"

"I need to get a little bit tighter, then we need to go into this football game," he said. He opened the envelope and checked the section and seat numbers on the tickets. "These are decent seats."

"I have a feeling that if you wait too long, fancy britches will go back to your grandfather's house to steal it. Whatever it is."

"Won't happen. Even if it matched one of his themed swinger parties, he wouldn't risk being in Dino's presence again to go back and get it."

"Care to wager on it then?"

"Wager? Wager what?"

"Here's the bet. If Auburn goes up by more than two touchdowns at any point during this game, we leave immediately and drive to Clarksdale."

"More than two? That's it? Must I remind you we were up 21-3 on Florida State when Jameis…"

"Don't you say his name! Don't say his name, Caleb. It's like saying Beetlejuice."

"Besides, Clarksdale is an hour out of our way," Caleb protested. "There won't be any time."

"Okay, then we'll really test the Fates. Make it three touchdowns. In the first half."

Caleb was much less confident regarding Auburn's chances. He smugly agreed. "Ok, if Auburn goes up by 21 points in the first half…"

"No, if I'm giving you the first half bet, then I get both teams. If either Auburn or Ole Miss goes up by 21 points at any time in the first half, we leave, and we drive to Clarksdale. Or would he be at the casinos today?"

"Not on a football Saturday."

"There's not a whole lot of risk in this bet, Caleb. It's an easy one to take."

"What's on the other side of the bet? What if nobody goes up big in the first half?"

"Then you get your wish, and we stay here in boring old Oxford. So, is it a bet?" I asked.

"I don't understand why you're so invested in going to Clarksdale. Something is up."

I knew I had to come clean. "If somebody swore on your father's grave to keep a secret, wouldn't you?" I asked.

"My mother called you, didn't she?"

"She called me. She told me about your cousin, and she told me that he might have news. She didn't say anything about a box though."

Caleb remained silent, his annoyance unvoiced but palpable.

"She really wanted to make sure that we got to Aaron," I explained, "And I think if she knew about what your cousin said, and the package, she'd really want you to go to Clarksdale, too."

"Trust me, I know. When it comes to my father, any morsel of his past that my mom stumbles upon is treated like sacred scripture. A couple weeks ago she found a sleeve of his old golf balls in the attic. She might as well have been staring into his eyes at the altar the way she stared at those old Titleists."

"I'm sorry I didn't tell you she called."

"I guess I'm glad you didn't."

"Why?"

"Because I would've never met Aaron in the first place," he said, and then he looked at me and added, "I'll take the bet."

When Caleb's mother called me about the tickets, she shared an observation that has lingered with me. She had seen a transformation in her son, a positive shift that predated his father's passing by several years, and in many ways, survived that tragedy. In her view, this change coincided with the beginning of our chance introduction and resulting friendship. She had dubbed me his "moral compass," a title I took seriously. As game time neared, a sense of destiny swept over me. The stars were aligned for Auburn to return the opening kickoff 103 yards for a touchdown, intercept the first Ole Miss pass for another quick seven points, hold them to a three-

and-out, fair-catch a punt, then throw a 75-yard bomb to put us up 21-0 in the blink of an eye.

And so, like the increasingly inebriated Ole Miss fans around us, whose handsome faces looked more threatening as game time grew nearer, I put on my own determined game face. From that point forward I would not give the Ole Miss people the time of day. I would not meet their eyes. I would not nod at them or smile. I would only peek at their wives and girlfriends and revel at how this light breach of etiquette upset those who passed me by, and to amplify their animosity, any time an Auburn fan was within reach, I'd yell WAR EAGLE at an uncomfortable volume, and I'd give out so many high-fives my palms would turn red.

I also took another Fireball shot and poured another beer, because more than likely, we were about to watch two above average teams play a relatively close game of mediocre football, and that meant we'd be stuck inside Vaught-Hemingway Stadium for the duration. Normally I'd be thrilled with that prospect, but the longer we were inside the stadium, and the drunker we got, the more serviceable excuses Caleb would find to avoid going to Clarksdale. I knew if the scoreboard wouldn't do the trick, if Auburn didn't jump out to that huge lead I needed, there were other ways of getting ejected from a stadium early - a task made much easier due to our status as the visiting team, the invaders. Running my mouth would be my Plan B. And so, I resolved myself to sacrifice my love of Auburn football, should it be necessary, for the good of my friend. I could tell, just by looking at Caleb, that something was eating at him. That's the problem with people like him, people who try so damn hard to be stoic about everything, the slightest twitch on their face or the tiniest twinkle in their eye reveals as much as any laugh or tear. Especially when revealed in front of their moral compass.

We followed the crowd out of The Grove and down a narrow flight of steps outside of a red-bricked pharmacy school building. I pulled Caleb off the main sidewalk to a spot at the base of a concrete wheelchair incline where there was a landscaped patch of thick shrubbery covered in pine straw. I stuffed my bag deep into the bushes and cloaked it beneath branches and pine straw. There were still a couple beers left.

"We're not poor college kids anymore," Caleb said. "Why don't you just throw that shit away?"

"Because we might need rally beers on the way out of here. That's why."

"Or, we might need misery beers," Caleb said.

"I'm not falling for that depressing Auburn pessimism. Today, I'm a 300-pound All-America offensive lineman, full of the Auburn Spirit, standing in the bell tower atop Samford Hall, bellowing the Auburn University Creed," I said. But, just in case, I also raised my head to the sky, closed my eyes, and began a silent prayer.

"I know you don't know the Auburn Creed, so what are you doing?" Caleb asked, when he caught me with my eyes closed, lips mumbling.

"Praying," I told him. "Join me," and I jokingly reached for his hand, but he slapped it away. "Lord, please guide Gus over the play-call sheet today, God, and let Coach tug on the waistband around his pleated khaki pants out of happiness from the multitude of touchdowns, Lord, so that..."

"Land the plane," Caleb grumbled.

"So that we may discover the grace you have gifted my friend that has guided him to Clarksdale, Mississippi, his family's ancestral home. Amen."

"Amen." Caleb rolled his eyes.

"And thank you for the blessed fall weather. Amen." I added quickly.

"Amen," Caleb agreed.

"Oh, and finally, Lord God, use your will to smite the smirks off these tight-jawed, handsome, stupid Ole Miss faces, with their stupid swoopy bangs."

"That's one too many addendums."

I opened my eyes. "In prayer, Caleb, there is no such thing as too many addendums." I finished my beer and reached into the bushes and got another one. "We must remind God that he is on our side, because though we may not be angels, at least we're not from Mississippi."

"I am," Caleb said.

"That was too short-lived to count," I said, feeling for the mini bottles of hooch I had packed in my jacket pockets. "Am I going to have trouble sneaking these in?" I asked.

"They don't care about adults. The student section is a different story. Used to be anyway."

"You ever get busted?"

"Egg Bowl in 2001, I think? I wore a trash bag as a poncho because it always rained at the Egg Bowl, too, and somehow, we always forgot to pack raingear. I had a glass pint of whiskey hidden in my crotch, but those dudes working security back then weren't having it. Even in the driving rain, they loved busting preppy white boys. The security guy patted me down, lifted the bottom of the trash bag up, and knocked on the zipper of my jeans just like he was knocking on a front door."

"Sounds hot."

"I tried explaining that it was just the erection I had for Ole Miss football, but it didn't work. I had to unfasten my belt and jeans to get the bottle out, then he poured the whole thing into the ground, right in front of me, and threw the empty into a trashcan that was already full of thousands of dollars' worth of other empties."

"But you still got to go into the game, right?"

"I walked inside along with eight of my cousins who smuggled in six more bottles of liquor between them. We were fine."

"Are you taking the pint in?"

"Why not?" he said.

"Here, let me have it," I said and took it from him. "I'll take this inside and make us a couple bathroom cocktails."

We waited for a gap along the walkway then squeezed into the massive flow of people moving toward the stadium. We were herded through a construction zone bordered on each side by temporary fencing that created the perfect logjam for my frequent shouts of "War Eagle!" or "Gus is gonna teach 'em a lesson today!" Each cheer was rained down upon by a loud chorus of boos that riled up the Ole Miss people until one loud voice shouted over the fray, "Are you ready!?"

The crowd joined him in unison:

"Hell Yeah, Damn Right!

Hotty Toddy, Gosh Almighty!

Who the hell are we? Hey!

Flim Flam, Bim Bam

Ole Miss by damn!"

We reached the stadium and the back of the jumbotron in the endzone, where the clouds lightened into a thin layer of white, allowing rays of bright sunlight to pierce through. This burst of light illuminated the day and electrified the school colors worn by fans waiting in line. Fortunately, the queues moved quickly, because the yellow jacketed security guards were bored and tired, and once we reached them, they barely paid me or my stash of hooch any mind.

I stopped at the first concession stand we found inside the stadium. I bought two large Cokes and my guilty pleasure: stadium nachos with extra jalapenos. I took them with me into the bathroom, and while Caleb took a leak, I entered a stall, closed the door, and carefully balanced the drink carrier and nachos atop the toilet. I had to move a couple of empty bottles around to create space, because I was clearly not the only person using the bathroom as a bartender's workstation. There were empty bottles of whiskey, scotch, vodka, and gin overflowing the trash can, balanced on the toilet seat, scattered on the floor, clogged atop toilet paper in the bowl. I poured enough Coke into the toilet to allow room for one light bourbon and Coke and one very spirited bourbon and Coke. If we were going to leave Oxford early and drive to Clarksdale, one of us had to be sober enough for the task.

Caleb was waiting for me on the concourse when I finished. I handed the less lethal of the two drinks to him, and we found the tunnel nearest our seat location. We entered the stadium halfway up the lower level on the Auburn side of the field at the 35-yard line. The light that still peeked through the clouds was captured in

Auburn's uniforms that shined whiter than any white I had ever seen, complemented by bright pops of orange, and the deep green turf. It was a fine day for football. A fine day for an Auburn victory.

I scoped out the crowd while we descended the stairs, and it did not appear that many other Auburn fans had been gifted tickets from their long-lost cousins who owned mid-to-high-level donor seats. I felt the mean glares of the Ole Miss fans, so I slowed down and let them have a long look. It felt good to be judged, to be hated, to fulfill their low expectations of Auburn people, like we had been lured out of a tin-roofed trailer on Wire Road, and now we were unleashed on the antebellum snobs for their amusement.

I faced the field and I shouted, "War Eagle!" then vigorously shook my orange and blue pom-pom. After several boos rang out, I added, "The Bagman is here! Y'all got any 5-Star recruits!?"

"Go to hell, Auburn!" a fan hollered from deep in the stands.

Caleb ignored my antics. He was already standing in front of his seat when I reached the far end of our row, where the most attractive woman I had ever seen in my entire life stood up so that I could squeeze through. She was in a red and white striped dress, with long flowing curls of brown hair, gold bracelets piled on her wrist, and puffy lips shaded Ole Miss red. The only thing missing from her getup was a diamond studded tiara on her head and a Miss America sash thrown over her shoulder. I scooted by her and looked her square in her flawless face when I went by. In the most restrained way possible she tossed me into the sky with her eyes and slammed me into the concrete between the metal bleachers, all with an eyeroll so subtle that I was the only one who could possibly see it. She had her boring husband next to her in a gingham Southern Tide shirt with matching Ole Miss Croakies. He looked helpless but wealthy, and I burped under my breath and exhaled the polluted scent of cheap whiskey and Coke toward his feet when I shuffled by him.

I joined Caleb in a padded chairback seat, an empty space flanking us on either side. I stretched out, draping an arm across the vacant seat beside me, drawing more jealous glares. I savored a long drink of my whiskey cocktail, and I scanned the Auburn sideline below us. It was nearly time for kickoff and the team looked amped up and jittery.

Auburn had a team full of good football names on the 2018 roster. We had Big Kat Bryant, Jarrett Stidham, Boobie Whitlow, Brodarious Hamm, but my favorite owned the best. Though I knew he couldn't hear me, once I spotted him stalking up and down the field, I cupped my hands over my mouth, and at the top of my lungs, I yelled, "Smoke Monday! You're my favorite player!" My cheer was drowned out by the blaring public address announcer, and the Ole Miss band, The Pride of the South, playing to loud applause, and the rising hum of thousands of excited conversations, and then one shrieking female voice with an accent culled somewhere deep in the Mississippi backwoods, who screamed with frightening clarity above the cacophony. "LET'S GO REBELS!"

It was the attractive woman at the end of our row. She straightened her hand and placed it atop her head to mimic a shark fin and she danced to the thumping beats blasting through the stadium speakers. She knew the players' names, too, but she called them by their first names like they were all her nephews. "Take it to the house, Elijah!" "Block your ass off, Jason!"

I bumped Caleb on the shoulder and got his attention. "As a feminist, a defender of all women," I said loudly into his ear, "if you forced me, barrel of a gun, to rank all of them based on who I would defend, first to last, the shrieking female voice at a football game would be the last category of woman I would choose to defend."

"I guess this one didn't wink at you on the way by?"

"She did not."

"Maybe if you stare at her long enough, she'll come to her senses."

Caleb was right. I was watching her more than the field, so I returned my attention to the game where the Auburn kicker booted the football over the backline of the endzone. When there was a lull in the crowd noise while the Ole Miss offense and the Auburn defense took the field, I stood up and added one more jeer. "Let's go, Referees! Remember what we talked about!" I yelled and I rubbed my fingertips together like I was sifting through a folded wad of cash.

Hundreds of people heard me. Not one of them laughed.

And then my nemesis down the way yelled back, "Take a seat, douchebag!" and of course people laughed at that, because she's attractive. Next, she directed her bitchy voice to the field and yelled, "Easy six, Rebels! These boys lost to Tennessee!"

Ole Miss' quarterback took the first snap out of the shotgun. The Rebels wore their sharp home uniform, red jersey with dual white stripes over each shoulder, navy helmets featuring the red Ole Miss script, and silver pants. The quarterback had white socks pulled up to his knees that somehow made him appear bigger and more athletic than anyone else on the field. He completed an out route on his first pass. An easy nine-yard strike to the sideline. The Auburn defensive line did not penetrate the Ole Miss blockers in the slightest and the cornerback was a full step behind the receiver. It only took one innocuous play to stir up my Auburn dread. The husky voice down the row didn't help.

"Does our band know the Tennessee fight song!?" she shouted and laughed.

The Rebels earned a first down with a short run play, then a quick pass in the flat gained five more yards, followed by a QB keep on a read-option that picked up another quick first down.

"Why do they always look bigger and faster than us?" Caleb asked.

"I was just thinking the same thing," I told him.

The Ole Miss QB threw a bullet of a pass in the middle of our zone defense for another first down, then on the next play their running back broke free into the secondary before he tripped making a cut after another long gain. Twenty-one to nothin' Ole Miss looked entirely possible, though I'm not sure the Rebel partisans around us would agree by the way they screamed at the referees about a missed facemask and hollered at their own players over a missed block. They wanted their team to score every time the ball was snapped, and they were so shocked when it didn't happen, the only rational explanation was their own common mistake or

Auburn's common cheating. In doing so, they played right into my Plan B.

First, we needed a stop, and we needed it bad, and I knew just who to look to for inspiration. I focused on Smoke Monday in the secondary. He always played with a war raging inside of him even when the defense was on its heels, and this attitude often permeated to his teammates and even to his fans in the stands. He looked ready. Like he was going to make something happen.

"Here comes a stop," I said to Caleb. "I can feel it."

"I don't know, man. It's not looking good," Caleb said. "We need to summon Tommy Tuberville. He'd have a defense ready for this."

"How do you summon Tommy Tuberville?"

"It's not as easy as finding his bones. You have to take 25 perfectly shaped, perfectly colored Golden Flake potato chips, crush them into a fine powder, and mix with two droplets of the blood of Fred Talley, then you must snort the mixture off a Miami hooker, body part of your choice."

"Who's Fred Talley?"

"He's an Auburn legend," Caleb answered, and paused, "who played for Arkansas. It's a long story."

On 2nd and 10, an Ole Miss player sprinted in motion out of the slot position and ran behind the quarterback, who forcefully slapped his hands together. This action drew anxious Auburn defenders offside. The center reacted quickly and snapped the ball while the defenders were stuck in the neutral zone. A yellow penalty flag flew in the air. The quarterback slung a pass deep down the sideline beyond a frozen Auburn cornerback that had his eyes locked in the backfield. When the Ole Miss receiver broke free, it looked certain he would catch the pass and jog into the endzone untouched, but just as the ball neared the receiver's hands, Smoke Monday burst toward the boundary like a screaming eagle descending toward its prey. From our angle, when Smoke Monday laid into that receiver, and there was an audible crash of helmets and pads, I thought he might have decapitated him. The ball trickled away, incomplete, and the Ole Miss cheerleaders nearby recoiled backwards and placed their pom poms over their faces, shocked at the violence of the impact.

A thunderous crack of sound rushed through the stadium as thousands of Ole Miss fans yelled at once, their anger directed at Smoke Monday. Every space of Vaught-Hemingway filled with fervent booing.

"TARGETING!" They screamed and put their fists against their heads, mimicking the referees hand signal for the penalty.

"GET THAT BOY OUTTA HERE!" They yelled. A penalty for targeting meant an automatic ejection.

The referees conferred with each other. The head ref announced the official call of offside and targeting, both penalties against Auburn, but then he notified the crowd the play was under video review. The initial shockwave of noise died down, and just as it quieted, I stood up from my seat, cupped my hands over my mouth, and shouted, "Attaboy, 21! We play tackle football at Auburn!"

My nemesis at the end of the row didn't waste any time with her retort. "Hey Aubie!" she yelled, "Kiss your favorite player buh-bye!!" She snapped her fingers and waved her hand over her head with her tongue out.

Caleb leaned into me and said, "She's definitely hot, but she sounds like she eats Krystal burgers in the daytime."

"I don't know what that means, Caleb! More importantly, was that a targeting penalty? I cannot handle losing my favorite player."

"I'm sure the replay guy is flipping a coin right now."

"Let's change the bet. If Smoke Monday gets ejected, we leave right now."

Caleb ignored me. "The targeting rule is far too punitive," he said. "The yellow card, red card system from soccer makes the most sense, but a system that efficient would take too much celebrity away from the referees."

"Change to a soccer system? In America?"

The Ole Miss student section continued their jeers toward Smoke Monday, who once again paced the sideline, this time with his helmet pushed up on top of his head. He wore an expression of bewilderment as he watched the replay on the big video board, while the students sang *Na-na-na-naaa, Na-na-na-naaa, hey, hey, hey, goodbye!*

I was convinced we had lost Smoke to the arbitrary targeting rules. This disheartening thought fueled my campaign against the spectators around us. I turned to Caleb and with enough volume to be clearly heard by everyone, I said, "I can see why Tuberville left this dump for Auburn. Did I ever tell you I was accepted to go to school at Ole Miss?"

Caleb just sighed. He turned his attention away from me and looked at the scoreboard. At this point, he knew resistance was futile.

"There I was having breakfast at my kitchen table," I continued. "I had just polished off a box of Lucky Charms. I used a purple crayon and finished the maze on the back of the cereal box when suddenly there was a knock at the door. It was a representative from the University of Mississippi's admissions department. She handed me a personal letter notifying me I had been accepted into the Honors College. I think I was twelve years old. It was like a…what was that movie…with the arcade game and outer space…"

"The Last Starfighter."

"Yes! It was just like that."

A silver haired old woman seated on the row in front of us shook her head so vehemently that her red and blue tasseled earrings slapped against her earlobes. Another target for Plan B.

Meanwhile, the referees in the TV booth completed their review of the Smoke Monday penalty, and they radioed the news to the head referee in the white hat, who rushed back onto the field and addressed the crowd. "After further review," the referee said, "there was no targeting by Number 21…"

The referee's words were swallowed by another thunderous crack of sound that swept through Vaught-Hemingway, followed by a unison of bloodthirsty boos. This time, when I stood out of my seat and clapped, the fans around us were allied in opposition, and there were concentrated rebukes lobbed my way.

I slowly pumped my fist, yelling over them, "The check cleared!"

In a rage, the angry, red faced Ole Miss gal screamed, "Cheaters!" When she caught me peeking at her, she bobbed her head while she pointed to the field. "We'll still take the five yards, idiot!" she added, and high-fived her husband and a few others around her.

Since Auburn had jumped offsides before Smoke Monday's questionable hit, the officials stepped off the five-yard penalty and marked 2nd and 5. Ole Miss tried a run play, but the Auburn defense, reenergized by Smoke Monday, stopped the ball carrier for a gain of only one yard.

On 3rd and 4, Auburn sent a heavy blitz that caused the quarterback to rush his throw. He threw it at his receiver's feet for an incomplete pass.

On 4th and 4, Ole Miss brought out their field goal unit for a 40-yard attempt. Auburn blocked it.

The energy inside the stadium evaporated, leaving only the roars from the Auburn minority in the corner of the endzone, while the sense of dread fell upon the Ole Miss faithful. With the air sucked out of the stadium, it became so perfectly quiet during a TV timeout, it provided the perfect backdrop for further inane trash talk.

"I've been meaning to ask you something," I said to Caleb, "what the hell is a Hotty Toddy? Is it a reference to the drink, or is it some kind of a code for white supremacy?"

The old woman in front of us threw her hands up and guffawed. She looked at her husband and her seat neighbors to make sure they too had heard what I said.

"It isn't any different than War Eagle, really," Caleb explained. "A fabricated phrase used ubiquitously to signal allegiance to Ole Miss and confuse everyone else."

"Are you…"

"It's why I think Auburn's toilet paper tradition at Toomer's is the best," Caleb continued. "Auburn wins a game, and we roll our own trees with toilet paper to celebrate. It's toilet paper. It's meant to wipe your ass. People should make fun of that tradition, but the more they do, the more the toilet paper galvanizes our fanbase."

"Has that gummy not worn off yet? Jesus!" I said. I noticed the old lady had now angled her body slightly to the left to make sure she faced me with her good ear, so I laid it on. "Anyway, speaking of white supremacy," I added, "I heard Eli Manning used to party with the best of 'em back when he attended Ole Miss."

I had clearly crossed the line. The old woman, stiff back and all, corkscrewed around and glared at me like I was trying to return a long overdue library book. "Are you gonna yap your ignorant gums all day" she growled, "or at some point will your pea brain empty of stupid things to say? God, the stink of Alabama makes me unwell." Her whole body shook as her frame struggled with the sudden spike in hatred, but she wasn't done yet. She put her hand over her chest to quiet her beating heart and added, "And it's little brother," she groaned. "Not even a full dose of Alabama!"

"I'm sorry, ma'am," I said and smiled. Faking a slight Southern accent, I continued. "In Eli's case, in the case of all the Mannings, a genteel family who rightfully command our love and respect, I meant white supremacist as in supremely talented person who happens to be white."

"Oh, enough of your bull crap!" she barked. "If you'd rather make fun of my beloved university, for God's sake, why don't you do it from a distance and leave us!"

Several rows of people were now aware of the incident. They stood on the bleachers and craned their necks to get a look at the verbal beatdown this woman was dishing out.

Suddenly, the husband of the striking Ole Miss woman at the end of the row appeared next to me, instructed to defend the row's honor. With anger clearly etched on his face, he asked, "Are you giving this nice woman a hard time?"

I got right up in his face, towering over him, and said, "I think she's holding her own just fine. Who wants to know?"

"How'd you get tickets over here? Who sold them to you?" he demanded.

My jaw tightened as I shot back, "That's none of your goddamned business."

I don't know what he intended to do next, probably nothing, but as he took an aggressive step forward, his foot landed on the tray of nachos I had slung under my seat. He slipped, and in a desperate attempt to regain his balance, his hand flung upward, inadvertently knocking the cocktail from my grasp. The cup hovered in the air momentarily, ice tipping over the rim, before it crashed into the old woman seated in front of me, spilling sticky coke and the sweet stench of bourbon all over her silver hair and the Ole Miss sweater she probably knitted herself. The husband collapsed into the arms of the surrounding fans, who propped him up, and he immediately turned his attention to the elderly woman, ensuring she was unharmed.

Though mortified, I must give Caleb due credit; he waited to confirm that no punches were forthcoming, before he scooted down the row, ignoring the death stares along the way, and hustled up the steps through the corridor. I had no choice but to follow. I took my time, basking in the small ovation that arose when the home fans realized I was leaving, too.

As I walked away, the husband puffed his chest out, triumphant like he had done something. His wife at the end of the row stepped completely out of the way when I reached her, like she was allergic to the Auburn germ infecting the stadium.

At the top of the stairs, I stopped at the tunnel and faced the field one last time, sad to abandon my Auburn Tigers so early, but confident that my mission on behalf of Caleb's mother was the more worthy endeavor. I looked past the gawking, angry Ole Miss fans, to that glorious, green field and found Smoke Monday on the sideline, and this time I whispered to him, "War Eagle."

When I reached Caleb, who was cowering behind a support beam on the concourse, I asked, "Is your cousin going to be mad?"

"I don't really care."

"We're going to Clarksdale, aren't we?"

"We could go to the other side of the stadium, if you want, squeeze into the Auburn section somewhere."

"Or, we could go to Clarksdale."

"If we leave now, you need to see The Square."

"What's so good about it?"

"Nothing, really. We'll find a bar, have a quick think, watch a little more of the game."

"Then go to Clarksdale?"

Caleb didn't answer, he started walking toward the exit, but I refused to let him off that easy. Channeling the Auburn Spirit, I belted out the first few lines of the fight song, causing Caleb to increase his pace to an Olympic speed walk.

"War Eagle fly down the field
Ever to conquer never to yield
War Eagle fearless and true
Fight on your orange and blue"

A handful of Auburn fans were nearby, and when they heard me call out those lines, they finished the whole song themselves. Their voices gradually faded and vanished as we reached the empty turnstiles and exited Vaught-Hemingway.

I decided I wanted a beer for the walk, so first we found the tailgate stash, then we walked through campus toward The Square. The cool breeze dislodged an occasional leaf from the branches overhead in The Grove, and I watched their winding descent onto tents and into the mud. In the pantheon of sports beers I had consumed over the years, maybe none were more iconic than that lukewarm Michelob Ultra, amidst the graceful tailgating chaos and the tranquility of the Ole Miss campus. Making it better, in the distance behind us, there arose another loud groan from the stadium, a good omen for Auburn.

Another column topped with a familiarly diminutive Confederate soldier guarded the white, neoclassical Lafayette County Courthouse – the centerpiece of The Square. The courthouse was surrounded by two-story buildings with porches, decks, and porticos reminiscent of the late 19th-century perhaps, but these old structures were now fronted by upscale restaurants, fancy boutiques, and a handful of bars. Oxford was not immune from the dull gentrification fad of the modern college town. Auburn suffered from the same affliction, and as Caleb put it, it will suffer forever as a graveyard of rotating corporatized pizza joints and fast-food chains. At least in Oxford, the façade remained well enough intact for frequent glimpses of the quintessential South.

Caleb pointed out several notable bars, but he warned they could be crowded and pretentious. As an alternative, I accompanied him down a side street, through a narrow entrance, and descended a steep staircase into a cozy, dimly lit basement bar. The place had TVs hung on the walls tuned to other games, and earthy graduate students seated at tables around each screen, barely paying attention. The only television showing the Auburn game was a small one behind the L-shaped bar, where one other person had bellied up. She was a chic Ole Miss fan, older, perhaps in her 50's, sporting a mid-century updo and noticeable bags under her eyes. Clad in a sophisticated navy-blue dress, that appeared both simple and expensive, she enhanced the look with several strands of pearls wrapped around her neck and silver and gold cable bracelets adorned with rubies on her wrists.

Caleb hesitated, and I beat him to the barstool that was one space away from Oxford's version of Audrey Hepburn. She had a half-consumed martini in front of her with a napkin holding extra olives, and I had a line charged up and ready to go. But just as I got comfortable in my seat, she threw me off balance when she initiated the conversation.

"You boys didn't want to be in the stadium for this?" she asked, making eyes at the TV, using the most delicate, buttery Old South accent I had ever heard in real life. The game was at halftime, but the score flashed across the ticker at the bottom of the screen. Auburn 10, Ole Miss 6.

"It was getting a little too claustrophobic for us," I answered. "We were seated in somewhat of a hostile area for Auburn fans."

The bartender interrupted us. He had a ruddy beard that matched his stoned eyes. I ordered a shot of Jameson and two beers – one for me, one for Caleb – and asked the woman if she was ready for another martini.

"Not at the moment, thank you," she said, then behind a charming smile, she added, "We might get there eventually."

"And what about you, ma'am?" I asked. "Since you look like

you're dressed for the President's box, why aren't you in the stadium? You didn't trust Ole Miss would win?"

"I am more or less obligated to dress in a formal way," she sighed, "because certain Ole Miss people, my husband especially, have made it a tradition to outdress the team's level of success. Though I have to get all done-up, I am not obligated to go into the stadium."

"Why not?"

"What did you call it? Claustrophobic? I prefer the dark confines of a sleepy bar anyway."

"And what about The Grove?" I asked. "They say it's the best tailgate scene in the whole country and here you are hiding out."

"If you must know, I am *supposed* to be in The Grove guarding the fine china and whatnot." She took a heavy gulp of her martini. "Ridiculous as that may sound to an Auburn fan."

"Well, I sure hope there aren't any devious Auburn fans pillaging about. We met a man today that said there wasn't an honest Auburn man alive."

"It's the teenagers wearing Eli jerseys that you need to worry about. Fortunately, my son, The Genius, has loaned me two of his Sigma Chi pledges. They're on guard duty so that I could sneak away for a little respite." She lifted her glass. "I think I will take another," she said loud enough so that the bartender heard her clearly.

When the TV broadcast returned for the beginning of the third quarter. Auburn received the football, and it wasn't long before Boobie Whitlow broke a long run into Ole Miss territory.

"Ma'am," I began courteously, "you said your son was a genius. What's he doing at Ole Miss?" I asked.

She covered her mouth with her hand when she laughed, showing off the three-carat diamond she wore on her ring finger. "The Genius is on his third major and his seventh and final Rebel football season as an undergraduate student. On his parents' payroll anyway. He can stay as long as he'd like after that."

"Sounds like a genius to me," I told her. "My advice to college kids has always been the same: stay in as long are your parents will pay."

"No real genius, by the way I define the term, ever carried a 2.5 GPA," she replied.

"Aren't there several notable cases where bona fide geniuses performed terribly in school? Wasn't Einstein like this?"

"Einstein wasn't floating around the liberal arts department at the University of Mississippi." She scoffed and shook her head. "Poor child. He began his collegiate career with Houston Nutt and he's ending it with Matt Luke."

Right on cue, Auburn ran a wide receiver reverse and handed the ball off to Anthony Schwartz, the fastest man in college football, who raced along the sideline and dove toward the goal line, stepping out of bounds just short of the line. We scored a touchdown on the next play to pull ahead 17-9, and the game cut away again for another commercial break.

The woman looked agitated. She sighed and said, "You know the worst thing about this sport? The outcome might be inevitable to everyone with half a brain and yet it still takes four and half hours of advertisements to get there."

Caleb had been noticeably silent since we arrived at the bar, and he barely flinched when Auburn scored, but when the lady started to complain about the length of the game, he perked up and said, "Ma'am, I will drink to that," and he took a small sip of the beer he was babysitting.

"And I swear on all that's holy," the lady continued, "if I ever run into Gary Danielson of CBS in a bar, and if it were he who bought me a martini, I'd drink half of it, then I'd throw the other half in his face."

"What did Uncle Gary ever do to you?" I asked.

"For one thing, he's got his head so far up Nick Saban's ass…But my real problem is this - how much do you think they pay Gary Danielson?" she asked.

"A lot," I answered. "Just a hunch."

"I guarantee you he's making too much money," she replied.

"Why else do they need ten minutes of television commercials for every 20 seconds of actual football."

"There should be fluidity to the game," Caleb agreed. "A flow of drives and momentum and field position."

The woman sneered and added, "The only thing that flows in a football game is the sober breath of the referees blowing loudly through their whistles so they can masturbate to another technicality in the rule book." She mimicked pulling a flag from her back pocket and tossing it into the sky.

"Personally, I think they need to get rid of the game clock all together," Caleb started to say, but I'd heard this spiel 100 times over. Caleb wanted newfangled football rules to scrap extra points, kickoffs, substitutions, and yes, the game clock, and no, I wasn't about to listen to the diatribe again.

"Ma'am," I interjected, "I must warn you, if he talks for even one minute about this, he'll talk longer than it takes to finish a triple overtime game. I mean, really, get rid of the game clock? Who would do such a thing?"

Sourly, Caleb answered. "Someone who'd rather not sit through a slog versus a directional Michigan school."

"The golden rule should be this," the lady said. She lifted her martini to her face and sipped, then she made eyes at Caleb from behind the rim of the glass and said, "If I walk into a ballgame drunk, by the time the game is over with, I should still be tipsy." She placed her hand over her mouth again and covered a tiny burp.

"Aren't you worried about the game getting out of hand?" I asked. "Won't that send your husband running back to the tailgate to discover that you're missing?"

"My husband comments on the football message boards, so, I can assure you he will be in his seat, arms crossed, until the clock strikes zero," she said, trailing off. She pointed at Caleb, and said, "What's with this one over here? Auburn's winning yet he's babysitting his beer?"

"Somebody has to drive us to Clarksdale," I told her.

"Maybe," Caleb said.

"What do you mean, maybe?"

He shrugged, held his beer in his hand like he was going to drink it, but left it on the bar top.

"What's in Clarksdale?" the woman asked.

Caleb hesitated, so I patted him on the shoulder and answered again, "Tribulations with his family."

The woman snorted. "Family issues in the Mississippi Delta? You don't say."

"Do you know the place?" I asked.

"I had an uncle we used to visit there when I was younger. Haven't been back in a long time. I got out of this state the day after I graduated, and I am only forced to return for the football revelry."

"When's the next home game?"

"Two weeks."

"Who do you play in two weeks?"

"Hell, I don't know. It doesn't matter. There's only one game I really look forward to all year."

"Egg Bowl?" I guessed.

"No way. That game ruins my Thanksgiving every year. The game I look forward to, it doesn't really matter who we play. It's whatever game falls when all the leaves have turned their most vibrant. We get yellows, and reds, and maroons, some purple, and the only orange I'll tolerate."

"It's starting to show already."

"Next game should be perfect conditions."

"It's too bad we missed it."

She reached into her purse and checked her phone, then quickly snapped the purse shut again. "Tell me, is your family in Clarksdale's thin slice of eccentric upper crust? Or are they from the cotton pickin' side of town?" she asked Caleb.

Caleb answered quickly before I had a chance to protest her disparaging language that sounded awfully sinister to me. "Is there an upper crust in Clarksdale?" he asked.

"Once upon a time…"

"Put it this way," Caleb continued, "my grandmother was a homemaker, a hoarder, and an alcoholic who married a man that fixed cotton gins and was also an alcoholic."

"And your parents? What did they do?"

"My father left via an academic scholarship at Mississippi State, where he met my mother, and like you, they left the day after they graduated and rarely come back."

"It would have been such a romantic story, if not for Starkville being a part of the setting," she said and frowned. "Now I must imagine all the key characters wearing hunting camo from head-to-toe."

"Let me just say," I jumped in, "I met one of Caleb's cousins today, and I don't think they're camo people. This guy was dressed like an Ole Miss dandy." I put my elbow on the bar and rested my cheek against my fist, peering at her curiously, I changed the subject and asked, "What did you mean earlier when you said the 'cotton-pickin' side of town?"

I saw Caleb's head sink out of the corner of my eye, then he took a legitimate sip of beer.

The woman laughed in response, deep in her throat, and said, "Darlin', please don't bring any of that political bullshit in here. Trust me, in Mississippi, in places like Clarksdale, they're already through the looking glass. Only thing that segregates people anymore are the haves and the have nots, and it sounds to me like he comes from the have nots, if that's a more delicate way of stating it for your precious little heart."

Caleb agreed. "I'll drink to that," he said, and took a second sip of beer.

"This shouldn't surprise you," the woman began, "given that you found me in a dingy little bar drinking all by myself, but I do love good gossip, especially about family – what did you call it – tribulations?"

I clarified. "It's more like a mystery, really."

"Oh, do tell," she purred.

"The only mystery," Caleb said dryly, "is whether it will be one disappointment or another."

I rolled my eyes and dismissed Caleb with a wave of my hand. "Don't mind his nonchalant attitude. It's all an act. You see, ma'am, there is both news and a package from an unknown sender that was intended for Caleb's father, may he rest in peace, but now his grandfather in Clarksdale is in possession of it all. The grandfather has kept both the news and the contents of the package a complete secret from the rest of the family, including Caleb's own mother, for reasons unknown."

"Could be money," the lady said.

"Exactly," I said.

"An inheritance of some kind? Property?" the lady guessed again.

"The only thing I stand to inherit," Caleb shot back, "is some rare form of cancer. Trust me, in my family, nothing good ever comes from looking back further than yesterday."

Caleb had unwittingly given me an opportunity to show-off the reading I had done leading up to the trip. I loudly rapped the bar top and said, "Wasn't it Faulkner who said the past is never dead, it's not even..." I began, but the woman nearly choked on an olive, and raised her hand to stop me.

"Lord have mercy, please don't start quoting William Faulkner in Oxford, Mississippi," she chuckled.

"Why not?"

"A little too on-the-nose, don't you think?"

Caleb's continued conversation spared me from furthered humiliation. "Given that I haven't warned my friend about Dino, more particularly, Dino's house, I'll explain it to you both and put to rest any thoughts of inheritance."

"Your grandfather is named Dino?" the woman questioned.

"His full name is Dean Orlando. Dean O. It's what everyone has always called him, even his own children, who mangled the spelling into D-I-N-O."

"And what warning does Dino's house come with?" I asked.

"Toward the end of my grandmother's life, the house started to turn. She couldn't move well so she'd sit at her table and chain smoke skinny cigarettes watching all of their hoarded shit pile up around her, waiting to die. When she did, we were never invited back to Clarksdale, and I can only imagine the house has digressed under Dino's watch since then."

"Sometimes slobs have buried treasure," I said.

"Or buried skeletons."

"Oh," I said, nodding along in agreement, "Like Tommy Tuberville."

Caleb laughed, but I watched the smile fade quickly, as he studied the condensation beading on his glass. He broke the silence, saying, "Most of the crazy Dino stories occurred long before me, and were retold by uncles and cousins. I imagine those stories were stretched to the limits of their truthfulness. But not necessarily their usefulness."

"Sounds like State people, all right," the woman joked.

"We'd visit during Easter and Thanksgiving, and first thing my father did as soon as we arrived was walk me into Dino's TV room where Dino would hand me a $50 savings bond, and in a big scary voice he'd ask me the same question every time: 'You gonna be a Mississippi State Bulldog?' I'd smile, and nod, and then hide from him the rest of the trip."

"It's no wonder you didn't go to State," the woman said, "but how'd you end up at Auburn?"

"I actually left that decision up to chance."

"How so?"

"I applied to every college that finished in the top-25 after the 1998 college football season."

"I'm sure your parents were thrilled. How many were you accepted into?"

"I didn't get into Air Force, Georgia Tech, a couple others. I don't remember."

"Was Ole Miss in the top-25 that year?" the woman asked.

"Nope."

"Probably our usual ranking of 'received votes,'" she added.

"How did Auburn finish?" I asked.

"Auburn was the exception. They were terrible in 1998. Fired Terry Bowden in the middle of the year, and began a butterfly effect that brought us Tuberville."

"So, you applied to 26 schools?" I asked.

"No, I substituted Auburn for the one school in the top-25 I wanted no part of attending."

"Who?"

"Syracuse."

"I don't blame you one bit there," the woman agreed. "But what did chance have to do with Auburn?"

"You remember that black and white Bo Jackson poster everyone had in their room in the 90's?"

"Shoulder pads with a baseball bat over his shoulders?" I asked.

"I had that poster, too." Caleb said. "Bo Knows. I played Tecmo Bo. I wore a Kansas City Royals hat. I cheered for the Raiders. I loved the interlocking AU logo because Bo looked good in it, so I added Auburn to the list, and I put them all in a hat, and I drew one."

"Picked Auburn?" the woman asked.

"Picked Auburn."

"You're full of shit," I told him.

"My parents thought I was full of shit, too, because I had never even seen the campus before. They made me take a tour of Auburn before I officially attended. It just so happened that on that tour I met the most idyllic Southern belle from Fairhope, Alabama. I thought about her for months after that day, until I was officially a student at Auburn, and then I searched for her, theoretically I suppose, for four years."

"You ever see her again?" the woman asked.

"I never saw her again."

Someone seated at a table behind us groaned. Auburn had regained possession of the football, and Boobie Whitlow took a delayed handoff, dodged through the Ole Miss secondary, fumbled the football into the endzone, where it was recovered by Anthony Schwartz for a touchdown.

"Is there a similar rite of passage in Auburn this time of the year?" she asked, "When you watch the season tumble down the drain?"

"It's the same in Auburn," Caleb answered, "just not as early or often as at Ole Miss."

After the extra point, Auburn led 24-9. I looked at Caleb and said, "That's all she wrote, so, are we going to Clarksdale, or not?"

Caleb thought about it for a second, then he looked at the woman at the bar, and asked for her advice. "What do you think I should I do?"

"You don't need my advice."

"I specifically asked for it."

Her eyes narrowed on Caleb before she said, "When I left Mississippi, I knew what I was running from. You can't truly escape something if you don't know what it is. It's a lot like the autumn leaves in The Grove. Their beauty may capture our attention, but to truly appreciate them, I think you must understand the tree that brought them into existence."

The front door upstairs jolted open, and a fresh-faced kid descended the steps with a heavy-footed gait. He wore skinny khaki pants that were rolled to his ankles, with blue and red striped socks, a striped tie to match, horse-bit loafers, and a blue blazer with bronze buttons. He carried a red shawl under his arm.

"You're early," the woman said when the college kid reached us at the bar.

"We've got a little problem, Mrs. Dansby," the kid said sheepishly.

"I know the problem isn't Mr. Dansby because there's still time on the clock, so what happened?"

"There was a little run-in with some Kappa Sigs," he stated, flatly.

Mrs. Dansby knew right away the full implication of an Ole Miss frat fight. She gathered her purse immediately while the pledge wrapped the shawl around her shoulders. She waltzed around the end of the bar and patted me on the back like we were old chums, then she said, "It sure was fun speaking with you Auburn boys. Be careful driving to Clarksdale, and if you can take barbecue advice from a woman who wore Louboutin's to a muddy football tailgate," Mrs. Dansby added and clicked her heels against the floor, "don't forget to eat at Abe's while you're in town."

She offered her arm to the Ole Miss fraternity brother, then she sauntered up the steps like an actress walking over the red carpet to accept an award, leaving us with her entire bar tab.

"I don't think we have any choice but to go now," I said. "While we've still got plenty of time."

Finally, Caleb agreed. I paid our tab and we hustled back to our rental car in the church parking lot, where I took the keys out of my pocket and tossed them to Caleb.

"You okay to drive?" I asked.

Caleb caught the keys and nodded, then climbed into the driver's seat and started the car. "Let's go through the checklist," he said, "just in case."

I walked behind the car and Caleb tapped the brakes. The lights glowed red. Caleb flipped the blinkers, left then right, both yellow lights worked, so I walked to the front of the car, and we tested those blinkers, too, and the headlights. Everything worked fine, so I climbed into the passenger seat.

Caleb said, "Every state trooper between here and Clarksdale is watching football right now anyway. We could do 100mph and all they'd do is flash their lights at us to slow down."

"Let's not risk that kind of exposure."

Caleb agreed with me. He removed the Auburn hat from his head and placed it in his lap while he drove us out of Oxford. I tuned the radio to the Ole Miss broadcast of the football game and listened to the misery and disappointment that filled the voices of the home team's announcers. We rejoiced in their torment, as we headed due west on Mississippi Highway 6 with Auburn leading 31-9 in the 4$^{th}$-quarter.

We passed through Batesville again, and the Waffle House, then continued to the Mississippi Delta. The landscape flattened into fields of soybeans, corn, and cotton, framed by thick forests of dark trees like looming shadows on the horizon. The mild autumn temperatures had only lightly dimmed the Delta's green fertility, and amid these emerald tones were boarded up cotton gins and rusted farm equipment lying dormant among the weeds. These remnants, evidence of a bygone era, were stark reminders of when the region was the golden buckle in the cotton belt. A buckle that was polished by the black hands of the enslaved, and then the socially oppressed, and then finally, the technology and machinery the white money preferred. What cotton we saw along the highway was up and ready to be harvested, and what had already been picked was baled and covered in bright yellow tarps arranged near the road. There was less of it than I expected. The crop had been reduced to a relic of a more prosperous time.

We reached the edge of Clarksdale around the time the clock expired in the 4$^{th}$ quarter. Auburn won 31-16. Caleb clicked the radio off and put the Auburn hat back on his head. He steered onto State Street where a picked over cotton field abutted a series of government duplexes. Laundry, weathered and faded, flapped on clotheslines staked between each unit. Then, the familiar, Southern landscape emerged. Churches, gas stations, Dollar stores, most of them instilled with a sense of struggle.

We passed side streets lined with shotgun shacks, ramshackle apartment buildings, and trailers covered in TV antennas and window a/c units. Within the same block, a divide was evident. Some homes were lovingly maintained with manicured vegetable gardens and terra cotta pots full of flowers on the porch, while other lots were destitute, overrun, or trapped out. There were vehicles everywhere, parked along the street or jammed into driveways and underneath carports, many of them broken down. As a contrast, every so often there was at least one mid-2000's Chevy Tahoe with shining 24" rims. Yet, there were still pedestrians walking around, lending an urban feel to this remote town, like Clarksdale had been plucked from the anonymity of a larger city and dropped into the open fields of Mississippi, unmasked and unhidden.

Catching me staring wide-eyed out the window, Caleb broke the silence, "Were you expecting a sweaty Ashley Judd and Matthew McConoughey to roll out the welcome mat for you?" he asked.

"I suppose it looks a little more impoverished than what I imagined, though I see plenty of signs of resilience despite the obvious hardships."

"Keep your eyes opened wide," Caleb said. "Clarksdale is a bona fide piece of American history. These people here picked it.

They spun it. They weaved the rug that, when it was all said and done, was yanked from under their feet, rolled up, and slung over someone else's shoulder, who skipped town without ever looking back."

We drove through an industrial ghost town with abandoned machine shops along railroad tracks and a big blue hardware supply building with boarded doors and busted windows. The rail lines were still running, but they didn't need to stop much in Clarksdale anymore; instead, the train cars continued through a canopy of trees and out into the fields, offering a panoramic of the Mississippi countryside that would have looked identical had it been Caleb's father driving by in 1955 or any year since.

We turned onto a small bridge that crossed over the sleepy Sunflower River and entered a neighborhood with houses more quintessentially Southern, though modest in scale. There were welcoming porches and yards big enough to mow, but still the occasional decrepit lot or abandoned house. With more room in this neighborhood, the trees flourished - magnificent magnolias, maples, and grand oaks framed every view.

Venturing further into the neighborhood, Caleb slowed to a stop in front of a small house with a steep roofline and jagged, tattered shingles that had collected rows of brown pine needles. The dead plants in the empty flower beds caught trash in broken limbs, while the front door, guarded by chipped wrought iron columns, seemed untouched for years, with clumps of wasp nests stuck to the door frame. The driveway overflowed with vehicles, so Caleb parked the car along the front lawn. There was a rusted tan Suburban and a Mercury Comet under the carport and two 90's era Cadillac sedans behind them, one forest green and the other beige, then a recent model Nissan Altima with shiny metallic rims and tinted windows that could not contain the bass from the rap music thumping inside.

The poor condition of the house made me anxious. Encountering unaccounted for strangers made the feeling worse.

"I had imagined it would be one lonely old man," I said.

"Are you nervous? You look nervous."

"I'm only nervous if you're nervous. Are you nervous?"

"Why would I be nervous?"

"I don't know!"

"Listen, you don't have to go in if you don't want to. You can just sit in the car."

"Aren't I obligated to go in?"

"Why?"

"Because I'm your friend and I've come all this way with you. And you might need protection."

"Protection from what?" Caleb laughed.

"I don't know. Who's in the Altima?"

Caleb shrugged and said, "Let's go find out." He got out of the car and spun his keys around his finger as he walked toward the Altima. Before he reached it, he stopped and warned me. "Oh, if there's an old black woman inside the house, she's mean as hell. You don't have to speak to her. She'll understand. Trust me."

"Okay," I said, confused.

There was an African American girl in the driver's seat of the Altima. She was 18 or 19 and had a Big K.R.I.T song playing at near max volume while she held her phone to her face at an angle and recorded herself angrily rapping the lyrics.

Caleb tapped a knuckle on the glass and got her attention. She turned the volume down and cracked the window.

"Dino in there?" Caleb asked.

She didn't look disturbed in the least by the two white boys interrupting her. She had looked angry rapping and she looked angry at us. "This his house, ain't it?" she said, and then she returned the song to full throttle and raised the window.

Caleb didn't seem bothered. He slipped between the vehicles underneath the carport to a Dutch backdoor with the top half swung open and a screen covering it. He punched the thumb lock on the screen and pulled it back. It screeched so loudly that a dog in the backyard next door reflexively barked.

"Tiffani!" the strong female voice hollered from inside, loud enough that the dog next door yelped and went silent. "I told you to keep your black ass in the goddamned car!"

Caleb took a deep breath then called out, "Tiffani is doing as she's told. I'm here to see Dino. He around?"

A long pause followed. Caleb just stood there, staring at his shoes.

"You the police?" the woman finally replied.

"No ma'am."

"You from Tunica?"

"I'm Dino's grandson."

"His what!?"

"His grandson!" Caleb said, louder this time.

After another short pause, she asked, "Which one!?"

"It's Caleb!"

One final pause, before she hollered, "Then what you standin' at the door for!?"

Caleb opened the bottom half of the Dutch door, and we walked inside to an appalling yellow kitchen surrounded by drab, wood paneled walls and contact paper along the ceiling decorated with the faded images of vegetables tarred from age, grime, and cigarette smoke. Pots were piled in the sink. Dirty dishes covered the countertops and unopened mail covered everything else. The pantry closet in the corner was left open and the shelves were mostly empty save one row of neatly packed, brightly colored boxes of sugary cereals – Smacks, Trix, Golden Crisps, and so on. The house smelled old, the bad kind of old, like sour milk left on the bedside table at an indigent nursing home. I put my sleeve over my mouth and alternated breaths through my nose and mouth, deciding I'd rather taste it than smell it.

An elderly African American woman wearing maroon scrubs and a shiny weave of black curls sat on a wooden stool at a nook adjacent the kitchen. Her silver name tag said Lula. She rested her elbow against a tabletop and curled her jagged wrist under her chin where two white hairs protruded in opposite directions.

"Dino ain't got no money," she said and peered at us like we here to sell something. Behind her, in a room around the corner, a whistle blew on a TV, and I recognized immediately the voice of CBS' Gary Danielson describing a play in the Alabama game.

"Isn't it obvious that there isn't any money to ask for?" Caleb asked, a precarious time to be sardonic, I thought.

"One of your cousins came by just the other day, and he asked for money."

"It was my cousin Aaron that sent me here. Was it Aaron?"

"Which one's Aaron? He the…" and she sat up straight and flittered her fingers in the air.

Caleb did not acknowledge her insinuation in the slightest.

Lula returned to her slouched posture. "Aaron came for Laverne's jewelry, worthless junk that it is, then asked Dino to invest in some damned political cockamamie bullshit he's got going on."

"I'm only here because I was told to come here," Caleb said.

The woman squinted and strained to see Caleb. She removed a pair of glasses from her shirt pocket and when she put them on, her eyes enlarged to an exaggerated size from the severe magnification. She blinked several times.

"Did your daddy ever tell you about Aunt Deidra?" she asked.

"Deidra, his nanny?"

"That's right."

"Just that she was generous with him."

Lula scowled. "Deidra? Generous? That would be the first time anyone called that sour old woman generous."

"That was the joke. Father's punchline was that Aunt Dee generously allowed him to pick the switch she'd whip him with if he spoke out of turn."

"Uh-huh. That's more like it," Lula nodded, familiar with the concept Caleb described. "And if the switch wasn't thick enough for her liking, she'd go back after the biggest, thickest motherfucker on the tree."

"Yeah, but Father also told me that even the thickest switches were better than the alternative," Caleb said and nodded toward the room with the TV.

The woman readjusted herself in her seat. She took a deep breath that whistled through her nose. "Dino is sitting on his chair watching the ballgames," she said. "I can't take this other cracker back there unless I know who he is." She narrowed her eyes on me.

"A friend of mine is all," Caleb answered.

"Hello, my name is Jeremy. We've been at the game in Oxford," I told her, smiling wide, so she would understand I posed no threat. Any other introductory niceties seemed wildly inappropriate given the tense mood.

"Dino don't like guests in the house," she said. "Especially not no guests wearing that silly Auburn shit."

"We won't be long," Caleb reassured her.

The broken thatch on the back of her chair crackled as she stood up slowly and braced herself on Caleb's arm. "Let me warn him," she said and ambled toward the back of the house like every bone in her body ached. "Dino!" she repeated at louder volumes as she moved into the living room. "Dino!!"

My instincts didn't want to see the rest of the house, but my curiosity was still spiked with liquid courage. I followed on Caleb's heels as he slowly walked behind Lula. There was a sitting area at the front of the room with an old cloth chair, green and covered in a layer of dust with spools of needlepoint thread and unfinished canvases stacked on the cushion. A brown plaid couch and a low rising coffee table were both buried beneath weeks old editions of the *Commercial Appeal* and the *Clarksdale Press Registe*r that were in turn littered with shotgun shells and Native American arrowheads displayed in small glass boxes.

Dino lounged in a grey La-Z-Boy in front of a 30-year-old TV, the big boxy kind that weighed a ton, where Alabama was up 44-14 on Tennessee. Hanging on the wall over the TV there was a framed, tattered Confederate battle flag.

The old man either ignored us or he couldn't hear us over Verne Lundquist calling the play-by-play at full volume. I could only see the wispy hair on top of Dino's fat head, the dark liver spots on his flabby arm, the pasty hand that held a blue can of RC Cola, and his pallid feet propped on the footrest with yellow toenails so long they curled where they hadn't cracked and broken. On a small end table next to the recliner, along with three empty cans of RC, there was a small box wrapped in brown paper tied with twine.

Lula walked in front of Dino's recliner and snapped her fingers to get his attention. She leaned over and said something into his ear, then waited with her hands upturned on her hips. Dino didn't move except to raise his index finger high enough to point at the TV. Alabama's quarterback dropped back to pass, stepped into the pocket to avoid a rush, got hit hard as soon as he threw, but floated a beautiful ball down the middle of the field to a wide-open receiver who caught the pass and scored another Crimson Tide touchdown. We all stood there silently and watched the whole play unfold, then Dino aimed the brick of a remote at the TV and mashed the mute button.

"Boy!" he called out. "Lemme see you!" His voice was a low grumble that sounded more like an old cop shouting demands than it did a grandfather eager to see his grandson.

Caleb casually switched places with Lula, who shooed me back toward the kitchen so grandfather and grandson could have their privacy. I moved slowly so that I could hear what Dino said.

"When you were a boy," Dino barked at Caleb, "you'd sit on my lap, and I'd ask you if you was gonna be a Mississippi State Bulldog! 'Yessir, I will be one day,'" Dino mocked in a boyish tone.

Caleb spread his feet and crossed his arms and looked down upon Dino. "Don't worry old man, I'm not going to sit in your lap this time," he said. "And I didn't go to Mississippi State because I got into a better school first."

"Then why'd you go to some cow college in Alabama?" Dino snapped back and coughed out a laugh. "Lula! You still back there?" he hollered after he gathered his breath.

Lula had dragged me around the corner when she stopped and said, "What you need, Dino?"

"My medicine."

"You already took your medicine, Dino."

"My other medicine!"

"What other medicine you talking about you big dummy?"

"The medicine I take with warm milk."

Lula froze. Her eyes slowly closed, and her hands clasped together in prayer.

"Lula!?" Dino yelled again. "You better bring me my medicine so I can tell this nigger boy here 'bout his nigger Daddy!"

The air rushed out of my lungs like I had been kicked in the windpipe, and my ears stung with a piercing ring as if a 12-pound cannon next to me had been fired across a field. The disgusting, thick twang he applied to that word sounded as red as any neck that ever hid beneath a white hood, as though Dino himself created that vile term and unleashed all the terror behind it.

Nobody else even flinched. Caleb's expression of fatigued annoyance didn't twist off his face despite the fact he had been called this name for some inexplicable reason, and Lula, the real victim of this awful slur, ended her solemn prayer and obediently walked into the kitchen to do as she was told. And so, it was left up to me to defend her honor, and to protest this racist piece of shit. However, just as I began to take one step toward Dino, and just before I hollered my admonishment, Lula struck me down cold as though she had read my mind and knew exactly what I intended to do.

"You better fucking not, White Boy," she said and scowled at me and wagged her finger.

The sheer severity in her voice removed any intention I had of cutting Caleb's grandfather down to size. Instead, I lost my balance. I took an awkward step sideways, tripped over a stack of *National Geographic* magazines on the floor, and balanced myself against the wood paneling on a wall next to a wooden gun case filled with hunting rifles. A framed needlepoint of Robert E. Lee tilted askew.

Lula rolled her eyes at me with a look of great disappointment, then she opened the refrigerator door and removed a carton of skim milk. She twisted the cap off the top, sniffed inside the carton, then retrieved a tall, cloudy glass, and filled it halfway with milk. She placed the glass in a filthy microwave, punched in a couple numbers, and while the milk warmed, she opened a cabinet door and found a bottle of red label scotch. When the microwave beeped, she removed the warm milk and filled the rest of the glass with booze, then used a butter knife from the sink to mix the cocktail.

"Take this to Dino," she told me, "My ankles hurtin'. You don't say nothin' in there, you hear me? It ain't none of your business."

I took the cocktail and followed orders. Caleb's demeanor and posture was exactly as I had left him, only now he held the package in one hand. He took a few steps toward me and spared me the uncomfortable embarrassment of meeting his grandfather.

"Sorry about all this," he whispered.

"You all right?"

"Absolutely not."

"I can't stay in this room, or she'll kill me."

"Go to the car if you want," he said. He reached into his pocket and handed me the keys.

I returned to Lula and found her seated in the same wicker-back chair where we initially confronted her.

"Sit down here in MeeMee's old spot," she said, and pointed to a chair at the empty dining room table, where she had placed a crystal whiskey glass that held three fingers of scotch. I sat down and sipped from it. I needed the drink.

"I got a story I'm going to tell you about a man named Charlie Ray Walker and I need you to listen and listen good. You understand me?" she asked and waited for me to verbally agree.

I heard her, but I did not understand. Not in the slightest. I had never heard the name Charlie Ray Walker in my life and without any frame of reference, Lula sounded completely insane. But I was too afraid to tell her, so I nodded again, affirmatively, and said, "Yes ma'am," then I listened, intently, like I would be quizzed about it later.

"When that boy, Caleb, gets done in there with Dino, I already know he's gonna run out of here without stopping to hear my side, you understand?" Again, she waited for my acknowledgement.

"Yes ma'am," I repeated.

"I knew Charlie Ray when I was a little girl. He was the most handsome light-skinned man I'd ever seen, with bright green eyes, and I know the history of how he came to be that way. His grandmother was a sharecropper. Black woman. She was raped by a white transient when she was just a girl, gave birth to Charlie Ray's mother, and his mother met a man in Atlanta who was a shade light himself, and they came back here to Clarksdale and it's here where they birthed Charlie Ray. He played jazz piano when he grew up, and he was good. Took a white girl to Memphis to see one of his gigs, and there he got her pregnant, and when he found out, he was so scared, he left for Chicago, leaving the white woman and her baby behind. That baby was Caleb's daddy."

Lula had made this revelation without any trace of emotion, and so I almost missed it. Dino was not Caleb's father's father. Dino was not Caleb's blood grandfather at all. Charlie Ray Walker was.

"Now here's what I want you to know," Lula continued, "Dino always knew about Charlie Ray Walker and MeeMee, because Dino came along just after the baby was born and he took that baby in like he was his own. He didn't have to neither. And he knew the repercussions. But he did it anyway and it's important that Caleb knows that."

She stopped and adjusted her weight in the chair, then just sat and stared at a plastic bird clock ticking on the wall. Apparently, she was finished talking.

"There is something I don't understand," I said, soft-spoken and respectful. "Why do you tolerate him saying that awful word in front of you?"

"That ain't nothing but a word my family says all the time, and Dino's done more for my family than anybody else in my family, so that makes him family. Not to mention, this is Dino's house. He can say whatever he wants."

"You might understand it caught me off guard. That's not how I feel about it. Especially not when it was directed to my friend while he's standing beneath a battle flag."

Lula laughed like I had said something ignorant. "That flag ain't nothing more than geography. I swear, this country has turned people into…"

But Lula did not finish her point. Just as she had predicted, Caleb turned the corner with the unopened box in hand, walking nearly as fast as he had when we escaped Vaught-Hemingway Stadium. For the first time since we had arrived at Dino's, Lula's eyes revealed something other than contempt. There was compassion in them as she watched Caleb breeze between us, intense compassion, that studied him up and down.

"Let's go," Caleb said and nothing more.

Lula offered me one more critical glare to let me know I was no longer welcome, was never welcome in the first place. I handed her the glass that still had a nip of scotch inside of it as a peace offering. She accepted it, drank it, and set it on the counter, where from the looks of the other items around it, the glass would sit for a long, long time. I followed Caleb out of the musky kitchen and through the squeaky screen door, through the carport and Cadillacs and Tiffani in the Altima.

We got in the rental car, but we didn't go anywhere. Just sat there with the car in park, each of us waiting for the other to begin. Caleb had one hand on the steering wheel and the other hand delicately cradled the unopened box on his lap.

"I was thinking…" I began to say, but Caleb silenced me with a quick, "Save it for a minute. There's some place I want to see one last time. Don't imagine I'll be back ever again. God willing."

I checked my watch to make sure we had time to make it to the airport in Memphis, then Caleb took one last look at the old house, its decay amplified in the waning light. We drove in silence around a bend where the road narrowed, and the sunset was swallowed by vine-covered trees. He veered onto a gravel path and stopped next to a white picket fence. The headlights illuminated a narrow stretch of the river, 30 yards wide, canopied by trees, where the water gently turned and pooled.

"We called it the Duck Pond," Caleb said. "The cousins and I would come down here with a loaf of bread and hide out as long as we could stand it."

Caleb turned the car off and got out, box in hand, and walked toward the river, where he stood on a slight embankment near the water's edge.

"Was I right about Lula? Was she mean?" he asked as I joined him.

"You're goddamn right she was mean."

"Father said that trait runs in her whole family. What did she tell you?"

"Hold on a minute, there is no way I'm going first," I said. "What did Dino say?"

Caleb shared Dino's revelation that was mostly in line with what Lula had explained to me. Charlie Ray Walker got Caleb's grandmother pregnant then abandoned his family, leaving only a legacy of mystery that ended suddenly, when he crashed his car over a bridge and drowned in three feet of flood water.

Caleb had finished without mentioning the most notable detail, so I said, "But you know why he called you a, uh…" and of course I couldn't finish the phrase.

"Charlie Ray was of mixed heritage, but as Dino informed me, mixed meant he was still a…meant he was black no matter what he was mixed with."

"He was a talented musician. Did Dino tell you that?"

"No."

"Lula said that he was trying to get to Chicago to play jazz piano with some musician he knew."

"I find it hard to believe she told you anything."

"I think she was sticking up for Dino."

"I'm not surprised. He always helped that family out if he hit anything at the slot machines."

"Dino also knew your father's lineage, and he chose to shoulder that responsibility, too. She implied there was something noble in that. Redemptive, I guess."

Across the water, a red-headed duck nestled on a ribbon of sandy shoreline. Caleb' soft chuckle broke his contemplative silence, and he said, "Dino wondered which was worse - being a poor, Mississippi-fied WOP named Orlando or carrying the miscegenated blood of a Walker."

"What an asshole."

"That's how he ended it. He turned the Alabama game back on, and that was that."

"Lula gave me your whole family history," I said. "Your blood family." I repeated what Lula told me about the family tree, verbatim, and though these somewhat bizarre, personal pieces of his family history were being assembled before him, Caleb didn't seem fazed in the slightest. "Aren't you shaken up about any of this?" I asked him.

"Why would I be?" he replied, voice steady.

"It changes things, doesn't it?" His indifference wasn't surprising, but it could still be unnerving, considering the magnitude of what he'd just learned.

"Changes? Like what?" he asked.

The question hung in the air. I didn't have an answer for this, so I gestured toward the box he hadn't opened, and I said, "Just open the thing already, will you, Caleb?"

I cast the light of my phone over the parcel, illuminating the worn twine and faded brown paper. Caleb carefully untied the string and unwrapped it, revealing a navy blue, felt box, unmarked, but old. He flipped it open and found a silver wristwatch. No logo. No brand. It did not appear to be working. Beneath the watch was a folded piece of paper that Caleb unraveled and held up to the light shining from my phone. It was sheet music, yellowed from age and use. The song was titled *Les Feuilles Mortes.*

It was a composition for piano with many added notations, some in blue ink and some in faded pencil, along with words, likely lyrics, written in French in the margins between scales. Neither of us knew how to read French, and I surmised that, if there was a hidden message, maybe it was in the melody.

Across the river and deep in the dark woods, a shadow of a man appeared after he lit a pit full of debris and dead leaves on fire. The flames grew quickly and when the breeze whistled our way, it carried the sweet aroma of soil and smoke, a scent that could turn even a man as cold as Caleb inward to investigate the mysteries of his soul. The same for me. A strange feeling swept over me suddenly, like there was somebody else there with us, watching. Though it was a ghostly sensation, the source felt familiar, and caring. It didn't originate somewhere behind us either, rather, it felt like it came from somewhere ahead of us. A Waffle House in some other Southern football town, where Caleb and I congregated before an Auburn game, and recalled this very moment for the one millionth time. As if, in doing so, we created a detectable entity in this moment, enshrined to signify its importance, and it felt so very real and true and so close to me that I wanted to reach out and touch it.

As the fire across the river grew in force and bright orange in color, Caleb looked down at the meager broken watch. He laid it over his wrist, contemplating whether it fit, whether he'd leave it on, but he returned it to the box instead. He folded the sheet music, then replaced the lid and slid the box into his pocket. He leaned over and picked up a smooth rock along the riverbank and tossed it across the water. It skipped several times and scared the red-headed duck that flew away to a safer spot downstream.

As his moral compass, I felt a duty to articulate the depth of what I was feeling, the entire sum of the significance discovered on this day, to make sure Caleb had experienced the same. It was his family after all, his history, his part of the country, his home. But I didn't have the words to describe in logical terms the implications of the sensation I felt, and I lacked the courage to convey it using an ethereal analogy that would be lost on Caleb. Perhaps the shared experience, the wonderful autumn day, the aroma of the burning leaves – perhaps that was enough. So, I resorted to our shared language, the one way we knew how to speak to each other in terms we'd inherently understand, to amplify meaning, to implicate a heightened importance. I said the same thing to Caleb that I always said after a day of football in the autumn, win or lose.

"Caleb, it's been one hell of an Auburn football Saturday."

And then I knew for certain that he had experienced it, that he understood the significance, as I had, because Caleb looked at me and I saw myself reflected in the gloss that covered his eyes, and he echoed back all those unsayable truths, when he simply said, "War Eagle."

# Acknowledgments

Matt McGowen

Aunt Cathy

John Garvin

Aaron Sisk

Ria Beach

Jack Livings was my editor. He is an excellent teacher and an author himself. Please check out his work. *The Dog* is a collection of short stories that won the 2015 PEN/Bingham Prize and the Rome Prize for Literature. He also has an excellent novel called *The Blizzard Party*.

# About the Author

Rich Varner grew up in Tyler, Texas; Auburn, Alabama; Lubbock, Texas; Midland, Texas; and he now resides in Burleson, Texas with his wife and three children.

 twitter.com/RittyRich

 instagram.com/rittyrich1

www.ingramcontent.com/pod-product-compliance
Lightning Source LLC
Chambersburg PA
CBHW020459310726
48979CB00016B/2717/J

* 9 7 9 8 2 1 8 1 8 3 5 7 8 *